# Boss Takes All

BOOK THREE OF THE AFRICAN TRILOGY

CARL HANCOCK

**Carl Hancock** was born in Aberdare, then a mining valley town in South Wales. After seven years in the local grammar school, he moved on to university where he studied for degrees in Classics and in English and became a teacher. His career took him to secondary schools in Britain, Cyprus and Malta. Latterly, he enjoyed six years in Pembroke House, a preparatory school up-country in the Kenya part of the Great Rift Valley, sometimes known as the White Highlands. He has two grown-up children and currently lives on a small farm in the Adelaide Hills.

Published in Australia by Sid Harta Publishers Pty Ltd,
ABN: 46 119 415 842
23 Stirling Crescent, Glen Waverley, Victoria
3150 Australia
Telephone: +61 3 9560 9920, Facsimile: +61 3 9545 1742
E-mail: author@sidharta.com.au

First published in Australia July 2011
This edition published July 2011

Cover design, typesetting: Chameleon Print Design



Hancock, Carl
Boss Takes All — African Trilogy Book Three
ISBN: 1-921829-28-1
EAN13: 978-1-921829-28-4
pp394

# Glossary

| *Swahili* | *English* |
| --- | --- |
| asante | thank you |
| askari | guard |
| chai | tea |
| dawa | medicine |
| dudu | trouble |
| fundi | expert |
| Hakuna matata | no worries |
| kidogo | bribe (literally, 'a little') |
| kwaheri | goodbye |
| mzee | old man |
| mzungo | stranger, foreigner |
| Saba Saba Day | July: Day of unrest in Kenya |
| sasa | now |
| shaurie | trouble |
| tackies (local usage) | trainers |
| uhuru | freedom, independence |
| wananchi | ordinary people |

*Land of a million pathways, land of the silken cords that bind the stranger and hold her in thrall, may you enjoy a future blessed with universal prosperity, harmony and justice.*

# Chapter One

Isaac Mumbo was up late, as usual. He sat close to the open fire that burned night and day in the heart of the rondavel village. His only company was the night askari. He thanked Luka for bringing fresh wood as he moved his fingers along the lines of his braille Bible.

'Luka, would you like me to read something out of the good book?'

'Maybe, when I get back from checking up at Big House. Isaac, why is it I never see you without that Bible in your hands. Two hours in the church on Sunday is plenty religion for me.'

'My friend, to worship in the temple of the Lord is a great honour.'

'This place don't look like much of a temple to me!'

'So peaceful out here at this time. I can't see the stars, Luka, but I know they are there. God never fails. And the moon is full tonight. I can feel her silvery glow on my face.'

'Yes, you are right, brother. She's up there. Yes indeed. But tell me, Isaac, if she is a she, how come we hear folks talk about the *man* in the moon?'

The two friends sat chuckling together by the fireside. The new wood crackled as the flames took hold, sending a rush of sparks up into the darkness above them.

'Yes indeed, Isaac. I bet you and me are the only people awake for miles around. Man, I do love this peace and quiet!'

A second later, a huge explosion cracked the night sky. The sound of it rolled out along the lakeside villages. By the time two further explosions rang out, the little group of houses encircling the gathering place where a bewildered Isaac sat clutching his Bible to his chest was pouring out a great noise of its own, screams mingled with terrified wailing and angry shouts. Big House was ablaze. Less than ten days before the flower fields and the plastic and cotton tents had been destroyed and the acrid smell had not been completely blown away by the breezes wafting in off the lake. Now Londiani itself was lighting up the night sky, a beacon that was visible for miles around.

In minutes South Lake Road was alive with the hundreds of Naivasha people rushing along in confusion to witness close up this second catastrophe to strike the McCall estate. There had been many deaths when the flames and the thick smoke had engulfed the work places of the young people who had just begun a new day cultivating their rows of flowers and vegetables. Surely, more lives had been lost in this new merciless inferno. It was not until long after dawn that the mass of people discovered that not a single person had died in the blaze that had destroyed the beautiful farmhouse. Fifty metres away one man had been wounded, not by fire but by a bullet.

Careful planning and not a chance miracle had been the saving of the people who lived on the farm. Nor had the fire itself been a random happening. Alfredo Rossi, a young American known to the McCalls of Londiani as Alfred Ross, had been employed, for a huge fee, to wipe out the very family who, in their only meeting with him, had shown him true up-country kindness. He had been the paid tool of another man's longing for vengeance, but he and his employer had been outwitted. As soon as he realised that the job had gone badly wrong, Rossi had fled in panic for the anonymity of Jomo Kenyatta Airport and from there had flown out to the safety of his New York home.

Abel Rubai, the very rich Mister Big of Kenya politics, had insisted on watching his enemies go down and nearly paid the price with his life. He had witnessed the explosion and the fire in a state of high excitement and just when he began to rejoice that at last he was free from a burden that he had been carrying for far too long was stunned by a horrendous shock. The McCalls who had caused him and his family so much pain, who had been behind the death of his beloved son, Julius, were part of history, or so he believed.

Rossi, against his better judgement, had given in to pressure from Rubai and set up a vantage point from where his paymaster would have a clear view of Londiani down to his left. But it was from the farmhouse to his right, Rusinga, the home of Bertie Briggs, that they came running. In the bright moonlight the rolling gait of Tom McCall was unmistakable as he ran towards his dying home, leading a dozen or more friends and family across the open plain.

With a massive effort Abel Rubai suppressed a scream of agony and blessed himself for bringing along his loaded Andrews repeating rifle. He shouted the McCall name as he pushed the smooth oak butt into his shoulder. There would be one chance on a certain kill. He had the blond-haired leader of the pack in his sights. A fraction of a second before he squeezed the trigger, he felt the searing pain in the small of his back and lost consciousness.

# Chapter Two

There was confusion in the small group of family and friends who had had rushed out of Rusinga Farm. They wanted to be close to Londiani however painful it would be to stand powerlessly by and watch the home of three generations of McCalls cracking and crumbling in the fierce heat. Before they had gone fifty metres the angry scream from a familiar voice and the muffled sound of a rifle shot drew their attention inland, to a grassy rise close to a farm fence. Tom had seen the barrel of the gun pointing at him from point-blank range, felt the pain as his shoulder struck the hard earth, watched Bertie Briggs calmly lower his rifle and bow his head.

Against the background roar, the small group changed direction. Rebecca Kamau was relieved to see Tom scrambling to his feet and, with their arms linked, the pair rushed towards two silent figures on the rise up ahead, one prostrate, one kneeling in a solemn pose bowed forward as if in prayer.

Reuben Rubai was not aware of their coming. He was in a state of deep shock. He passed his hands along the chest and face of his dead father, as if he were searching out some magical key place where he could press and restore life. He turned and looked up to see all 'round him the faces of those who had no business to be alive. They were watching him and barely containing their anger. In his eyes he was the more offended.

He rose, trembling, and looked into the eyes of each of the hostile faces of those surrounding him before exploding into a fit of ice-cold rage.

'You murdering bastards, you will pay for this! You have robbed me, my family, our country of a great man. McCall, your life is finished. You and your whore will soon be rotting in your own private hell. I swear to God, Papa, that they will not escape.'

Hosea Kabari, in his sergeant's uniform and his wife, Maria, were hurrying towards the rise from the direction of the fire. Reuben saw a first sign of help.

'Just in time! Sergeant, arrest every one of these animals. Look! My father, Abel Rubai. You know him. You know him! Now do your duty by him. There's his gun. Use it.'

Maria Kabari paid no attention to the distraught young man's anger. Instead she knelt by Abel's side. She, too, ran her hands along the body. She was not looking for some magic place. She bent low and listened at the chest. With her husband's help she lifted Abel's limp body to a sitting position and examined the back.

All the while, Reuben watched her. His dazed stare was the outward sign of the turmoil that was churning inside him. He was overwhelmed by the succession of shocks that had bombarded him in the previous half hour. And then he remembered. He had seen this woman before. It was at the Daniels' house on the evening of the funeral of Simon Mboya. He had come face to face with her while on an errand for his father looking out for the woman, Lydia Smith. Father Rubai had made a serious error with this street girl and it was Reuben's task to get her to his father double quick. She had heard things, very private things. If she blabbed, there could be danger. Abel could take no chances. She would have to be moved on, permanently.

His encounter with this woman weeks before had been over in seconds. No words had been spoken, but the look of cold contempt in those dark eyes had stayed with him. In spite of this and against all the hostile instincts he knew he should be feeling towards this person meddling with his father's body, something about her was giving him hope.

From her kneeling position Maria looked up into his face. Was that the suggestion of a smile? Was she mocking him? He tried to assert himself.

'I don't know who you are, but I want you to leave my father in peace. Come away now. Now, curse you! And you, policeman, do your duty. You're supposed to be the law in this godforsaken hellhole. You'll be damned sorry if you don't. I know people who could make you an ex-policeman by morning!'

Maria, ignoring his big talk, took his breath away with a single short sentence. 'Do you think that your father is dead?'

A mixture of fear, amazement and wild, blind hope made him speechless. She continued.

'This man is still with us, just.'

This time Maria's words had an opposite effect on Reuben Rubai. The blind hope swelled into excitement. The speech returned, but it was without a coherent focus.

'You mean that … look, you'd better not … who are you, anyway? You're no doctor. I'm warning you …'

'He is with us. Just. He is very close to the edge.'

Reuben, chastened into silence, meekly waited. This woman, this witch, had humbled him.

'What must I do?'

'There is nothing for you to do and everything you can allow someone else to do.'

Reuben screamed out in frustration. 'Please, none of this clever crap! I want my father back.'

'Then, listen! Listen! A bullet is lodged in your father's spine. He cannot be treated here. Help lies sixty miles from this place, in a house that we both know.'

'You must get him to a hospital ...'

'What is it about your family and "proper" hospitals? Let me be unkind but honest for a moment. The only people who can help your father owe you and especially your father nothing. Nothing! He has brought them nothing but the bitterest grief. But they can and they will help him. Listen! You will travel with your father.'

'We have a car, close by, on the road up there.'

'I'm not sure. Any journey will be dangerous. Time is against us, so, okay, we will have to use it.'

In the near distance, in the direction of Londiani, they could hear the rising hubbub of people in gathering numbers. There were the noisy outbursts of a crowd caught up in a state of wild excitement. They were thrilled to be witnesses to a great event. They would have stories to tell. Tom McCall expressed the fear that all in that dark corner of the farm felt. 'There's danger. Those people must not find us here. They'll soon piece together some kind of story and, Rubai, it could be the end of you. You're coming with me to that car. I'll drive us down. You can ride in the boot.'

'McCall, you'll be sorry for this!'

'Fine! Stay here, then. Rebecca, will you sit with me? Maria, what do you think?'

'I wish we had six or seven pillows.'

'Sorry. We're right out of them just now in Londiani. Bertie, could we borrow a few pillows? We'll charge this pair for them.'

'Sure, Tom, but not none of their blood money for me, thanks very much!'

'And, Reuben, when we arrive at our destination, you will travel on to your home and wait for the morning. Tell your mother that your father has been called away unexpectedly on government business. You will be a fool if you let any news of this come out. It will be your choice, but if you want to help you father … Got that, cretin?'

# Chapter Three

Sally Rubai enjoyed her early mornings. The new baby was only a few weeks away, so there were always some words to share with the new Julius. She could not wait to hold him in her arms. Her maid, Monica, spoiled her mistress, making sure that there were plenty of sugary treats on the breakfast tray. Sally looked forward to reading the early edition of *The Nation* fetched by one of the boys from the Karen dukas. She leaned back and scanned the front page. Nothing special there, but today she could look forward to the features supplement and especially for her favourite, 'Mary's recipes from the country'. When Monica turned on the radio to catch the latest local news, the word Londiani made Sally sit up.

'Reports are still sketchy, but we understand from an eyewitness that there was a series of explosions at about two am followed by a large conflagration which completely destroyed the rambling farm complex. Regular listeners will recall that less than ten days ago we reported on the fire that struck the working part of this lakeside farm. On that occasion there were forty-five deaths, mostly from among the young workforce who had just arrived to start the new day in the fields.

'So far there have been no reports of casualties from this morning's tragedy. Our eyewitness who was at the scene only minutes after the first of the explosions stated graphically,

"No one in there could have survived even a few seconds of that fire from hell."

'We will keep you up to date on this breaking story. Now, to other news.'

Sally, in slippers and dressing-gown, was soon on her way to her husband's screen room. Abel was usually there first thing, that is if he had not spent the whole night sitting in front of those blue and green squares of light that fascinated him so much. He was not there, so she went on to the breakfast room.

'Reuben! You are very early, boy.' She paused to take a closer look at him. 'Is there something the matter? Your eyes are very red. Have you slept?'

'Fine, Mama. Yes, I was a little late in. Out in the "Carnivore". Ziggy Kormai is up from Zim for a few days. We were in school together. A few of us invited him out. And, you know how it is …'

'No, I most definitely do not know how it is. More about that later. Terrible news about Londiani. I'm looking for your father.'

Reuben stifled a gasp. *How could she …?*

'What is the matter with you, boy? So, you haven't seen Papa?'

'Well, look, I got this message. Someone down at the Carnivore. He got it from someone else.'

'What is going on here? Are you sick?'

He suddenly felt very weak. There had always been something in his mother's manner that made it almost impossible for him to lie to her. She had a way of narrowing her gaze that made him feel that her eyes were burning a path into his brain and his closest thoughts. He made a massive effort.

'The message was that Papa was called away at short notice. Government business.'

Sally slowly poured herself a glass of milk, all the while scrutinising the minutest shifts in her son's expression. She drew in an extra long breath before speaking again.

'Now, this time, the truth. What's your Daddy's expression? "Strictly no bullshit!".'

Reuben was emotionally drained. He sat down at the table and looked across at his mother. His personality and his strength of mind were being tested to their limits. Above all things, he wanted to be honest with this woman who for all his life had been his loyal, loving supporter. Wave after wave of warm currents passed through his tired mind blocking his thoughts like an electronic jamming machine. Deep inside were the words he needed, but they were out of reach. She was asking for truth. Yes, he could have managed to bring out some version of what, just then, he perceived as reality, but at what cost? In one or two sentences he could come close to breaking her heart.

'Mama, Papa is not very far from us here.'

'So?' In the five minutes that she had been in that room with her son, her original mild concern about her husband and his whereabouts had curved upwards through fear to the edge of terror. She wanted complete knowledge in a single instant, to be presented with a single huge colourful picture where she would be able to see the beginning and end in front of her.

'Mama, I have made promises.'

Sally raised her voice in mounting anxiety and anger. 'Do not speak in riddles. Can't you see how you are torturing me?'

Reuben lowered his eyes. He summoned what was left of his courage.

'Papa is very sick. He has been badly hurt.'

'You mean that he is dead.'

'No! No!'

'Tell me.' The resignation in her voice told him that it was time to give her everything he was capable of. As he spoke she watched him with her hand to her mouth and the sadness of a wounded animal in her eyes.

'He is with the family of doctors, the people with the garden you like.'

'I know these people, but if he …'

'Mama, he has a wound in his back. Yes, in his spine. I was there.'

'You? It was a gun, I know it. Your father has many enemies. Has someone been arrested yet? But why not in a hospital? Or at home here? And why were you there? It was at the Carnivore?'

'Naivasha.'

The illumination was instant. 'The McCalls, they did not say if any of them survived.'

'No deaths there. It was the Briggs man. He was the one. Mama, I thought we had lost him. A strange woman, a policeman's wife, she said that there is life. But also much danger. She is over there with him now.'

'Then I must go there. Now.'

'But the story must not get out. They said this.'

'I am going, alone.'

# Chapter Four

The night askari at 'Cartref' escorted her on foot to the door of the Daniels' surgery. He led the way with an honest reverence. He recognised this lady. It was the only way he could express his sympathy.

She went in unannounced, the unexpected visitor whose arrival was not a complete surprise. She saw him at once, even before she took in the pleasant coolness and the scented air of the high-beamed room which put her in mind of the Catholic church her mother took her to when she was a child up in North-West District. Abel was lying face down on the raised table, close to the open door. Five white doctors wearing green gowns and masks were standing 'round him. His three sons and his younger sister were watching David Daniels completely engaged in the delicate job of removing the bullet that was lodged tight between two vertebrae in the lower part of his patient's back. Sonya Mboya, the only person there that Sally recognised, turned, removed her mask and gave the visitor a warm smile.

'So your son could not hide the news. This is good. It is right for you to be with him. Please, sit with me. There are chairs on the other side.'

Maria Kabari made no attempt to introduce herself. Sally's every move was hesitant. She was the child who had entered a strange, new land where all the humans seemed friendly, but where a dark cloud hung down threatening to engulf her at any moment. Maria took her hand and rubbed it gently with her own like a mother bringing back warmth to her child's chilled fingers.

Sally's agitation was not helped by her sitting down. 'Please, being still makes my fear worse. Perhaps if I could walk in the garden. It will give me something else to think of. I know that the garden here is beautiful.'

'Yes, very beautiful, but there is work for you here.'

Sally turned to look into the face of this stranger. She was comforted by the serenity she found there. The dark eyes and pursed lips combined into an expression of firm confidence.

'You were the one who helped my husband. Reuben said that, without you ...'

The stranger's face lit up into a smile of pure compassion. She began to sing. The words were in a language new to Sally and she understood instinctively that the lilting melody was something that was reaching out to her from an ancient past. Maria's gentle nod was an encouragement to Sally to share. The singing paused briefly.

'Sally, you are a woman of prayer. We can work together.'

The melody began again and paused. 'He needs you.'

For the first time since entering that room she felt assured enough to look carefully at the raised table that dominated its centre. The back of Abel's head and his bare shoulders were all that she could comfortably see. They were motionless. Her prayer became fervent. Her voice blended with Maria's as a background to the work being performed by the five doctors standing above and across from them in that cool place.

David Daniels held out his hand towards Sally Rubai. In the palm, the offending piece of metal gleamed.

'I am showing you this to prove that this part of the job is done. I must keep it. The police will want to examine it, of course.'

'Is he going to be all right?'

'Ah, well, yes. Um, let's just say that, if everything goes according to plan. He's a very strong man. Look, his body has suffered a deep trauma ...'

'In other words, you don't know.'

'He'll live. That's for sure. But actions have consequences.'

'And what does that mean?'

Sally was on an armchair next to Rebecca in the Daniels' sitting room. She had reluctantly come away from the surgery, leaving her unconscious husband in the care of Maria Kabari. She found no friendliness in this room. With her mind freed from the most acute of her anxieties, questions began to surface. Who had fired the bullet that had almost killed Abel? What was her husband doing out in Londiani in the middle of the night? Why had he not been taken directly to Nairobi Hospital or the Aga Khan? What were these people trying to hide?

Abel had enemies. She had always accepted that this must be so when a good man who loved his country dearly had to deal with opponents who were out to serve their own ends whatever the cost to the wananchi. He had been lured into a trap. Reuben would have some of the answers about how this had been sprung. What had he seen? How did he escape unharmed?

Abel had many friends. It was time that they found out what was going on. They would have the skills and the connections. She must talk to doctor friends. She would implore them to move Abel from this excuse for a medical centre, which was probably illegal anyway.

She must talk to this Maria, get her to promise to stay with

Abel until she could organise proper help. She would pay big money. Abel would have understood what she was up against. She must be as innocent as a dove but as wise as a serpent. She smiled when she recalled that this was just about the only quotation from the Good Book that he approved of. There in that comfortable European style room she was becoming aware of a presence in her and around her, a transformation, a kind of possession by a benevolent force. It revealed itself in several ways.

Her concern for Abel was as strong as ever, but just as strong was a certainty that all would be well with him sooner rather than later. He was being cared for. Her prayer was being answered. 'My cup runneth over', the words of King David dropped into her mind as a confirmation. While she was in this place she must contain her excitement. The thoughts and ideas teemed. She was the gold miner who had struck the mother lode. The dam wall was being breached and streams of living water were pouring over her.

When she returned home she would have so many things to do. She was almost afraid to identify the source of this new energy but was ready to be rushed along.

Her first task was to speak to Reuben. Together they would prepare the Rubai counterattack. He knew the facts, she had the contacts. When she was ready, she would call in the people who could help her to put her plans into action. First, though, she must take advantage of the lucky chance. They were no friends of Abel, but they were in this house and she must use them.

* * *

'Thomas, Rebecca, I heard the news. The girl said that they did not know about ... the people.'

'We are all safe. We have lost everything. Tell you the truth, it hasn't hit me yet. We got a bit busy. I can't say that I spent more than a second or two actually watching the blaze. There's work to be done. We ... what can you say?'

'Abel?'

Rebecca moved in quickly. She had caught the despair in Thomas's face at the mention of the name of Mister Big. For the third time in less than a year, his life had been under a mortal threat from a Rubai. He saw the rifle pointing at him not ten metres away, heard the angry scream, felt the thud of pain as his shoulder slammed into the earth. He could not find it in him to tell his truth and let her know that it had been Bertie who had saved his life with a single shot into the body of this woman's husband.

'Sally, everything happened so quickly and it was dark out there on the plain.'

'But why was he there? Reuben, too.'

After a long and painful silence, the best that Tom McCall could manage was a curt, 'I don't know.'

* * *

'I must go out to your surgery again. This Maria has a good heart.'

'She has many gifts.' These were the first words that Sonya had spoken to Sally that morning. 'David will tell you. They were together when my Simon was brought down from Kericho.' Sonya was ready to go further and risk upsetting Sally. 'His hands, those healing hands, were mutilated by his killers. I pray that you will be more fortunate. Abel has his life and soon, perhaps, the return of his full health. Sally, you are right, Maria has a good heart.'

Sally left that sitting room in a state of misunderstanding. Her newly rediscovered insight was telling her that there was a conspiracy going on in this Daniels' house. For whatever reason, envy or plain malice, these people were out to get her husband. But she had seen through them and, with God's help, they would pay for the harm they were doing.

Over many years Sally Rubai had become accustomed to having her way, to believing that her truth was the truth. Part of this gentle arrogance was a readiness to ignore the uncomfortable signs that would have told her that all was not as well as she wanted to believe, especially when it came to understanding what her husband stood for. He loved her, he spoiled her and he protected her. How could he possibly be a ruthless thug who would stop at nothing to protect his position, for whom killing, wiping out opposition was a ready option?

When the honest, hardworking, creative people whom she had just left showed her compassion by not spelling out for her a much more accurate truth about her husband's part in the horrors of the night that had just passed, she had conveniently, but by her light, honestly misunderstood.

She returned to the surgery with a relieved mind. The worst of a bad experience was behind her, and Abel. The scented air and the coolness of that room gave her spirits a lift. Abel was safe here.

She joined Maria on the raised platform and was taken aback to see that the woman whom everyone saw as a gifted healer was kneading lavender oil into Abel's bare shoulders. Sally's first reaction to this soothing process was one of resentment. This beautiful woman had invaded an intimate privacy without consent. And that strange singing again with the haunting melody did not please her either. But Sally knew that, for now, she must not upset this woman.

'Soon I shall be meeting a very dear friend who is also the most gifted physician in the country. With his help I will be taking my husband away from this place. Until I return I ask you to stay with Abel.'

'But, Madam …'

'You will be rewarded well.'

'You do not understand. When Rebecca and Tom come for me I am going home. Do not worry about your husband. He will not be left alone and he will be in good hands.'

'Yes, and I will see to it.'

# Chapter Five

When the wild fig trees are in fruit in the gardens of Karen, flocks of starlings can be seen swooping down to feast on this abundant special treat. When one garden is stripped bare, the birds fly on until their sharp eyes light on a fresh feeding ground. Fields and woodlands are their world. They are indifferent to the ways of humans, so they would have shown no interest in the large lady in the white suit as she crossed below them. She was on her way home. She was walking. Rich, heavily pregnant women, the wives of prominent citizens do not normally behave like this. But Sally Rubai needed to be away from people and houses, even for a few minutes. She had thinking to do.

It was no great distance between the homes of the Daniels and the Rubais. They were next-door but distant neighbours. On another level a large gap separated them. For media people, the events of the night at the farmhouse on the shore of Lake Naivasha were being sorted into a comprehensible shape. An eager audience would devour this version of the truth avidly, though the offering was little more than a competent recital of some of the facts.

Many hundreds of thousands of shillings would have been gladly offered by these same media people for access to the two very different versions of the what and especially the why of these same events.

When Sally arrived home, she found that Reuben was having a shower after spending the morning in bed. She was pleased. The boy would be rested and refreshed, ready for some hard work.

While she waited for Monica to prepare lunch, she sat at the table in the room where she kept her Bible. For the first time that she could remember, she was reluctant to delve into its pages. She did not expect to find help and consolation at this worst of times in her life. Instead of turning to one of her many favourite passages, she sat quietly contemplating the events of the day and her reaction to them. There had been revelations. Her emotions had been deeply stirred. There had been moments of exhilaration followed by others of near despair. But, at the end of this roller-coaster ride for her heart and mind, she had bottomed out.

Her resolve was strong and she saw a clear path stretching before her. Until Abel recovered his powers, she was the family leader. She was ready to cause a few surprises even to herself.

The lunch dishes were not cleared away early that day. For several hours Sally and Reuben had separated themselves from the rest of the household. Reuben had found it a trying experience to be closed off with his re-energised mother while she grilled and pushed him mercilessly.

'First thing, son. Let's get the stuff about the fire all straightened out.'

With a little sympathetic massaging of the facts they soon created the Rubai truth on that issue which at first look might have seemed to be loaded down with evidence damning to Abel's cause. The case would have been presented to the high court judge in these terms.

'Your Honour, Abel Nathaniel Rubai is a deep lover of his country, a patriot of the highest calibre. Late in the evening of the night in question he received telephone calls advising him that a very serious crime was about to be committed. Londiani Farm and its inhabitants, the McCalls of Naivasha, were the target of the attack. There was no time to alert the police, so Abel took it upon himself, in company of his son, Reuben, to race up to Naivasha. (He made the difficult decision not to alert and so trouble the McCall family, just in case it was a false alarm.) On arrival at the lakeside property, they found that all was quiet. They waited and watched for an hour or more but, just when they were on the point of moving away, the now famous explosion shattered the peace. As we all know, that outrage is being investigated by the relevant authorities and forms no part of this brief.

'We have arrived at the heart of the matter. Abel Rubai was cruelly rewarded for his effort to be of service to his fellow citizens. An attempt was made on his life. He received a gunshot wound in his lower back that almost killed him. We confidently trust that proceedings will soon begin to deal with this matter. There is a defendant and we hope that he will soon appear before yourself or another of your esteemed colleagues to answer a charge.'

On the other side of the murram road, the Daniels family and their guests were in low spirits. Out in the surgery Rhys Daniels, the youngest of the three doctor brothers, was taking his stint at keeping an eye on their wounded patient. They were expecting that before nightfall an ambulance would come to take Rubai away to a 'proper hospital'.

In Cartref no story was being concocted about the events of the night. They had the would-be murderer with them. Just as, ten days before, Abel Rubai had not set the charges down on the farm to cause fires and kill forty-five young workers, so now he had paid someone else to do his work.

'No doubt, when he comes 'round and returns to his old self, he will open his arms and say 'Who, me?' and give us the old bilge, 'Prove it, then!' The trouble is that the courts will believe him. And think about this. Who put the bullet in his back? We know and we know why. But, ditto the above! Pretty serious stuff.'

'Thomas, there is no Londiani any more. What will happen?'

'I know that we are insured. I also know that there are a few broken hearts back there. This could kill Rafaella.'

'You are wrong, Thomas. She is stronger than any of us.'

'Yeah, right, 'Becca. I think our best hope is Paul. He understands how the law works in this country. More important, how it doesn't work! Maria, do you think he would mind if we called in on him in Langata on the way home?'

'No. Comes in handy sometimes to have a lawyer for a brother!'

Sonya was the only one in the room who was crying. 'I have a very ungodly thought in my mind. How easy to go out into the garden with this cushion in my hands. How long would it take? Two minutes? A kind of justice? I think so.' A smile broke through. 'Trouble is, just as I was beginning to press down, I'd see Simon fluttering his eyes with that disapproving look on his face. Simon! Simon! God, how could you let such a thing happen to our boys?'

Rebecca pressed her friend's face into her chest. 'There's no answer, darling.'

In the late afternoon, Sally Rubai, alone again, sat with her head bowed over her family Bible. She had sent Reuben out. 'Go and be with your friends, boy. Get away from this witch of a mother!'

She had taken some big steps and the effort had left her

tired out. But she had spoken to Alfred Koyane, Abel's most trusted friend and a lawyer. He was going to come for dinner with his wife, Eunice. 'Hakuna Matata, Sally. Let me have some time to work on a few things. Meanwhile spoil yourself. Talk to the baby. Abel tells me that he will be called Julius. Good choice, good choice!'

Ten minutes before, she had stood by the lodge gate and waved off an ambulance on its way to Nairobi Hospital with Abel on board. Austin Mwegi, the family doctor, and three nurses were looking after him. Doctor Austin had been impressed with the work done by David Daniels in removing the bullet from a very tricky part of the spine.

'Couldn't have had a better man. Brilliant hands, cool as ice. I'll pick you up at around nine tomorrow morning. I think he will have come 'round by then.'

So the news for Sally was as good as it could have been. The afternoon sun fell across her table. A great weariness hung about her. In itself that might have been pleasant, even satisfying after the high-octane effort she had put in since early morning. But there was more. The spirit had drained out of her. Sally had always lived with a close awareness of the Holy Spirit. It had sustained her in her dark days, especially in those weeks after Julius had been taken from them. The presence had always felt warm, reminding her of the tongues of fire that had fallen on those gathered in the room in Jerusalem on the Day of Pentecost.

Today there was something different. With her belief system, it was quite easy and natural to acknowledge that she had been inspired, energised by some outside force that, in its mysterious way, had filled her, guided her thoughts, brought her hope. It was time to give thanks, but she could not do so. There was no afterglow of warmth, left behind as a kind of calling card. She sat over her book willing herself to search the pages. 'He that hath clean hands and a pure heart'. She had forgotten where to look for these so familiar words.

Thoughts of her mother came to her. Her happiest childhood hours had been spent sitting in the kitchen before bedtime. The fire still held its warmth and cast a glow across the room. Mama was the godliest woman she knew but, sometimes, dark memories had been stirred in her.

'Sally, my grandmother was the first in the family to be baptised, as I told you before. She warned us girls that not all the spirits who move about us are from the Good Lord. Some have a special cunning and mean to harm us, even to destroy us. You will recognise them by their coldness …'

Sally sat bolt upright. When she came into her special room, there had been a coolness in that place where normally the afternoon warmth had lingered longest. Her mind was in a delicate state and very quickly shocked itself into a state of panic.

'God forgive me! God forgive me!' She was fingering the pages of the book in front of her. She read aloud all the verses of King David's psalm. 'Yea, though I walk through the valley of death … I will fear no evil… for Thou art with me …'

Then it was on to the Sermon on the Mount.

An hour later Monica came in to remind her mistress that her guests would soon be with them. Sally was leaning back into her chair. There was a contented smile on her face.

Two days later and a hundred kilometres north of Karen, afternoon was moving quickly on. The site where Londiani had stood was busy with activity. Peter Bellengeri had brought his heavy equipment up from the other side of town where it was working on the first of the preparations for the new Naivasha Hospital. A good deal of the wreckage of the farmhouse had been scooped up and carted off.

The focus of the moment was on the area of the veranda and front of the garden. The women had been rescuing plants, potting them and setting them down in the shade. Rafaella had been pleasantly surprised to find so many of her old friends alive. And, close up, the rich brown soil gave off the wholesome perfume of earth alive.

The men were cleaning up on everyone's favourite part of the old house. The veranda looked bigger when it was cleared of the piles of damaged bricks and broken furniture.

'My father always said that they put good stuff into this place when they built it. Run a stone cleaner over this floor for an hour or two and she'd be as good as new.'

'Dad, do you think there's a machine for clearing the stench of burning?'

Bertie had the solution. 'Tom, two heavy rains should do it. That and dig up the scorched trees. They remember the insult longer than anything else.'

'Trees remember?'

'Certainly do, Rollo. Don't worry. When you and Eddie get back here on a permanent basis, you'll soon pick up the old ways again.'

Eddie, the younger of the McCall twins by half an hour, countered quickly. 'But we are home on a permanent basis. Brought all our stuff with us.'

'Eddie, your Ma and I are not wearing that one. Two more terms and you'll be done.'

'No, Dad. We're eighteen now. Remember?'

'Just about as old as one of those poor blackened acacia out there.'

'Yeah, but acacia are not good at arithmetic. Two terms' fees for Rollo and me.'

'And no money coming in from the farm. We can still take the dreaded A-levels next June.'

'Straight As times two. All sorted. Let's move on. Look, Mum and Angela with the chai! Come on everybody. Tea break. Tools on the bar!'

When he had taken his mug of hot, sweet tea, Stephen Kamau, Alex's senior foreman, right-hand man and good friend made sure that he was sitting next to his much respected bwana. There were thoughts and feelings he needed to share.

'Bwana ...'

Alex raised his arms in protest. 'Stephen, my name is Alex. I'm your friend now, not your boss.'

'Asante for that. But you wouldn't grudge a friend using words that are... comfortable?' There was a broad grin on the big man's handsome face.

Alex joined in the smiling. 'Fine. But! Soon Rebecca and Tom will be married. We'll be family ...'

Stephen's melodious chuckle brought a warm feeling of pleasant reality to everyone sitting around and trying to keep spirits high. 'Got me there ... Bwana, but soon to be ... we'll have to wait and see.'

The two men, hunched and weary, leaned forward in their seats, their shoulders almost touching. Alex was contemplating the truth of a lifetime of work destroyed. Stephen was inwardly thanking the Lord that everyone who, a year before, had been bustling about this thriving farm ... The thought was stopped in a burst of shame. Forty-five of his workers were in the earth, in graves scattered around the district. There had been no miracle for them and, for a moment, he had forgotten them. All around his people with him there hung the stench of destruction. The power of Satan had revealed itself with devastating force.

'Stephen, what happens now?'

The strong man wiped away the tears with the back of his hand. 'The light on the path is mighty dim. I walked around the fields this morning. The canopies were gone and the last of the flowers ploughed in. But the earth felt good, resting, waiting. It came to me. We must have been saved for a reason. Only ...'

'We haven't discovered it yet ...'

'Too impatient. The Lord's time is not our time. And down there just me and a fish-eagle or two, with the sun shining on the lake, I felt good. And I had you to thank for it. You're still here and you are working. Bwana, yes, Bwana, you have let us stay in our homes. You are paying us when we can do no work for you ... Not all would do these things. And you ask me what happens now.'

Alex and Stephen, furthest away from the veranda steps, were the last to notice the two cars arriving. They pulled up on the blackened gravel. Eight heavily built men stepped down and looked around. These Nairobi policemen had seen the pictures on the television, but the reality, the terrible smell, the deathly blackness against the different blues of the sky and the lake, this piece of battleground made them hesitate briefly.

Chief Inspector Karumi soon gathered himself and led his men towards the steps. He wanted this job done quickly. That was why he had brought this squad of top city boys.

# Chapter Six

When he had formed his men into a semicircle behind him, the inspector stated his business.

'I understand that a Mister Bertrand Briggs is here among you people.'

Bertie, who was sitting on the veranda wall, closest to the line of policemen, stood up.

'Bertrand Briggs, I have a warrant here for your arrest.'

'Oh, yes? May I see it?'

When the top Nairobi cop held back from handing the official piece of paper over, Bertie reassured him and surprised him with his relaxed manner.

'Don't look so worried. I'm not going to set fire to it. As you can see, we've had quite enough of those around here recently. And I certainly wouldn't want to eat it.'

'Mister Briggs, are you well?'

'Of course not. Whatever the charge is, I'm going to plead insanity. That's allowed, I suppose?'

'It is not allowed to hand over warrants for criminals to look at.'

'There, you see – criminal. Guilty before I even get to the court. I'm sorry, I don't think I'll bother.'

On the surface Bertie was putting on a show of the suave English public schoolboy. His tall, slim figure, the neat head with the swept-back dark hair, the laconic, carefree manner and the affected plummy voice, all combined to give performance authenticity.

Rafaella was afraid that this rough group of lawmen would soon lose their patience and take off her much loved friend by force.

Underneath, Bertie was assessing the chances of escape. He was eyeing the police car furthest away from the house. It was pointed in the right direction for a quick getaway. Would the dumb driver have left the keys in the ignition? He could skip over the veranda wall, throw down the two brushes leaning next to him in front of the lumbering cops. He would drive down South Lake Road as far as Kingoni, get out and escape into the forest. Some time later he could return to pick up Ewan.

He never did discover if that key had been left in the ignition. They grabbed him before he reached the first car and bent him over the bonnet, slipped on the handcuffs and manhandled him back towards the steps. The chief inspector began again.

'Bertrand Briggs, we are arresting you for the attempted murder of Abel Nathaniel Rubai three nights ago on this property, Londiani Farm in the district of Nakuru South.'

Again there was resistance, this time in the noisy confusion of angry shouts. Everyone who had been working to clean up the veranda moved forward towards the platoon of policemen. Out came the guns. This move silenced the menacing group, except for Thomas McCall.

'You are taking the wrong man. Bertie was saving my life. Your Abel Nathaniel Rubai was trying to kill me. We can show you his gun. The thug is in Nairobi somewhere. I drove him down. People on this veranda saved his life! Goddammit, look around you! Do you think we blew ourselves up? And what was he doing here at two o'clock in the morning?'

'You, too, are known to us. Please, you are not helping here, Thomas McCall.'

The inspector was struggling to sound calm. He could understand now why the minister had insisted on sending up two squad cars on a routine job. European born criminals rarely gave problems when it came to taking them into custody. He wanted to get back to town quickly.

'So why don't you take me instead? I had a better motive for taking out that excuse for a human being. Is he on your books? No! You won't find his fingerprints —'

'McCall, shut your mouth! Now! There is room for another one in the car.'

'Where's your warrant?'

A nod from Karui's sergeant and Tom was carted off by three powerfully-built constables. They were out of sight for less than a minute. There was no visible mark on the farmer boy's body when they dumped him, barely conscious, back on the veranda steps. His angry resistance had been crushed. Two other members of the visiting constabulary frogmarched their prisoner to their car.

Leaving her son temporarily in the care of his grandmother and his wife-to-be, Maura pursued the chief inspector and pulled him 'round to face her. Karumi listened to her with a snarl of contempt on his face.

'Where are you taking this innocent man? He has a son. Let them see each other before you take him away. You will break his heart!'

The reply was an amused snort and a curt, 'Send the kid to a home! He'll soon forget!'

# Chapter Seven

'But, Caroline, we don't know where they took him. Were they real policemen even?'

'Well, Maura, there is a big wig called Karumi down in Nairobi. I know that for sure. Normally the city cops leave the locals to do the arresting. I've got friends in the CID on Nairobi Hill. One of them is bound to know.'

'Yes, and I hope they'll be willing to talk. Allowed even.'

'That's true, Paul.'

'No one down there is going to risk confronting the master thug if he values his job, his life even.'

It was now more than two hours since the brief but violent visit of the boys in blue. A group of twelve sat around in the darkness outside the cottage adjacent to the main house on Rusinga Farm. The warmth of the day was still with them and to the east the lights of the farms on the plain further along the lakeside helped to create a scene of calm. The waters of the lake itself were like rippled slate and in the distance merged into the black mass of the hills of the Rift. Above, the picture book sky of dark violet was crowded with low-hanging stars. Everyone there had enjoyed the wonder of nights like this a thousand times. They made their homeland special.

Alex took a long draught on his White-cap before he spoke.

'He was afraid something like this would happen. Told me yesterday when we went over to the new hospital to do some measuring up.' He raised his hand to forestall his wife's comment. 'He thought about … disappearing. Waste of time. Where can you hide from that lot? With young Ewan in tow.'

Paul was able to introduce a new line of thought.

'There have been rumours. The press has lost interest in the fires up here. The usual thing. A bigger fish has swum into the pool. Assassination! Now, think about that. And the Big Man in the firing line. Kenya's version of the John Kennedy saga.'

His sister, Maria, pointed out something else.

'This Big Man has survived. He'll be some kind of hero and the person who tried to kill him … He'll need police protection.'

Rafaella, matriarch of the McCall family, was deeply hurt by the destruction of the house that had been built for her by her husband, Don, as a wedding present on her arrival from Verona and had been her home for over half a century. But new stones would be bought and fresh timbers would be laid.

Minutes before she had sat at the bedside of a beautiful child as he cried himself to sleep. Tom had read from Ewan's favourite storybook and Rebecca had sung to him.

'The boy knows that we all love him, but children are not stupid. Our lies do not fool him. Only Bertie can soothe this heartache. I fear for Bertie. Do those people feel nothing?'

'Please, forgive the ramblings of an old woman. I think that I have lived long enough. I do not recognise this world as God's creation any more. I would be happy to go now.'

She felt a hand take hers. She looked up from her chair and was surprised to find Angela Kamau standing over her. Apart from surprise, she also experienced a deep sense of shame. Angela had been a maid in Londiani since the day that Stephen had brought her there when he had begun to work on the farm for Don. Rafaella and she had never had a cross word. But why was it at that moment of personal anguish that she had noticed the beauty of this Somali woman's face? The smile of compassion, the feminine purity reminded her of the face of the angel painted on the wall behind the altar of Saint Veronica's Church in the village of her own grandmother.

Rafaella did not secretly chide herself for not being a good mistress. That would have been unfair. But had she been guilty of pride, a sense of superiority? She was not allowed time to dwell on this unexpected new piece of gloom that had entered her life.

'Memsahib, tomorrow you and I will go on a small journey together. We have work to do.'

When would these strange happenings cease? Angela loved her life on the lakeside. Her three girls had been born there. On the night, many years before, when she had fled her home village in the north to escape the fate of becoming the second wife of Ahmed, the rich man who was old enough to be her father, she had cut herself adrift from family, friends and settled patterns of life. It had been a desperate move for an innocent country girl to go down to the city where hundreds of young Somali beauties like herself survived by hiring out their bodies. But Angela had met first the Shah family and then the big coastie boy on his way up-country to take up a job in the flower business. She thanked God every day for protecting her.

She was a woman who enjoyed being in the background. She had a husband who was known and respected in Naivasha town and the villages 'round about. Her firstborn had been acclaimed for her beauty and her voice in the great United States. So to be in the laundry garden, thrusting her arms into the warm, soapy water of the deep metal troughs or being in the kitchen at Londiani with two mistresses who treated her like a friend, what more could she ask for?

And now, this self-effacing woman was giving instructions to her older mistress. This was not the way things were done in the farms in the White Highlands. And this was why everyone sitting out in the garden of Rusinga Farm was riveted into silence, especially Stephen and Rebecca. Had the housemaid crossed an invisible but real line in the antiquated system of hierarchy?

'And may I ask where this journey will take us? I hope it will not be too far. You know that I am not happy driving a car these days.'

There was no hint of sarcasm in Rafaella's tone. Quite the opposite, Rafaella's spirits had been given a lift by Angela's bold move.

'It is a long way, but I shall ask Bwana Thomas to take us.'

'Bwana Thomas will be happy to drive two beautiful women to the North Pole, if that's where they want to go.'

Tom was also excited and wanted to know more.

'North Pole is too far to go in one day. Too cold for Kenyan people. Last night I sat up by the village fire. You know that Isaac is there every night. He was reading his Bible to me. And we prayed together. Many hours. Many times, over and over, the words came. Every time the same. I spoke to Isaac about these things. He tells me that I have been blessed. I must obey. Rebecca will come, too. And one other.'

# Chapter Eight

George, the day porter at the Karen home of the Rubai family, was having a busy morning. Since eight o'clock hospital vans and cars had been coming and going. Bwana was coming home in the afternoon. The doctors had warned him about the dangers of leaving the hospital environment too early. Abel had insisted that he was ready to leave and a compromise had been reached which involved temporarily converting a large ground floor room into a hospital ward.

Just after ten, three unexpected visitors had arrived at the lodge gate. George explained to Sally.

'Yes, Madam, there was a car. I did not recognise it. Three passengers stepped out and crossed the road to our gate. No, Madam, I have not seen them before, but two of the names are familiar. Certainly, Madam. Rafaella McCall and Angela Kamau. The third is a white toto. They will not give his name. Yes, I will escort them myself.'

Sally went to the front door to greet the newcomers. They were not welcome, but she had always been welcomed at Londiani. The least she could do in return was to be polite and hope they would not stay long. And who could the toto be?

Rafaella introduced the little stranger.

'Ewan Briggs. You have met his father.'

Sally could not hide her shock, but she managed to hold

back the angry words that this rude intrusion was stirring inside her. A maid had accompanied her to the door.

'Alice, take the child into the kitchen. He has come a long way this morning.' And to Ewan, 'Child, go with Alice. She has some special treats for boys who know how to behave themselves.'

A bewildered Ewan looked up at Rafaella and when she gave him the nod happily skipped off down the passageway.

Sally was in for more surprises. When the door of the sitting room was closed behind the three of them, Sally was expecting to launch into a lesson on proper behaviour when one was bent on visiting good company. Angela was too quick for her.

'Madam, I am very sorry for the trouble that has come to your family. I feel the pain deeply. Perhaps you know that recently I thought that my Stephen had been taken from me.'

'Yes, I know this.'

Sally was not enjoying the coldness she was effortlessly injecting into the tone of her voice. She sensed danger. This housemaid had not dressed up in an elegant blue suit that highlighted the handsome figure and the fine head just to deliver a few clichés about sympathy. Neither did Sally relish what she saw as a disdainful smile on the lips of the McCall woman. In fact, Rafaella was simply standing in admiration at the performance of this new confident housemaid.

Sally tried a counterattack. 'Ladies, how wonderful to see you both looking so … well. But you will have to excuse me. The master is coming home this afternoon. He has suffered much these last few days.'

Why did she, the mistress of this house, feel so trapped, so unable to send these two off with a few sharp words? She was about to try again when there was a gentle tap on the door.

Alice's timing was awry. Sally had not wanted the child to be brought into this room. In spite of herself, she warmed to the boy's enthusiasm and (she hated the idea) his vulnerability.

Angela was in no mood to hold back. She was perfectly aware that her behaviour was not the kind that would go down well in bwana land, black or white. But these were circumstances that cried out for something else. A fine man's life was in danger, a small boy's life was on the edge of ruin. Self-pity was not an option.

'Madam, you know this boy's father?'

'Yes, of course. Bwana Briggs. I have seen him in Londiani.'

'He has been taken. Eight policemen from Nairobi came for him yesterday.'

'Eight?'

'So you know?'

Sally had not invited her visitors to sit down. She wanted the meeting to be brief. Rafaella took Ewan's hand and led him across the room towards a large bay window where he knelt on the cushioned seat. While he looked out onto the terrace and the garden beyond, she watched the exchanges continue from a distance. It was like a scene in a courtroom. On the one side she was seeing a totally new Angela, a woman grim-faced and determined. Sally was uncomfortable under this barrage of relentless questioning, apprehensive about the state of mind of this normally gentle, polite maid.

Rafaella considered stepping in to end the embarrassment. Her attention was drawn away by Ewan pointing to something going on outside. A very large man was moving towards them along the drive, struggling under the weight of a wooden box. The boy was anxious with both hands pressed to his face, afraid that the man would fall. The man passed out of sight to the relief of Ewan.

In her own tense state, her reaction to the brief incident was to remind herself of why Angela was across the room from her, being impolite, being aggressive to the mistress of this grand but ugly house. The wounded master would be returning that very afternoon, the ruthless, murdering power maniac, unchanged by his close brush with death, still in pursuit of anyone brave enough or stupid enough to stand in his way.

The result was that all trace of embarrassment at the way Angela was grilling Sally was gone. She was silently cheering her on.

'Yes, I know. I also know why this has happened. In this country, you cannot go around trying to kill people because they have offended you.'

'Madam, you are right. You say you know. But do you know why?'

'Why do you talk in riddles?'

'No riddles, Madam. I will tell you.'

Rafaella sat back, fell back onto the support of the window seat and grasped Ewan's hand. Surely not! Angela, be very careful. No, darling, just be brave.

'Yes, the father of this child here did fire the bullet that almost took the life of your husband. But at that very moment your husband had a gun in his hands, too, and he was about to pull the trigger and take the life … of Thomas McCall.'

'That is not true!'

Angela swept on. 'Oh, but it is true.'

'You cannot prove this!'

'In this country, you cannot go around trying to kill people just because they have offended you. There are many witnesses. Bwana Briggs has been taken because he saved a life. I am very sorry to have to say these things to you, Madam.

A good man's life is in danger. Even at this moment we do not know where he is.'

At the end of moments of silence, Angela began again. Her manner was gentle, compassionate but also pleading.

'You can save this man's life. You can bring happiness back to this child. This child never knew his mother. You would understand the pain of this.'

Pleading but calculating. It was not only Sally Rubai who knew the teaching about serpents and doves.

On the short walk between the Rubai house and the Daniels' house where Rebecca and Tom were waiting for them, Angela seemed drained of energy. She offered to carry Ewan, but the little man refused. Angela was not offended by the rejection.

'I could murder a mug of chai. Plenty of sugar, Angela. How many times has Bwana Alex come into the kitchen and said this?'

'Murder.' Rafaella was surprised that Angela could use this word so casually. But this was the old, familiar Angela. She had followed the instructions of the message. The job was done. Time to move on.

# Chapter Nine

Abel arrived home late. Even as the porters were transferring him from the trolley to his bed, his doctors were making a last attempt to get their patient to change his mind.

'Situations can change quickly at this stage of recovery. We may need —'

'That's why you're leaving me two of your top nurses, at great expense, I should add …'

'Abel, your life could be in danger. Money is not important.'

'Mmn, not important, Sally?'

'You know what I mean. I am so pleased to have you back with us.'

Sally was not being entirely truthful. The reverberations from her confrontation with the housemaid of Londiani were still troubling her. Perhaps it would have been better if she could have had another twenty-four hours to absorb them, to deal with their implications. She had spent the hours since the departure of her unexpected visitors on her own. Uncomfortable thoughts had been swirling around her mind. That woman had been so sure of herself. So sure, and so unlike the shy maid she remembered from times when their paths had previously crossed, so driven. Why did she bring the child? She had caressed her own belly, felt the movement of her own boy. In three weeks her new Julius would be with her. This white toto would be back home by now, in a place where he had never known the love of a mother and deserted by his father.

Her own home had been her fortress, but however hard she tried in the loneliness of that dark afternoon, she felt a great certainty that the walls were crumbling around her.

'Abel! Abel!' She lay her head down on the open pages of her Bible and wept herself into a fitful doze.

And now he was with her again. Her love for him was as strong as ever. She found it easy to keep desperate thoughts hidden.

Just before the doctors left to return to their other patients in the hospital, a last visitor arrived. He took pictures of her smiling husband sitting up in bed, flanked by his two new carers, and was gone.

'Sally, tomorrow morning when you send the boy over to Karen Dukas for the paper, tell him to bring half a dozen copies of *The Nation* and *The Standard.*

He chuckled to see the big-eyed puzzlement on her face. 'I can tell you the headlines right now. "Assassination attempt. Big Man survives attack on his life" or some such words. They could not hold the story back any longer. Too many rumours.' He chuckled again. 'I was a dead man in most of them!'

They were alone by now. The time for light-heartedness was over. He knew that.

'Sal, you know how much you mean to me.'

'I know it.' She was not ready to meet his gaze. This and the deadpan expression in her voice troubled him.

'The new boy will be with us soon. Right? So you will have two babies to look after.'

His hearty good humour began to shift her mood, but her tone remained down-beat.

'Husband, you have never needed anyone to look after you.

Even as a young man in Western District. Your mama told me this.'

He changed the subject. 'They've caught the one who did this.'

'Bertie Briggs. I know it. His boy was here this morning.'

'His boy!'

At last she had said something to startle him.

'He was with Rebecca's mother and the Italian one.'

'But why?'

'To sympathise.' She lied. She did not care that he knew this. She needed to be alone again. She rang the call bell. 'They have told me that you will need much rest. I will see you in the morning. I will bring the newspapers. Sleep well, Abel.'

'One last thing, Sally. The house phones will be off for two days. Use your mobile. And there will be policemen around the place. Reporters, too. They will not trouble you.'

'Thank you, Abel.' He watched her make her way wearily towards the door. She hesitated before going through as though about to say something more. Nothing. Sally cried herself to sleep that night.

# Chapter Ten

'They are holding him in Nakuru police station.' Inspector Caroline had brought the news herself. 'John Wambui is still the inspector in charge up there.'

Tom was the first to remember. 'The one who brought me home in the squad car after my enforced camping night out in Kakamega Forest? Funny chap. Said the plumbing was out of order in the police block. He wanted me to hang on to my filth 'til I got home. Make him look better as my rescuer.'

'Yep. Damned sight different from the gang of thugs who took Bertie off from here. Seemed eager to help.'

'Yes, Alex, but I hate to remind you how he sucked up to Rubai when he arrived unannounced with Sally to cover up his own part in Tom's … ordeal.'

'I'd forgotten, Maura. So he's just another of Rubai's boys. Bugger! Thought we were getting a bit of good news. Tell you, I'm scared stiff.'

'But surely Bertie's got some rights. You know, seeing a lawyer and stuff.'

Paul Miller had a suggestion. 'No, Tom. They've got him. There aren't many Carolines around in the system. But, what about this? I know Wambui quite well and he will listen. I suggest that we set off for Nakuru straight away and take our chances. Those reports in the papers this morning will raise the stakes for us and especially Bertie, of course. The hotheads will be out looking for the person who tried to take out their beloved – no kidding – beloved leader. When they find out that it is a white man, well, just think about the kind of savagery a little old election can spark off in this country.'

'So who goes, Paul?'

'Me for a start. I'm good at waving official looking bits of paper around in policemen's faces. They rarely read them. Rafaella, could you take another one of these, well, mercy missions?'

Rafaella arched her eyebrows in surprise. 'Delighted! Thought I was a bit past this James Bond stuff.'

'It's my experience that Kenyan policemen always have a respect for, shall we say, European ladies of mature years. Something to do with their country upbringing. And when they are also beautiful … And Tom to drive.'

'Perhaps he'll remember me.'

'Come on. Let's get going.'

The road between Naivasha and Nakuru had been recently resurfaced. This improvement to travelling conditions had its drawbacks. The large intercity coaches hurtled along the A104 faster than ever. The number one rule for the sensible car driver was to look constantly in the rear-view mirror watching for a *Kisii Executive* or an *Eldoret Express* bearing down on you. Rule number two was never to try to outrun these field marshals of the highway. They took no prisoners.

Tom and his passengers used the forty-five minute journey to prepare themselves for whatever they might meet when they climbed those steps to the police building on Odinga Odinga Avenue. On that morning the extraordinary beauty of the Great Rift of Central Kenya was simply a backdrop to help them form a perspective to their thoughts. The familiar sights of the Sleeping Masai, the thick pink border of flamingos feeding on the edges of the soda lake at Elementeita, the lines of jacaranda in full blossom on the long, gentle incline down to the old railway bridge that marked the boundary of Nakuru town were a comfort.

They left the car in the safe haven of the Rift Valley Club and walked through a quiet part of town to their destination. They were almost there when they were hailed from the other side of the road by two women wearing nuns' headdress. Rafaella knew them well.

'May and Phillipa. They're from Ireland, been here thirty years. We must talk to them.'

The chance meeting turned out to be a blessing though it delayed their arrival at the police station. May surprised them, not only with the attractive Limerick brogue that was as strong as on the day she had arrived all those years before.

'You've come to visit. Now, there's an answer to a prayer. He's not happy in there. Missing the boy something terrible. Come inside for a minute. It will be safer to talk.'

The Catholic Cathedral in Nakuru is almost exactly across the road from the police station. Rafaella and the sisters had been friends for years.

'We meet every month when I come for confession.'

'Bertie and Anna were married here and the boy baptised.'

'The saddest day of my life. We haven't seen him or his father since. Too painful for him.'

'Until three days ago. Phillipa and I were returning from visiting 'round the town, just like today. There was a big fuss over there, again! Some poor soul was being dragged from a car. Big, ugly brutes, not our local boys. We know most of them. This one was struggling, shouting. European voice. English.'

'We got the one look. Anna's Bertie.'

'After supper we went over. They usually let us in.'

'They've learnt. We've got a great line in shouting and screaming ourselves if we can't have our way.'

'Poor man. They'd given him a beating. Worse than usual. But it was his boy that was giving him the real pain.'

'We hope you can get him out. Bail or something.'

'Paul, we know a lot about Serena. The father and we often talk about it. There's a lot of support here. You're giving us hope.'

Paul was smiling. 'Ladies, you, too, are an answer to prayer. Bless us before we go over there. As for bail, I'm surprised they don't give it more often. Think of the money they're missing. But … I have, well, there are other ways of fighting back.'

John Wambui was tidying his desk when the duty sergeant came in to report.

'Boss, some folks in the office want to speak with you.'

'Like who, exactly?'

'Smart fella, 'bout your age. Name of Miller. Says he's a lawyer. Two white folks. The woman don't look too young, but, well, nice ass, a heavy pair up top.'

'Matthew, do you have to talk like this? Seems to me you got some kind of problem with your dick. Just let's be a bit more careful with our words here. And the other one?'

'McCall. Name ring a bell? A few months back …'

The Wambui face lit up. The inspector was recalling the happiest day of his police career.

'Thomas, the kid from the Kakamega Forest? Bring him in! Bring them all in! Wait a minute. What do they want?'

'A visit. The farmer the Nairobi boys brought in. Attempted murder. Hey, by the way, did you see the papers yet? Assassination.'

'Attempted ... attempted. Get your facts right. You're a cop, don't forget.'

Wambui was in a quandary. He liked the people waiting out in the office and he wanted to oblige them. But this Briggs, he was a high priority prisoner. Mmn, what to do?

'Okay, bring them in. Executive decision. Matthew, watch me and learn.'

As the inspector feared, this Miller was a tricky operator. So many questions: diet, exercise, visitors, did he think this place was some kind of hotel? In the end Wambui gave in.

'Right, twenty minutes with Prisoner 22146.'

'No supervision.'

'No supervision, okay. Twenty minutes and then you all disappear.'

Bertie had been hit about. That was obvious from the difficulty he had crossing his tiny cell to greet them and the bruises and cuts clearly visible on his face. None of this was a concern for him.

'Ewan, how's he going, Raf?

'Missing his daddy.' She was smiling through her tears. 'He's smart, that's for sure. When he gets one of us on our own, he's full of questions, usually the same ones to each of us. If the answers don't add up ...'

'I've asked them if they'll let him visit. They just laugh. "Bwana, you would not be allowing your son to come into a dump like this! That's bad, man, so bad".' After a long silence he began again. 'I don't think I'm going to get out of here. Seen the papers? Assassination. I'm a fool. Could have finished him off. No trouble. Left him for the birds and the ants to clear up. Probably turn their guts over. Do you think ants have guts, Tom? Instead, I'll be the one having the little accident. Probably take me down to the park. You know, late at night job.'

The tears were flowing freely now from Tom as well as his grandmother. Paul, conscious of the passing time, stepped in.

'That's enough! Bertie, you are not going to rot in this place or another one like it. And the scavengers are not going to be picking at your bones on some mountain top.'

Paul had been inside his country's jails on many occasions, visiting friends or clients. They were places that bred a sense of despair, hopelessness. Bertie, like so many others, was in a state of deep shock. He himself had to fight hard to keep down the feelings of helplessness that threatened to overwhelm him. In a few minutes he would be back on the street, but for now, on the inside, he knew that the best he could do was to share the anguish, to try to understand the cold reality of what it was like to have the precious gift of freedom suddenly wrenched away. Words or silence, which helped more? He was never sure.

The look in Bertie's eyes frightened him. A sensitive man brooding on feelings of injustice created a dangerous situation. In those moments when the blackness was at its deepest, the urge to create one's own peace became seductive and the balance of the mind was easily disturbed. Paul knew that to survive intact Bertie would need to have deep inside him a core of belief, a hard centre that no one, nothing could destroy. His sister, Maria, was the only person he knew who could foster this kind of hope. She had the gift of making the delicate mind feel strong again.

Self-belief, the possibility of change for the better, mental toughness, so easy to talk about, to think about as ideals.

'Bertie, ever read *The Count of Monte Christo*?'

'Yeah, as a kid. Loved it.'

'What a man, eh? Edmund Dantes. I think about him often

when I come into places like these. Words on a page. Cheap talk. Yes.'

Bertie laughed. 'I see. For Edmund Dantes, read Bertie Briggs.'

'Sorry, Bertie. I get these … notions sometimes. Out they come. Talking too much. Runs in the family.'

'Yeah, the Chateau d'If, another hellhole. Bloody marvellous. Best book I ever read.'

'Bertie, listen.' Paul spoke quietly but with a sense of urgency. 'I think we can get you out of this place.'

'We?'

'Daniel and I. You remember Daniel Komar. You met him at the Rugby Sevens in Pembroke. His nephew was playing for the Banda. Another lawyer, I'm afraid.'

'So?'

'Fighting fire with fire. Just think about us like we are that little old man in the next cell to Edmund.'

Bertie's gaze narrowed. 'You believe this, don't you?'

'Not just a story to help make you feel good. Bertie, patience. I didn't want to come out with it yet. And, please God, remember …'

'That it could all go down the gurgler …'

The cell door creaked open. 'Time's up. Time to go.'

Wambui himself had ventured down to the cell to let the visitors out. He watched the long embraces of farewell and as he bent to lock the door, he said to Bertie, 'Mr Briggs, it is my wish that some day soon I will walk down to this place to open this door and say goodbye. Perhaps I could get Matthew to polish up the squad car and we could drive together to Naivasha.'

# Chapter Eleven

Jim Sawyer had broken off work to come to the meeting. He had left his two stonemasons to finish the job of pointing the outside walls on the bungalow that would soon be the home of Rebecca and Tom. He could see the building set on the knoll just about a hundred metres away and from where he sat on the veranda of the ruin of what the farm workers referred to as 'Big House', he could understand why his men had started calling it 'Long House'.

'So, Jim, what should we do here?'

'Spoilt for choice, Alex. This veranda has polished up well. Wonderful stuff, not a crack in it. Blue marble. Can't get it any more. I suggest that you keep this as the heart of the house. If you still want to rebuild, that is. On the phone a couple of days ago …'

'Yeah, yeah, I know. But they'd just taken Bertie then. Now I feel we owe it to him to stay. Last thing Ewan needs is a big move.'

'Okay. Debbie will tell you that I was speaking to her just before we sat down. I feel happy with a pile of bricks to look after or a few lengths of new timber. Love the smells of my work. But, Debbie, I'm confused. You're American, but your dad …'

'Was born in Western District. Luo. Barnie is Paul's brother and their sister, my aunt, Maria.'

'Wow. I just about follow that. But even an up-country boy like me can see that, well, this is a bit more than putting up a house here or getting a hospital going. Not sure if I'm up to it.

'I took my degree in Boston, Public Building … but you know all this. I really came over to work on plans for the hospital with Rebecca. When we were kids, Daddy used to tell us stories about home here. They were just crazy sometimes. "Oh, Daddy, come on!" "Ah, but you see". And he ended them all in the same way: "Always something new out of Africa". I can see what he meant now. But I guess I didn't expect so much so quickly.'

Maura set down her empty tray on the wall next to where she was sitting. 'Neither did we. To be honest, we toyed with the idea of taking off for the coast for a week. Taking Ewan, letting him play on the beach or something. We were pretty down.'

'Maria, you soon knocked us on the head for that.'

'Alex, Luo women are headstrong. You know that.'

'My father had his expressions, too, Debbie. "A spade is a bloody spade, son. Tell it like it is." So "selfish", "self-pitying", "running away", Dad would have approved.'

Maura took up the thread again. '"Dead man walking". There's another one for the collection. Bloody, bloody depressing and all the other negative words rattling 'round in my head.'

'Leo Mackie's butterflies. He had cases of them in his old shack in the grounds of Pembroke. Beautiful creatures, every one held down on its bit of parchment by a steel pin through the guts. Powerless. That's me, too.'

'Thomas, forget us. What about Bertie? Too much time to think, mostly about Ewan. Perhaps … I am afraid. He can't cope.'

'But, Rafaella ...'

Jim looked across at Alex. 'Shall I go back to the house? Help with pointing. I'm upset myself, but for you people ... I don't know what's for the best.'

'Listen!' There was anger in Maria's voice. 'Listen! Carry another person in your hearts for a few minutes. Simon Mboya. I was one of the first to see him after Hosea's men found his body on the side of the road in Kericho. Knife wounds in his back and his hands, a doctor's healing hands, hacked so badly that his fingers were hanging off. And another person and this one sitting over there between his wife and daughter. Burned in the fire where forty-five of his friends lost their lives. And you, Thomas ...'

'Maria, you're right, but you are also strong.' There was a tremble in Maura's voice as though she was pleading for forgiveness, mercy even.

'So we sit round here and wait for the butcher to pick out another target. Why don't we all just drive down to Karen and stand in line outside that monstrosity of a house and invite him to get it over with? I'm sorry. I'm going too far.'

'No, Maria.' Stephen Kamau's rich, melodious voice turned heads towards the place where he was rising to his feet. 'No, Mister Sawyer, you must not go back to your work yet. I see that you are almost finished with that house. Well, I for one want you and you, Miss Debbie, to make your plans for the new life that will soon be growing here. We cannot allow them to suck the marrow out of our bones. I miss my plants. I want my hands to be busy again. There is no choice.'

The emotional temperature was rising. Maria judged that the moment had come to share her news.

'Daniel Komar and my brother are on their way to join us here. Paul tells me that lawyers have to take good care how they act and how they speak. They have been working very hard and now there is a plan. They are ready to take a big risk, to be reckless. I'm excited.

* * *

'Paul and I have been getting a case ready. We're usually in the business of defending, mostly someone who's being screwed by our beloved government. This time we're bringing the case. We have a defendant. The name of Abel Rubai. Yes, we know what you are going to say and we agree with you. No judge in this country who values his life will take this case on.'

'Not to mention your lives.'

'Right, Alex. The thought has entered our heads. But … we have a judge who is willing to give the charge a hearing. Joshua Gombo.'

'Crazy Josh. I thought he was dead.'

'Old, but not dead. He was around in 1963, best young lawyer in the country, friend of Tom Mboya. Even the Brits thought he was quality when they gave the country back to us.'

'Too good, of course. And another Luo. That didn't help. When they got rid of Tom, Joshua … He told us one late afternoon. He was lecturing in the uni law school. Brilliant. His courses were always oversubscribed. This day he asked us to stay behind. I think he saw something promising in us. "Men, Tom was the best political man this country has ever had, but dead bones, what use are they? I'm on the list. I know it. So I teach and I write and sometimes I do something a little bit, shall we say, odd. Keep them guessing. One day, my chance will come. I've watched you two. Keep an eye out for each other. They want to make me a judge. I'll do a good job but quietly. I want you to know before the news comes out. Trust me and don't forget me. One day, perhaps you will need me. I'll be ready." The day has come.'

'More bones on the mountain tops!'

'Alex, we're telling you just in case.'

'Yeah, Daniel and I have talked that one through, several times!'

'And this is all we are telling you. Keep your eyes open. It is safer this way. So why did we come all this way to …'

'Tell you nothing?'

Tom McCall understood. 'You've told us all we need to know. Maria, I'm excited, too!'

The following Saturday *The Nation* carried an article written by the editor, Laurie Patel. It was one of what he called his 'occasional pieces'. Laurie was the youngest editor in the history of the paper and, at first, had been a very reluctant one. A year before, Adil, his father and predecessor in the job, had called him home.

'The paper needs a young man's energy and new ideas. Come and show us some of the smart things you have learned in that University of Oxford and at those parties in London that you keep writing to your mother about.'

To Laurie's surprise, he had loved his new job from his first morning down at the Nairobi office. Within a month, circulation had begun to rise. Very early on, he had seen that, as boss, there were special treats to enjoy. He chose to combine his love of writing and fascination for liberal ideas to conjure up articles on subjects that interested him but always with a Kenya slant. Mildly disapproving of such indulgences, Adil had given the pieces the title of 'sophisticated ramblings'.

Readers loved them and every time they appeared, they sparked discussion in the lounges of the Nairobi Club and Muthaiga and on the street corners and in the cafes where the wananchi chewed on their roasted maize cobs or sipped their glasses of strong coffee. And when the editor of *The Washington Post* had asked permission to reproduce a piece entitled, 'Aid or Aids, which is the greater villain?' even Adil was impressed.

So, on that Saturday, 'Time to speak up for the little people' intrigued the huge band of faithful readers. None of these was aware of the influence that two Nairobi lawyers and founders of the newest political party had had on the writing. The theme was a call for more equality in the courts, a well-worn topic, but there was an edge, an aggression in the writing that angered a few but delighted the vast majority, one paragraph above all.

'Perhaps the situation is about to change. I have heard a rumour that one of our big boys is about to feel the heat of the blowtorch. Now that would be a case worth watching in court! What would the charge be? Would it be a police prosecution? What judge would be ready to put himself forward to conduct the case, knowing the risks involved in a failed prosecution, or even a successful one?'

What the readers did not know was that the article was not simply a piece of ordinary journalism. Mister Komar and Mister Miller were making their first move. Others would follow very soon. The first came on that very afternoon.

All Saints' Cathedral on Kenyatta Avenue was full to capacity. The youngest daughter of Alfred Shimba was marrying the son of the most prosperous tea-planter in Western District. The father of the bride was one of the twelve, the mysterious band of brothers whom Abel Rubai had gathered around him. In theory, they were meant to be seen as advisors to the president. In theory. In reality, they took their orders from the King of Karen. Membership was fluid. Displease Sir Abel and you would find yourself in the outer darkness, cut off from all the privileges and deal making that the big man watched over.

An invitation was a must for anyone who wanted to think of himself or herself as a member of the social elite on the Nairobi scene. Alfred and Mrs Shimba had requested the presence of the company of Daniel and Ann Komar and Paul and Marion Miller out of reluctant respect to the founders of the latest in a line of insignificant protest parties with delusions of grandeur. Their places were far back in the nave, but they were happy to be present at the marriage of two young people they had never set eyes on before that day.

The ceremony over, the celebrations continued further up the hill at the Nairobi Club. The buffet lunch was followed by entertainment in the great lounge, cleared of its solid oak tables and its leather chairs. A heavily pregnant lady soon tired of the noise and the exuberant behaviour of the young set of Nairobi socialites. When she stepped outside to take the cool afternoon air with a stroll around the boundary of the club's cricket pitch, she had company.

Sally Rubai had not seen Ann Komar for at least twenty years, since the days when they had worked together at Neisland, Kapper and Reed, the city accountants. She was excited to have met her former colleague and the bond of friendship was instantly renewed. Ann introduced Marion and the three women ambled happily towards the pavilion, at ease with each other and filling the minutes with unbroken conversation.

'Ann, you haven't changed one single bit.'

'Nor you.'

Sally let out one of her gravelly chuckles. 'Where did you learn to tell nice fibs like that? This is all me, you know.' She wobbled her body briefly to prove her point. 'This remind you of something? Like the jelly they used to sell in that café at the top of Kamathi Street.'

'The place we went to for lunch on a Friday.'

A shadow passed across Sally's face as she stared for a moment out towards the line of pine trees sheltering the club grounds from the Ngong Road and its Saturday traffic.

'You two are lucky, you know. I can't do that any more. Just wander where I please. Is that place still there?'

Ann shrugged. Marion was able to clear up the mystery. 'It's a bar. Yes, another one. Rough place. Paul had a case about six months ago. Somebody hit somebody over the head with a chair, or was it a table? I forget.'

'This used to be such a beautiful city. I remember the day when Abel and I moved into our first house. On Wiaki Way. A palace. Then Julius came along and I finished work.'

Sally noticed the exchange of anxious glances between her companions. She reassured them. 'It's all right. I'm getting over it. Well, you never do, I don't think, but you know …'

She sighed and made an effort to lighten the mood. 'Anyway,' she caressed her belly. 'My new baby. My Julius. Yes, I know it will be a boy. We talk a lot! Crazy?'

'No. Beautiful.'

'Thank you, Marion. Look, if you don't mind, I think I ought to go back. Go home. I enjoy this blubber, but I'm not so happy with the walking these days.'

Ann had a deep affection for Sally and this made the pangs of guilt bite more deeply. Daniel and Paul would have to look for some other way. And at that precise moment, Sally paused and laid her hand across Ann's arm. She had an idea.

'Listen. Come to lunch tomorrow. Bring a man, your husbands if you have to. Alfred and Molly, the bride's parents, are coming 'round. I could do with some help. Cheering up poor Molly. The nest is empty. She's very weepy about the whole business.'

* * *

Paul drove the four of them back to Langata. The mood in the car was gloomy on the feminine side.

'Daniel, she's such a good girl. I always thought she was better at the work than he was. I feel a bit tainted, dirty, using her like this.'

'Sweetheart – dirty. That's the perfect word for this kind of business. But, to be blunt, she must have switched off somewhere along the line. You say she was bright with figures. Yet there must have been dozens of times when she couldn't make two and two add up to four.'

'Typical man's answer. She loves him.'

'And love is the coverall.'

'And, do you know, I think he loves her so much that he makes sure that she never gets a sniff of all the, the stuff he gets up to.'

'So the big butcher has a tender side to him. I could be cynical and suggest that he uses her as a kind of front in some inexplicable way.'

The remainder of the journey passed in an uncomfortable silence. Ann Komar's discomfort was born out of an acknowledgement that her husband's take on reality was stronger, braver than her own. He had no hiding place. He had to make uncomfortable choices and stand or fall by them.

For his part Daniel, and Paul, too, was fighting hard to keep a firm hold on anxiety. Their plan was outrageous and very risky. They would be heavily dependent on the element of surprise. They would be up against a formidable and ruthless opponent, fighting a battle on his territory. But the adrenalin rush was already beginning. They were excited and had not the slightest wish to back off and settle for some safe and useless compromise.

* * *

The food for Sunday lunch in the Pink Palace was delicious, but Paul Miller and Daniel Komar had no relish for what Sally repeatedly described as 'La cuisine française', prepared by Marcel, some famous French cook from some even more famous French restaurant. To have said that they had no stomach for the delights on offer was literally true. Their insides were churning with uncomfortable thoughts. Their digestive system was temporarily out of order. But their conversation was sparkling, witty yet inoffensive. There was plenty of laughter in that elegantly designed but garishly furnished dining room.

But Abel Rubai, recovering fast, was feeling particularly good-humoured. Perhaps that was why he made a miscalculation about why these two unwelcome luncheon guests looked anxious and uncomfortable. He saw plainly that they were a little too manic in their conversation pieces. They were fine, eloquent speakers. He had seen both of them perform in court. Perhaps they were overawed. Perhaps they were conscious of the aura of power that hung about the place. He surprised himself with his feelings of sympathy for them. When Alfred had been forced to leave the little party early to take his inconsolable Molly home, Abel decided that a display of his resources might be a good idea. Might help these two lightweights to understand what they were up against when they started playing politics.

'Gentlemen, come and have a look at this.'

As he led the way down a wide corridor towards the east wing of the house, he affably explained something of what they were about to see.

'I call it the green heart of the house. Don't usually bring visitors here.'

He stopped by a pair of double doors and, using a remote control, caused what sounded like a heavy bolt to be released. He led the way into the windowless room and, again using the remote, brought to life a bank of screens that stretched the length of the facing wall.

'Green, you see?'

Abel was purring with self-assurance. The elegant city lawyers exchanged looks of wide-eyed amazement. Abel was beginning to think that Sally's idea of inviting these people to lunch was doing him a favour. These potential election rivals were getting the message in the clearest possible way. KANU versus Serena, what a joke.

'Awesome, don't you think?'

Paul searched his mind for a reply that would not give away his real opinion. He settled for a limp, 'Most impressive, sir. Don't you think so, Daniel?'

'Never seen anything like it. Man, this must cost you a mighty lot of shillings for the electricity alone.'

Abel narrowed his gaze. Why was he getting the feeling that these two punks were far from impressed with what they were seeing?

He pressed another button on his remote and the two lines of six screens directly above his desk were no longer blank. Faces in close-up appeared on each of them and, behind these faces, more banks of computers. Abel was eager to explain.

'Each of these screens is linked to stock markets all over

the world. I call these the big twelve – London, New York, Tokyo and so on. They never shut down. I want to tell you something else.' He hesitated briefly before making his big statement.

'You know that it's a common insult put about by those who don't know the facts that the people who help to look after this country are on the take, have their hands in the till, say it how you will. Well, this man,' and he pointed both hands dramatically towards his heart, 'has never taken a single shilling out of the money that belongs to the wananchi. Not a shilling. This is where I make my dollars, my pounds. I go out there into the global marketplace and compete.'

'That is a wonderful thing to be able to say.' Daniel, though tempted, did not go on to pose the supplementary question about the rest of the big man's colleagues and their financial habits. Instead he shifted the conversation to where he and Daniel wanted it to be.

'Can you pick up other things here? Films, newspapers, books. You know.'

'What do mean specifically?'

'Well, take newspapers. You could save money …'

'For one thing, I don't need to save money on newspapers. I never read them. Too full of crap.'

'Not even *The Nation*, with all the local news?'

'That rag. Sally's got an addiction that I can't cure.'

'So you didn't see the article by Laurie Patel?'

'That communist!'

'He's no communist.' Paul was ready to move in. 'Did you know that his wife is a Catholic?'

'She could be a transvestite gorilla for all I care.' Abel was rapidly becoming bored. He realised now that he had made a big mistake in inviting these two smart-arsed pygmies into his inner sanctum. 'Time we rejoined the ladies. I'll just switch off in here.'

Daniel could feel his heartbeat racing. The moment had come.

'Sir, can I quote you something? Very brief.' He did not wait for a reply before reading from a small square of paper. 'Here it is, about law and order in this country: "I have heard a rumour that one of our big boys is about to feel the heat of the blowtorch. Now, that would be a case worth watching in court! What would the charge be? Would it be a police prosecution? What judge would be ready to put himself forward to conduct the case, knowing the risks involved in a failed prosecution, or even a successful one?"'

Abel shrugged. 'So?'

Paul made sure that he was standing directly facing his host when he dropped the bomb.

'You, Mister Rubai, you're the big boy.'

Abel went for his mobile, but as he moved to turn it on, Paul added a caution.

'Before you call your boys to begin the process of turning our two wives in there into widows, just hang on a moment.'

Daniel continued. 'Hear us out. We've taken a few precautions you ought to know about.'

'Let's be honest with you here. We know your style. You don't like somebody, pouf! Instant history. But if we do disappear rather suddenly, then some pieces are going to appear in some pretty important places. *The London Times*, *The Washington Post*. How does that grab you?'

Abel moved forward until he stood toe to toe with Paul Miller, so close that Paul could smell the flavour of the wine that Abel had taken with his lunch.

'You do not have a single thing on me that would stand up in a court in this country. Got it? You are committing delayed suicide.'

'Is that a threat?'

Abel roared with laughter and mimicked the restrained tone in Daniel's voice. 'Is that a threat?'

Paul moved in quickly and confidently. 'We've got a day picked out. We've got a judge and we've got witnesses, one of whom will be Reuben Rubai.'

Before Abel could let rip with his next burst of anger, Paul continued. 'And we are not stupid.'

Daniel, smarting after Abel's little dart of mockery, picked himself up and resumed the attack. 'We don't go along with the Rubai way of doling out punishments, but we know that, for the moment, we can't knock you over.'

An amused Abel interrupted. 'Is that a threat, Miller, Komar, whichever the hell you are?'

'The name is Komar, Daniel Komar. And, no, we don't go in for threats, just promises.'

'So if you have got the sense to see that you cannot "knock me over", what are you two idiots who claim not to be stupid actually after?'

'Bertie Briggs out on the street by tomorrow morning, at the latest, all charges dropped.'

Abel was stunned and turned his red swivel chair and sat down heavily.

'Unbelievable! Unfucking believable! That bastard shot me, damn near killed me.'

'You have no witnesses, no proof. It could have been your American friend.'

'American friend?' Abel sat forward, incredulous.

'Friend, hired gun, whatever. Strange man, but a real pro.

Had every reason to get rid of you. Do you want a name? Alfredo Rossi, Alfred Ross.'

'Now, Mister Bertrand Briggs, back in Naivasha by tomorrow, early enough to take his son breakfast in bed.'

Abel had been caught off guard. He was shocked that anyone but himself had known about Rossi. He was inwardly furious that these two nobodies had managed to manipulate him into a position where he might be vulnerable. He could tough it out, get rid of them even, but he was shrewd enough to see how easy it would be to make a bad situation worse. He hated the idea, but it was time to go on the defensive.

Paul was becoming impatient. Rubai's hesitation was a worry. Time to press the issue.

'At six pm this evening we shall telephone the duty officer at Nakuru police station to check that you have sent a message telling them to release Mister Briggs into the hands, custody if you prefer, of two officers of the Naivasha force. We will contact these two people and they will escort him home. Sorry to be so formal. By the way, I think you should know that we have been making a recording of …'

'That's enough! I will do what you demand. Now, I want you out of here in five minutes. And don't you think that this matter will end here.'

'That goes for us, too, Mister Rubai. Now if you will just allow us enough time to collect our ladies …'

'Just get the hell out of my house.'

It was ten minutes before Abel Rubai returned to the dining room to join his wife who was sitting stony-faced in her chair, sipping from a cup of cold coffee. She looked up as he came in.

'Why, Abel?'

He was in no mood for gentle apologies.

'Those two snakes tricked you.'

'What are you talking about?'

Sally was hurt by the sharpness of his tone. She was bewildered by his reply, but it was obvious that he was deeply upset by something that had happened between him and the two lawyers who, minutes before, had swept in to collect their wives and bring to an abrupt end what had been, for her, a very pleasant reunion with an old friend.

'Abel, do we need to talk? What have I done to upset you?'

Abel pinched the top of his nose as he released a long, slow breath. In a matter of seconds his expression had changed dramatically. The old, familiar tenderness was back. He shifted a chair so that when he sat down he was able to look directly into her eyes and take her hand in his. He sensed that somewhere deep inside him a massive tension had been released.

'Sally, we should have had this conversation a long time ago.'

# Chapter Twelve

'Rebecca, I'm so glad you could come.'

'It's nearly twenty times now. Papa brought me here for the first time when I was three. Mister Freddie was very old then. I remember him playing the piano under the tree next to the veranda. You and your mama were singing.'

'You know Daddy hated to see the flower farms coming to the lake, but he would have been so sad to have seen all this terrible trouble at Londiani. He and Don McCall were good pals. They had their disagreements, but Don never failed to send us beautiful boxes of roses for birthdays and Christmas.'

'Ah, here's Papa. He's the one who always packed those boxes. I helped sometimes.'

'Miss Mollie, no flowers this year. First time Londiani Farm has not sent something to help to decorate the stage for the music festival.'

'Stephen, you two are here. That's enough.'

Mollie Nash reached up to grasp Stephen Kamau's broad shoulders and pull his face close to hers.

'I hear we nearly lost you. Please, forgive the tears. Every year you sing for us and every year, as I watch and listen, I think of those thousands of people in opera houses around the world who will never hear that glorious voice.'

'But, Miss Mollie, you've got Rebecca now. She, we owe you so much.'

'Listen. I must have told you all this before, but I like repeating this story about the family. Father was barely out of school when he came over the mountains with Delamere all those years go. Saw our beautiful lake, fell in love with it and went back to Britain to find a woman ready to share this paradise. Not many living around these parts then, but ten noisy little Nashes soon changed all that.

'Mama said, "Freddie, we could form a choir," and Father said, "Lizzie, we are going to have a festival, every year on your birthday."

'I heard about this music making when I was a youngster living on the coast.'

Mollie hesitated about finishing her family story. She was the last survivor of the original Nash ten. The future of the festival was in good hands, but with each passing year, Mollie became very emotional about the past and about the chances of her surviving to see another one.

'I've never told anyone this bit of the Nash saga. You were just eight, Rebecca. You had sung at the festival. Father was too ill to join us out here, but he listened through that window.'

'And I came inside the house. Bwana Nash was sitting in an armchair by the fire and I sang two songs. I remember them. 'Annie Laurie' and 'The Lord is my shepherd'.

'After you had gone home, he said to us all. "Today, someone came down from heaven to sing to me. I'm ready to go anytime now." Three days later he did go.'

'My heart is beating fast to hear such a thing. Perhaps, if you wish it, I could sing those songs again. Papa …'

'Stephen.' Mollie hesitated again. This time she was afraid that her words would hurt Stephen. 'Stephen, you know that there was something my father loved more than his music, almost as much as he loved his family.'

'I know this thing. We talked about it often. He asked me to leave Londiani. He wanted me to come down here to help with the cattle and the conservation work. One time he asked me to grab a big handful of the rich brown earth and let it run through my fingers. He said, "Stephen, I don't think the good Lord gave us these waters and this soil to grow food and flowers for rich Europeans." We parted friends. Miss Mollie, cattle, conservation, this is not work that I could understand. I told him that Bwana McCall is a good farmer and that he will never hurt the land. And the farm brings work to many, many people, feeds the children.'

'Stephen, there will never be such farms down at this end of South Lake Road. Perhaps flowers will never again be grown on Londiani. Perhaps this will be the beginning of a great change.'

Stephen sighed deeply and put his arm across Rebecca's shoulders. 'Who can know the future? Not a coastie like me, that's for sure. But I do know that many bad things have happened around our part of the lake.'

'Many of our young people have died. We nearly lost Thomas. We nearly lost Papa. We know where many of these bad things come from. We know this man, but we do not fear him.'

# Chapter Thirteen

'No, Sally, don't call Monica. We can leave the coffee and the other stuff 'til later.'

'Abel, you don't look so good. You are doing too much too soon. Give yourself some free time.'

'Yeah, later, later. I need to clear a few things up first.'

'Perhaps you could start by explaining why our guests left so fast. Us ladies were enjoying a real good time and then in come Daniel and Paul … What happened out there, Abel?'

'Yeah, Sally, yeah. It was pretty quick.' Abel was taking longer than usual in organising his thoughts into a 'case'. Abel was always very careful in his conversations, his exchanges, even with, especially with Sally. It was as if he believed that everything he said was being recorded in some mysterious way and might be played back to him at some inconvenient time in the future. He was an A-one expert in covering his back.

'Those two fellows wormed their way into this house. It wasn't your fault …'

'But I'm an easy touch. Is that the way to put it?' Sally was not prepared to take the blame on this. 'I meet an old friend and I invite her to my home.'

'True, sweetheart, but … Look. Miller and Komar, smart in appearance but two very slippery customers in their line of business, and I don't just mean in the courts.'

'So, they upset you in some way and I take the punishment.'

'Okay, let's start again. Ten, twenty minutes ago I took a big risk with those two punks.'

'Why punks? Abel, they must have really upset you big time.'

'Not at all. I'll show you. Bertie Briggs. Remember that name?'

'His toto was here with Angela, the McCall maid. He's in the lock-up somewhere up-country.'

'He tried to kill your husband. Damn near did. Well, by sunset tonight he will be a free man. A free man courtesy of this same husband. This was the news I was giving to Miller and Komar. Over lunch here, it came to me. I could give these dreamers a lesson, show them how a real statesman behaves. Do something … spectacular, unexpected. And you know what, Sal, they were not happy. Not happy. I tell you. Like they were upset, yes upset. They would have one less thing to beat me over the head with. That's the truth.'

For a time Sally sat wide-eyed, pleased, amazed, proud. At last, she smiled, patted her belly and spoke a few words to the new Julius.

'Now, that's your daddy over there …'

'And your daddy hasn't quite finished yet, boy.'

'There's more? Now you listen carefully, Julius. When Daddy speaks, you take notice!'

Sally chuckled, wobbled and seemed about to summon Monica.

He raised his hand to stop her. 'Sally, what was that religious stuff you used to say to me? You know, when I was having a hard time after we lost the boy. "Confessing is …?"'

'Confession is good for the soul.'

'Whatever the hell a soul is! However. We've known each

other a long time, Sal. We've done pretty well together. You know that you're my jewel.'

'This sounds like bedroom talk to me. And you know that I'm ... unavailable just now.' She smiled, patted her hair and fluttered her eyelashes.

He was too preoccupied with his next 'case' to pick up on her reaction.

'Sometimes I have had to hide things from you. You know it's more than twenty years since I started helping the old president with his money problems. Back then I was full of, well, ideals. I was going to be Mister Open Door. Hard knocks can change you.'

'Can change us all.'

'And hard knocks can make us hard.' Abel was faltering. As he spoke he began to realise that in 'confessing' he was not able to go beyond generalities. Confession was also a very dangerous road to travel. Examples of where he could show that he had done some dirty stuff, (dirty in Sally's eyes) passed through his mind and moved on out of sight. Simon Mboya. Would she understand that, for the greater good, Abel had made the decision that this popular but subversive doctor must be eliminated?

Sally saw clearly that he was struggling and moved in to help.

'Abel, I trust you. I know what this country means to you. And I know that men of good will bless themselves that they have such an honest man guide them. But this is your home. I am going to get Monica bring us some of that coffee you mentioned and for "stuff", how about a couple of slices of that chocolate cake that Marcel made this morning?'

Sally was no innocent. She understood what Abel was trying to get out much better than he could know. She had learned to live with these things many years before. There were private places in her heart and mind that only she and her God knew about.

# Chapter Fourteen

Inspector John Wambui liked working the Sunday shift. There was never a quieter time in Nakuru, so he rarely had a big case on his hands. Even the many petty thieves around the town seemed to have found places to take time out from their hectic times on the streets.

When the call came through, Inspector John became so animated that Humphrey, his desk sergeant, thought the boss had been at the bottle.

'Humphrey, great news! We've got some tidying up to do. And get one of the boys to give the car a polish. I just could be going on another official journey… to Naivasha.'

'Like with that McCall kid?'

'Correct, young man! Who was the fool who told me you had no brains?'

'That was you, boss. Last week when I got you those vegetable samosas which I swear …'

'Delicious. We'll buy a trayful tomorrow.'

'I suppose that someone by the name of Briggs was mentioned in that call you just had?'

'Genius. I may allow you to come this time.'

* * *

'Yes, release the prisoner. Without charge.' Wambui had not recognised the voice of the man who had given him the amazing news. 'And, Wambui, make sure that there is plenty of gas in the car, in case you have to do the delivery job. And don't let him go before six. No talking to the press boys. One more thing. Wait until the last minute before you tell Briggs.'

Half an hour later some of the shine was taken off the news. There were two more calls. The first, from Miller, the lawyer who had visited Briggs three days before who asked the inspector to have the prisoner ready for dead on six.

'There will be a car waiting outside the station.'

Ten minutes later he was talking to the smart, oldish woman with the Italian accent. She was asking if she could speak to 'my friend, Bertie'.

'Regrettably, Madam, prisoners are not allowed calls in or out. I must remind you that this is not the Waterbuck Hotel.'

'No. Of course. I recognise your voice. Inspector, I am glad that it was you who has been looking after him. You have been a blessing to this family.'

After putting down the receiver, Wambui sat quietly at his desk, beaming. So he did not make it out to Naivasha this time. But a compliment from a very attractive European lady was a satisfying consolation prize.

There were two cars waiting outside the station five minutes before the appointed time. The news of Bertie's release had caused such excitement in the Naivasha district that there could have been a dozen more to join them. Inspector Caroline Miggot had four passengers in her Volvo; her own sergeant, Hosea Kabari; his wife, Maria; her brother, Paul Miller and his fellow lawyer Daniel Komar. They were the kind of official group who would make sure that there would be no hitches to hold up the release. The idea was that these professionals would not be distracted by the emotion of the occasion. But Paul and Daniel were in a state of controlled euphoria.

Rubai was keeping his word. The plan had worked and for the second time in a matter of days they had put one over on the Big Man. Their hard work was paying off and a little crack was appearing in the steel-coated monolith that Rubai had built to help him keep control over the running of the country.

Tom was driving Bertie's Pajero. There had been some brief talk back at Rusinga about bringing along Ewan to greet his father as he stepped out of his captivity. The idea had been quickly rejected as risking emotional overload. Maura would see the boy off to bed and Lydia would read him a story, as she had been doing since the day Bertie had been carted off to jail by the rough group of Nairobi police heavies. Rafaella and Rebecca would travel to Nakuru.

Hearts in both vehicles were running wild. The time lapse between hearing the news and witnessing the reality had been brief, not long enough for them to put the amazing turn of events into a comfortable perspective.

* * *

There was something different about the tap on the steel door of his cell. This one was not the usual simple warning telling him that someone was coming in to present him with a new unpleasantness. Instead this tap was asking his permission to allow an invasion of his privacy. It suggested that he might still, after all, have some control over some minor part of his existence.

The illusion continued after the key had been turned in the lock and the door swung open. The Inspector and the sergeant made no move to come in. Even after the Inspector's opening words, Bertie did not grasp the full meaning of his changing situation.

'Mister Briggs, you are a free man. I am so happy to tell you that your people are waiting …'

The sounds became blurred, heard through some opaque material and addressed to some stranger. 'The sergeant will see to it that all your possessions will be collected together and returned to you …'

Bertie was being hustled along a corridor, past a duty desk and towards the front door. Where were they taking him? Sunday night, a good time to take poor bastards like himself …

The door opened and he was in the arms of dear friends. They were all around him. They were laughing and crying. It took another few seconds before the truth struck him and it came like a bowl of ice-cold water being thrown into his face. For the first time in his life he almost fainted. The suddenness of the shock took away his power of speech. Rafaella had never seen such a look of terror in a man's face. She was afraid that he might suffer a heart attack.

The change, when it came, was lightning quick. A long, trembling sigh and he sank into the arms of Tom and Hosea. The energy melted away briefly only to announce its return with a loud, uninhibited whoop of delight.

'Bertie! You are safe! We have you back!' Rafaella could hardly contain her joy.

'Ewan, is he all right? Can I see him?'

'Tonight, there will be fairy stories all 'round at Rusinga, old friend.' Tom hugged Bertie very tight. Then he noticed. Across the street, standing outside the open doors of the cathedral, Sister May and Sister Phillipa were waving a large white flag emblazoned with a yellow rose. Inside the majestic sound of an organ struck up on full power, like a hymn of celebration rolling up and down Odinga Odinga Avenue.

Without warning, Bertie broke away and crossed the street, murmuring as he went, 'It's been so long, too long.'

As he reached the sisters, they each grasped a hand and led him inside. Father Robert had hurried from his lodge to see what the commotion was. He knew all about Bertie's trials. He had been the priest when Anna had been buried and Ewan baptised. He had known, too, about the arrest but had delayed visiting. So, this was the first time in almost three years that he had set eyes on Bertie, a man he still considered to be one of his own.

The impromptu thanksgiving put a proper seal on Bertie's release, a perfect climax to an ordinary Sunday.

Dusk was moving into night as the two cars cleared the roundabout at the edge of town and crossed under the railway bridge on their way home. Normally travel by night was not considered to be a good idea on the great highway that was the A104. Unlit cars and trucks were a hazard and there was always the fear that you might run into desperados out and about for a spot of hijacking.

But on this Sunday night for these people a journey under the stars was sheer delight. The skies were big and free and the mysteries out to their left and their right were kindly. Tom, in Bertie's Pajero, kept the speed steady and when he took a moment out to glance at his fellow passengers, Rebecca by his side and Rafaella and Bertie behind him, he saw faces that glowed. Very little was said until the lights of Gilgil came into sight over on their left. Bertie frequently placed his hand over his face as his mind gradually came to terms with his sudden and startling change of fortune.

After Gilgil, there was a change as Bertie, especially, began to anticipate his homecoming. The picture of Ewan scarcely left his mind. His heartfelt sighs of 'Oh, God!' came to his lips, accompanied by the cold shiver of realisation of what so easily might have been. In those lonely hours in that small cell he had rationalised himself into the certainty that he would never see his boy again. Never.

In Caroline's Volvo, the mood was happy, too, but more subdued. And there was one concern, minor for the moment but with the potential for future danger. 'All charges dropped' had been a clear part of the deal with Rubai. Daniel and Paul had quietly asked the Nakuru inspector if he had any documentation on this.

'Did the people on Nairobi Hill send a fax through with the terms of the release?'

'Nothing, Mister Komar.'

'Nothing?'

'The machine has not worked for the last two weeks.'

'Was anything said on the phone? Or was that not working either?'

'Oh, the phone works fine.' Wambui looked over his shoulder to check before going on. 'Confidentially, I don't believe it was a police voice that gave the message. I've been on the force for a long time now. You get a feel for these things. Understand me?'

'Oh, yes, we understand.'

* * *

'You people, everything must be recorded somewhere, then stored away in some file and then … forgotten.'

'Maria, how else are you going to get justice in this country?'

'And what justice is that, husband?'

'Paul, was she like this when you were kids?'

'I just remember she was the bossiest kid in the school. The boys, even some of the teachers, were scared of her. But, Maria, if something is not written down on paper, then, in law, it doesn't really exist. In Bertie's case it means that a fox like Rubai ...'

'Tarantula!'

'Whatever, but he can say, "Charges dropped? Where's the evidence?"'

'So, the Nairobi thugs could come tomorrow and pick him up.'

Daniel took over the job of setting Maria's mind at rest. 'In theory, but tomorrow morning, your brother and I will pay a visit to CID on Nairobi Hill. We'll check it out. We have some contacts who can tell us what we need to know. And Caroline is the police boss in Naivasha District, so ...'

'I need a piece of paper to —'

'And if one doesn't exist, we, er, manufacture one, signatures and all.'

'Paul and I know a first-class forger who owes us ...'

By the time the passengers in the Volvo had sorted out the logistics of the police work, they were halfway to Naivasha. Hosea, idly staring out of the window to his right recognised two landmarks clearly visible in the moonlight. First there was the soda waters of Lake Elementeita, with its faint rim of pink on the shoreline, flamingos busy at a late supper and then the outline of the Sleeping Maasai, flat out on the low hillside just a couple of hundred metres further on.

'Sorry, Bertie, but we're going to ask you to make a decision.'

'Decision? I haven't made one of those for days. Try me. See if I remember what to do.'

Tom explained the dilemma. 'Do we go straight to Rusinga?

Or, I know there are people on our veranda, cleaned and polished, by the way, wanting just to catch a glimpse, a sort of impromptu welcome home.'

'Hakuna matata. Haven't said that for a while either. Can't be rude, but I would love to see some friendly faces. Help me to know that I really am coming home.'

For Bertie, there was a single White-cap, a lot of hugging and kissing and, after about fifteen minutes, a walk home across the open plain with his blood brother of a friend.

'Let's take our time, Alex.'

Their feather-like footfalls carried them out of range of the rigged up lighting on the refurbished veranda. They weaved between the scattered waterbuck cropping noisily at the thick, damp grass. Their first stop was at a low flat rock that as boys they had named 'Home View', their usual meeting point on their safaris through the bush when they were on holiday from school.

'Alex, so many people have been making a fuss.'

'Well, it's not every day we can get to welcome home a —'

'Jailbird! Thank God I can have a bit of a laugh. Not much of one just yet, but give me time.' Bertie paused before turning to his friend to recall a memory of their Pembroke days. '"Chateau D'If". Remember the name?'

'Common entrance English, Miss Cullen, her of the beautiful legs. Edmund Dantes. What a man! If there were more blokes like that in books, I'd read a bit more than I do.'

'Paul asked me about him. You know he came to visit …? Anyway, just now back there, he was talking books again. Raised a can for a toast. "Restored to life." Surprised him again.'Tale of Two Cities', Doctor Manette. You know, Alex, one half decent thing about prison? Gives you time to think. Half the time it was Ewan, the other half, you people over there.'

'Your ears should have been red hot on times.'

'But you've lost everything – house, farm, cars, even your clothes.'

'Funny you should say that. Friday night, Maura and I were sitting on the veranda wall, just before bedtime. Mother's still over in your guest cottage and we could hear the boys over in the new house, noisy as usual. Maura decided to draw up an imaginary inventory. Try saying that after a few beers. Anyway she started her list. One aeroplane, not even scorched. Three horses, thank God for the Buckles. A laundry garden, with heated water, could be connected up to a bath, perhaps. An excuse to buy a new wardrobe. A building site with a great view and plenty of hard core for foundations. Then she broke down. Cried for ages. Words kept coming. Still got each other. Wonderful friends. No house but still got a home. No mementos but a million memories.'

'It was the poison, pus. It has to come out somehow. You'll never drain it all. Well, I don't think that's possible.'

They lay back on their rock and looked up into the stars. As boys, it had been the place where they would say their final goodbye to the day and to each other, to spend time on that cool place and draw the adventures of the day together. That night the grand sweep of the Milky Way held them in thrall as strongly as ever and it was just as impossible for them to believe that those millions of tiny dots that, seen close up, were huge lumps of molten gas sending down their light to two little boys in love with the wonder of it all.

'Shirley's dropping in on Tuesday. You know she lives on that little island on Lake Baringo.'

'Next to the club?'

'Right. She's going to give us tips on what Rollo calls "open plan living". Her house is fantastic. Mabati side walls and roof with the front open to the sky and the garden. Just like us for the next few weeks, at least.'

'Alex, it never ever gets cold up there.'

'Yeah, right. Just another adventure for a middle-aged couple on the look out for a dose of pneumonia. Shall we move on? You must be itching to see Ewan.'

'Damn right, but I'm holding back. I love the idea of having him just a few hundred yards away. See, there's no light on this side of the house. He must be asleep.'

'Bertie, in a previous life you must have been a fish-eagle and they've let you keep your eyes. I can't even see the house properly.'

'Practice, old chap.'

More stillness, more looking up, more stirring of happy memories of schooldays long ago in Gilgil.

Bertie began, 'The owl looked up to the stars above as he sang to a small guitar ...'

Alex took up the line. 'Oh, lovely pussy, oh, pussy, my love, what a beautiful pussy you are. Annie Brown, form R. Haven't forgotten a word.'

Bertie chuckled. 'Ewan is learning the same poem in Hippo House. I was testing him, well, the other day, I suppose. Cracks up when he got to that bit. "But, Daddy, an owl can't marry a cat!" Sad, isn't it? They're trying to ban fantasy from a boy's life.'

They stood up and stretched the stiffness out of their limbs before moving on to Rusinga.

If they had been ten minutes earlier, it probably would not have happened. They discovered this later.

Bertie, alone now, crept up the carpeted staircase, guided by the blue light on the outside of the open door of Ewan's bedroom. He stood over his son for a very long time, watching every movement, listening to every sound. At last he found himself a blanket, kicked off his shoes and snuggled into the big armchair within touching distance of the bed. It was a full three hours before he found sleep to be irresistible.

A little before four o'clock in the afternoon of that same Sunday, a telephone call had gone out from the Pink Palace in Karen to a second floor appartment overlooking Mama Ngina Street.

'Uchome?'

Patrick Uchome threw down his newspaper. He had recognised the boss's voice. He was afraid that he was in for another tongue lashing but could not think of any blunders he had made in the previous few days.

'Yes, Boss?'

Abel Rubai chuckled. He had picked up the panic in his boy's voice. He liked the sound of that. 'Calm down, man. Got a job. Naivasha. Take your wife with you.'

'Margaret?'

'Yes, Margaret. You've been to this place before ...'

Fortunately the boss could not see the grimace of pain on Uchome's face. Rubai had no interest in Patrick Uchome's emotional state as long as it did not interfere with his competence on the job. After all he was giving his Nairobi man the chance to make up for the blunder he had made last time he had been sent with a big crew to do this same simple errand.

'Listen. Certain things are happening that I don't like. When I move away from the table, I want to be in profit. Do this right and there will be profit for you, too. And a bonus for Margaret.'

Abel was a man who was deeply annoyed and just a little bit uncomfortable. The threats of the two joke lawyers had caught him off balance. The control of a situation had been taken out of his hands – temporarily. He swore to that. He needed to strike back straight away. Almost at once a possibility presented itself. Three phone calls raised his hopes. His scheme could be a winner. The girl no longer had any real importance, but to have her in his power, that would be a big blow to those who thought they had Mister Abel Rubai, the next president of Kenya, trapped in a corner.

So what if in the planning of the move he had not had time to cover every angle? He knew that there was more risk involved than he liked, but he would build in precautions.

'Uchome, take a small car, one that has seen a bit of life. Park back from the turn-off down to the farm. From six o'clock only she and the kid will be in the house, the big house this time. Come up from the shore side. Are you getting all this?'

'Every word, Boss.'

'Make like you are a couple out on an evening stroll. Wait around close to the house. Plenty of trees for cover. Any doubts and come away. Use Margaret to get you into the place. Take your gun but don't use it. Got it? Bring her to the farm. Only phone when the job is done.'

The first attempt to kidnap Lydia Smith had been a mess. Uchome had half convinced himself then that the boys were right. There were evil spirits hanging about that place. This time he made up his mind that if a twig snapped in the wrong place, if the breeze blew in any suspicious sounds, he would be on his way home.

'Boss, like you said, if things look bad …'

But things were not bad. In fact, getting the girl out of the house and up to the road ranked as the easiest job he had ever done. He must take Margaret out more often. It was as if the

Smith whore had been expecting them. One glance from him up the stairs to where the kid was sleeping and she was ready to go anywhere. Margaret had been surprised.

'Patrick, this kid ain't scared of us. My God, she's a pretty thing. What's he going to do to her?'

'Sweetheart, let's just get her to the car. I'll feel a whole lot happier when we get to the dual carriageway on top of the Escarpment. You go in the back with her and …'

'No gun, if that was what you were thinking.'

It was three am on Monday when it was discovered in Londiani that Lydia was missing. Rafaella had returned to Rusinga and gone straight to her room, assuming that after putting Ewan to bed, Lydia had done likewise. The jangle of her emotions made it difficult for her to sleep. After one long doze, she woke with a start, realising that she had not seen her house companion since she had set out for Nakuru many hours before. With a sense of foreboding she tapped gently on Lydia's door. The bed had not been slept in.

The hastily gathered meeting of friends threw up only one strong speculation.

'The cunning bastard!' Alex's words summed the opinions of everyone sitting around that veranda in that chilliest part of the night.

'He's got her. The poor child. Where can he have taken her? Not that bloody farmhouse again!' Maura was wide awake, burning with anger, mainly at her own, all their carelessness. She dismissed the first lapse into an 'if only' before it could reach her lips.

Bertie was openly in tears. 'My bloody fault. You should have left me in there. I'm not worth it.'

'Rubbish, Bertie.' Tom's tone was quiet but forceful. 'A kick in the guts for us all, but you, my friend, have no blame in this.

Look, we've been through this before. And we are going to get her back. First job, I'm going to let Caroline know.'

Rollo agreed. He was in favour of some action.

'But, son, headless chickens, blue-arsed flies don't get things done.'

If they had but known it, all that could be done had been done. Neither Alex McCall nor Abel Rubai could change any of that. Everything had been accomplished within the narrow confines of that ordinary small car that had seen a bit of life.

* * *

On the wide open plain beyond Naivaisha to the turn-off to Narok, Patrick Uchome had relaxed at the wheel. The land to his left sloped steeply until it reached the A104 where it topped out at nine thousand feet and he felt protected by its dark bulk. The whore was giving him and Margaret no trouble. In less than an hour he would be handing her over and collecting a wad of notes for his efforts.

'Why you do these things? Why you work for this wicked man who loves to kill people? Don't you have kids of your own?'

'My, the little dolly girl has a voice. And no, we don't have kids and glad of it.'

'Leave it, Margaret. A silent drive is a safe drive, believe me.'

'But, Patrick, show a little kindness here. We may be the last people this kid will ever have seen.'

'Margaret, cut it!'

'What are you so afraid of, fat man? I can't hurt you. I got no gun. I been in trouble before, lots of times.'

'And you shut it, too, or I'll —'

'Open the door and throw me out. You won't get your blood

money then. My blood. I like my blood. It is such a lovely colour. One time I saw my uncle kill a goat. One sharp knife. Over in seconds. All that lovely blood. Do you know that a goat's blood is also red?'

'Shut the hell up! We could have an accident here.'

Lydia laughed mock hysterically. 'Why would I worry about an accident? Why would I want to make it easy for you?'

'I'll put a gag on you. Margaret, try to shut her up. I'm going to start climbing soon. I think we took the wrong car. The gears are useless.'

'I know this place. Mister Briggs brought me down very steep hill. Twists like a snake. There is a church. He called it "the Italian Church". Said we could visit one day. I want to visit now. Stop the car when we are close by.'

'You crazy bitch, what would you do in a church?'

'Pray for forgiveness, of course. You could come with me. And I would thank God for reminding me to bring my friend. See!'

Lydia slid into the corner of her seat and waved her knife.

'Give me that!'

Uchome's lunge caused him to swing the car very slightly. It was enough. The skid gathered momentum. The car ran off the road and plunged into the undergrowth. The trunk of the tree was not thick and strong, but it was enough. Silence.

Fifty metres directly below in a house on a lonely track off the main road there was a party going on, celebrating a homecoming. Even though the scream of the skid and the thud of the crash had been muffled by the forest trees, the host heard enough of the noise to know that someone was in trouble up there. He groaned and called out to his brother.

'Alan, give us a hand. Another bang on the top road. Got to go and check. Got the stuff. Come on.'

They were soon speeding on their way in the Land Rover. 'Don, how many times is this? Sell the place and come back to the city.'

'You're getting past it. Can't say that I enjoy this kind of nonsense, but I've got my bit to do … Oops! Always take that corner too fast. And you'll have a story when we get back. Look, over there. Something's knocked the stuffing out of those thorn bushes. Thankfully it's not a truck.'

On foot, and with beams of their power torches lighting the way ahead, they were soon up to the small Datsun with faded orange paintwork. Every window had been shattered.

Donald Dawson knocked away the few remaining jagged bits of glass on the driver's side, lowered his head and peered in. His assessment was swift.

'Three poor bastards, probably a family and probably on their way up to the top.'

'All dead?'

'Think so, but I'm no doc. Daughter was a looker.'

'So what do we do? Get onto the cops?'

'Sure, but first we tow them out.'

'That's illegal. Scene of the crime and all that.'

'Let's grab the rope. Hope this old banger won't fall apart on us when we start to pull. Alan, come on. I've done this before. Just watch an old pro at work.'

Alan Dawson took very little part in the recovery of the Datsun which his brother pulled out of the undergrowth and then manoevred into a parking position in the open space in front of the Italian church.

'We can go home now. Have a shower, phone the police and back to the party. But I want you to meet some people first.'

The shocked expression on his brother's face sent Don into a burst of loud laughter.

'You thought I meant … No, they are over by the church door. Alan, meet Peter and Gloria Katami, my collaborators, partners in crime to you.'

The caretaker had opened the doors of the church in readiness for their part in the gruesome business and was not unhappy when the two brothers climbed into their vehicle and drove off down the road. While Peter examined the car and looked in at its occupants, Gloria entered the church, lit the altar candles and took down three linen sheets from the cupboard next to the organ.

In the half hour that passed before the police car arrived, the old couple was busy. Tenderly they removed the bodies from the car. They made no effort to tend wounds or clean away any mess before wrapping them in the sheets and laying them in the space in front of the altar. When this was done it was their usual practice to sit in the dim light and let their thoughts wander. They rarely spoke.

This time was different. A small observation had far-reaching consequences.

'Peter, the girl's face, there was warmth in it.'

'She is young. The warmth is slower to leave.'

'I will listen to the heart.' She lifted the sheet and bent low. 'Peter, feel her hands. And there is breath. The child has life. What can we do?'

'Wait, and pray. It is out of our hands.'

* * *

'So is that two or three for the morgue? The old woman says there is life in the young one.'

'You been on too many of these accident call-outs, Naluki. Your heart is turning to stone.'

'Sergeant Leah, this is your first one. I know that.'

'You are right. I wanted to see for myself. And there are surprises. For instance, who brought all the evidence over here? You are not going to tell me that these unfortunate people conveniently rolled their vehicle into this little area …'

'Okay, okay, it is not the proper legal way, but in the end it works. Nobody suffers and the police save money.'

'But who did all this … organising?'

'Don't know.' His reply was too pat.

'We talk about this later. First thing, get this girl to a hospital.'

'The ambulance, I can hear it coming. She can travel with the stiffs. I'll drop her off somewhere on the way down to the city.'

'But where?'

'First one we come to. I know a few. They never survive.'

'That's it! I'll take care of her. I know a place where they'll give her a chance.' She turned to the old lady. 'I want you to come. Help me to lift her into the car. We must hurry.'

'Fine, fine, Sergeant. Shall I start a report when I come back from my delivery?'

'You do that, Naluki. I'll write my own later.'

* * *

Leah Marang and her twin sister, Ruth, were from one of the string of villages and townships that dotted the very top of the Escarpment that separated Nairobi from the Central Rift. Up here the soil was rich and the rain plentiful. The family farm was prosperous with enough money to allow the girls to finish their education in a city boarding school.

Farming held no interest for the sisters and when they left

school, Leah became the youngest recruit in the city constabulary and Ruth landed herself a job in the American hospital up in the hills above the Naivasha plains.

'Ruth, you are on duty tonight, yes?'

'Right ...'

'I'm bringing someone in. Car accident. Unconscious. Pretty bad, I would say, but my friend Gloria, she says that she is going to make it. Hope so. She's a beautiful kid. Give me twenty minutes.'

Gloria had one or two other opinions to express to her driver on their way across the hills.

'They are not a family. The English say that she is the child of the two dead ones. She is not.'

'Do you know these people? Do they live near you?'

'No, I have not seen them, no.'

'Then ...?'

'I spend much time in the church. I polish. I dust. I talk but mostly I listen. It is a place of peace. It is very easy to hear things.'

'So someone told you this?'

Gloria smiled and nodded her head knowingly. 'And you think that poor Gloria spends too long in that place. Police lady, you have a good heart and I want to tell you that those two we left back in the church, they wanted to hurt this one. When I was wrapping them in the linen sheets, I saw these things, I felt them so clearly.'

On arrival at the hospital, Lydia Smith was whisked away on a trolley while Leah and Gloria were ushered into an empty waiting room.

'I'll drive you home.' Leah tried to cheer her friend with this piece of small talk.

'I like this place. If I am sick, I would like to come here.'

An hour later, Ruth brought news of the preliminary diagnosis.

'Well, Gloria, perhaps we ought to offer you a job here. The girl is going to live. She has broken bones … in her foot! There is a nasty cut on her left arm, probably from a knife. And concussion that knocked her out. And the other two died …?'

'Probably on impact. The car's a mess.'

'But who is she? Not a single thing to tell us this.'

Gloria had a question. 'Is this a safe place?'

The twins exchanged puzzled looks.

'Hide her. Until she wakes. Then you will know where to find her people. It is a small thing to ask but for her, I have this fear.

# Chapter Fifteen

Abel Rubai did not suffer the inconvenience of fear, but there were times when bouts of anxiety troubled him. He thought he had had his share for that Sunday when two overreaching lawyers cornered him briefly in his very own screen room. But now, close to midnight, he was being given another serve of this uncomfortable emotion.

He was alone in the farmhouse just outside the city. But where was Uchome? More important, where was the girl? If something had gone wrong, why was there no telephone call?

At last there was news from a trusted source working in police CID headquarters on Nairobi Hill, and it was not good. 'Half an hour ago, two bodies were brought into the city morgue on Ngong Road. Patrick Uchome and his wife, Margaret. Car crash on the bottom of the twisting road out of plains outside Naivasha.'

'Two bodies, not three? Are you sure?'

'Sure, but I can recheck.'

The ten minutes between calls from Nairobi Hill passed unpleasantly for Mister Big. Uchome gone. How long since that first job, a farmer down in Machakos, if he remembered properly? Died on the job. Even in this time of misfortune for someone else, Rubai's thoughts were for himself and his own mortality. So simple, so final. Hell, a man could get depressed thinking like this! The second call brought relief and sparked new vitality.

'There was a third person. The constable who brought the bodies down said there was a girl. He thought she was gone as well, but his sergeant, a woman, took her off to a hospital.'

'Which one?'

'Not much information on that. The constable is still around here somewhere. I'll track him down and put him on.'

'Without letting him know this number.'

Rubai's inside man at Nairobi pulled the handset from his ear and looked down at it scornfully. He controlled his spasm of anger before ending his conversation.

'You know me better than that, I think.'

'Constable Nemuti …'

'Naluki.'

'Okay. Okay. You brought the body of Uchome and his wife down to the city, yes?'

'Two bodies, no names. No ID, nothing. Nothing. I never seen this before. Oh yeah, a gun and a knife on the floor.'

'Have you been drinking? Listen, start …'

'No, I never drink on duty. One more thing. Sergeant Marang will not be happy to find —'

The telephone was removed briefly from the constable's hand. Words were spoken on the Nairobi side that an angry Abel Rubai could not make out. When the constable took the receiver again, his tone was more submissive.

'Yes, there was a girl. The daughter, perhaps.'

'Nalubi, stop assuming, start thinking carefully. This woman sergeant took this … girl to a hospital.'

'In the police car. I accompanied the deceased to the city in an ambulance. I offered to bring the kid. Could have dropped her off.'

'Now then, big question. Which hospital? Take your time.'

The silence was so long on the CID side that Abel thought …

'Sir, the sergeant looked as if she would be ready to pay, so my guess would be Aga Khan or Nairobi.'

'But she didn't mention a particular one.'

'No, sir. I think, sir, that perhaps by now this third person is also down in the morgue. Thank you, sir.'

To Abel's mounting fury, it took a half an hour for him to clear the two big city hospitals from his list of possibilities. He began to wonder if this extraordinarily caring policewoman had taken the nuisance whore to some private doctor. He took time out just to think. He stood out on the front veranda of the farmhouse and found his concentration being disturbed by the racket that the crickets and cicadas made out there in the darkness. Abel's interest in the outdoors was limited to the profits he could make from tea plantations, from chopping down old forests and, soon, from a flower farm on the big lake just up the road.

In the enforced idleness that he was enduring in the middle of that unsuccessful night, he recalled a book he had bought at some airport book stall one time. It was a sort of primer on thinking. He had found the exercises amusing and saw they could be useful in certain circumstances. Lateral thinking, thinking outside the box, expecting the unexpected.

'So, this bright policewoman might know a private place where she could take badly injured person, not too many questions asked.' He closed his eyes for a few moments to allow his brain machinery to grind its numbers and words. And come up with a brilliant inspiration. Clearly the theory did not always work out in practice.

All the while that Rubai was trying to work out where he might find his elusive quarry, he had two cars out on the road, ready, like a kind of criminal flying squad to do his instant bidding. He was shocked when the report from the first dash came in.

'No, Boss. That weird clinic just across the road from your place. Dead quiet and no patients, dead or alive.'

Next came a shock of a different kind, a burst of initiative from an unlikely source. From his car parked and waiting at the very end of the dual carriageway running north out of the city came a very tentative suggestion. Zac Gusil, good friend and colleague of Patrick Uchome and brother of Drongo who had been killed on a previous attempt to get this woman, had a question for the paymaster.

'Boss, you ever heard of a hospital up in these places? Folks around the villages up here call it "The American hospital". It's in Kijabe.'

'Goddammit!'

'Sorry, Boss, did I say something wrong? It's just that me, Buba and Caleb were sitting here waiting …'

'Nothing wrong. You boys been thinking outside the square and for the first time in your lives you've hit a target.'

'I don't get it.'

'Well, get this! You got the picture of the whore with you?'

'Yep. Buba's looking at it right now. I think he fancies her.'

'Then stop fancying and start moving.'

At last all the ideas fitted together. The sergeant, a private hospital, close to the where the car crashed. She must be there.

'How far away?'

'Mmn, half an hour. We know where it is, so …'

'Got some casual clothes?'

'Always bring them. Patrick insisted.'

'Put them on. You're Patrick's brothers. Give them the story. Be polite but get into where she is. Use a silencer. I'll be waiting for news, good news. Get going!'

# Chapter Sixteen

'I'll take you home now, Gloria. You should be a happy woman. You helped save her life.'

'Sergeant, not yet.'

'But I have to go back to the station.'

'Ask Ruth. I can get home later. I have money for the bus fare.'

'But why? She'll be safe here. You say those two were not her parents. Okay, tomorrow I'll find out where she belongs. I'll come down to the church to tell you.'

'Ask Ruth if I can sit with her, close by.'

'You are one stubborn woman, Gloria. This is an American hospital. They have strict rules.'

'She is in danger. I know this.'

'But we are not in the church now. How can …'

'Sergeant Leah, you are a good lady. Ruth, too. I ask a small thing, but for this girl it could be very big.'

Ten minutes later, a new nurse, dressed in an ill-fitting uniform, sat on a hard chair at the side of the bed of the new patient. She wore a big smile as she looked across at her companion. She touched the girl's arm and nodded contentedly to feel the warmth there. Indeed, this was a very pretty girl. Her face, her hair were well cared for. This was no village girl who spent her time out in the fields under a warm sun.

Nurse Ruth had granted her wish and checked it out with

the tall American lady. So why was her heart still troubled? How could she know that down in the city much effort was being put into the task of finding this girl lying at rest in this very bed? The people down there knew exactly who she was. The search was being narrowed down.

Gloria began to rock back and forth on her chair. She closed her eyes. Her lips began to move soundlessly. Then, as the minutes ticked by, she began a whispered humming. She directed her closed eyes upward as though searching for some invisible guidance. The intensity of her will became stronger, more insistent. She was beginning to make demands. She became aware that she must not yield whatever the cost. The pressure mounted relentlessly in this internal struggle. Perhaps she was asking too much. Perhaps she would fall and be lost.

And there was a collapse but not of will nor of effort. Gloria felt a clear sensation that she was being watched. She prepared, fearfully, to open her eyes.

'Who are you? Where am I?'

'My name is Gloria. My home is not far away. You were in a car. There was an accident. I have been with you for many hours now.'

'Is this a hospital? Are there people waiting outside?' Fear compelled her to lower her voice to a whisper. 'Please, do not call them!'

'There is no one there. No one but the nurses and the doctors.'

'Are you a nurse? You are not young and your uniform …' Lydia smiled.

Gloria clapped her hands for joy. She was ready to probe further. 'Your parents …'

'My parents?' Lydia's eyes opened wide and made an

attempt to move that she at once regretted for the pain it set off in her head.

'The ones in the car with you.'

Lydia's reply was a pained shake of the head.

'I knew it. And they were not friends.'

Another shake, more vigorous this time.

'Little one, do you need a drink? There is water here.'

There was a long pause while the patient tried to size up her unusual companion. It did not take much thinking for Lydia to accept that this person meant her no harm. Obviously she was not a regular nurse.

'Why are you sitting with me? Is this your work?'

It was Gloria's turn to pause. How could she explain without scaring the child or, worse, causing her to laugh?

'My name is Gloria Patami. My husband is Peter. We look after the church at the bottom of the hill. The Englishmen brought you to us. We took you out of the car. We sat together in the church until the police came. The constable, Naluki, I know his mother. He said that there was no life. He was wrong and I knew it. Praise God, the lady sergeant believed me. And so you are here.'

The pause on Lydia's side was longer this time. There were some big things to take in. She listened to the sound of her own heavy breathing and let her thoughts seeds take root and blossom.

'Gloria, that is a beautiful name. What you say makes me think of my friend Maria. She saves lives, too, just as you have saved mine.'

The tears were flowing on both sides. Gloria stood up and moved closer to the bed. She reached down to exchange a painful embrace.

They shared the comfort of the island of peace in that cool, bare, whitewashed room. Even then Gloria was troubled, restless without knowing why. There was a threat to their peace, to their very lives.

'Tell me your name. The sister asked me and I could not say. The doctor wants to know where you live for when you are ready to go home.'

Lydia felt a deep shame for the shaft of suspicion that crossed her mind. Could all this be a part of a trap? She struck the side of her bed hard with her hand, angry with herself for her lack of trust.

'Lydia Smith. I am from Nairobi. I am not a good person.'

'Thank God. Neither am I!' Gloria paused briefly. 'So, you were on your way home?'

'Home. That is a big word but,' she decided that it was time to make, for her, a bold claim, 'this home is in Naivasha, at Rusinga Farm. I have many friends in those places.'

'Lydia Smith, we must speak with those friends very soon. Do you have the telephone?'

'I have nothing, not even a number. But I have a person who will know. Inspector Caroline will tell us.'

* * *

The key fitted and, in no time, the door was opened. Caroline was sitting on the wall of the veranda of Londiani Farm when her mobile rang. It was a familiar voice. American. Angie Summers and Caroline had been friends since their days in Langata when the ambitious young police sergeant and the Peace Corps girl from Montana had lived in adjacent apartments.

'Caroline, we've got a patient who says she knows you …'

One astonishing leap and one triumphant punch into

the air transformed the hearts and minds of the previously gloomy and uninspired group slouched around on that open veranda. While the glorious hubbub around her spread upward and outwards into the enveloping night, Rafaella McCall sat incredulous, trying but failing to find suitable words of thanks for a new miracle.

The mystery of Lydia's disappearance was solved. Caroline was able to tell her Naivasha people about the car crash, the deaths of the kidnappers and the rescue of Lydia herself. At last they knew where she was.

'But I have a dark thought. Others will be searching for her. Perhaps they know where she is, too. Angie tells me that Lydia is fit to travel if she has to. We need a fast driver who is a little bit crazy, ready to go right now.'

'Or a plane. The mad American spared us that, by accident, of course.'

'Alex, no. Impossible. Bertie, will you let Tom …'

'There's a strip right next to the hospital, you know. I flew there once. Maura, you were with me. The Kingoni boy, shattered his arm …'

'That was in broad daylight.'

'They've got lights. Listen. This is what we do. And now. Tom and Bertie take the Pajero. Okay, Bertie? I'll race you. Caroline, phone your friend. Explain about the lights. Expect me in twenty minutes. I'm off. On my way back, I'll snake along the road. If I dip, turn back. Anyone fancy a ride?'

The skies out of Londiani were as empty as the roads. Rollo, chosen for his better eyesight, was the twin who sat next to his father in the cockpit of the white Cessna. No pilot in the whole Central Rift knew the routes in and out of the valley as well as Alex McCall. No one was more aware of the risks involved in this desperate night flight. There would be no margin for error. It was almost three years since his father, Don, cool and concentrated, lost his life because of a trivial miscalculation on a straightforward landing on their home strip.

He flew out over the lake and then banked to his left. He climbed until he was parallel with A104. Rollo spotted it first. They were onto the rectangle of light quicker than they had expected. He allowed himself one trial run before coming down, tense and tight-lipped. The landing was rough but safe.

'Alex, two passengers. Okay? I think you're just in time. We heard that there's some action at the main gate. Some guys are having trouble with our night guards. Two Marine Corps youngsters. Yes it's true. We've had our military up here since they hit our embassy a few years back. Well done, Gloria! Kwaheri, everyone. Thanks for bringing some excitement into the lives of two young men! Downhill's best for a quick lift-off!

The Cessna was barely fifty feet above the Mercedes that was waiting with its engine running outside the stone-built compound wall. Two of its occupants, standing outside, swung hard 'round as the plane passed directly overhead. Mister Zac and Mister Buba sighted their pistols on the broad white metal of their target, only to be distracted at the last minute by a volley of rifle shots. The front tyres on the Mercedes exploded at the same moment as the powerful engine burst into flames and sent up a thunderclap roar that jolted ten thousand villagers near and far out of their sleep.

* * *

Confusion and disturbance broke out below and above. Caleb and his companions were transformed in seconds from unwelcome invaders to vulnerable patients. The unexpected extra passenger in the little machine that was swinging its way south-east across a moonlit sky had created a minor logistical problem.

After helping to belt a flustered Gloria into the seat next to his father, Rollo had to move backwards to find a place to squeeze his bulk into the cramped rear area. Two attempts by him and Lydia to accommodate each other left them both in acute discomfort. Alex saw danger. One unforeseen jolt or lurch could mean that one of his passengers would be tumbled into his lap, making the plane uncontrollable.

'Rollo, take the seat and hold on tight to Lydia. That should be interesting for the pair of you! Home in fifteen minutes. I hope Tom and Bertie will spot us. I dare not dip with you two on the loose up here. Lydia, we meet again in strange circumstances. See that moon over there? In my head I've just been over it, if that makes sense to you. Okay now, you two? I'm about to go into a bit of a dive.'

Alex barely knew his co-pilot's name. He was pleasantly surprised by Gloria's calmness. It was probably her first time up, at least in a tiny, cramped machine like this, but her eyes were constantly on the move taking in the details on this, her new view of her world.

There were new views for the passengers behind him, too. They were enjoying the enforced closeness. Being pressed up against a man's body was something she was very familiar with, but never with a man so young, so muscular, so masculine. Doctor Angie had given her painkillers for the journey, but the throb in her injured foot and the ache in her head were as uncomfortable as ever except that the feel and the smell of this companion made them much easier to bear.

Rollo was familiar enough with Lydia's story. According to

that he was holding a Nairobi street girl in his arms, a high-class tart. Only she was neither of these things for him. He understood that she had more courage than he would ever possess. She had offered to sacrifice her life to save his father. She had been pursued mercilessly by Rubai thugs. She was loved and trusted like a young aunt by Ewan Briggs. And she was beautiful. It embarrassed him to have such a lovely creature in his arms. She was probably hating the experience.

* * *

It was too late to cancel the heavy equipment. The hope was to have all the clearing finished in a single day and that would mean an eight o'clock start at the latest. Three hours to go and not a single one of the ten people out under the stars on the veranda at Londiani had been to sleep that night. Lydia had spent part of that time in a bed, but that had been no relaxing experience. Five am and the chatter was noisy and excited. There was plenty to talk about.

Tom and Bertie had arrived at the American hospital minutes after the Rubai men. Tom kept his distance when he saw that another car had beaten them to the main gate. They had a grandstand view as simultaneously a familiar white shape had appeared out of the darkness climbing steeply while far below the car up ahead exploded and sent flames into the slipstream only seconds too late to do damage. The gaps in that story had been filled in by an animated Angie Summers.

'We don't have a burns unit up here, but we are giving them first aid. Some rich city guy is sending an air ambulance to collect them. The Lord knows how he found out about all this stuff. I'm only a humble gynaecologist, but I'd guess that they all have over fifty per cent burn damage. Our two marine guards have zero sympathy. Their poor mothers …'

For the first time Lydia and Gloria understood the danger they had been in. They exchanged solemn looks before embracing. Gloria had her explanation and gave thanks.

'God was in front of us and behind us, like always.'

A bewildered Lydia shuddered and over Gloria's shoulder caught the relieved gaze of a sympathetic Rollo. He was pointing the thumb of his right hand upwards.

The quiet of private contemplation replaced the high spirits that had come when they had discovered that Lydia was back amongst them. Alex looked at his watch, unnecessarily, for one glance towards the east told him what the time was. For him the coming of a new day was a moment for stillness and waiting. He had watched the unfolding of the dawn thousands of times from that veranda, not always with the luxury of the leisure to rejoice in the wonder of it.

That first light was the purest of the day. It seemed to have come to wash away the failing darkness. Its power intensified relentlessly and rose to a climax when lines of grey puffs of cloud hung above the horizon against a background of a strong red that began to fade quickly before vanishing with the irresistible rise of what was for a few seconds a plate of molten gases.

Two hours later the rumble of the heavy procession ceased and the large vehicles stood in a line twenty metres back from the shell and the rubble they were about to carry away. In ten minutes the site was clear of people. The veranda would stay, but the rest of the old house would be carried off. The broken pieces of stone, brick and plaster would be dumped in piles on the other side of town ready to be used as hard core for the base of the new hospital. Burnt trees would be uprooted in the house garden and with the considerable remnant from the flower farm built into a huge bonfire. Villages around would have the picking of this heap for firewood or charcoal before a final burn-off.

None of those ten who had seen the arrival of the new dawn would stay to watch the wrecking crew at work. Gloria, still bubbling with energy, was anxious to return to her Peter and her church. Did she have stories to tell him! Inspector Caroline would ferry her along the lower road back to her home and combine her role as social worker with a professional inspection of the car crash the night before.

None of the McCalls could stomach the prospect of watching the final destruction of the family home. They had their distractions lined up. Their first stop was to be Nakuru Park.

# Chapter Seventeen

In the morning after his disastrous night away from home, Abel Rubai returned to his Pink Palace in Karen in a state of almost total exhaustion. And there was nothing to show for the energy, physical and emotional, he had pumped out of himself. If there was any consolation, it came in the form of some new realities, some changed perspectives that had forced themselves on him, none of them comforting in their individual selves.

Less than twenty-four hours after sending Patrick Uchome and his wife in pursuit of Lydia whatever – 'See, I cannot even remember her name' – he found it difficult to understand why he had ever attached such importance to a nobody like her. Her physical attractions had served him well for a brief evening. It was also true that it bothered him that she might have evidence on him about the silencing of the meddlesome Mboya. How foolish of him to have contemplated even the slightest threat to him posed by this frightened … child.

He understood why the nonsense had taken hold.

'Papa, you taught me too well! Remember that night when a lion had taken one of the village boys and you kept me from my bed until you had made my head weary from repeating that single word: "Control! Control! Control!"'

'Yes, it was a good word. I lived by it and, in my turn, I tried to teach it to Julius… It is a fine thing to be able to control an elephant or a buffalo, but to waste my time trying to swat an ant because she might sting me, this is a crazy behaviour.

'And today I will have to tell a mother that I helped to kill her son. I will give her money to buy a new house. She would laugh at me if I told her my truth.'

Envy. Sally, in one of her attempts to get him to spend more time in the church, told him that this envy stuff was one of the killing sins. 'Seven of them, and each one can kill a soul stone dead.' There was a time when he could have recited them off pat. He had thought then that the one that would trouble him least was looking at what other folks had and worrying and wanting to grab some of that for himself.

Wrong. This was a reality that had taken its time to dawn on him. But there that morning, lit up in bright lights he saw it, gnawing at his mind like an infection of the brain. The McCalls, the Mboyas, the Daniels, the Briggs. He had tried to hurt them all, succeeded in part, but they all shared a bond that he could barely comprehend. 'Superiority complex.' He had laughed when Sally suggested, only partly in jest, that he was in danger of developing one.

'Sal, that's not a complex. That's just a little touch of reality. I am a superior being!'

On that worst of mornings, there was no person he could go to and share the secrets of his heart. That heart had become too private, too secretive. He was a hard man and could live with that. He would have to. But for a time he could see what it was like on the other side, where the weak people and the soft people lived their lives.

For an hour he dozed in his red armchair in his screen room. It revived him. The household would soon be rising. He would enjoy a leisurely breakfast. Perhaps Sally would want to read him snippets from *The Nation*. Her boy would be on his way over to Karen dukas right now to fetch her copy. Perhaps she would read him a piece about yet another accident on the sharp bend by the Italian church on the lower road to Naivasha. He would like to know the truth behind that one himself.

* * *

'Patrick Uchome. Haven't I heard that name from somewhere, Abel?'

'So *The Nation* got the story already. Yes, I know him. Did some jobs for me once in a while. Police called me last night.'

'Says here that his wife was with him in the car. They were both taken.'

'Yep. I went into town late last night. You know the morgue on Ngong Road? No family down here, so …'

'You identified them?'

'His father has a small tea plantation up near Kericho. Usual story. The eldest son doesn't want to be stuck on the land, so there's another young man who packs his bag and climbs aboard the *Eldoret Express* or the *Kisii Executive* – you know the names.'

'Just like a certain Abel Nathaniel Rubai …'

'Yeah, hoping to make the golden shilling in the big city. Actually, Sally, he was a fine painter. Studied art. No money in it though. That's why he helped me out sometimes. Anyway, I arranged for the local police to let his people know. I got business I can do up there today, buying a bigger share in a plantation. I'm taking him home. Late morning, after I've checked on that new slice of old forest that's coming down in the next month.'

'Abel, you'll have the papers writing nasty things about you again. And those European conservatives …'

'Conservationists. The same Europeans who've been plundering this country for a hundred years or more. Ask yourself how many local Africans own one of the flower farms on that lake you're so fond of.'

'I'm sorry, Abel.'

'Me, too, Sal. Hey, isn't this the day you got an appointment down at the hospital?'

'Should I cancel it and come up with you?'

'No. Look, by the time I get there, the grave will be dug. Your job is to care for the living. I think Reuben ought to come though. He might as well start getting used to experiencing other people's grief. When he's the MP …'

'Abel, there's been plenty of grief around lately …'

Abel closed his eyes and sighed in a whisper, 'But not always in the right places!'

# Chapter Eighteen

Breakfast at Rusinga was a quiet affair. Freed from his recent ordeals and back home with Ewan, Bertie was keener than ever to please his guests. From the tables set out behind the thick cei-apple hedge there was no view of the demolition going on at Londiani, but the grinding noise of the machinery at its work was carried across the plain on the still morning air.

'Shall I play some music? Can't be too pleasant to hear the old place being bashed about.'

Rafaella's reply was swift and decisive.

'No need, Bertie. The strange thing is that now that it's all started, I no longer see this bashing up as the end. More like a new beginning. When I get home tonight, I want to walk around the garden, push my hands deep into the soil and start dreaming, again.'

Bertie had laid on more food than his guests could cope with.

'Thought so. But after we've gone, the girls will take it across to the workers. Encourage them to do a good job!'

Rollo had a question.

'Why am I not feeling knackered. Sorry Grandma ...'

'I'll sorry you with this handbag. Knackered, that's fine. Don used it a lot. But you know how I dislike ...'

'Yes, I know, Madam McCall Senior, but are you feeling exhausted? You don't look it ...'

'Oh, shut up, Rolls. I saw you having a nap.'

'Eddie, you fibber. That was not me having a nap. I was in deep contemplation, trying to figure out what might have happened to Lydia ...'

Alex intervened. 'Boys, the trip to the park is not compulsory, you know. Just the place to get away from, I don't know, but please forgive the French, some of the shit that has been hitting our fan lately, if you get my drift.'

The twins exchanged amused expressions. Eddie nodded, so Rollo handed out the reprimand.

'Dad, we've left school now, but to prove to you that you didn't waste all that money you spent on our education, over to you, brother.'

'Father, it really is not good form to mix your metaphors as you just did.'

'Mixing my metaphors! Who was your English teacher?'

Maura was pleased and relieved at the show of light-heartedness on display in Bertie's garden.

'I think most people are demonstrating that they are full of beans, single metaphor, on this lovely morning, so I suggest that we drink up, shut up and be on our way!'

Alex touched his best friend on the arm as they all made their way around to the front yard.

'Sorry that we need to take both vehicles. The insurance company says they are almost ready to pay out on the Land Cruiser.'

'You know I'm pleased to do something for you for a change. So it's back to Nakuru, but this time with the boy, and hoping to come back to sleep in my own bed tonight.'

The Pajero and the farm Land Rover stuck together for

the whole of the leisurely drive from South Lake Road to the Lanet Gate entrance of the park. The twins were delighted to be entrusted with the job of driving. Bertie, against the law and against common sense, sat next to Eddie with Ewan in his arms. Behind, Alex sat between his mother and his wife, from time to time grasping the hand of each. They had made that journey hundreds of times. Riding the highways of the homeland was never a dull experience, but this one was special, not only because they were together and well when recent events could have made for a very different situation. Nothing that they saw through the windows of that comfortable vehicle gave them less than a thrill. The orange sellers seated on tiny stools with their bulging nets of fruit in the shade of the yellow fever trees on the rise up to Gilgil, the breathtaking view of wide open country for miles ahead as they ran down towards Kikopei on the steep drop out of Gilgil, the ancient flanks of the Great Rift to their left and their right on the undulating road between Soysambu and Greensteds. The idea of coming away for the day was turning out to be inspired.

The journey in the rickety farm Landy was much less smooth but just as high-spirited in its own noisy way. Tom and Rollo spent a lot of the journey swapping stories about their days in their English boarding school, mimicking teachers, describing hilarious adventures that sounded more like disasters, to Rebecca and Lydia. Rebecca listened with an air of tolerant amusement, Lydia with a bewildered credulity.

Once inside the park, they were all glad to see that the storms of the previous week had left everywhere, trees and bush with a feel of freshness. Their passage along the gravel tracks did not raise clouds of dust behind them. The chances were good that the soda lake would have plenty of water. In their early visits, when the boys were young, the idea had been to move slowly to make sure that they did not miss out on the sighting of a single creature. Seeing rhino was a bonus, getting close to the pride of lion a special treat, but the top encounter was catching sight of the master of camouflage, the sinuous, gorgeous leopard.

On that day being there was enough. Except for Lydia, who had never seen one of these animals of the homeland and who marvelled at dik-dik, gazelle and warthog as enthusiastically as she stared unbelieving at the huge ridge of a buffalo horn, the ride was the pleasure. They trailed around the Euphorbia Forest and still felt no affection for what Maura described as one of nature's misfits. They drank sodas on the rocks of the Baboon Cliffs and watched a family of Eddie's favourite giraffe below them as they stepped their dignified way into a thick clump of woodland.

An eleven year old Tom had been challenged by his grandfather to describe the essence of what the boy had dismissively called the 'Lake Nakuru pong'.

'Do you know what essence means, Tom?'

'No, but I think it stinks like animal manure, wet sand and flamingo droppings. Is that essence?'

'It'll do, son.'

Tom put his arm around his grandmother's shoulders as they stepped out again on the familiar wide stretch of brown and black sand that was always blessed by a cooling breeze.

'Do you still like the pong?'

'Love it!'

Without looking he knew that the smile on Rafaella's beautiful face was heightened by a glint of tears in her eyes.

The big decision of the late morning was where to take lunch. There were two choices: stay in the park and eat at the lodge – delicious food but lots of tourists. They took the second option and chose to go to the Rift Valley Club – predictable fare in familiar surroundings. They could relax and melt into the background, a quiet interlude before going on to Gilgil to organise an important piece of family business.

Wrong. Their arrival caused a minor sensation. Alerted to the news that the McCalls had arrived in the car park, the club secretary rushed out to the top of the steps, camera in hand, asking for a group photograph for the club archives. The dining room was unusually crowded for a Monday and members and their guests were soon on their feet to greet them with a round of applause. A bemused Alex caught sight of Toby Barclay, a farmer friend from Njoro, at his usual table close to the door.

'Toby, what are they putting into the beer here today?'

'Come off it, Alex! First time in here for a while, isn't it? Your family, a bunch of bloody heroes. We've been following the stories. They could make a film. The chairman's in today. Look, he wants you to sit at his table.'

After a warm handshake and a hug, Toby waved Alex on his way. Progress to the centre of the room was very slow. Tom and Rebecca, Alex, Eddie and, most recently, Bertie had all featured on the front pages of *The Nation* and *The Standard* in the previous months, every one of them in some kind of serious danger. Everyone they passed wanted a word, often several. The 'well dones', the 'good lucks' went on and on until the chairman, Edward Narong, came to their rescue.

'How is it, Alex, my friend? You have suffered some mighty blows recently. Those fires. So many of your people taken. What is happening to us all?'

The downcast expressions on the faces of Maura and Rafaella alerted Edward's wife, Mary. She refocused the whole direction of the table talk.

'Ewan, I hear you have been in the park this morning. You must be thirsty and no one has brought you a soda. Bad manners. I'll see to it. Henry, this young man would like you to bring him a …?'

Ewan glanced at his father to check that he was allowed. When Bertie smiled his approval, Ewan surprised the company.

'Papa likes the White-cap. Uncle Alex and the boys, too. And can I have the lemonade?'

A smiling Mary queried. 'And for the ladies?'

Ewan buried his shaking head into his father's arm and added shyly, 'My friend, Rebecca, says that ladies are special.' And added more perkily, 'Rebecca can sing, you know.'

Edward took up the spirit of enthusiasm. 'Yes, you are right. And I think they would like champagne. Henry will need help to bring all these drinks.'

Ewan caused more amusement when he slid from his chair. 'I can help. Sometimes, when we are waiting for our supper I will go to the fridge …'

'But, Ewan, you don't know where the fridge is in this place.'

'Yes, Eddie, but Henry can show me …'

Bertie had another moment of feeling pride in his son and, as usual, the joy of it was shot through with the pain that Anna was not there to share it with him.

Leaving the club through the bottom gate they found themselves held up straightaway. Gilani's supermarket was reopening after the lunch break and the mass of workers was packing the road as they filed back through the partially open door to begin the afternoon shift. After that, with the Land Rover in the lead, they were soon climbing out of town along the avenue of jacaranda on the A104, the main road to all parts south.

There had been an exchange of passengers. Lydia had swapped places with Maura and Tom was now driving the slower, hardworking Landy with Rebecca by his side. They were passing the entrance to Greensteds School when Rollo broke a long silence.

'Feeling nervous, Thomas?'

Tom let the Land Rover drone on another hundred metres before responding to but not answering his brother's question.

'Do you know, I reckon that at least half the times I've driven home on this road, we've had rain somewhere between here and Lord Delamere's Nose. Amazing, don't you think?'

It was Rollo's turn to let the silence drift on before picking up the point.

'Shall I take that as a no?'

Maura, who was a little apprehensive about the business that was awaiting them in Gilgil, specifically in Pembroke House, was not enjoying the brotherly sparring and cut in.

'At this rate, you two would not have proper conversation if we were going all the way down to the coast.'

'There you are, Rollo!'

'What are you on about?'

'If you want to know about nerves, you should be asking Rebecca.'

'Can't do that until you're married and she's my sister. You are still going to be my sister, Rebecca.'

Maura was regretting leaving the vehicle where the conversation was almost civilised.

'Rebecca, sweetheart, don't answer that. The only way to shut morons up is to starve them of oxygen. Took me years to work that out.'

* * *

Their arrival at Pembroke was perfectly timed, just fifteen minutes before lessons for the day ended. In the shade of the line of pepper trees close to the Prefects' Lawn the tables for the afternoon tea break were being loaded with cakes and biscuits and slabs of honeyed bread. All three McCall boys had boarded for seven years in this the second oldest English prep school in the country and this afternoon break and release from lessons ranked equal top for their best time at school. Just as much they loved the Sunday evening chapel service. Another week had passed and the whole school came together in their greys to sit quietly in that time when outside half light merged into full darkness.

The headmaster's study overlooked the Prefects' Lawn from the opposite side to the children's tables and the four oldest of the new arrivals were able to have a more private tea and yet watch what their young companions got up to. Of these, only Lydia had not been to the school before. It had been the first place outside Naivasha that Tom and Rebecca had visited after their first engagement. Tom was ever the hero after his amazing escape from captivity and almost certain death in a hut in a remote part of the Kakamega Forest. But it was Rebecca who held their hearts. Through the windows of the main school block two classes of eleven year olds had seen her arrival and promptly lost interest in their Geography and English lessons.

When the chapel bell clanged to signal the end of lessons, the noise in that tree-lined triangle of greenery was so loud that it drew staff from their offices and the house to see what was going on. Nothing could calm the excitement until Rebecca climbed onto a low stool and charmed them into rapt silence. First she gave them 'The elephant and the buffalo', the only comic song that Toni Wajiru had ever been able to finish. Then she surprised them.

'I hear that you have a new school song, written by two of your clever teachers. I know this song, all three verses. Thomas tells me that you must go to your places to change for your games. Please, if we hurry, we can sing this song together.'

And they did, loud enough for the goats on the top of Big Hill to be disturbed by the sound, especially when they came to the last two lines of the little chorus: 'O, Africa, O, Africa, I take my stand in thee. And the peaceful paths of Pembroke are ever dear to me!'

The children went on their way, the hubbub died away and the real business of the afternoon began. Rebecca and Tom stayed in the study while the rest followed the children to the playing fields. There was something for everyone down there. The twins had golden memories revived when they watched the senior boys batting and bowling in the cricket nets. Bertie and Alex took Ewan over to a corner pitch where the youngest boys were chasing a football with noisy enthusiasm.

For the ladies, the setting offered the best reward of all. Rafaella and Maura had strolled around these flat, grassy fields hundreds of times when they came to watch their three boys at school matches.

'Lydia, this is the paradise within a paradise. Why do all these children have to rush around so madly like this and miss all this magic around them?'

'Maura, I once suggested to Eddie and Rollo that, for a change, they put down their bits of wood and the rest of the stuff. "Just sit on the mound there for half an hour and look around you. Do you more good than getting sweaty and having your legs kicked."'

'And what did they say?'

'Lydia, they looked at me then looked at each other, smiled at their idiotic grandmother and told me that I must speak to Mister Wilson or Mister Williams, the games fundi. See them over there. They love this place. I think they understand now what I was trying to tell them.'

* * *

'You know that we would love you to have the marriage service in the chapel. Five weeks time?'

'Well, Bill, we've had a bit of trouble lately, but headmasters are used to bits of trouble, aren't you?'

Bill Foster smiled. He had been in the job for just over two years now. Even behind his desk, those wide shoulders, the easy smile on the sunburned face and the mass of curly grey hair would have made it clear to any newcomer that no child in his right mind would want to upset this man in even the most trivial way. He was a giant of a man when he stood to his full height, sure like a terrifying sight to a six year old in trouble for the sin of tugging a little girl's pigtails.

'House burned down, farm destroyed, Tom, and that's a bit of trouble? I don't know what it was like in your day here, but as far as Susie and I are concerned, Pembroke is as near to paradise as you'd find in any school.'

'Bwana …'

'Hold on! Rebecca, my name's Bill.'

She hesitated, found the 'Bill' bit too difficult but went on anyway. 'Does the idea of getting married in a school sound foolish to you?'

'If I was in Tom's shoes, I'd be ready to marry ten times to make sure I got you signed and sealed.'

'He asked me to explain. The chapel at Pembroke is his

only church. "The Christina Chapel". I know about it. He has told me. The boys built it when the troubles were with us. Long time ago now. The Mau Mau. They were bad times, but a beautiful place was born then. When his time came, Tom was in the choir. On Monday mornings he took his turn to put up the flag. When we set the day for the marriage …'

'Bill, I was happy for the service to be at home, in the garden. My grandmother – you know Rafaella – is a friend of the priests in the cathedral in Nakuru. She's a Catholic. One of the fathers came when Grandfather Don was killed in, well, nearly three years ago now. So there is a new one. Went to school in England. Father Peter. He's only about my age. Why do they call them father? Look, I'm not doing a good job of explaining …'

'You are right, Thomas. You are not. There is no garden today in Londiani. Everything was destroyed in the fire. But, tomorrow a new garden will be born. I think in five weeks it will be ready for us, new growing for a new marriage. On Saturday here at Christina. It will be my present to my new husband. On Sunday, at home. The families want this.'

'And so do we. I suggest twelve-thirty. The children will be at early lunch …'

'No, no, they must be there …'

'But the chapel … your guests.'

'Perhaps some of the very young ones and the choir. Next week we will come up again. It will be a wonderful day. I am very excited.'

# Chapter Nineteen

At the very same time that the McCalls and their friends were enjoying lunch at the table of the chairman of the Rift Valley Club, Abel Rubai and his entourage were travelling under the line of jacaranda into Nakuru. At the roundabout just beyond the railway bridge, they did not take a left towards Kenyatta Avenue but bypassed the town centre on Geoffrey Kamati Road on their way to the tea capital of Kericho.

Four Mercedes and a Daimler hearse, all black, travelled in convoy, turning the heads of passers-by.

'Hey, I wonder where the funeral is, Zacharias.'

'Yeah, Jonah. Must be some Nairobi bigwig on his last ride up to the family farm.'

'Didn't read about the death of no bigwig in the paper this morning.'

The only bigwig in that little procession was very much alive, pleased with two successful pieces of business completed in short order that morning. He had a reluctant Reuben by his side. The boy was not happy. His father had made him miss out on a lunch at Muthaiga with two friends who had recently returned from a month long holiday in the United States and Canada.

'Papa, we're a rich family. How come we never get to take a holiday in some exciting place?'

Reuben kept the question firmly in his head. No need to

provoke another lecture from his father about the virtues of careful living to go with the one he was presently enduring about smart business practice.

'Know exactly what you want before you start talking. And do precious little of that. Let the other fellow make the running. And always be in ...?'

'Control. Yes, but ...'

'I'd like it if you could sound a little more enthusiastic, son.'

'Papa, you know that I think you are the greatest man in the country, but what's wrong with a person my age having a bit of fun sometimes?'

'Let me tell you, Reuben, that there are lots of ways of having fun besides going to clubs to get drunk in the middle of a Monday.'

'But, Papa, we are on our way to a funeral. Where's the fun in that?'

Abel chuckled. 'When I was your age, I was a father and I was financial adviser to the president, no less. I had my fun by keeping my eyes open, watching how the big people did things. Soon enough I became one of those big people myself.'

Beaten into submission yet again, Reuben withdrew into himself and willed the day to hurry along. They were beginning to climb out of the valley floor. The countryside was beginning to green up. He tried focusing on what he could see out there through the window on his side. Fence after fence, field after field. All the fault of those early pioneers, those Europeans who had killed off the wildlife, the native African animals to set up their boring farms. So, after perhaps half a minute staring out into a nothing landscape, his head swivelled 'round and he was forced once more to fix his eyes on the back end of that extra wide hearse carrying Patrick Uchome and his wife home for the last time. In spite of himself, he visualised the couple flat out in their separate coffins, dressed in their smartest clothes, their bodies juddering in uncontrolled response to their vehicle hurrying along that rough road. He shuddered. He was desperate to see a few lions running about. Okay, that was impossible, but what about some rain, a downpour to cheer things up?

In less than twenty minutes his second wish was granted. Rain fell on the tea plantations as it did every afternoon, another short, sharp shower to feed the tea bushes and keep the rolling ridges green. The downpour was heaviest as they travelled along Moi Highway and for a few seconds it overwhelmed the windscreen wipers with its ferocity. The meeting place was just beyond Hospital Road where the highway veers down to the right en route for Kitale, Kisumu and the lake.

One of the boys in the leading cars came back to report to Abel.

'Boss, this old fellah up ahead says he is Patrick's uncle. He's got a bike. Knows the place. Mile, mile and a half, mostly good road.'

'Mostly? Don't like the sound of that. Reminds me of my village and the red mud when the rains came. Tell him to ditch the bike and climb in with you or it will be dark by the time we get there.'

Now when he looked through the car windows to the left and right, Reuben saw nothing but an apple green landscape.

'Papa, I never knew there was a place like this in Kenya. Like being in a different world.'

'Perhaps we should buy a place up here. Your mother likes her tea. Just down the road, sugar plantations. Plenty rain, too. No, I think I prefer it down south these days.'

Abel was pleasantly surprised when they turned off the metalled road. The murram was firmer than he expected and they soon covered the distance to the Uchome place. He was glad to get down to stretch his legs and look around. He soon discovered that Patrick's extended family owned three large plots in the area, all producing tea. There was a big turnout for the funerals and he and Reuben were led through the crowd to a small group of well-built stone houses. To one side of a large vegetable garden heavy with crops, he could see the two graves with the mounds of earth stacked neatly all around. Just beyond, and in the fields, stood a large, open shed, a simple structure of pine poles topped with a thatch of reeds and straw. On working days the pickers brought their baskets here to be weighed. Today it was transformed into a gathering place for family and friends. Abel groaned.

He had known that there must be a service but had not given much thought to how it would be. He would have liked a simple but speedy farewell. This set-up suggested something more elaborate and, more important, longer. Regular churches made him feel uncomfortable. On the few occasions when he had been obliged to go along with Sally to the cathedral or one of the other big Nairobi churches, he had his technique worked out. He let Sally belt out the hymns or spill the overflow of emotion while he let his thoughts wander or, better still, fixed his concentration on a minor problem. In those places he found that he could work without distraction.

Here he knew he would be a focus of attention. Eyes would be on him. He would be expected to react … properly. He had seen to the Nairobi side of the arrangements, had the bodies removed from the morgue before there had been a full autopsy, paid for the expensive oak coffins, hired the only double hearse in the country. To the casual observer, these might have seemed to be the actions of a considerate friend anxious to demonstrate his compassion and his sympathy for the bereaved family. In fact, they were little more than a mask to protect his own interests. He wanted Patrick in particular safely under ground as quickly as possible.

His personal ordeal was about to begin. He and Reuben led the Rubai contingent on the walk to the tea shed. There was plenty of give in the grassy verges. He did not enjoy the suck of the mud pulling at his shoes as they squelched towards the waiting family. The bottoms of his trousers were soon saturated, making his ankles feel uncomfortable.

'Bwana Rubai, my name is David. I am Patrick's brother. My mother and father want me to tell you how grateful they are to you for your kindness to them in bringing their boy home and coming yourself …'

Abel was switching off. Twenty years on the political scene had helped him hone the art of presenting an interested face to company, to filter away the parts of exchanges that had no relevance to him and to be alert and attentive when it suited.

So the ritual began. The coffins were carried in, the bodies inspected and grieved over painfully. Words were spoken impassionately, songs were sung interspersed with prayers. The big man looked on with an impassive expression. He cast an eye out into the rolling fields and noticed that the afternoon was far gone. Just when he was wondering if the burial would take place in the dark, everything stopped abruptly.

There, directly in front of him and supported on her husband's arm, stood Sophie Uchome, Patrick's mother. And he who was no friend to her son, who had been wishing himself a hundred miles away, looked into that beautiful, old face and wept, sobbed with total sincerity. He was overwhelmed by a sense of loss. This unexpected reaction stunned Reuben and shocked his men, but in Abel there was only a feeling of release. He reached out to grasp the two old people in front of him and held them in a tight embrace. The room might have been totally empty to judge from the silence of the two hundred people gathered there. Every one of them heard the whispered plea from Abel's lips.

'I am so sorry!'

The seconds ticked by and the moment was passed.

Half an hour later, the powerful motors of the four Rubai cars were started up. By now the hearse was well on its way back to its Nairobi yard. On the short journey back to the main road, they caught up with Patrick's uncle on his way to retrieve his bicycle and Abel invited him to sit by his side. For the last few metres Abel got down and walked with the cheerful man who had such an impressive zest for life.

'Do you have a lamp on the bike, Shadrack?'

'Bwana, why would I need a lamp? I have been living in these plantations for sixty-five years and more. Even on the darkest night, there is some brightness up there. On my way home tonight I will be singing because I am happy. Bwana Rubai has brought honour to our family.'

'But how will you find your bike now? You have come too late.'

Reuben, riding in the car that was moving at walking pace, was watching his father with curious interest. Since the outburst of emotion in the tea hall, some of the sharp edge had left him. He was giving time to people he would normally have ignored. Listening in to the conversation with the Uchome uncle and seeing his concern for the old man's bike, he would not have been surprised if his father had pulled out his wallet and handed over a few thousand for a new machine.

'To find it, that will be easy. Ah, we are close now. I left it near that pile of stone just where we turn onto the big road.

They are special marble, paid for by businessmen in Nairobi. I expect you will know them.'

'And why would they do that?'

'A Kericho stonemason will soon be building a place where we will remember the good doctor. They found him just there. They had killed him with knives, left him naked by the entrance to the big plantation.'

Abel snapped back into his old self in seconds. His system had been struck by a second shock, this one unpleasant and totally explicable. Without another word, he left the old man to look for his cycle and slid into the seat next to Reuben.

'I have changed my mind. We will not go to the farm to spend the night. The road through Kakamega Forest can be dangerous. I know that the President will not be at State House Nakuru. I will phone ahead. Obi, pick up the speed!'

He was regathering his composure.

'Yes, yes, a much better plan. I can get in some practice for when my time comes. I should have thought of it before. Yes, Reuben, when you are elected, you will come and visit. Perhaps you will bring your family.'

'If they elect me.'

'I don't like that little word. You will be the chosen one.'

It was Abel's turn to will the journey to pass more quickly. He would like to have had some interesting conversation to distract him on the way. He was well aware that Reuben was not up to the mark on this score. There was not much common ground of shared interests.

'Your mama went to the hospital today. A check-up on the new child. He is coming soon now.'

'She asked me to go with her. I don't like hospitals much.'

'So I rescued you.'

'Well, yes, except ...'

'That you don't like funerals either.'

'Not all the way up here and for someone I never even met.'

'Okay, son, we'll agree on a truce. I'll just lay my head back and let the tyres eat up the miles. They are getting dinner prepared for when we arrive.'

He closed his eyes, but the hoped for doze into temporary oblivion did not come. Instead he felt the uncomfortable presence of someone he had thought he had rid himself of weeks before. 'The good doctor' were Shadrack's words. Abel had no regrets. Simon Mboya would have been as big a threat to the stability of the state as his Uncle Tom before him, another Luo meddler. They were popular with some of the wananchi. Their careless tongues could blab all the nonsense they liked. Dreamers do not make sensible leaders.

At last, the lights of Nakuru gleamed in the distance. In twenty minutes he would be in State House, back in familiar territory.

After sending three cars straight on to Nairobi, he noticed that his driver, Obi, had a wide grin on his face as he sorted out the formalities with the guards on duty at the gatehouse.

'Hey, boy, share the story. Me and Reuben here could do with a smile ourselves.'

'Bwana, just thinking how lucky I am to be driving your car. This place is so … relaxing.'

'So I made a smart decision to spend the night here? You approve.'

'Bwana, any decision you make, I approve. But I get on well with the staff here and I like the garden.'

'Given me an idea. Reuben, make yourself useful. Go inside and check on things. Treat it like a test, practice for the future. I'll go for a stroll and have a chat with Mama Nature.'

Abel was not far into his walk along a wide path when

he remembered that it would bring him to a wooden bench on a grassy mound at the top of the garden. Sitting there brought him a double bonus. The line of jasmine bushes that encircled the base of the mound gave off a scent that was made more intoxicating by the evening dew. The view was special, too. From there he could look down on lower ground that stretched out to the lake and beyond. There it was half a mile beyond the lights of the A104, a flat, glassy, irregular shape reflecting light from some, to him, invisible source. One of the askaris had once told him that on very still nights up there he had heard flamingos paddling noisily around the shallows eating their way through the night.

After half an hour in that place, the low moments of the day were already fading into insignificance for him. He was renewed and had returned to his confident best self.

Before supper he phoned Sally to check on her day.

'Abel, in two weeks little Julius will be with us. He has been a very busy boy today. I have had to ask him to remember that his mama is not as young as she was. Makes no difference. This one will be his own bwana. Oh, sorry, I am forgetting. The funeral, how was it?'

'Huh. It passed. What can one say? I suppose the one person I will remember will be Patrick's mother. She reminded me of Mama. Caught me by surprise. I'm over it now.'

'Pity.'

'And what does that mean?'

'Oh nothing. You are such a strong person. Sometimes it is good to have some tears.'

'But I did. You can ask Reuben. I think he was shocked.'

The pause on her side was brief. 'Abel, I will be happy to have you home. Are you at the farm?'

'No. Much closer. Reuben and I are, shall we say, trying out the facilities at State House in Nakuru. I think you know why. We will be home tomorrow.'

Next morning Abel decided that he would make a small diversion on the last leg of the journey back to Karen. His confidence was high and he was ready to negotiate the sale of a piece of land. He had failed to buy twice before, but circumstances had changed since those days. He felt lucky.

Alex McCall was standing at the end of the driveway that led up to South Lake Road. He had walked over there to have a panoramic view of the house and garden now that the site had been cleared. A dozen and more bodies were bent over or kneeling in the earth on this the first day of the new creation.

So firmly was he focused on the work going on in front of him that he did not hear the large black car gliding down the track behind him. A door closed and Alex swung 'round. He was shocked to see the bulky figure of Abel Rubai sauntering towards him with a hand outstretched.

Alex restrained the reflex reaction to scream at the brass-necked intruder to get off his land. He ignored the proferred handshake. He found it more difficult not to launch himself at this smiling, arrogant, hateful lump of humanity. Rubai was in first.

'McCall, I hear there's a piece of land for sale here.'

'Now which one of your bonehead acquaintances gave you that stupid idea?'

'Is it just the farm or are the fields included?'

'I would have thought that with all your money, you could have afforded a hearing aid! I hear there's a doctor in New York who can fit you up with the newest piece of technology. If you hurry, you could be there by Christmas.'

Abel chuckled. 'Hey, sarcasm doesn't suit you, boy!'

'Boy, is it? Would you like me to call you bwana, too? Look, let's get this finished quickly so that you can be on your way to the next poor sucker on your list. Not a square inch of this place is for sale, especially to a person of, I'll put it delicately, of dubious character. Now, please, shove off!'

Abel shifted awkwardly. The smile on his face was long gone. How was it that these McCalls knew the way to needle his family so easily? He would never be able to forget how the piggy face son had been bad news for Julius from they moment they crossed paths up in that European man's school in Gilgil. What a fool he had been to send him there so that he could learn to act like a proper English gentleman.

He looked towards the house. Obviously a lot of work had gone on there already. These stubborn fools were going to rebuild. That crowd was fixing the garden. How did these bastards manage to win out all the time? He could feel the control slipping, and fast. There were Africans over there kneeling in the deep soil and they were singing. He never noticed any singing from the workmen converting the bush into parkland on his Karen estate. The next stop in the logic of this painful train of thought was the memory of the lines of burnt corpses stretched out in lines on the lawns that used to be over there by that ruin of a farmhouse.

Abel's breathing was heavy and his expression a scowl. Once again in his mind he was absolving himself from guilt, from accepting the fact that he was the motive force behind the death of forty-five young people. This is what can happen when invaders from up north come down to steal pieces of the sacred homeland. So the Rossi man went too far, but that was not his fault. And still these white bastards would not give the land back.

He must suffer the ordeal again. These people, this family from hell … but he would think about that later. The storm was passing. This stubborn farmer was staring at him. He must not lose face. Thank God he had left Reuben in the car. The boy would not have understood what was going on. And now he must create a smooth departure for himself. He signalled to Obi to turn the car around.

Abel masked his anger with a smile, a hint of a nod.

'Bwana McCall, I am here with the best of intentions. You are in deep distress and I came to offer you a way out – the full value of the land and the buildings before these misfortunes struck. The offer will stand for a year from today.'

Alex was staring blankly over Rubai's shoulder at the shiny black car being skillfully manoevred until its nose was pointing up the driveway towards the main road. Under his breath he whispered a single word.

'Surreal!'

Everyone in that bare garden saw the meeting of the two men but could hear none of the words exchanged. Maura and Rafaella moved close together as they watched a shocked and weary Alex plodding towards them. Maura broke the silence.

'Coffee time, everyone. I'll get the kettle going.'

One mug of sweet coffee and two Mcvitie's chocolate biscuits later and Alex ended the wait.

'Maura, if you hadn't been so quick off the mark with the kettle, I would have been into a large straight whisky by now.'

'What did he want, Dad?'

'Tom, that generous man wanted to save us all the bother of working ourselves silly making Londiani an even better place than it was before he tried to wipe us out with his murderous ways.

'Yeah, I know that's putting it a bit strong for our first day back on the job. Perhaps I should pretend that we had no visitor out there, just a nasty stench of a bad memory.'

Stephen Kamau, Alex's good friend, still on full pay for being chief foreman at a nonexistent flower farm, broke in gently.

'No, Bwana, no use hiding away from trouble. Look Mister Danger straight in the eye. If you bury your head, you can't even see who's kicking your backside.'

'Like some silly old ostrich.'

'Well, Rollo, perhaps someone hasn't been telling us the truth about those creatures. One time I took some of the older village boys on a cycle ride 'round to the other side of the lake. There's an ostrich farm over there and we had our picnic on some rocks close by. Young Stanley, he was only eight at the time, sat up close to the fence. He was there for an hour or more. Never took his eyes off those big birds.

'Stanley, time to turn back now, unless you want to spend the night out in the bush. I heard that there's a couple of old leopards got a place around here.'

'Bwana Kamau, I don't think that these birds are real ostriches. No, never saw one of them try to dig a hole and hide his head down inside. Ostriches? I do not think so!'

'Stephen, your grandchildren are going to love having you come across to the house to tell them bedtime stories.'

'Yes, bedtime stories. Perhaps I was wrong to speak like that. These kids are so clever and it wasn't anything made up out of my head. Next day Stanley came up to me. "Bwana, if we had stayed longer. Maybe they only do it at night when nobody sees." Coasties like me never grow up. Just can't help ourselves sometimes. Anyway I don't think Stanley will find any ostriches around Londiani.'

Maria was sitting next to Stephen on the veranda wall. She reached out to grasp his hand.

'Stephen, you're the most grown-up person I've ever met. And if Stanley had been here a few minutes ago he would have seen an ostrich going off in that big car.'

'Hang on, Maria, why would he need to bury his head? He's got nothing to be scared of.'

'Wrong, Rollo. Men like him scent danger when it's still a long way off. But be careful when the rat is cornered. And you know the best thing we can do? Plant this garden. Create the work so that there will be flowers and vegetables to look after in the fields over there. Start building the hospital. It will make him even more crazy.'

'So he will send his thugs to get rid of a few more enemies, burn more kids he's never heard of.'

'He might do just that. But Stanley is right. We must not pretend. Hide and hope, hope that he will be blown away like any other bad stench. Of course, he is a monster, a murderer. I do not forget a single one of those young persons whose bodies were lying in this very place, burned to death. But Abel Rubai is also a coward. He has money and he has men ready to do his dirty work.'

Eddie was as distraught as his brother. He had just seen the man who had tried to wipe out his whole family arrogantly invade their farm and pretend to be a potential benefactor. This man feared nothing.

'Maria, there is only one sure way for us to be rid of him. We could have done that when he was here. Put one between the eyes.'

'Solve one problem and create ten more. Listen. We are all country people here. Think of the story of the tall, strong tree, perhaps the biggest in the forest. One morning, a farmer comes along and finds the giant flat on the ground. When he saws across the trunk, he finds the inside is rotten. The preparation for that fall was going on long before it happened.'

Maria held the little audience spellbound. The beautiful Luo woman was on fire with passion. Her brothers, Paul and Barnabas, were both successful lawyers, but they would have been hard put to outshine her in the dynamic presentation of an argument. Like any competent lawyer, she had arguments to back up her case.

'In a moment of weakness our rulers, two months ago, appointed Andrew Rafiki to investigate corruption and graft in the government. Unfortunately, Andrew, an honest man, took the job very seriously. Some of the power men discovered that he was wanting to look into their books. Last week, we read in *The Nation* that Andrew has fled the country. His life was in danger. But the evidence he collected is not lost, and when the time comes ... The rot is inside the tree.'

'Maria, what happened?'

'What do you mean, Maura?'

'Why aren't you a lawyer, or an MP, or running some big thing in this country?'

'What could be more important than helping to plant this new garden? And later I will be going to join Rebecca and Lydia over where the new hospital will be. And, Eddie, there is much rot gathering unnoticed in the heart of the big tree. Many, many policemen want to be part of the change ... when the time comes. Ask Inspector Caroline.'

'Yeah, but when?'

Maria smiled. Rollo and Eddie had known Maria for less time than the others having their extraordinarily long coffee break on that open veranda, and they still found her smile comforting and at the same time disturbing. When those dark eyes were focused on them, it was as if she was able to read their minds or at least work out in which direction their thoughts were moving.

'The tree will fall sooner than we think. And it will not topple over in the darkness of the night. The axemen are sharpening their blades. They are in danger, more even than any of us.'

'So there!' Rollo nodded towards his mother and grandmother with an amused grin.

# Chapter Twenty

When the Mercedes reached the junction at the end of South Lake Road, Obi asked for instructions.

'High or low, Boss?'

Abel considered the matter before surprising Reuben with his answer.

'Mmn, go back through the town and up the Escarpment.'

'But, Dad, that's so much slower!'

'Yeah, I know it, but today it suits me to go that way.'

Abel wanted to avoid the unpleasantness of passing the Italian church and close to the place where Patrick Uchome and his wife were killed. He could not know it, but taking the longer route was simply avoiding one distasteful experience to move into another before he even left the town.

'Hell and damnation! Look over there. Obi, turn right, yes, in through that gate!'

'Into this field with the big piles of earth?'

'In case you haven't noticed there are people there, too.'

'Yes, I saw them when we drove in. You and the boy were talking.'

Bertie had driven Rebecca and Lydia across town to the site of the new hospital. The first plans had arrived from Debbie Miller in Boston and they wanted to make rough measurements on the site. Lydia and Bertie worked with the tape measure while Rebecca called out the numbers and made notes.

For the second time that morning Abel had the advantage of surprise on his side. Obi had parked just inside the gate and it was the crunch of feet on the gravelly surface that alerted the three busy surveyors to the presence of company.

A shocked Bertie dropped his end of the tape. The unexpected confrontation had him trembling. He was angry but desperate to hang on to his self-control. Abel smiled blandly, delighted to see his nemesis caught out and in a panic. Each one of this trio had caused him a lot of trouble in their different ways. And now this wild idea about a hospital could be a source of more embarrassment to him personally and politically. No such building would be put up on this site or any other in the town without his say-so.

The stand-off was prolonged. For a few moments, isolated from each other in their reaction, Rebecca, Bertie and Lydia stared incredulous at the intruders. The melting feeling in the pit of their stomachs took away the will and the energy to speak out.

For Reuben, standing a step behind his father, this was a demonstration of the power of his father's personality. His unexpected arrival was making these people rigid with fear. They were like naughty children caught out by their father in a prank and now scared of the consequences. He was wrong in his assumption.

Bertie made the first move. He picked up his end of the tape measure and wound it in slowly, all the while focusing his eyes on the smiling Abel. When the tape was all in, he walked resolutely towards his car that was parked twenty metres behind where the Rubais stood. He chose to pass much closer to the father and son than was necessary. Reuben thought that this mad white man was about to attack his father and Abel hoped that he would. The physical pain involved would be nothing compared to the benefits it would bring. Before nightfall Briggs would be back in a prison cell, this time in a Nairobi jail.

But Bertie passed on and climbed into his car.

Abel broke the silence with a stab of sarcasm.

'Ladies, I think that building is over for the day. Your friend has taken the toys away.'

'Mister Rubai, this is private property.'

This was the best reply that Rebecca could think of in her confused state.

To the accompaniment of Reuben's guffaws, his father went on.

'A house girl and a street girl playing at being civil engineers. And your friend there hiding from visitors in his car.'

'He is not hiding from you. He is not afraid of you. He is afraid of himself.'

'Very clever. I said that building is over for the day ...'

'But we are not building. The farmers say that the soil here is very rich, just right for growing macadamias. We are measuring out the beds.'

Abel did not try to hide his mounting anger. As he spoke, he prodded the air with his finger. For the second time within an hour an attempt was being made to belittle him.

'That's enough. Do not waste your money and your time. There will be no hospital built here. There is a perfectly good hospital here already.'

'Mister Rubai, I know that your own wife is soon to have a child. Would you like him to be born in the maternity ward up there?'

Reuben saw his father's head jerk backwards. For a few

seconds Abel said nothing and when he spoke the tone was calm but tense.

'I preferred it when you were the shy wash girl. Money has made you arrogant and foul-mouthed with it.'

'No, sir. That is unfair. Mrs Rubai has always treated me with kindness and I love her dearly. Is it wrong to want the women of this town to have a place where they, too, can be properly looked after when a new child comes?'

'You don't understand, do you? Do you think that you are the first one to come along believing you can solve with your amateur ways problems that the government wrestle with every single day?'

'So there is a problem?'

'Of course, you fool! But Kenya is a poor country. Things take time to put right.'

'Yes, but if in one small place we can solve one problem.'

'And make other small places first jealous and then angry.'

'No, give other small places hope, Mister Rubai, hope. And hope makes all the difference. You were a village boy once. Have you forgotten so quickly?'

As he listened to the words of this wash girl, this singer, Mister Abel Rubai, he who will not be opposed, found himself unexpectedly moved. The expression of deeply felt passion on the Kamau girl's face added a kind of sublimity to her youthful, fresh beauty. 'A village boy'. The notion struck hard, catapulting him back thirty years to the clean days when the scholarship boy worked tirelessly at his lessons and had hopes for himself and for those hundreds, thousands of his people. To have any chance of turning these hopes into reality, he would have to take the well-worn path to the capital. He would, but he would return.

Close by, Reuben watched the transformation in his father.

The anger subsided. Even the outline of his body seemed diminished. Without warning, he turned away from Rebecca and Lydia. He seemed to have lost interest in beating down the arguments of the young woman who could so easily have become his daughter-in-law.

Obi had the engine running and the door open, ready for his boss's arrival. The chauffeur had never seen Mister R look so downcast. The Mercedes was soon out onto the A104 and climbing the Escarpment at a steady speed. Reuben was relieved that his father had no interest in making conversation. Instead he spent most of the journey looking out at the commonest sight any traveller in the Great Rift of Kenya would have witnessed – hundreds of people, young and old, on the march on the red earth footpaths.

Measuring work at the hospital site was over for the morning. Rubai had been right about that. Rebecca and Lydia joined a solemn Bertie in his Pajero. While Rebecca slid up onto her seat wearily, Lydia's entrance was sprightly. She was eager to talk about the meeting with the Rubais. Rebecca's fearless confrontation of a man she had feared since first encountering him had given her confidence, but she knew that it was not her place to speak the first words.

Bertie's retreat to his vehicle had been the right move. He was pleased with himself for that. At first, from his vantage point at the driving wheel, he had been ashamed to have left his two young friends to deal with the unpleasant confrontation, but shame soon turned to admiration and pride when he saw how Rebecca stood her ground and then went onto the attack. He had heard every word spoken and at one point feared that, in his temper, Rubai might become physically violent. Mister Big was wily enough not to risk doing harm to the most popular woman in the country. Bertie was surprised and pleased to watch Rubai's limp departure, seemingly a beaten man.

'Let's go home. We can join the gardeners.'

Bertie drove slowly through the town. It turned out to be a royal progress. He saw for himself again how popular Rebecca was with the local people. It was waving and smiling all the way to the railway crossing. Lydia loved her for many reasons, but sitting behind her on that short journey back to Londiani, she felt awed. This beautiful woman so talented, so much loved was her friend.

'Rebecca, you are amazing!'

'I don't think so.'

'I was watching. My heart was pounding away. I was afraid that they had come to take me with them. You had no fear. In the end, I think he just wanted to get away. You told him hard, true things. It was impossible, but I saw it. And, then, in the town, the people are so happy just to see you pass by. It's like they … worship you or something.'

'Now that is really crazy talk, Lydia!' There was no sharpness in the reprimand, just a kindly correction delivered with a smile. 'You are forgetting. I am just a Naivasha girl. They have known me all my life. My friends are here. They would be in fits of laughter to hear you say such things.'

Bertie smiled to himself. There was a truth in Lydia's words, but he was sure that Rebecca's head would not be turned by any such talk. He had never met anyone with so keen a perception of the reality of a given situation. She was modesty personified. What a fool he had been all those months ago when he heard that Tom was planning to marry the wash girl, and disapproved, prophesied all sorts of problems. A lot of learning by a lot of people had taken place since then and this girl was responsible for a good deal of it.

'Rebecca, it was impressive. I've never seen the old bugger – sorry, girls – the big man look so small. You had him on the run. Tell you something else. Watching that little lot made me believe that Maria could be right. Rubai could be toppled, beaten or whatever.'

'To tell you the truth, I felt no fear standing there facing him. It's only now that I am trembling. But Maria also warned of the danger of a rat when he is cornered. Thomas's mother calls him a snake, the king cobra with the cold, hooded eyes. He is strong and the three of us know that he will strike and strike until he has his way.'

They were turning off South Lake Road when Lydia came out with her wistful observation. 'There will be only one winner here. Is that right, Mister Briggs?'

'Lydia, I think it's the people's turn this time.'

# Chapter Twenty-one

Stephen Kamau had taken his six workers over to the flower fields. They were his foremen. They had finished their heavy work in the garden and it was time to do some groundwork ready for the return of another hundred Londiani people eager to begin the much longer task of preparing the ground for new planting.

Rafaella, the organiser, was having a wonderful time. She was busy creating and leading a team of enthusiasts. The rich soil had been fed and the seedlings, the young shrubs and the saplings were ready to be put in position.

When she saw the Pajero of Bertie Briggs returning early from the morning out at the hospital site, Rafaella called a ten minute break. The coffee and biscuits were finished in that time, but the talk kept them from their work for much longer. The reaction to what they heard from the new arrivals was mixed. The McCalls were impressed when they listened to Bertie's account of Rebecca's face-off with Rubai Senior, but Tom, especially, was apprehensive about a backlash from the other side.

'Sent off twice in one morning. Wow! He'll love that.'

Maria broke in. 'Tom, no. The Abel Rubai of a year ago would be on his way home right now spitting blood, planning revenge, red hot with anger. Today, whether he is willing to acknowledge it or not, there are cracks in the wall of that pink palace. Little dark clouds of doubt are floating about in that twisted mind.'

'Maria, please God, you are right. It is not many weeks since Sonya and I were in a sitting room in that pink palace, pleading for the life of Simon. I'm shuddering at the memory of it. Ruthless, mean, arrogant and with those cold eyes and lying tongue, in one word, evil, he treated us like grovelling fools. In my case he was right. I had persuaded Sonya. I feel the shame of it. Maria, he hates this family.'

'Maura, please, forgive me for my talk of cracks and clouds of doubt. But soft words are dangerous. Believe me, however hard you find it to do so. We cannot wish him away. We cannot. Sometimes in our lives we become raw with fear and pain. At these times we have to cling on hard. There are other forces much stronger than our human powers … Maura, I must stop. All is going to be well.'

Rafaella saw that her much loved daughter-in-law was allowing her emotions to work her mind into a state of turmoil. She was losing her sense of proportion.

'Darling, let us trust the good earth. It longs for us to create new beauty in this place.'

Alex and his three sons were feeling uncomfortable in this atmosphere of high-octane emotion. He did not want to be caught up in it. Tom found the words for him.

'In five weeks Rebecca and I will be married right here. That is going to mean a lot of work. I just want to get stuck in.'

Eddie chimed in. 'Got a great idea. We play music to get us into the swim of things.'

'No power.'

'Okay, Rollo, we sing! Like our people in the fields. And, think of it, they'll be back singing soon.'

'But you've got a terrible voice. Probably kill the plants.'

'The ladies can cover up my racket. Let's give it a go.'

And singing there was, but not straight away. The tools were picked up and the soil worked, slowly and quietly by a garden crew who were looking inward and allowing their thoughts and emotions to work their way through.

At last, Rebecca began to hum the melody of one her most popular songs, 'Mombasa Sunset'.

An hour later, the music of the voices, good and the ordinary, was rising out of the patch of garden where the work was concentrated, was disturbed. Two large trucks were bumping down the track towards them. Alex dug his fork into the earth and went to greet them.

'It's stuff for the build. Sawyer said he'd get most of it on site this week. Maura, a good omen?'

'A good omen.' She was smiling through tears.

In the late afternoon there was an unexpected visitor. Only the three McCall boys were still on the job. The car pulled up on the gravel area close to the veranda. The passenger door opened and a small, smartly dressed old man stepped out with his hand outstretched in greeting. Tom took the hand and smiled uncertainly.

'You must be the McCall boys. I knew your grandfather, Don. Used to meet at the farmers' meetings in the Rift Valley Club.'

Tom and his brothers were puzzled.

The old man chuckled. 'You don't know me, do you? Well, that's no surprise. I've never visited before. I meant to and I should have, looking for you to vote for me. I've been the MP for Nakuru South since long before any of you were born.'

'Simon Nyache. Blow me! I knew I'd seen you before. Last election. You were making a speech in town, from the steps of the bank. I remember you were standing on a little box.'

'Old Charlie. I take him everywhere. My wife persuaded me long ago. She's a big woman. She said it would make me look more important. It got to be a habit.'

The brothers hesitated before Rollo began the question.

'Mr Nyache ...'

'Simon, please, and you want to know what I'm doing here.'

'Yes, but you're very welcome.'

Eddie went on. 'As you can see, even in this light, we've got a problem with inviting guests inside.'

'There's no inside.'

'Eddie's right, but if you look out to the edge of the plain,' Tom pointed, 'you'll see the stone and wood Jim Sawyer had delivered today. He's building for us.'

'My neighbour. Built our house. Best builder in this part of the Rift.'

The next brief hesitation was ended by Simon.

'I understand, Tom, that you're standing for Serena in the election, whenever that happens. I've come to tell you I'm going to be supporting you.'

'But you're a KANU man.'

'Yes, all my life. I'll serve out my time, try to be loyal, but after that ...'

'Have you got a few minutes? I think a few more people need to hear this.'

'Sure. Like Mister Dracula, as long as I'm home by sunrise tomorrow.'

All told there were sixteen people in the sitting room of the guesthouse at Rusinga. By the time Maria, Inspector Caroline and Sergeant Ezra, the last arrivals, had taken their coffee cups and sat down, Tom had discovered that Simon was no stranger to anyone in the room except the youngest. But even to Caroline who had met him many times it was a surprise to see him out here in the territory of the flower farmers. Surprise turned to mild shock when Simon repeated the news he had given to the McCall boys just half an hour before.

'I am sure you have all noticed that I do not come at the sensible, polite time of day for calling on comparative strangers. And I come unannounced. And why do I do this? Friends, and I hope I do not give offence by using that word, I confess that I have a strongly developed sense of self-preservation. Not fear, notice. I think I am too old for that but not an old fool either.'

'KANU people would not be too pleased to see you sitting down talking to the enemy like this.'

'Mister Briggs?'

Bertie nodded.

'Forty-five of my young constituents murdered as they worked in the fields of this farm. This farmhouse itself blown up ten days later. Another of my constituents arrested and put in jail for attempted murder. There is a dark force at work in our party and a single individual wielding too much power, the power of life and death. A young doctor, a creative force working for our poorest people, murdered as he travelled to his home village in Western District and the culprits melt into the night.'

Maria interrupted. 'Mr Nyache, what you say is true, but it is your party that wields the power in this country. And yet I know that there are many good men and women in KANU. Where were the protests from them? Why the silence?'

Simon fixed his eyes on Maria, but it was several seconds before he could give her an answer.

'Yes, self-preservation. It is the other man who is hurting. It is too costly to speak up. I am guilty. What does our reverend minister call these things? "Sins of omission". Men of the church are clever with words. "Passing by on the other side". That doesn't sound too bad. Hiding violence and bloodshed under a civilised cover. I'm sick of it. So why have I come here? Have I gone too far, too fast? Perhaps you want to get rid of me, but you are too polite to tell me.'

Alex cut him off. 'Simon, welcome! And I have a feeling that my wife will think that your coming is a good omen.'

Maura followed up. 'Alex is right about that. It is wonderful to see you. Brave, but you are taking a big risk. You must know that. Unfriendly eyes everywhere.'

'Madam, what risk? It is nothing. I want risk. I embrace risk. Eighteen months ago, there was a headline in *The Nation*: 'New party on the scene'. Daniel Komar and Paul Miller – now they were taking a risk. Serena, our people called it the joke party, the new home for political misfits. That first day, I became a secret member. Tonight I become a free member. And I am proud to be sitting here next to my successor.'

'Now just hang on a minute. That is too far and too fast!'

'Perhaps. But, see. You trust me. You don't believe that I am some spy sent by the big boss. Thomas, the wananchi are longing for someone they can trust. I speak to people on the streets every day. Many of them tell me that they want you. Reasons? So many. They see that you have suffered like they have. Reuben Rubai? They'll take his daddy's kidogo, but they won't vote for a young puppet.

'Soon you will be married to the most popular woman in the country. They will vote for you to keep her here!

'And then there is the hospital. For fifteen years our bosses in Nairobi have promised that there would be funds for a new hospital. Big mouth Nyache stands up in front of the people and I share the great news. I am tired of being a fool. But now, when the passengers on the *Eldoret Express*, the kids pedalling by on their bikes, they see a big piece of land and men in machines working. They ask questions and when the answers come, they are excited and they have real hope.

'I too am excited. That is why the words are tumbling out of my mouth like water down the falls of Niagara!'

His small audience was spellbound. In her time in the police force Caroline had served in small towns and in the capital and had listened to and usually been bored by speeches from hundreds of politicians. What she had just heard was completely new for its openness, for a kind of innocent vulnerability in Simon's manner. The old man was risking his life. He must know this and yet there was no hint of fear.

And there was something else. As she listened, her mind was unconsciously drawing together little signs she had gathered from a variety of sources, sometimes not much more than a sentence, a look, an attitude. Together they suggested there were green shoots of change poking their heads above the soil of the homeland. She felt a lift in her spirits and a change was coming after all, just as Maria kept telling them.

Maria Kabari, sister of Paul Miller, wife of Sergeant Ezra, was a woman of many gifts. One of these was what seemed to others to be a clear foresight of the way things would be, a gift born out of spiritual strength and ancient knowledge. She had come into the lives of the people in that room when to their amazement she had, with her husband, accompanied the body of the murdered Doctor Simon Mboya from Kericho to Cartref, the home of the Daniels family of the Nairobi suburb of Karen. Her work there had won over a sceptical group. Out of the eight members of that family five were doctors, one of them Simon's wife, Sonya.

In the little private surgery close to the house, first Sonya and one by one the others in the family witnessed not a miracle but a demonstration of an extraordinary medical healing. With her oils and ointments she did not try to imitate the ways taught in the great modern schools of medicine. She followed a tradition of ancient skills. David Daniels had tried to restore Simon's hands, sadistically mutilated by his killers, but failed miserably. Maria, with painstaking effort had seemingly brought those fingers, so skilful in life, to look as they had looked when Simon was at his working best. As she worked she sang melodies and words that might have been sung by those women who worked on the body of Jesus himself after he had been laid in his tomb.

Sonya had trusted from the beginning. David was won over from doubt to awe. This beautiful woman with the penetrating dark eyes was the most amazing person he had ever met.

So it was a smiling Maria who had listened to the testimony of the old politician.

'Simon, we salute you for your courage and for the reassurance you bring us. Recently among us there has been talk of omens, tiny glimpses into the future. Suddenly there is a shaft of light shining in the dark clouds. Risk. Risk is surely no less than life lived to the full, not recklessly but with hope.'

'I know you. Two years ago, you remember?'

'Yes, everything.'

'I brought my neighbours to a church meeting in Kericho. A healer from … Nairobi?'

'America. Benjamin Johnstone.'

'Phyllis and Seth. Their boy, Eb, very sick in his mind but strong in his body. The gentle child had become a violent young man. At home, sometimes and without warning he would harm himself with sharp stones, pieces of wood.'

For a second time Simon held his companions in thrall.

'Eb Joseph. I remember that young man.' Caroline was animated by an unpleasant memory. 'I was coming to the end of my time in Gilgil. There is a … place, they call it a hospital. It is close to the police station. One afternoon a car pulled up in the yard. Seth Joseph got out and asked me for directions to the home.

'I have a boy. He needs special help.'

'That was a very bad day.'

'Caroline, they came home heartbroken, like they did from the church in Kericho. The Reverend Johnstone tried really hard with his praying and the laying on of hands. Maria, you sat with him and held his hands and you sang. Phyllis told me on the way home that the hour with you was the happiest time of her life. Now Eb spends most of his day strapped into a chair. I am sorry. I am bringing you more pain. I have to go.'

Bertie was anxious. 'Back to Nakuru? Don't you think …?'

'I am often on the road at night. Never had any trouble. Perhaps I have been lucky. Festus, my driver, likes it better when only the night coaches are about. And the truck boys have pulled in to rest up. But when I am in Naivasha, late, I stay with Peter and Lilian Lawrence, great people, and two more votes for you, Tom.'

* * *

Next morning, Inspector Caroline stepped out of her Volvo. She had parked in the yard of Gilgil police station where she had some routine business in the office. Her passengers waited in the car until her work was finished. She had brought Rebecca, Lydia and Tom to see the 'home' or whatever it was called officially. Rebecca had not been able to get the young man, Eb, Simon's neighbour, out of her mind. She had to find out what went on in that place.

'Caroline, what is it really like? You must have seen it a hundred times.'

'Many hundred but, well, it is not an easy thing to tell you what it is like. Being there, spending time with the people, it makes some "visitors" want to run away. Some become very angry. I have known a few who find tranquillity there. If you want my opinion … No, I will take you there in the morning.'

The part of the A104 between Naivasha and Gilgil had recently been resurfaced. The endless potholes, enemies of the strongest suspensions and the toughest tyres, had been replaced by a carpet smooth bitumen. European Union money had covered the cost and payment had been made directly to the contractors, much to the annoyance of the bosses in the local public works department. No chance of any kidogo there!

'Tell your mother, Tom. Another good omen!'

'Caroline, it seems crazy, but this neat bit of black stuff transforms the whole place. Look at that chunk of green hill out there above Gilgil. Pembroke kids called it the Lion's Head. For the first time I can see what they mean. Even these scrubby bits of plain look like a proper piece of Africa.'

Rebecca was too preoccupied to pay attention to the chatter. Her mind was full of thoughts about sick people and hospitals. She was apprehensive, more so the closer they came to the heart of the busy, untidy, colourful township. Now, as she stepped down from the car, she took notice of a hedge. Through a gap she could see the edge of a patch of thick, rough grass. Caroline pointed the way through the gap.

'Through there. It's a warm morning. We'll see a lot of people out sunning themselves today.'

She was right, but it took a few moments to realise just how many residents there were scattered across the large stretch of open ground. There were two reasons. Almost everyone out there was sitting or lying on the firm, comfortable surface. And they were all dressed in dark green, short-sleeved Roman style tunics that blended into the background. The only sounds were the noise of the town traffic in the near distance and the low whisper of a light breeze through the branches of the few trees that would offer some shade in the heat of the day.

At first there were no human sounds, no conversations, no calling out.

Caroline set off through the middle of the field. 'We'll walk through slowly as far as the town clinic over there and come back a slightly different way. See what happens.'

They saw no women and the men were of all ages and sizes. Many seemed not to notice their visitors passing, lost in their own worlds with some enjoying conversations with themselves. A few fixed a narrow gaze on these strangers and kept a close eye as they passed by.

Caroline had crossed this way many times and she felt the old sadness rising in her. So many men lost to the world and destined to spend their time, perhaps their whole lives, watching and waiting.

Lydia and Tom were struck by the sense of peace that the men seemed to share. Tom whispered mainly to himself, 'Such a different world. No worries, no cares. Perhaps.'

Lydia felt no fear but wanted to be away from the place. She considered returning to the car but was afraid to walk back alone.

Rebecca was bewildered. For several weeks her mind had been full of thoughts of hospitals and her hopes and ideas for the new build in Naivasha. Unwittingly, Simon Nyache with his talk of this place in Gilgil had opened up her mind in uncomfortable ways. She had spent a disturbed night and on the journey that morning felt more and more tense about what she would find.

And now she was in the heart of it. Less than twenty-four hours before she had never dreamed that it even existed. If it was a hospital, where were the nurses, the carers? Was there some building where the serious cases were looked after? 'Looked after?' The idea did not fit well with what she could see all around her. But by what right could she pass judgement? How had all these men found their way to this … this gathering place for those with troubled minds? There, she was judging again, forming conclusions. Was she so naïve, so wrong-headed? Sentimental, even arrogant. She had money, so she would oversee 'her'creation. Money, compassion, hope but next to no knowledge and now a big dollop of confusion.

Doubts poured in on her, some so quickly that she could not register them in her conscious mind. The strongest of these hit her hard. Should she turn her thoughts to helping these men first? The need was immediate and crying out at her. A moment's rational thought had her reeling again. Suddenly her newly acquired wealth seemed to be more of curse than a blessing. Rebecca, you fool, who do you think you are? I must go.

'I'm so sorry, so sorry. I …'

'I know you.'

She gasped with surprise and turned sharply to her right. It must be one of those three men stretched out at ease on the grass not five metres away.

She had been lingering behind the others who, by now, had reached the far hedge and were turning to cross back to the police station. Caroline was hurrying ahead to catch up with her when the voice spoke again.

'I have heard you sing. When I go home today, you can come to my house and sing to me.'

It was the oldest of the three, a handsome man with a mop of grizzled hair. He showed no emotion except for the excited brightness in his dark eyes. In her overwrought state she was not sure whether to take this look as a sign of happiness or madness. By now Caroline was with her.

'Rebecca, what's wrong? What's upset you?'

'One of them just spoke to me.'

Before she could say more the same man spoke again.

'Caroline, why did you leave us?'

'That's the one.'

'I could have guessed. That's Michael. He's from Naivasha. I know his family.'

'But why would they let him stay in a place like this?'

Caroline hesitated and looked across at Michael before replying. She kept her voice low.

'Rebecca, Michael was born to an ordinary family. He was a kind of wonder child, a freak some said. As a young man he went to, believe it or not, Oxford University. Came home to be a professor down in Nairobi. Philosophy or something. Very bright. Too bright, perhaps. One day, in a lecture he ... lost it. Started raving at one of the students, said that a woman was laughing at him. Three, four more times something similar happened. Michael had to leave. He came home. Didn't work out. Once or twice his sisters said that he was violent towards their children. Three years ago he ended up here. Big families, small shambas, it happens a lot. Rebecca, he's a lovely person. They mostly all are.'

Just as Tom and Lydia were joining them, Michael spoke

again. This time he sat up, his face wreathed in smiles and pointing his finger towards Caroline.

'Telling my secrets again, Inspector. I don't mind you doing it to this lady. Perhaps she will sing a song. I read the papers. She sings in America.'

Rebecca shook her head. 'My head is all over the place. I really …'

'Don't worry. It won't bother them. Michael's probably the only one who knows about you.'

Rebecca climbed nimbly to a raised patch of bare earth. She spread her arms out wide.

And she sang. 'The monkey's wedding' was one of Toni's rare light-hearted pieces that involved a lot of hand clapping and body swaying. As usual, she put all her energy into her performance and felt the adrenalin surge that both calmed and energised her whenever she stood in front of an audience. Caroline, Lydia and Tom mimicked Rebecca's gestures, but otherwise, for a time, she seemed to be putting on a show for just Michael. He was up on his feet and moving rhythmically, totally locked into her every word and movement.

As the song rocked along, heads began to turn further out on the field. Tom moved off to encourage patients, residents or whatever to move in closer. Some seemed to be unmoved, even unaware of what was happening in their safe and normally tranquil home. But most were more positive. They stood up and peered over to where the new noise was coming from. When a fat young man made the first move and trotted in across the thick grass with short, pattering footsteps, green tunics were coming in from all sides.

'This is something new! I've crossed this field hundreds of times, but look at this!'

Part of her was thrilled to see this animation, this life

bursting out on a recreation ground where inertia was normally king. There was a risk that these men were about to have some fun and enjoy themselves for the first time in years.

But Caroline, the professional guardian of law and order, saw danger, too. Rebecca was stirring the emotions of potentially volatile, in many ways, childish men. The excitement must not be allowed to boil over. When she looked up at Rebecca, she saw from her expression that she, too, was aware. What Caroline could not see was that Rebecca had been in front of large audiences and understood a lot about the dynamics of group emotions.

Gradually she reduced the pace of the song and calmed her movements. Without a break she moved into a wordless lullaby. Instantly the clapping and the swaying ceased. The rise and fall of the beautiful voice and its power held them firmly in her emotional grasp. A hundred men, most of them bewildered by what was happening in front of them and inside them, stood silent and motionless.

Caroline touched Tom on the shoulder and, without a word, started on her way towards the police station. Lydia followed while Tom held out his hand towards Rebecca as she stepped unhurried from the mound. There was no break in the lullaby, but she raised and let fall her arms gracefully like some fish eagle coming in to land on the surface of a calm lake. Distracted by the movement, her audience hesitated and, in the brief interval, the four friends were united.

Caroline, well aware that the harmony of the moment could easily be shattered by some hasty action, slipped back to walk with Rebecca. Someone watching from a distance would have been puzzled but held by the scene opening in front of him. At the head of the procession four people dressed in blue jeans and an assortment of other colours were leading a large platoon in dark green uniforms. The leaders were moving in unison, following the rhythmic rise and fall of a soothing melody sung by one of the three women in the group. Some of those behind were imitating the example of the gliding movement, but as the slow march continued towards the hedge that marked the boundary of the field, there was a gradual falling away of the followers as each felt he was straying too far from his territory, the area where he was used to spending his long days out in the field.

The Volvo was visible through the gap in the hedge. They were left with a single follower.

'Michael, I saw you singing. You knew all the words.'

'I'm feeling very good, just like in the old days. I know this because I am remembering things. Today I would be no trouble at home. I would like to see the lake again. Someone told me that if I climb that hill, in the distance the lake will be there. Perhaps tomorrow …'

'Michael, I wish we could take you.'

'Yes, but this is a peaceful place and I have friends here.'

He smiled sadly and held out his hand. She took it and felt his firm grasp tightening briefly.

'Kwaheri, beautiful Rebecca.'

'Kwaheri, Michael. Thank you for being a good audience.'

* * *

It was quiet in the car on the bumpy road out of Gilgil town. The contractors had not been in to fix this loop off the A104. Tom knew every speed bump and most of the potholes from travelling this way to school in Pembroke. When they had passed the tollgate and were cruising down between the groves of yellow fever trees, Rebecca broke the silence. It was obvious to her companions that she had been shaken by their visit, but her reaction was not what they had expected.

'Wow! Now that was no easy way to learn a good lesson!'

'So it wasn't a mistake for me to take you.' The smile returned to the face of a relieved Caroline.

'My stomach still feels like liquid jelly, but I can't feel my heartbeat any more. My, my, I was one very confused person there for a while.'

"Becs, are you all right?'

'Yes, Tom. And thank you for being anxious about me.' She sighed before going on. 'This may sound crazy, but seeing all those men made me feel like a, what's that word you like, Tom, a prat, stupid, arrogant, naïve, all in one lump. What kind of fool would think that she could go on some kind of crusade to save the women of Naivasha? Tom, when you become the MP for Nakuru South, those men will be your responsibility.'

'Oh, gawd!'

'Donkey, don't look so scared. You can make those big shots down in Nairobi take notice of the little people.'

'Salina Amin, I've told you about her. She owns hotels in Kisuma. She's in Serena, another female dynamo.'

Lydia was puzzled by what Rebecca was saying.

'Do you mean that there will be no hospital in Naivasha?'

'Lydia, yesterday I was sure. Today, I just hope.'

# Chapter Twenty-two

Obi pulled into the lookout point at the highest part of the Escarpment for the boss to take a call. It was his secretary ringing from home.

'Joan, an hour ago?'

'I waited to make sure they arrived at the hospital before I let you know.'

'The doctor and the nurse travelled in with her. Everything was fine.'

'But a week early. Okay, we'll go straight there.' Turning to Reuben he continued. 'You've worked that out? Your brother's on the way. Obi, straight to the hospital.'

'Congratulations, Boss. Nothing like a new baby to make a man feel young.'

'So, Obi, my friend, you think the bwana is a mzee already!'

Looking in the mirror, Obi was relieved to see a smile on the boss's face.

'Oh, no, Boss. It's just that my seventh ...'

'Made your point. Seven eh, Obi. You need a raise. I won't forget. But, for now, I want the inside of this car to be as quiet as an empty room in the middle of the night. Time for a little silent prayer.'

Reuben looked across at his father with a quick double take. Prayer? This was a first. All the same, he was glad to hear the call for silence. Pa was into one of his unpredictable moods, angry one minute, friendly the next. Reuben pushed himself into the corner of his side of the seat and closed his eyes. He considered making a mumbling movement with his lips, make out he was praying, just like his daddy.

But prayer was the furthest thing from Abel's mind. He liked to be driven at just above a sedate speed, way below the capacity of the powerful German engine.

'Slow it down, Obi. Try being a racing driver with me and you'll soon be behind the wheel of a taxi downtown.'

Abel wanted time to take in the passing scenery and the sight of his countrymen going about their daily business. It was never dead time. He did some of his clearest thinking in these interludes of peace. Unfortunately for Mister R, joyful thoughts were not uppermost in his mind at this special time. Yes, it would be good to set eyes on the new Julius. He hoped he would come out of the womb heavy, with strong bones. But Abel counted himself as an expert in the processes of thought. He fully understood that the mind too often had its own agenda. On this occasion he could not shake off events of earlier that morning. The anger that had grabbed him hard when he was sent on his way twice by those jumped up farm people had loosened its grip but not released him. The stone that plopped into the centre of the pool sent its unpleasant eddies out to trouble him. It severely tarnished the image he had built about himself and his career, the village boy who made it big through natural talent and hard work, the Kenyan version of the American dream.

The line of successes was unbroken for so many years stretching back to his schooldays. He had been a good servant to his president and his country. He had cut profitable deals, charmed foreign envoys, never touched a shilling of the wananchi's money. Alongside this, he had married his childhood sweetheart, raised a family and made himself the richest man in the country by simply understanding the ways of money and having the nerve to back his own judgement.

For the last ten years it had been accepted that it was not the president but Abel Rubai who was the strong man of Kenya, the shadowy figure who had no official position but made the big decisions. It was well understood that it was unwise for his countrymen to oppose his wishes. He was ruthless and had the boys to deal with the fools who tried.

The list of achievements was long and as a special bonus he had preserved good order and stability in the country.

Then along came … Londiani. Looking out as they joined the dual carriageway that would bring them down to the city centre and the hospital, he winced and saw the reflection in his window of a face twisted by anger and regret. That insignificant flower farm that he could have bought out a thousand times over had bred the scum that turned his life upside down. The eldest McCall kid whom Julius had called piggy face should have been dead long before he engineered the death of his own boy out on that accursed golf course. His own hesitation, his weakness at a crucial moment had helped to send his world crashing down.

His hate was as strong as ever, but even since that morning he had felt an involuntary shift in its focus. At last, he understood. It was the woman, the wash girl. It had taken a long time for him to see the truth of it, but her defiance when he had caught her fooling about on that rough land, talking rubbish about building a hospital confirmed it. She had had her revenge and her careless tongue was giving her away.

He recalled the afternoon almost a year before. He was visiting that place with Julius and Sally. He and McCall were going through the usual banter about selling the farm. He had just laughingly trotted out the street vendor's cliché, 'I give you good price,' when he was astounded by the sight of his son naked and unconscious in the arms of the witch's father who, minutes before, had beaten the boy senseless.

Whether the talk about rape had any substance or not, he understood how that hour in that place set in train the tragedy in the lives of his family. From that moment Julius became her target. She would bring him down. She sang her way into the hearts of the people. She played the innocent, simple country girl part to perfection. Perhaps she had used piggy face and her 'love' for him as a front.

He looked up through the trees that lined the road into town and saw the peaceful blue of a beautiful African morning. Surely he had earned the right to a share of the wonderful gift of peace of mind. But he had been a blind fool, a blind fool! He also saw the danger of being swept along by the storm of anger. It would be so easy to be careless and overreach himself. He must not lose control.

When the hospital came into view, he experienced another mind shift. An involuntary smile formed on his lips when he thought of the ironic link between the death of one Julius and the imminent birth of the new child. As he stood in the lift taking him up to be with Sally, excitement got on top of his hate. When he peered through the porthole window of her room, he saw his wife sitting up with the child lying on her breast.

'Papa, let me introduce you to the new man in the house!'

'Sally, what's happening here? You have just given birth but …'

'But I am sitting up like the queen of the world? Well, let me tell you, no queen has ever had such a beautiful jewel to show to the world.'

'He is a big boy for his age!'

'And something else. It was so easy. He gave me not a moment of pain. I hardly knew that he was coming. And …' The smile was replaced by a serious, solemn expression. 'We share everything, Abel, but don't think me crazy. When the nurse took him to give the smack …'

'Is something wrong, Sally?'

'No, but when the little cry came, I swear to God that little fellow looked into my eyes … and smiled.'

'You sure he didn't give you a wink as well?'

'Abel, my heart is beating so fast. It was like he knew me.'

Abel broke down in tears. Even if they had not been alone in the room with their new son, he would not have been able to hold back the surge of the conflict of emotion.

'Sally, I am so sorry. It's just that Julius, big Julius …'

'No need for sorry, Abel. Perhaps there is a cleansing here. The child is starting his work.'

'Work?'

'Don't forget where he has come from.'

Abel was baffled. His eyes narrowed. 'You mean …'

'Of course, all children come from God's presence.'

'Oh, yes. I forgot.'

'Time for the old poison to be drained away.'

Abel let the sobbing pass off. He sat silently with his head lowered and his eyes closed. He was taking the chance not to have to speak. 'We share everything.' Did Sally really believe that? Perhaps she was stronger than him and could shut off thoughts that were uncomfortable and inconvenient to the point where they did not exist. He looked up to find her smiling down on him with pity in her eyes. He shuddered.

'Abel, the people expect too much of you. The burden is too much. Jesus is willing to share that burden.'

Abel groaned inwardly. He was fighting hard to find even the tiniest spark of real hope and Sally comes up with the old mantra which she had pounded him with so many times. But Abel, the master of deception, managed to dig out a smile, even a throaty chuckle.

He leaned back, languid and content. 'Perhaps it is time. Tell you what. First time you go down to church, I'll come, drive you myself. Just now when I looked up, you seemed to be pitying your old man. Ah, much better. Those eyes are sparking again. No prettier sight in the world. Sal, do you think I could hold him for a second?'

'God has blessed us. Here's our son. Take him.'

Abel stood and took the boy, lifting him tenderly and letting him lean into his chest and shoulder.

'Now, young man, you take a good sniff of your daddy. My, my, Sally, this is one big child you've brought us.'

Abel closed his eyes again but this time not to hide away. The solid, warm flesh and the clean, new smell were intoxicating, thrilling.

'Sally, how many times have I heard you say that we must live for the moment? What a moment! When are you coming home? But, hey, I'm forgetting. Reuben is sitting out there some place. I'll get him.'

He pushed the door open and, without checking to see if his son was in hearing distance, shouted along the corridor.

'Reuben, get yourself down here! Your brother wants to say hello!'

Before he let the door close, Abel spent a few seconds checking out the surroundings. 'Mmn, clean, lots of activity, smart looking staff, quiet. Nothing much wrong with our hospitals. This country doesn't need any help from singing witches.'

Reuben was enjoying a pleasant conversation at the desk of the maternity block when he heard his name called out somewhere in the distance. The order signalled the end of his freedom for the day. He knew where his mother was holed up, but he insisted that his new companion show him the way. He wasn't quite done with showing off and besides, having a pretty girl by his side would distract him from unwelcome thoughts.

Alone at the door, he stood back and looked in. He psyched himself up for the ordeal that was awaiting him inside. He was not excited about the prospect of the new Julius making his entrance into the world. This unexpected latecomer would be fussed and pampered from morning till night. His first tooth, his first step, his first word would be for family and friends to drool over. He pushed open the door, determined to be a successful hypocrite.

'Con-grat-ulations, Mama and Papa! I thought you were never going to invite me in.'

Sally saw through him straight away.

'Aw hush up, Reuben. I remember you when your brothers and sister came along. Couldn't get you to hold any of them for a kiss and I do believe that you disappeared into your room for days.'

'I'm older now. I understand these things a whole lot better.'

'You know, Sally, I think the boy may be telling it like it is. He's been a model of common sense these last couple of days. Said the right things at the funeral and, this morning, when there were a few problems, he was right there behind me. If he carries on like this, he's going to be a top rate MP.'

Sally seized on the word that troubled her.

'Abel, what do you mean "problems"?'

'I picked the wrong word, Sal. All the excitement …'

'Won't wash, husband. You called in to Naivasha on the way home.'

'Mama, how did you work that out?'

Abel cut him off.

'Now, son, that is not a smart piece of that common sense I was just talking about. And yes, Sally, we did call in. But problem? No. Some people over there think that they can take over from the government …'

'You mean the Kamau girl and the idea of a hospital.'

'Sally, what are they feeding you in here?'

'So far nothing. Haven't been in here for that long. But, Abel, long enough to think some more about that girl. I've had two Juliuses on my mind. Remember what I said about poison? Not so easy to get rid of, is it?'

'Sal, this a day for celebration, not gloomy thoughts.'

'Just had a crazy thought. Do you think that our little one can take any of this in? Anyway, some day …'

'He's going to understand that she has been bad news from the start. Some day she will pay the price. Ever heard of the word "karma"?'

'Oh, yes. "You reap what you sow."'

'Jesus talk?'

'Jesus talk. But this karma doesn't always turn out the way you might have expected. But, gentlemen, this child and I have shared the most wonderful experience. Now we are emotionally drained. And, even more important, Mama must give Julius his afternoon tea. And, Abel, tomorrow, I'm having a check-up. I hope to be home for coffee at eleven. Perhaps we could talk a bit more about hospitals. If we made a contribution to Rebecca's project, that would make it semi-official and …'

'Sally, you've got that naughty schoolgirl look on your face. Yes, tomorrow. I think I need to explain a few things to you.'

* * *

Now there were just over four weeks to the wedding. By that time every last vestige of fire damage would have disappeared from the farm and from the ruin of Big House. Already the tents were going up on the flower fields and the first stage of planting around the new, infant garden was almost complete.

But as for the house, it would be impossible to have even the ground floor finished by then. It would be a very tidy building site. Jim Sawyer would see to that. The unexpected arrival of four young men changed the time scale considerably.

* * *

Two beautiful women were moving from plant to plant around the garden, 'bowling up', as Rafaella had described the work.

'When we feed our little children we make sure that none of our precious water is wasted.'

Rebecca loved a dirty hands job, sweeping the fertile soil up into little craters. When she knelt she always made sure that she was facing in the direction of the lake. Every time she sat back on her haunches and looked out across the plain, there it was on the raised piece of meadow, her own house, 'Long House' as everyone had begun to call it. Having Maria for company gave the work an added delight. They had shared so much in such a short time.

Rebecca had just finished a bowl around another young plant. She leaned back, shaking her head gently but smiling.

'That first time when you called my name. I felt so …

irritated. You were inside the Daniels' little surgery with Simon. Really, I think I was plain scared. I still can't work out how you knew I was there.'

Maria laughed. 'And I cannot give you a sensible explanation. Suddenly, a thought comes into my head and, well, I have learned to trust them. Tell you the truth, I was the one who was in awe. There I was in the presence of the beautiful singer, the most famous woman in the country.

Rebecca moved on to her next plant, focused hard on it so that her face was hidden from Maria.

'You changed my life, a lot of lives around here. Without you, Papa, we would have lost him. "Blood Sisters". If men can be blood brothers.'

'Wonderful. I've never had a younger sister before. Two of the most talkative brothers in creation and you can't always share with a brother.'

'Martha and Jane are a bit young for sharing.'

'Especially ugly, painful thoughts, maybe about a certain Nairobi man who was here yesterday. Lydia told me. You know how much she looks up to you. She said she was so proud of you. Sent him on his way like he was some naughty schoolboy.'

'Was it wise though?'

'Were you speaking the plain truth, Rebecca?'

'My truth.'

'The more he hears the truth, the more it will eat into that shell he has built around himself. The tiny worm will eventually destroy the whole apple. We all know that he is a rotten apple to start with.'

'But the people love him. When he makes speeches …'

'They simply fear him.'

'There was so much hate in his eyes. I even felt some pity

for Reuben. He looked frightened standing behind his father, embarrassed, too. "You don't meddle in government business. There will be no new hospital built on this scrubby bit of bush". I think he's a little bit crazy.'

'Not so much of the little bit! Doctors have a name for his condition. I have two words, "murderer" and "coward". Just remember Simon Mboya and the forty-five young people burned to death on the flower fields of this farm. Burned to death, Rebecca. Sonya and the boys are coming up this afternoon. And there is another word, from a wise man's teaching. I don't suppose he ever thinks about it. "Karma".'

'She's bringing material for the boys' suits. The page boys. I should be excited about the wedding.'

'Sister, be excited. I'm excited. The whole country is excited. Got an idea. We need a coffee break. How about if we go for a walk over to that house on that little hill and take in the views?'

* * *

'Noah won't even come over. Seems that he's a bit old for being a pageboy. Says he'll do it if he can wear his football kit! He's got it on now, teaching Ewan how to kick the ball like a proper player. He's got this idea that since we lost Simon, he's the man in the family. He wants to look after us all. He can be so serious sometimes. I want him to be a nine year old.'

'Sonya, it's so touching. I can feel my throat tightening up.'

'So you don't mind, Rebecca?'

'Tom says we are short of someone to show people to their seats up in Pembroke. Perhaps he'll be willing to do that. Bertie will help him. There are so many strange rules in these English weddings. Tom says it's all right. The "real" wedding is down here at the farm. It's a mystery. I'm glad I was born in Africa.'

'But so was Tom, Rebecca.'

'I know that, Maria. I'm getting confused. Perhaps it's wedding nerves.'

'You're reminding me.' Sonya bit her lip hard and closed her eyes before she went on.

'About a hundred years ago, when I got the news that Simon had been taken, I had just been to a wedding, in Kidwelly, a small town near Carmarthen. The boys loved the place because it had a castle. A Welsh wedding can't be so different from an English one, except that this one was in Welsh. I'm pretty good on what goes on. Any questions, ask Noah and me.'

The long and solemn silence that followed was set against the sound of building noises coming from somewhere behind the veranda where the three friends were sitting at a small table while Moses and Sammy were finishing their Coke and cake on the steps, waiting for the call to be measured up.

Half an hour later, at four-thirty, there was a general gathering at the official time for tea at Londiani. Jim Sawyer's men were making their noisy way to their transport while Jim himself joined the group on the veranda to make his daily report on progress on the site. Jim had a surprise when he took his place at a table with his tea and biscuits. Sitting opposite him was a familiar face but one he had not expected to see at Londiani. He shot to his feet.

'Sonya! I never expected ...'

Jim was a big man, in his fifties now. He was of old European stock. His grandfather, one of the early pioneers who had travelled down from the Aberdares, bought a fertile patch of land just north of Nakuru and never left. Jim had followed his father into the building trade. A Sawyer house meant top quality work. But at the end of a day on site, pulling his weight with his men, he looked as immaculate as when he stepped down from his pick-up eight hours before. His bronzed face revealed his disturbed emotion. His lips were moving but not bringing out any coherent words and his eyes flickered rapidly as though they were struggling to hold back tears.

Sonya understood and was moved. There were no tears in her eyes. A nod and a warm smile persuaded Jim to sit back down.

'Sonya, I feel ashamed, bringing it all back again for the nth time.'

'Don't be! Of course, it hurts, but that will never go away. Our Simon has left a big, big gap in so many lives. How many weeks is it since we saw you?'

'I remember you telling Ruth that you were going overseas to a wedding in a few weeks. Forgive me, but that was such a happy day for everyone in our church. Having Simon to speak to us. He was like bright light amongst us.'

'And he talked about bringing one of his clinics to the town. Jim, tell your people that there will be a clinic.'

'We still have the money in the bank.'

'We're smiling. The light hasn't gone out. It reaches a long way. Listen to this. When I was in Wales, I went back to the Methodist church that our grandparents helped to build. It is like the churches over here, full of people, and not just on Sunday. You see so many young men and women. Some came from Korea and China to brush up on their English and learn more about gospel teaching. But, when it comes to living a Christian life, they are further along the path than most of us.

'Simon had often visited when we were students in London. They loved him even back then, especially when he told them stories about Kenya. There's a Methodist church down on the coast and the congregation in Calfaria took it into their hearts to help their brothers and sisters in Malindi. Well, four young Welshmen are just finishing a project down there, three builders, and a doctor taking a year out. They've been working with the locals to put up a new hall. Coming to us tomorrow for a few days. David and Dot are looking forward to trying out their Welsh again.'

'Builders? What trades? Do you know?'

'I was told. Um, Ivor's a builder, a brickie man, Dai's a carpenter, Phil an electrician or a plumber. Iolo calls himself the medical dogsbody.'

'Wonderful!'

'Synchronicity! Modern for "God at work"! The money for the work the boys have done in Malindi was put up by a certain Nairobi lady, Sally Rubai. She wanted it kept a secret.'

'Amazing. I wish I could have a bit of synchronicity here, on this job. My boys are great. Never stop all day, but they could do with a bit more leadership, inspiration. They'd love … Sorry, the Sonya effect is carrying me away!'

'Jim …' She shook her head in wonder. 'I'll have a chat with them at Cartref, but I can offer you three tea-boys ready to start today, as long as you don't mind half empty mugs of tea.'

# Chapter Twenty-three

'Where did you get him from, Rafaella? What a beautiful voice, so soft and lilting. And there are three more?'

'So musical, Caroline, just like Italian! They're Welshmen. That one was Iolo. Going to be a doctor. He's the tallest.'

'A Welsh doctor working on a building site in Naivasha. Wow! And I only came over to check with Tom and Alex about security on the big day.'

'They're both down the fields. Most of the tents are up. Things are hectic around here. Come and have a look at how the new house is going and you can meet the other Welsh boys. Jim is so excited and everyone is getting on so well. Jim says it's the first site he's been on where the house is building itself. And they sing hymns, in Welsh! I didn't expect to hear so much laughter in Londiani again so soon.'

'But how did Jim get onto them?'

'No idea. Sonya will tell you. She's bringing the boys up for a final fitting this afternoon. Well, Moses and Sammy will be trying on their suits. Big brother Noah will be helping out with the builders. He's growing up fast and he wants us all to know. They're staying with Bertie.'

'What about the Welsh boys?'

'They're renting rooms in Gilgil Club. Such charmers. Someone down at the coast gave them a car. They have been early for work every day of the two weeks they have been coming here. Jim's boys love them. You've got to meet them, Caroline. They're staying on for tea today, for the first time.'

It was the noisiest teatime seen on the veranda at Londiani since the days when the McCall boys brought their pals back after one of their bike safaris around the lake or up to Hell's Gate.

'Yeah, Tom, Ivor the Brickie they call me. There's only four of us and three of us are Joneses and not one of us related.'

'Explains a lot. Inbreeding causes madness. Our science teacher passed on that little nugget.'

'Hark who's talking. David W Davies, Dai the Chippie, not to be confused with Dai the Chips.'

'Do you like it in this country?'

'Love it. How many weeks since we had any rain, Ivor?'

'Not a drop. Four weeks in Malindi and a couple of weeks up here. That would be a record back home.'

'I was a student in Reading. Went to Wales about four times a year. Only once it didn't rain. Out here rain is a good friend who can't visit too often.'

'Don't think we'd use that word. Not an enemy, more of a challenge, especially when it's sheeting for days on end off the Irish Sea. But it keeps the pavements clean.'

'And the Daniels family, great people, so many doctors. David saved Eddie, my brother's, life.

'Spent two days with them, and Sonya and the boys. Very relaxing. Iolo spent half his time in that surgery. Given him ideas for back home. We only went out once. That was to deliver a thank you letter for Pastor John and his people. That was our main reason for stopping in Nairobi.'

'Sorry, I took so long, gentlemen. Sonya's been cooking on the new stove. Something special, she says. I've never seen them before, but they look delicious.'

Rebecca removed the white cloth from the tray with a flourish.

'Dai, I've heard about those mirages you have in Africa, but they look real to me.'

'Ivor, now I know we've landed in heaven. Welsh cakes! Where's Sonya?'

'She's finishing off. Excuse me. I'll bring the tea. I was too scared to carry them together. Give me a minute. Let me put the cloth back, just in case the flies take a fancy.'

With his two companions silenced by Rebecca's surprise, an amused Tom resumed the conversation.

'So the pastor was pretty pleased?'

'Well, without her money, there would have been no hall built.'

'Right, Dai, but, Tom, when we said where we were going …'

'At the time we couldn't work it out. I mean the house was just 'round the corner.'

'But, Ivor, I don't think they realised we were actually going to call on them until Phil mentioned it at the lunch table, just casual like.'

'Better go, we think. Show a bit of respect. What are these Rubai neighbours like?'

There were serious faces for a while around the table, a bit of tension till Dorothy brought it 'round.

'They haven't been living there all that long. Sally seems nice. We've heard she's often in on her own, with the children, that is. You're right to go over there. She'll be thrilled. That was it. After lunch, everyone in the house had something important to do, so off we went.'

* * *

'What an amazing place. Disneyland comes to Nairobi. Couldn't make up our minds how they managed to get that pinky colour. Brainbox, alias beanpole Iolo, the only one with any A-levels, knew straight away. "Coral. We saw tons of it in Malindi. Must have cost a fortune". Plenty of jokes about that.

'Tom, you must have seen it. What do you think?'

'Oh, yes, Ivor, I've seen it. Never been inside.'

The pleasant exchange with this sparky pair of Welshmen was becoming uncomfortable. He was hoping that Rebecca would be delayed until he could move the conversation away from where it seemed to be heading, but the fiery Ivor seemed eager to share their experience.

'Quality everywhere you looked, the materials, the finish, the lot. And the pinky colour, washed into the concrete. Just like Roman concrete. Learned about that in night school.'

'And, Ivor, wasn't she thrilled with the thank you letter? She insisted we call her Sally. I gathered that the old man knew nothing about the money.'

'I wouldn't bet on that, Dai.'

'Do you know them, Tom?'

'You could say that our paths have crossed.'

'She was a lovely person. "Dripping with gold", my gran would say. Bubbly and very kind to us ruffians. It was the poshest house I've ever been in.'

'Yeah, by a mile! And for a while, we got on really well. But, Tom, you know how it is sometimes with strangers, especially as we were scared of saying the wrong thing Conversation dies the death.'

To keep things going, doctor educated Iolo had a bright idea. Brought up the subject of Simon Mboya. We all knew him. He'd been to our church. 'Sally, I suppose you heard a lot about it. Even a big spread about it in *The Carmarthen Times*.

You could see the anger rising in him. Poor Iolo still can't get over about what happened and out it came: "Sally, what kind of twisted mind can gun down or whatever the most compassionate doctor in the country?" I think he expected one of those, "Yes, how terrible" nothing replies. You know Iolo, innocent face and big blue eyes. You could see he was stung by the look she gave him.'

'Right, Dai, but it got worse, Tom.'

'Her husband arrived back early. Maybe she heard him coming and that's what upset her. Didn't want her secret to get out. He welcomed us and sat down. He's a very impressive chap.'

'Smart suit, built like a boxer. Scary, too. I think it's the eyes. Someone said the night before that he was a pretty big man in the country. Didn't pay much attention then, but sitting there on one of the family's gold chairs, different story. I was holding my breath.'

'From Wales, eh? I have visited. Cardiff, do you live near there? Tell me, where are you staying in Kenya?'

'Just 'round the corner. The Daniels family. We know Sonya, Ms Mboya. She's looking after us.'

'For a few moments he said nothing but he's even better than his wife with the drop-dead looks. We were getting the message hot and strong.'

'Five minutes later, we were back out on the road, chucked out but very politely!'

'Fair play, everyone back in Cartref was very apologetic. Then it all came out. Shocking story. Unbelievable!'

A very relieved Tom had no intention of elaborating on the saga of the sins of Mister Big. Rebecca's timing was perfect. The tea was refreshing and the Welsh cakes scrumptious.

# Chapter Twenty-four

On the day of his wedding Tom McCall enjoyed a special thrill even before he left the house. For the first time in many weeks he woke up in his own bedroom. The camp bed was comfortable enough, but like the rest of the house, his room was little more than a bare empty shell. That Londiani had reached this advanced stage was mainly because of the four foreign young men. They had worked with unsparing energy and a high level of skill. More than that, they had inspired everyone around them. They had broken the back of the build and every day they were on site, Jim had shaken his head in grateful disbelief.

Tom had been up early to stand at his window. The first light, slanting across the lake as the sun lifted above the unseen ridge of the Aberdares far away to his right was an old and much missed friend. He had slept badly, kept awake by a worry that had troubled more and more the closer he came to this day of days. How selfish was he being to have wanted and been granted two day of days. Standing there looking out across the plains towards the waters of the lake, it seemed plain ridiculous that he was dragging so many people up to Pembroke House school with all the inconveniences involved so that he could marry his Rebecca in the Christina chapel and then draw so many of the same people to Londiani to go through a similar process. He wasn't even sure which event marked the true marriage. His regret, his remorse was far too late. The day was underway in many practical ways, not least up in the school itself.

Up there those involved had a much less gloomy take on Tom's selfishness. The duty staff had no problems on getting the children out of bed as the six-thirty wake-up bell clanged in the chapel tower. The din of breakfast was noisier than ever and the chattering and rushing continued undiminished through bed making and chores. The three normal lessons before break passed at lightning speed with even the toughest of the teachers being ready to be drawn off subject by the most obvious red herrings.

'Miss, why do women have to wear a white dress when they get married?'

They even allowed the variety of answers to come from the class.

'Women don't have to do anything that men tell them. I'm getting married in my swimming costume and tackies.'

'Yeah, Melanie, just cos you're so stingy. And your husband will only be wearing a pair of underpants.'

'George Smith, why do you enjoy being disgusting so much?'

'Sorry, Miss. But you've got to admit, Miss, that it made everybody laugh, even Mel.'

At ten o'clock, the early break was over and the school was gathered on the Prefects' Lawn, listening to the headmaster setting out the plan for the day. As he was talking, a procession of four cars was leaving the A104 at the first Gilgil turn-off making their way into town and the climb up the Nyharuru Road to Pembroke. Bertie, with Ewan, Sonya and the boys on board, led the way as usual. And, as usual Bertie had a loaded pistol in the glove compartment. In the rear,

Eddie was driving Tom who had been long reassured that forcing a lot of friends to spend a day out in one of the most lovely parts of the valley was no selfish act.

'Tom, look. The zebras are out in force on both sides. Rollo and I always saw that as a good sign at the start of a new term.'

'Saw them but just here I always make sure I can pick out the Bata Bridge. Did your lot used to make a palaver as you went under on the way back from away matches?'

'Sure. We'll give it belt as we go under.'

In the second car Rollo's passengers were the bride, her mother and Rafaella, and, behind them, Alex drove the rest of the Kamau family. The outfits of the bride's party were waiting for them on hangers in the darkened bedroom of the girls' housemistress, Tammy Moss.

The four Welsh residents of Gilgil Club were well-known to everyone in the school. The children looked on them as extra gap years and enjoyed having them to take games on Saturday. But it was in the Sunday evening chapel services that these four Christian boys touched the zenith of their popularity. They had a lot of experience of passing on their message to unsympathetic audiences. They had good voices and led by the red-headed Jones, the Brickie, a natural comedian, they dazzled their eager audience with their all-action mixture of fun and teaching.

So they had volunteered to keep the hundred and sixty highly excited Pembroke people occupied and, if possible, reasonably calm. They relished the prospect, but after ten minutes lost the attention of their audience to a superior attraction.

Slowly, from the direction of the top car park they came, an assorted group of young and old, some known but most not. They were heading for the chapel, as everyone had been told would happen. Necks were craned and eyes were riveted on one person above all. It was not only the children who gasped when they caught sight of the tall, smiling woman in the lavender trouser suit.

'I always thought that there was a tradition the bride and groom met for the first time at the altar on the big day.'

'This is Africa, Pete, the land of free spirits.'

'Thank you, Marge. I'll remember when my time comes for the chop.'

'Chop? I don't think you'd find Tom McCall talking such rubbish today.'

The head girl and the head boy led the way into the stone chapel. The visitors took up the last two rows. Rafaella made sure of her place where she had the best view of the procession of the school coming for their morning service. They came, youngest first. Rafaella wished they would walk more slowly, but many of the smallest were shy and wanted the ordeal over quickly.

The headmaster took the service.

'Welcome students and guests to the Christina Chapel and to our ordinary, extraordinary service. Do you understand that, Thomas?'

He pointed to a very small boy just below him.

'Yes, sir. It means a bit weird.'

'Brilliant answer!' The sincere compliment shut up the few half-hearted guffaws coming out of the large choir who were waiting nervously to sing their anthem.

'And where do you come from, Tom?'

'Naivasha, sir.'

'So why did I ask you the question?'

Thomas Walker stood up, screwed himself 'round and pointed to the back of the chapel with his arm bent.

'My friend. We play football sometimes.'

Tom McCall stood up and acknowledged the polite ripple of applause and blew a kiss to his young neighbour.

The service moved on quickly. The head girl read the gospel story of the wedding at Cana. Six children popped up from various parts of the chapel to recite the prayers they had written to honour the occasion.

'And now a little touch of deja vu. Don't worry, Thomas, no questions this time. How many of you remember last year's Londiani Sevens tournament?'

A hundred hands shot up, ramrod straight.

'And the hymn we ...'

Even more hands just as quickly.

'Well, then, here we go again, but this time ...'

Rebecca was already on her way to the front of the chapel. The radiance of her smile, the poignancy of the moment and the vulnerability of the beautiful creature standing before them set off a rush of quiet tears all over the place, especially in the last two rows of the chapel.

Those arriving early for the wedding proper were greeted by an empty school and a full-throated sound of singing bursting through the open windows of the chapel and out across the valley.

The service ended, the children scattered and the bride and her party went off to get ready.

Rebecca and Tom were to be married outdoors. Rows of seats had been arranged in a large semicircle under the shade of the large branches of the pepper trees just across from the chapel. Facing the large gathering was a low platform and, in front, an altar with a dark wooden cross resting on a colouful tapestry decorated with scenes illustrating Jesus's baptism in the River Jordan.

The ceremony itself was low-key. Sisters May and Phillipa from Nakuru Cathedral assisted their priest, Father Robert, in a ritual he had composed that was Christian but not Catholic. Instead of readings or a sermon, he had invited Alex and Stephen to say a few words of thanksgiving and blessing.

The words both fathers had prepared were never heard that day. The handsome bulk of Stephen stepped forward. He clasped his hands together in front of his stomach, but before he could begin to speak, the calm assurance in his expression changed. He had seen something that upset his composure, something that most of the guests could not have noticed from their different sightline. Behind them, three dark blue cars had edged silently around the curve of the lawn and pulled up.

Doors banged and three policemen stepped out from each car. They covered their uncertainty with the measured swagger of their movement towards the front of their cars, as if they wanted to make sure that they looked good on camera. Caroline and Hosea Kabari, out of uniform for the day, moved quickly to check on the unexpected callers.

'Inspector Caroline Miggot and my colleague from the Naivasha, Sergeant Hosea Kabari.' (She smiled but did not introduce Maria who was giving the mostly young officers the full force of one her aggressive scowls.)

'We know you, Inspector.'

The spokesman, the oldest in the group, a hefty man with bulging neck and stomach sneered, confident and challenging, a bully who had never made it above sergeant for all his many arrests he had made of the street scum he had brought into the station, usually in a damaged condition. He had little respect for policewomen above the rank of constable. Caroline vaguely remembered him from her time down in Nairobi.

'Sergeant, do you realise that you are trespassing on private property? And there's a wedding. If you think you have business with anyone here, get back into your cars and wait outside.'

'Not so fast, madam!' The sergeant cleared his throat dramatically and then lapsed into police mode. 'We believe that you are harbouring four aliens somewhere on these premises. They do not have the proper permits to be in Kenya. The government wants them out. These people must be at the airport by six pm this evening, ready to board a night flight to London. Now you will understand why we cannot delay. Help us to do our job and we will leave you in peace.'

Before Caroline could reply, Maria moved from behind her husband's back.

'How long did it take you to learn that speech, Constable?'

'About thirty years madam and ...'

'Maria, leave this to Hosea and me. I take it, Sergeant, that you have written instructions giving you some kind of authority on this. May I see them, please?'

'No, Inspector, our boss has them. He'll be with us shortly. Mechanical problem with the vehicle. His driver has radioed through.'

'Then wait outside.' Irritation was beginning to show through in Caroline's voice.

But the sergeant was up for a contest of words and wills. He had ammunition to fire.

'Inspector, I have to point out that if you had done your job properly none of this shaurie would have happened.'

'What!' She had a problem. She wanted to get rid of this pompous man, but he was enjoying his stubborn resistance. Above all she did not want to let down Rebecca and Tom by allowing this ridiculous situation to continue.

'If you had bothered to check their passports, when they were working in your area. Their work at the coast, sponsored by Mrs Sally Rubai, was sanctioned but finished and …'

'Ah, now we're coming to it.' Caroline had recovered her composure. 'Just one moment.' She turned to Hosea. 'Ask one of the Welshmen …'

'They never travel anywhere without them. Mister Iolo …'

Iolo handed his passport to Caroline. She flicked through the mostly empty pages until she found what she wanted. Unusually, the visa was handwritten by someone who had mastered the art of calligraphy and was unequivocal in its statement. The signature of the Archbishop of Nairobi was endorsed with the stamp of the Department of Immigration.

'Now, Inspector, if you would be good enough to look at this document, which I first checked some five weeks ago, you will see that this man has permission to stay in this country "sine die" while engaged on legitimate, charitable work. His fellow "aliens" have similar entries. Read it carefully.'

The sergeant was not done.

'So, working for a local building contractor on a house owned by a flower farmer counts as charitable work? I don't think so!'

'Sergeant, and in what part of the universe have you been travelling in for these last few weeks. We have a family of our fellow countrymen who have their house – and farm – completely destroyed by criminals, whom we have yet to catch, who are helped in rebuilding their lives by four young men who receive not a shilling for their efforts, and this is not charitable work? I remind you. This is private property and you are trespassing.'

This kind of treatment was a new experience for these big city policemen. They were being bullied and they swapped puzzled glances hoping that one of them might find the inspiration to reverse the situation or at least find some way of making a dignified exit.

Maria Kabari was ready to send them on their way with a fiery farewell.

'What a bunch of jerks. Sergeant, you know this word "jerk"? American. My brother lives in America. He keeps sending me these new words. He is here today. Would you like to speak to him? He is a lawyer.'

'And I'm her other brother, a lawyer, too!'

'I recognise you, Mister Miller.' The sergeant's puff and bluster were gone. His men were climbing back into their cars. He was eager to join them.

'Sergeant, my sister is normally a gentle lady, but get her angry and well … But I have to say that she has expressed our sentiments with her usual sharp precision. Kwaheri!'

The interruption was over. The wedding guests applauded. The bully boys had been routed.

The two mechanics sent out from the motor pool in police headquarters to fix the immobile vehicle were astonished when they found the cause of the problem.

'Inspector, your driver knows less about how a car engine works than my Uncle Solomon and he's been dead two years. You've run out of gas!'

'But the red arrow is pointing to full! See!'

The inspector who did know a lot about cars felt some shame. He had doctored the gauge, a simple job. He had also made sure that the vital warrant had not left his pocket. A colleague had told him the first source of the order to send four cars up to the school in Gilgil. As a secret member of the Serena party he had taken a big risk by virtually sabotaging a piece of police business. He had thrown a few grains of sand into the well-oiled machine of Rubai Inc. It was time.

Back up in Gilgil, Father Robert, after a few words with Stephen and Alex, moved to the microphone. 'I can't speak for all of you but, for me, I thank God for a piece of very witty deliverance just now. Ivor, David, Phillip and Iolo, my Celtic brothers, I am so glad that you are not already on your way back to the beloved land of your fathers! And, to answer a question I have been asked several times today: of course, these two wonderful people are joined together as man and wife in the presence of God.

'Now, children, everyone, Maura and Angela tell me that it is time to celebrate in the good old up-country way.'

For a wedding feast, a surprising amount of business took place in the following hours before sunset and young and old went their ways, most of it around two large round tables set in a corner of the field. The music played and the people danced, but for once Rebecca, the new Mrs McCall, did not sing.

At the ladies' table a lot of the talk was about hospitals and the building of one special one. Debbie Miller had returned from Boston with her parents. She had brought detailed drawings of the plans and some pleasant surprises.

The men's business was more sensitive. A party out under the open sky was not the place to risk being overheard even by friendly ears. And there was also the important matter of drinking the health of the happy couple. Barnie Miller had his news from Boston and New York. It would wait for a more convenient time.

# Chapter Twenty-five

'Simon, how are you? Good to have you with us. I see Sally has taken Margaret off to see young Julius.'

'Yes, Abel, and congratulations on the new arrival. And the new house. You seem to be creating a park out there.'

'You haven't been here before? I think it's four years since we moved in.'

Simon was uneasy and on his guard. He had travelled down to Nairobi to pick up his personal belongings from Parliament House. When the next session began there would be someone else sitting in his place fighting the cause of Nakuru South. Forty years was probably too long to do the job properly all the time. He had sat with Margaret in the empty chamber, quietly remembering.

'Margaret, I should have gone ten, fifteen years ago. I suppose I got into the habit and enjoyed being a somebody, but what did I accomplish for our people?'

'Simon, you have been honest, hardworking and the people loved you. Think how many of them have asked you to stay on.'

'Better the devil you know.'

Now he was sitting alone in the presence of Mister Big for the very first time. Abel Rubai was being friendly and attentive, but Simon was waiting for him to come to the end of the small talk. He had an idea about why he had been summoned, but the essence of this man remained a mystery. How could a person who never stood for let alone won any public office dominate the happenings in the country like this? He was very clever with money. That must have been the key to his rise from financial adviser up the magic ladder to the very top rung.

'Simon, Nakuru South. How many years now?'

'Too many, Abel! We need some young blood up there.'

'My thoughts exactly. I've been giving a lot of time to how we move on in this very important constituency.'

Abel did not miss the sudden raising of the eyebrows and the expression of surprise.

'Of course, Simon. Think about it. You have the army camp. The road and rail links pass through. Then there is the wealth and employment generated by the farms around the lake. More than just important, vital.'

'Can't say that I've noticed much interest in the place from Nairobi in my time up there.'

'Because the government knew they had a man up there they could trust. You must have been aware of that.'

'Abel, let me be frank with you.'

'I would want nothing less. Fire away.'

'The hospital.'

Abel was the one caught off guard. He felt his gorge rising. Surely Simon Nyache was not supporting the crazy idea of the Naivasha tart! His mind was soon put at rest.

'There is a desperate need in Gilgil. We have abandoned five hundred or more of our people who have some sickness of the mind. Three, four million shillings would transform lives.'

'That's a disgrace! Why have I never heard about this? You must write a memo. Send it directly to me.'

Simon hated the hypocrisy. Memo. Treating me like a

bosom friend. Nauseous stuff. But there was something else to come.

'Next time I'm travelling up that way I must call in. Your successor will have to give it high priority.' A slight pause and Abel Rubai had reached his destination. 'While we are on the subject of the man to take over from you, I should like to ask your advice.'

Simon smiled. 'That's a first.'

'What do you think of the idea of my boy Reuben taking over from you?'

'I know nothing about him, not even how old he is. Is he keen?'

'Perhaps you would be ready to take him under your wing, introduce him to some people.'

'They would take a lot more notice if you took him around.'

'What if the two of us … just had an idea. Take him to see that terrible place in Gilgil.'

'Mister Rubai, I've been 'round the area saying my farewells.'

'So I hear. Someone was saying that you were seen visiting some of the farms on the lake.'

Alarm bells clanged in Simon's head. So this was what it was all leading up to. And how much more had this 'someone' told him? But wily old Simon had prepared an answer for just this situation. If it didn't work he would give him the real works about supporting the McCall boy and Serena. It was time to step out of the shadows.

'Yes, that's right. There's no secret. In all my years as MP I never once went to any of those farms looking for a vote. I had some spare time one afternoon so I called in to introduce myself. They all knew me …'

'All, Simon?'

'They were really friendly, thanked me but said nothing about where their vote would go this time.'

'Did you call in on the McCalls?'

'First stop. That family has suffered so much and their workers even more. All my people, and I could not offer them even the smallest bit of assistance.'

'European thieves. Got what was coming to them. But that's not our concern here. Let's organise a meeting for some time next week. I'll make the arrangements and let you know. You'll stay for tea?'

'That's kind, but I have to get Margaret home. She's promised our daughter that she will babysit tonight.'

* * *

'Simon, you are trembling.'

'Margaret, in a minute. Let me drive us out of this place before I talk.'

Simon turned right at the gatehouse and right again at the crossroads. He parked on a verge close to a pair of open wooden gates. He leaned back in his seat and closed his eyes.

'He knows everything. That night I went to Londiani. He has spies everywhere.'

'You mean that someone at the meeting …'

'No, no, no. I would never believe that. Someone on watch outside. Money buys him everything, or so he thinks'

The handsome old couple sat silently, calculating the fallout of the hour-long visit to the pink palace that Margaret had enjoyed. Ahead of them were a hundred metres of a wide verge, bordered on the house side by a well-built sandstone wall. The grass on the verge had had been cut short and broken up by beds of flowers in full bloom.

'You chose a beautiful place to stop. I wonder what the inside must look like.'

'No coincidence. I know the family who live in this house. I was here not many weeks ago. The Daniels family. Welsh. See the name, "Cartref" means home. You have forgotten?'

'Um, give me a moment ...'

'If I said "Simon Mboya"?'

Margaret clasped her hands to her mouth. 'Oh, Simon!' Margaret had been associated with the politics of Kenya enough to draw a frightening conclusion.

All fear and trembling had vanished from Simon's mind and body.

'I feel safe here. If we went inside now we would be made welcome. I could tell our story and they would look after us. I was here for Simon's funeral.'

'Are you afraid ...?'

'That I could be next? Not afraid, not for me. Annoyed, yes. I missed my chance to spell out – what did Don McCall say – "a few home truths". But in that place, he is so intimidating. Me a little flyweight against the big bully heavyweight.'

'Are you enjoying this?'

'No, my dear, but my tail is up. The big old lion will not find this dik-dik so easy to catch! And I have the beginnings of a plan.'

'You sound like you've been down the Lucky Bar!'

'I'm going back into the city to drop you off at your sister's place. No arguing. Then I'm going to call in the troops.'

'The troops!'

'Yes, and this time, Mister Rubai, you're going to be the one with the bloody nose!'

'Is it wise to talk like this?'

'Wise? Perhaps not, but here I am, eighty years old and

about to be put out to pasture and, all of a sudden, I find myself in the middle of a big adventure!'

# Chapter Twenty-six

On the day of her 'second' wedding, Rebecca McCall woke up in the same bed she had slept in for the whole of her life. For company she had her sisters, Martha and Jane. Her mother knew that her firstborn had done this to please her. Rebecca was the first one up in the village, but she knew that she had company waiting outside. In the last darkness of the night, Maria Kabari had borrowed Hosea's bike and ridden the short distance to Londiani along a quiet Sunday morning road.

The two friends greeted each other with a long, close, swaying hug.

'Good morning, Madam McCall!'

'And good morning to you, Mistress Kabari!'

They sat close together on the flat rock seats that encircled the hearth fire that was at the centre of the small scattering of rondavels. The embers were more grey than red, but there was enough warmth to ward off the chill of early morning.

'Maria, is this wise?'

'Tom was full of worries yesterday and the bride today? Sure it's wise. The day will open out like a rose. Its perfume will fill the valley and the guests will go home full of hope.'

'Where does all this peace come from? Being with you, it's … it's like listening to sweet harmonies.'

'Rebecca, listen to me. Even before I met you, I knew that this day would come.'

'I don't understand.'

'Good. It's better that way. That first concert in the Bomas with Toni and Mary, I was there. The moment you stepped onto the stage, did you hear the gasp of wonder? Maybe not, but I tell you that anyone sitting in that place who had the eyes to see could have understood so many things about you.'

'But how can you say this, Maria? And who would be interested in a wash girl from Naivasha?'

'The great teachers talk about vibrations, auras. Hosea smiles when I try to explain. Remember, Julius Rubai and his family were in the front row there. Thomas was further back. Even in that crowd the pain screamed out. What was in your heart was also in your voice. Am I telling a truth here?'

'I am getting married today and you talk about Julius!'

'Yes, my darling, because sharing that pain in your heart was love, the purest love I have ever seen in a human being. In those moments of agony the spirit of the universe was with you. Rebecca, this is no crazy idea. What happened to you happens to millions of men, women, children. Children see it clearest. When it comes to us, we are aware of it, but it is hard to understand, to believe, so we hide it away because we are afraid that our friends, our family will tell us that we are mistaken or plain foolish.'

'Maria, this is too much. You know that I love you and I trust you. I am so glad that you have come into my life, our lives but …'

'Today is special in ways that I do not understand. I have been carrying these thoughts in my mind for many days, a message, not for me.'

'For me? What you are saying sounds like a burden.'

'But a burden that will be light because, even though they may not realise it yet, many, many people will be eager to share it. Without you there would be no dream. Sing on, Rebecca. Look, I have brought a flask of chai with lots of milk and sugar. A girl should spoil herself on such a day.'

By chance the seats they had chosen were facing east. All the while they had been talking, the regular drama of the morning had been unfolding in front of them. Darkness had become full light and the villagers were stirring.

'I must go home. Hosea will think that his bike has been stolen in the night.'

Rebecca drank down the last of the chai. There was a broad smile on her face.

'Maria, what dawa did you put in that drink? All of a sudden …'

'I feel the excitement, too. I must check the sugar when I get home. I have delivered the message. It's like I am getting married myself. All right, Hosea, I'm coming!'

Eight hours later a red bus bumped its way along the track leading down to Londiani from South Lake Road. For the second time in less than a year a group of singers from Nakuru had been invited to celebrate an important occasion in the lives of a young Naivasha couple. Earlier, Rebecca and Tom were having their first engagement party at the rondavel village. Now, for the second wedding, many of the guests were already gathered a stone's throw away on the open ground in front of the new Big House.

Four relieved young Welshmen had spent the morning hard at work finishing off a second upstairs bathroom. After a dawn service at the Catholic church, Rafaella and her two gardening boys had been prinking the soil and watering the hundreds of vigorous plants flourishing in her new pride and joy.

No more than thirty of this day's guests had been up at Pembroke. Father Robert and the two Irish sisters from Nakuru Cathedral were thrilled to be invited to join the locals on a farm rising out of its ashes on a day when the warm afternoon sun had transformed the waters of the lake into a vast, gleaming silver tray.

Following their tradition, the twenty-five members of the Nakuru singers began their performance as soon as they stepped down from their bus. As each man, smartly dressed in blue blazer and grey trousers, got down, he placed his hand on the shoulder of the man in front. The totos in the crowd pushed to the front to get a good view of the drama. When they were all down, the men moved off with slow, rhythmic steps, chanting a wordless lament.

It was the biggest wedding ever seen in the town. So many people dressed in their colourful best, so much orderly chaos. The choir sang from the veranda steps. Their audience responded with tribal songs, with hymns, then, following the briefest lull, a woman's powerful voice struck out with a sweet cooing of the names of the bride and groom.

'Re-becc-a, ahhhh, Re-becc-a, ohhhh!

'Tho-mas, ahhhh, Tho-mas, ohhhh!

'To-geth-er, To geth-er,

'For ever, for ever, for ever!'

Soon the throng was standing, clapping and moving rhythmically from foot to foot. The excitement was building rapidly. On and on they went with calls shouted from all corners. What had begun as a peaceful gathering of friends and neighbours was turning into a spontaneous prayer meeting.

'The nightingale and her Lazarus

'More beautiful than the rose of Sharon

'Stronger than Samson himself.

'O, Lord of the wedding feast, bless your two children here this day.'

'Alleleuia, praise God for his goodness.'

Without warning, the hero and the heroine were standing in front of them on top of the veranda steps. A gasp of silence was followed by a noisy rush to the semicircular wooden barrier festooned with a mass of white ribbons set up ten metres out from the steps. The singers stood aside for a group of five to pass through. The Reverend Elias Mbathi was followed by the two fathers and, two steps behind, by Rebecca and Tom holding hands. They would be married facing the people, the lake and the sun that was beginning its decline towards the western shore. As the bride's maids and pageboys were moving in from the side to stand behind the bride and groom, Stephen Kamau raised his arm. He had a request to make.

'Sammy, Sammy Koskei, where are you?' He explained. 'Many of you know my good friend, but I cannot … Ah, here he comes.'

Sammy, an eight year old but small for his age, was lifted over the barrier. Stephen took Sammy's hand and gave it a single shake.

'That's better. Sammy, is there anything you would like to say to Rebecca and Thomas?'

Sammy had his eyes closed and was scratching his forehead as he replied.

'Will I have to call you Memsahib when you are living with Bwana?'

'If you do, I will not be your best friend! So watch out then, young man. And just tell our friends why you have the best seat today, there on the veranda. I have to tell you all that his teacher told me that he is a fine artist. So?'

'I am drawing two pictures of the wedding, one for Rebecca and her Thomas. The other one will be for my sister, Rita and our brother, Thomas, if Jesus will let them come back to visit us.'

Very few people present did not know that the Koskeis were the only family to lose two in the explosions and fire that had devastated the flower fields of Londiani just weeks before.

Sammy had been to village weddings before. The young boys saw them as great places for playing around without being told off too much and after the boring part was over being allowed to eat and drink too much.

As the ceremony began, Sammy sat with his chin resting on his hands, watching carefully. He did not draw a single line. Yes, he had been to weddings before, but this was the first time he had paid attention to what was going on. He knew that the big business was between Rebecca and Bwana McCall, but he soon became bored with what they were doing. They were having a chat with the old man in the black suit who sometimes read from a book that looked like Isaac Mumbo's blind man's Bible. He liked drawing pictures where people and things were on the move, like a car crashing into a big bus, or the cops chasing after crooks and firing their guns. He did his best picture ever the day he returned to school after the fire down at the flower fields.

Teacher gave him a big sheet of paper and a new box of coloured crayons. He kept them with him until home time. When he showed the picture to Ms Mbarka, she had taken one long look and started to cry.

'What's wrong, Miss? Is my work very bad?'

'No, Sammy, it's the best picture I have ever seen from a student in my class. It's beautiful. It's the fire, isn't it?'

'Rita and Thomas were there. Can I take it to show Mama?'

'She will cry, just like me. Let me show it to your friend Bwana Kamau first.'

'Bwana Kamau, God let him come home from the fire. I pray with him and we ask God to let Rita and Thomas come back home, too.'

Sammy shifted in his seat to look at the people who had come to share in the wedding. He had never seen so many gathered in one place. They were not so still. There was plenty of moving about, plenty of chatting going on out there. Some of his friends were swinging from branches of trees. Boys and girls were walking towards the lake with the four young mzungos who had been working on Big House. Better watch out for the hippos. They sometimes come out of their water on warm afternoons.

And suddenly, without him thinking about it, his picture of the wedding was sitting in his mind as if it had been waiting for him to come and collect. Such a lot of colour. He would ask Martha and Jane if he could borrow their crayons.

The fire he saw a hundred times a day was there, but this time, like in Bwana Kamau's stories, there was a happy ever after ending. Tommy and Rita walked out. They were wearing their Sunday clothes. Look, standing there with Mama, they were waving at him.

Rita pointed at him and nodded seriously.

'Oh, so we have a new Mister Big in the family! We only have to turn our backs for five minutes!'

'Rita, you look so beautiful again.'

* * *

Evie Koskei was proud to see her Sammy in a position of honour at the wedding. By now all the guests were sitting on the soft grass, so she had a clear view of him alone up there on the veranda. She turned away for a few seconds, drawn by the last few moments of the ceremony and hoping to catch the climax, wondering whether Rebecca and the bwana would actually exchange a kiss in front of so many hundreds of people. When she stole a quick glance at Sammy, he was gone. She rose and made her way over the tangle of outstretched legs and 'round to the back entrance to the house. She found him sitting against the wall and talking to the woman, Maria, the wife of the new police sergeant.

'Mama, Mama! I have seen them. I have just told this lady. Mama, listen!'

She would listen but was fearful of what she would hear. When would her boy be free of these memories of fire and destruction? If only she had been home to keep him back from rushing down to the fields with the other children!

'Mama, they were here at the wedding. I saw them …'

'But, Sammy, you know that …'

'Mama, this lady believes me. Ask her. I will draw you a picture. Rita spoke to me. She called me the new Mister Big in the family.'

'Memsahib, tell him.'

'But I believe him. Sammy, your mama will look at your picture and she will understand. And so will you. Sammy, you know what love is?'

'I know it.'

'Your love brought them back, for a visit. They wanted to tell you that they are well in their new home.'

Others joined them.

'Bwana, Kamau, I have something to tell you.'

'And perhaps you will show me your picture, too.'

'I have seen Rita and Thomas!'

'Wonderful news. I want you to tell me when we are together in the village later. In private. But you are needed elsewhere. Ivor and David have brought their football.'

'Yeah, the mzungos need a goalie for the match against the village totos. We've got Eddie and Rollo on our team.'

'Give the brain a rest. Half an hour until the feast and the singing and the dancing.'

'And then I will draw my picture!'

* * *

The new married couple were chatting to the Reverend Elias when, from somewhere out of the back rows of the guests, Rebecca heard her name being called out by a group of voices in unison. 'Rebecca McCall. Paging Rebecca McCall!' As they called, the group began waving.

She climbed the steps to have a better view. There were ten familiar faces dressed in band uniform and ready with their instruments.

'Mary, Toni, I was afraid that you wouldn't come.'

The long distance conversation continued from Toni Wajiru's side.

'We got a new song for you. "Wedding of the Year". Corny, but we think you'll like it. Bring Tom and the Nakuru boys.'

The music played, the singers hummed a melodious background and, arm in arm, Rebecca and Tom led their helpers in the samba rhythm through the crowd parting in front of them. Mary broke off from her singing only long enough to give her oldest friend a whirling hug and a sheet of music score. Holding her at arm's length she looked into Rebecca's eyes.

'To think that we almost missed all this. Rebecca, wonderful, wonderful day.'

So began a concert that went on and on until the sun was about to sink behind the glowering bulk of the heights of Eburu. Filled with food and drink and exhausted by the most exciting day of their lives the children were ready to be led home long before darkness fell. By six the red bus was bumping back up the track. The singers wanted to be clear of the A104 and safely back in Nakuru before dusk. At seven minibuses arrived from the country club to take Toni and his entourage back to their accommodation and their evening concert. Charlie, the drummer man, had been impressed by his first visit to Naivasha.

'Rebecca, to think that I used to feel sorry for you wanting to stay in your piece of up-country bush. Paradise more like. Any land for sale in these parts for a rickety old drummer boy?'

The wedding was over, but an even more important event of the day was about to begin. With only a half moon to lighten the full darkness, Luka and Erik were on constant patrol around the house and garden. The lanterns hanging from the veranda ceiling gave out enough light for those scattered in a loose circle around a large low table. For the first time there was to be a completely open discussion. Everyone was aware of the danger posed by unwanted eyes and ears. Abel Rubai had his paid spies everywhere. Paul was first to speak.

'Rebecca, Tom, not a great choice of times for you, but this is our best chance for getting ourselves organised for the final, big push.'

'Tom and I are an old married couple now. We all know how important this meeting is.'

'So some of the wedding guests stay on to put the day to sleep. What could be more natural than that?'

'Right, Tom. And I would like us to remember that there are hundreds, no, thousands of silent supporters out there ...'

Hearts sank when a breathless Erik hurried up the steps and went straight to Alex.

'Bwana, we have caught someone, a man creeping down the driveway. Luka is bringing him. He pretends that his car is broken down.'

Paul Miller and Daniel Komar exchanged wry smiles. Daniel defied his mounting sense of tension and spoke calmly.

'Let's just wait and see. Won't it be great when we no longer have to jump out of our skins just because some driver forgot to put enough petrol in his car to get him home?'

Luka had his prisoner in an arm lock, pushing him along at a speed that the little old man could not handle.

'Bloody hell! Simon, what are you doing here? We thought ... I don't know what we thought.'

Simon Nyache was fighting to get his breath.

'I haven't run so fast in fifty years ... Paul, I am so glad ... your people in Langata said you might be here ...'

Maura and Rafaella eased the old man into an armchair while Sonya moved in to check him over. The feeling of relief in that open-sided room was palpable, on both sides, Simon because he had reached a safe haven and the others because the fear of discovery and exposure seemed to have evaporated.

'Could I have a glass of water, please?'

'I'm sorry about the welcome, Simon. Luka, Erik, great job. Memsahib will look after you later.'

There was quiet while Simon sipped his water, gathered himself and began his explanation.

'He knows. Someone must have seen me coming or going. My God, it was frightening. I made up a story about visiting the lake farms as a kind of farewell to folks who never voted for me. Didn't believe me, of course. He can hide his thoughts, but those eyes, half smiling, half threatening. You all know what I'm talking about. Yes, and he wants me to show his boy around Nakuru South, an introduction for my successor. Next Wednesday. For a while there I thought I'd never get out of that house alive. I should have realised he never does his killing himself and it never happens on his own territory.'

A downcast Stephen voiced his fear.

'Bwana, seems to me that the whole country is his territory. Maria, you know about these things.'

'Stephen, I know you're a coastie and there is a lot of black magic down there, but this man makes his own magic.'

'That is for sure. From the moment I left that place until your boys brought me here, Alex, I've been expecting … something bad, a bullet, a knife, a pick-up. I drove Margaret to her sister's house by the back roads, parked under a tree in the garden. Covered the car under two big blankets.'

Paul and Daniel crossed to Simon and shook his hand.

'Welcome to Serena. Sorry we don't have membership cards, yet!'

'Too risky. Get picked up with one in your pocket, it could lead to big trouble.'

Bertie, from experience, knew as well as anyone in that place how dangerous it was to fall into the range of Rubai's interest. What this tough old trooper needed above all was a sense of safety, as far as that was possible.

'We stick together. We'll get the murdering … fill the gap. Bastard will do. Sorry, Raf, I know …'

'No, Bertie, this time you have found a very suitable word.'

'I want to get one more thing off my chest. I know why we are all here, but … why don't we take a short cut. I mean one bullet in the right place … play him at his own game.'

Paul was in very quickly. 'Very tempting, Bertie. Quicker? Easier? Not even in the short run. Gun a villain down and you're in danger of opening the floodgates of sympathy. When they worked out who got him, we would become the villains.'

Daniel backed him.

'The law is slow. Mister Dickens tells us that the law is an ass. But it's our only real hope. And, let's not fool ourselves. We have just one chance. If we miscalculate …'

'He's going down. That's lawyer talk, isn't it, Paul.'

'Maria, I'm glad you're on our side. I'm being very serious here. When we get into court, you're going to be right next to Daniel and me. You'll have a title. "Amicus Curiae", Friend of the Court. If we get into a jam sometime, we are going to turn you loose. So pay attention, sister. Now, what evidence do we have? Will it be enough to, Maria, "send him down"?'

Maura was puzzled. 'How many murders does a man have to commit before he gets punished in this country?'

'Actually carried out with his own bare hands? Possibly none.'

'But what about the word "accessory"? Our law teacher in Oundle said that was almost as bad …'

'Right, Tom. And this is where we are strong.'

Bertie was relieved. 'Surely, Paul, not almost as bad but just as bad. Dickens was being too polite. The law is not an ass but an arsehole. All right, Rafaella?'

'Bertie, still too polite! And, Alex, don't look so surprised. I know lots of juicy Italian words!'

'So why was he pointing a rifle at me from twenty metres the night that Londiani was blown up?'

'Yes, Tom. And what was he doing out on the farm at two o'clock in the morning with that nutcase of a son? Waiting for a bus?'

'Alfredo Rossi, alias Alfred Ross, we all remember him. Why do we have a photograph of him paying a visit to Rubai's secret farm outside Nairobi?'

'Barnie, this is where you come in.'

'Sure. Most of you know that I am Paul's brother, another lawyer. My practice is in Boston. I think the ruthless Mister Rossi could be a very expensive weakness in Rubai's defence. I have associates in several New York law firms and friends in the NYPD. Mister Rossi has a thick file with the FBI. Normal families run stores or go on the subway early in the morning to work for accountants or construction companies. The Rossi family of Brooklyn have an unusual line of business. They kill people to order. I'll spare you the details on his work in Kenya, but we are close, very close to making a deal on evidence from Rossi that will be acceptable in a court here. We have him on toast or over a barrel, take you pick!'

Paul had warning.

'There are fifteen of us in this room. Doesn't sound a lot. But, Maria, remember Papa's favourite Bible story?'

Maria smiled. 'Well, wouldn't that be the one where little David gives that philistine Goliath a nasty headache with a couple of pebbles?'

Barnie took up the story.

'And the moral, children, is, shall I put it this way, if a little guy wants to whip a big guy, he must have surprise up his sleeve and move quicker than an angry cheetah!'

While everyone pondered the implications of Mzee Miller's teaching to his children, Sonya shifted uncomfortably in her chair.

'You know, perhaps I shouldn't have stayed on for the meeting. I think I'm inhibiting you.'

'You mean by not talking about Simon?'

'Maria, you are the most sensitive person I've ever met. You understand that my thoughts on Simon never stop, like some endless painful background music.'

Paul took over in his compassionate way.

'Sonya, you are half right when you talk about some of us holding back. Simon is never far from my heart. We all see the bloodstained hand of Rubai in this. But … Hosea will explain better.'

'Madam Sonya.'

'Just Sonya, please.'

'I'm sorry. This word, "accessory". We try very hard to find a link to tie in Rubai. Patrick Uchome, he was Rubai's Kenya number one man.'

'The one killed with his wife on the road by the Italian chapel?'

'He was in charge of the kidnap. His boys drove Simon up to Kericho, expecting to … I'm so sorry to be so cruel, harsh, to … so sorry for the tears. They expected to finish their work and return to Nairobi that evening. They were angry when Uchome said that the boss wasn't ready.'

'But, Hosea, how do you know all this?'

Hosea forced himself on. 'Two of them did return to the city, without Simon. They drew lots. Simon was kept in a hut outside the town. Two local idiots saw a big payday for helping out. Two days later at noon, Uchome sent word …'

Maura moved to Sonya, knelt down and burst into tears.

'Sonya, it was just before twelve when we left the Rubai house. If I hadn't forced you to go to that place, perhaps Simon …'

There were no tears from Sonya. When she spoke her tone was calm and businesslike.

'No, Maura. There would be no mercy there. But where are these men now? They were not at the inquest. Why?'

Paul took over again. 'Sonya, often criminals refuse to speak. It can be like signing their own death warrants. Some very angry Kericho cops, shall we say, persuaded them to tell their story. Almost killed them. On advice from some anonymous CID man on Nairobi Hill, they were kept in custody. They were nursed over the worst of their injuries by two Sisters of Mercy. That took weeks. Now they are holed up in an old tea store on one of the estates and under constant watch. Daniel was up to see them last week.'

'Sonya, they won't be the best of witnesses if we manage to get them to court. Rubai's money might get someone to let him know who they are and where they are.'

# Chapter Twenty-seven

'Tell me, Albert, Walter, what do you really think of me?'

Albert Latani and Walter Wambui were bewildered and frightened. They exchanged frowns, each hoping that the other would take the first bite at an answer. Just because they were part of the group of twelve that Boss Man Abel had gathered around him as sounding boards and yes men, it did not mean that they were bosom pals and permanent members of the inner sanctum. Why had he invited them to lunch at Muthaiga for the very first time and afterwards closeted them in a private room for a 'chat about how things are going in your neck of the woods'?

'What kind of a question is that, Abel?'

'Well, Albert, with the three of us here on neutral ground, I thought we could be more open than when the whole thirteen of us get together at my place. If friends can't be frank ... Look, I'm a Kalenjin boy and you are a Luo, both successful in our own ways, but you know how this tribal thing is in our blood. And, Walter, from good Kikuyu stock, how long you been the MP for Nakuru North?'

'Twenty years and hoping for more, Abel.' Walter chuckled. His fears were easing, but he was well aware of how unpredictable Abel was. And it would not be a wise move to upset the man who would soon be the president.

'And you see how it is. With me in the big job, I have to feel sure of my people. And I want to be frank with you. One or two little things have cropped up. I hate to admit it, but there are times when I can be just somewhat remote from the … the pulse of the nation.'

Abel was trying to prompt a reply, but his solemn companions remained tight-lipped. Neither of them was comfortable. The Rubai spotlight was probing, testing. The real agenda of the Big Man was never easy to work out. After a suitably unnerving lapse of time, Abel shifted slightly in his chair until his focus was firmly fixed on Albert, the very rich Luo businessman.

'Albert, a few weeks ago now, there was a most unfortunate incident involving a Luo medical man.'

The polite terminology briefly deceived Albert: 'unfortunate incident' and 'medical man'?

'Oh, you mean the cowardly murder of one of the finest, most caring doctors this country has ever had.'

Abel, stung by the unexpected aggression in Albert's tone continued, unruffled.

'It's true then that Luo people are deeply upset?'

'Abel, why all this soft language? Outrage, anger, fury. Take your pick. After all this time the cops keep churning out those limp statements: "We think we are getting close to a probable suspect", and "No, no, the trail has definitely gone cold". Not Luo cops. But they are as powerless as the rest of us. God help the man behind this when we find him.'

'I'm with you on this, of course, but it disturbs me to think that this could become a tribal matter. But thank you for helping me feel the pulse on this one. Now, Walter …'

'Now, Walter'! Abel wanted to pass on to 'item two' on the agenda. Albert wanted to scream out his disgust at having this crime against the nation passed over so glibly. He held himself in check and even managed an ironic smile when he recited in his head the Kenyan motto of self-preservation: 'Discretion is the better part of cowardice'.

'Walter, I have a more specific problem that you could help me with. How well do you know your fellow Nakuru MP?'

'You mean Simon?' It was Walter's turn to have his mind start to spin and flutter in confusion.

'Who else? Tell me, do you think we can trust him as a loyal member of the party?'

Sharp-eyed Abel noted with interest Walter's slight hesitation.

'Abel, Simon Nyache is our oldest, longest serving MP and an honourable man.'

'Yes, I studied Julius Caesar at school, too. Brutus, wasn't he the honourable man? Just assassinated the boss man! What if I told you that our Simon has been having meetings with members of the new joke party.'

'You mean Serena, Miller, Komar, that mob?'

'Very sharp, Walter. A couple of days ago, I had him here. I wanted him to show my boy, Reuben, 'round Nakuru South before the election, just in case they vote him in. I swear the old fellow wet his pants! Scared out of his wits. I pressed a little. Quite reasonable, I think. I said I'd make the arrangements and let him know. Got a phone call yesterday. "Can the boy, notice not Reuben, can the boy meet me at Gilgil police station. I want to show him …"'

'Around the mental hospital next door. Abel, he's always asking people that. The place is his passion. Every budget time he asks the government for money to improve the place.'

'Perhaps he's thinking of joining up himself. And, while I'm on the topic of hospitals, what do you know of the idea to build a new hospital in Naivasha?'

'Never heard him say a word about that.'

'You've heard of the Kamau girl? Come into money and she's got the mad idea that she can walk in and do what she likes.'

'She's a McCall now. Married on the weekend. Big affair, so I'm told.'

'Tried to smuggle in a couple of aliens – whites, of course. What's going on up there, Walter?

Mention of the wedding brought instant and unexpected relief for Abel's guests. The inquisitor suddenly lost his edge and his interest.

'Well, thanks for coming. Hope you enjoyed the lunch. When you're in the car park ask my driver, Obi, to come in. Got some things for him to carry.'

* * *

'What did you think of all that, Walter?'

Albert was giving his lunch companion a lift into the city.

'Not as bad as I thought it was going to be. I was glad I wasn't the only one invited. When I get the call from Abel, I think about checking my will.'

'He is so unpredictable. He works on it, to keep us guessing.' Caught in a queue of traffic, Albert cleared his throat. Walter had noticed several times before that this trick of the nerves usually meant that Albert was weighing up an idea in his mind, wondering whether or not to bring it out. Albert began again. 'Confidentially, I got the feeling that the great man is uneasy about something. I mean why did he need to talk with us at all? Is he looking for reassurance?'

'Same here. I think it's that Kamau girl. Does that sound crazy to you?'

'Not a bit. Stunning looks, great voice. My girls are always singing her songs. Everyone seems to love her.'

'They say Abel blames her for the death of Julius. Lucky escape for her, I'd say. And Simon tells me that with her as his wife, Farmer McCall could take his place as the man for Nakuru South.'

'Walter, a lot of Luo think that our Doctor Simon … Did you hear him, just now? "Unfortunate accident". I don't want to spell it out. You know the rumours.'

'And Rebecca McCall is a great friend of Sonya Mboya. You were at the funeral.'

'Big, big mistake, Abel.'

'Albert, you used the word "uneasy". I'm beginning to see that it's more than that. The great Abel is becoming desperate.'

# Chapter Twenty-eight

Jim Sawyer left the three Welsh craftsmen in charge for an hour. His own boys would enjoy that – plenty of work and plenty of fun. The four 'aliens' were glad to stay on site until the work on Londiani was complete. He and the 'almost' Doctor Iolo were excited as they skipped down the stairs on their way to the kitchen.

The other four were already standing around the large breakfast table, waiting for them before they began the meeting-cum-consultation. A big moment had arrived in the drive to build the new Naivasha hospital. Peter Bellengeri helped Debbie Miller to lift her large leather document holder onto the table.

'Open it up, Rebecca. You're the boss here, you know.'

'I'm going to need some help. My fingers are trembling.' But the clasp was easy and the task soon done. Rebecca stooped to take a sidelong look into a holder that was still flat on the table. 'Debbie, so many sheets of paper, or should I say …?'

'Sheets will do fine. Don't forget these are plans for a hospital. I've done two sets so you can have a choice.'

Peter and Iolo slid the documents out and Debbie began to spread them on the table in order. Rebecca had only ever seen one set of architect's plans and those were for Long House, and she barely understood the lines and figures on those.

She shook her head in disbelief at the sight of these beautiful, complicated works of art.

'But how could one person ...?'

'Ah, but it was not just me. I'll explain. When I got back to school, I couldn't wait to start on the drawings. When my friends found out what I was doing, they were as excited as I am about this, er, work. Bad word but, you know. In the end there were enough plans for ten hospitals. "My God, this for an actual place in Africa!" By the way, I stored away all the other plans.'

Debbie focused on her first and largest sheet, a general impression on what the hospital would look like when it was built.

'This is number one plan, my favourite. What do you think, Rebecca?'

'Unbelievable!' The emotion showed through in the tremble of her voice and the moistness of her eyes. 'I think it will be the most beautiful building in the whole country!'

'You can add Wales to that list.' Iolo was wide-eyed and already wondering if he could persuade this brilliant young woman to come to Llanelli where plans were being made for a new hospital.

Jim Sawyer had been a builder all his life. When they started to look at details in the plans, he was very impressed.

'You're right, Rebecca. And I can tell straight away that whatever contractor is lucky enough to work from these plans will have the best experience of his life. Everything is so sharp and clear.'

The discussion around the table became animated and technical. Sonya pored over the drawings of the large maternity wing. She wept for the joy of seeing them and for the sadness that Simon was not with her to share what would have been a fulfillment of his dream.

'Almost' Doctor Iolo was looking at measurements and the facilities planned for staff as well as patients. His heart sank a little when be began to think about the cost of materials, construction and the expense of running the place. Would there be, could there be enough money for all this?

Rebecca moved away from the table to sit alone with her own tumble of thoughts. She wished Papa could have been with her to calm her, give her a sense of proportion. But she knew where he would begin. She closed her eyes in silent prayer and meditation.

As usual, when she longed for her prayer to be totally focused, she could not shut out the interruptions.

'Rebecca, don't forget that the Father knows our needs better than we do, so I reckon that listening is better than talking. And always stay relaxed.'

Relaxed? For her trying to pray soon saw her mind turned into a battleground. Scenes and ideas flashed in and out of her mind like lightning strikes.

A married woman has new responsibilities. Three days a wife and she saw the possibilities of divided loyalties up ahead.

Such a wonderful building would cost so much money. Sooner rather than later she would have to confess that her dream was too big. The thrill of a dream fulfilled would turn into the drudgery of failure. She would let so many people down.

Cold thoughts chilled her imagination. Into her fevered brain stepped Julius Rubai, Reuben Rubai and, towering above them like a wicked, leering genie, their ruthless, arrogant father. She had heard the plans to bring him down. Their hopes were high, but even Paul and Daniel warned that risks were higher.

There, just across the room, the enthusiastic chatter

continued. The plans were as real as ever. So why were the tears of despair wetting her cheeks?

A single low sob drew Sonya's attention. She, quickly followed by Debbie, hurried to her side. Within seconds the three women were stepping down from the veranda and striding, arms linked, slowly, so slowly across the spring grass of the plain. For Rebecca the gold of the morning had turned to dross. The cool breeze and the presence close by of a hundred familiar and much loved sights failed to revive her spirits. Sonya and Debbie were shocked by the sudden turn-around but knew that the way out for Rebecca and themselves would involve patient waiting. At last, Rebecca, calmer now, was able to share her fears.

'I'm so sorry. I have built up so many hopes, but now, coming close to the real mountain, I see that I cannot climb. Mama was right to call me the dreamer of the family.'

'But, Rebecca, you are not just close to your mountain, but you are not far from the summit.'

'Sonya, I am overreaching. Such a building will cost —'

Debbie broke in. 'Ah, I think I can help with that one. I wasn't intending to speak about it until after checking out the plans. Jim has already mentioned the next stage. The word is "costing".'

'I understand that.'

'Yes, and this building is not going to fail for want of dollars and shillings. I can promise you that, hand on my heart!'

'So you know how much it will cost.'

'No one does yet, Rebecca. Listen. Boston is a rich city. In the university we have a campus radio, run by students. My friend, Mimi Adams, broadcasts a program twice a week, called "Science in action". She knows all about you and the work you want to do here. Three weeks ago, she invited me on the show. We played part of a concert recorded in the Flamingo – you, Mary and Toni's boys. I gave background information. One of the Boston stations picked it up and rebroadcast the whole bit.'

'These people were interested in Naivasha?'

'Sure, very interested, and they wanted to help in some way. Money began to come in. The accounts department in my dad's firm has opened a bank account, "The Rebecca Kamau Hospital Fund". It's a backup. I hope you're not offended. I didn't want to ...'

'Why offended, Debbie? Come to the hospital that we have today and ask the new mothers if they are offended. Only one person can stop us now.'

There was no need for an explanation. They had walked some way from Londiani, across the plain to a ridge above the lake. There was a sturdy wooden bench facing inland. They sat down and, for a time, no words were spoken. Each of them took in the hundreds of aspects of the broad landscape, stretching for many miles from the heights of Eburu to north-west, across the shadowy mass of the Aberdares to Longonot, Rebecca's old friend to the south-east.

The beauty of the view and the sweetness of the cool air filled Debbie with an unlooked for pride in the homeland she had hardly visited. Sonya leaned against the bench, closed her eyes and, lifting her face to catch the gentle breeze, asked her Simon to stay close and touch her with his wisdom. Rebecca silently blessed her companions and fixed her eyes on the clear outline of Long House, her new home. Recent memories, none of them pleasant, returned to her, Tom lying in his hospital bed, bruised and wounded after the ordeal of the kidnapping that almost took his life, her own father rescued from death by the mysterious gifts of Maria, the body of

Sonya's Simon being prepared by Maria for his final passing in the sanctuary room of the Daniels' family. The memories were not pleasant, but she was not troubled by them.

'Another good omen, Maura!' Sonya laughed at herself. 'Where did that come from?'

'And what does it mean?'

'Oh, it's become a kind of family saying that sprang out of a dark moment, Debbie. We must seem to be a gloomy lot to be living in such a lovely place.'

'That's a joke, Rebecca. You are the toughest, most lovable group of people I've ever even heard of. This Rubai character, he's scared stiff of you.'

Rebecca and Sonya leaned forward to look at each other wide-eyed with arched brows. Debbie watched them with mild amusement.

'Have I said something outrageous?'

'Sitting here in the sunshine, at home, with friends and family close by, perhaps, for half a second, Mister Big is cut down to size. Scared stiff of us? How does Tom put it? "In your dreams".'

'Yes, Rebecca, but "in your nightmares" would be nearer the truth. He's a murderer, Debbie. Just talk to father and Paul for five minutes. He specialises in planting daggers in innocent peoples' souls. I know it's a sin, but, last week David and I were talking about things for the thousandth time, since … well. David went to a drawer and took out the gun a Scottish friend gave him years ago. "Sonya, we use knives to help preserve life, but this little fellow …"'

'"David, let me hold it for a moment." It was heavier than I had expected and … beautiful. I pressed it to my cheek and it felt cool. "David, those knives, we use them to cut away diseased parts of flesh. Would it be so wrong to use this different piece of metal …?"'

'Yes, wrong, but I would be willing to do it.'

'God forbid …'

'That's it. God does forbid. Remember what Mam called guns? One of the devil's playthings.'

'David, promise me …'

'I can't, love.'

'I'm so sorry. My big mouth! There I go blathering on about the plans and I'm so excited.'

'Debbie, sweetheart, you must keep "blathering on". Please! We're excited, too! Sonya, I've just got married and I feel defenceless. We're in the risk business and I have never felt so high in my life.'

'Rebecca, if your father-in-law saw us now, he'd be offering us whisky to calm us down!'

'And I might just take him up on the offer!'

# Chapter Twenty-nine

Once they were completely clear of Nakuru, Sonya began to show signs of agitation. She fiddled with the sheaf of notes she had brought so that she would not forget the uncomfortable questions she must ask once they reached their destination. She talked much more than usual and regularly shifted around in her seat in the front seat of the Pajero.

She could not have had two better companions for the journey and for the ordeal that lay ahead. Bertie had volunteered to drive and had left a happy Ewan to spend the day at Londiani where Jim Sawyer and his men were in the last stages of rebuilding Big House. She and Simon had been good friends with Jim long before the day when Anna was taken away from him minutes after she had her first and last sight of her miracle baby. He would make sure that Ewan and her three would enjoy their day among the big men. Maria had lived in Kericho for years and knew exactly where to find the two men they were going to meet later that morning.

Sonya's nervous state had not improved by the time Bertie pulled up close to the house of Charlie and Sue Mossly. Charlie was the owner and manager of a medium sized tea plantation in the heart of the rich, green hillsides and he and Sue had loved their lives in the 'wild north' as their Nairobi friends had described Kericho when they sold up successful businesses on the huge estate off Mombasa Road south of the capital.

'We thought we'd have early elevenses out in the garden. Don't worry, plenty of shade if you want it.'

'Best time of day to sit idling out here. Try having a cup of afternoon tea on this very spot and likely you'd be soaked to the skin.'

Sonya recalled Alex's words to her before they had set out earlier that morning.

'You'll love them. They really do have hearts of gold. But chalk and cheese. Just being with them will make you feel better.'

Sonya could not fail to see the truth of what Alex had said about the contrast between husband and wife. He was tall and powerfully built. It was no surprise to learn that he had played rugby for the army for several years. In his time in the service he had learned to be a first-class mechanic. But in his wanderings around the world, his voice had lost nothing of its Yorkshire accent.

Susan Mossly (nee Marlowe) was the film director's cliché of the typical English lady, in looks, at least. Slim, blonde and vivacious, she too had travelled extensively and everywhere she went, she always attracted attention with her unaffectedly posh voice – minus the plum in the mouth, not a surprise in the former head girl of a leading English boarding school.

They had met by chance at a polo match in the small up-country town of Gilgil. He had flown a friend up from Nairobi to play in a tournament and stayed on for the beer. She had wandered across from the Coulson house where she was spending a leisurely last weekend before returning home to London. She had stayed on. Within a month they were married and, two years later, had quit the city for a life in the hills.

They were into their second cup of tea when Sue decided that it was time to get down to business.

'Adam and Andrew Karume, you want to see them, Sonya. I think it's a wonderful idea and so does Charlie.'

'I must say that it was a bit unexpected. You'll be their first visitors.'

'Don't they have family or friends close by? I thought they were Kericho men.'

'Certainly, but everyone around here thinks that they are both dead. They almost were an' all. The police gave them such leatherin'.'

'Not a good way to persuade men to tell the truth. I can't agree with Charlie about everyone thinking they're dead. Impossible to keep something like this a complete secret. At the moment, they're living in an old tea store.'

'Sue's put in new beds and a few home comforts. You'd think they were our boys!'

Sonya was puzzled. 'I understood they were a couple of local criminals.'

'That's the story. Maria, you must remember them. Paul tells us that they are going to be important witnesses later this year.'

'I do remember them. Sue, I take it that they know Sonya's coming.'

'I told them this morning. Come on. Let's go and see them.'

'Just before we go. Maria and Bertie know that I've agonised over whether to come or not. In the end I decided that I want to find out even a tiny bit more about how it all happened.'

'Sonya, all I know is that I don't think it's in me to do

something like this. Not the right moment for saying this, I know. I hope … There are no words.'

But there were tears. Sonya and Sue, strangers an hour before, embraced with the warmth of sisters.

* * *

The double doors of the tea store were wide open and two young men stood on the threshold waiting. Both were smartly dressed in T-shirt and jeans. The meeting did not begin well. As Sonya, Maria and Bertie got close to the shed, one of the men became agitated. He pointed his arm towards Bertie, letting out a stream of words so quickly that they were almost incomprehensible. One word was clear and repeated several times: the name, 'Rubai'.

'My name is Andrew. I come from the New Testament. My brother is Adam, from the Old. I will explain.'

Andrew put his arm around his brother's shoulder and, with a few words in a local dialect, calmed him and then led Sonya and Maria into the stone-built store. He smiled at Bertie.

'Bwana, forgive my brother. Patrick warned us that if we did not obey him, this Rubai person would find us and hurt us badly. He thinks you are this man.'

A relieved Bertie understood and turned to go. 'Andrew, I'm with your brother on this. Tell him that I am sorry that I frighten him. I'm no friend of Rubai. I'm glad I've met you. Kwaheri, ladies. I'll withdraw to the garden.'

Inside the store, the furniture was basic but adequate. Though there were wooden chairs, Andrew invited Sonya and Maria to sit on one of the widely spaced twin beds.

'You are on my bed. Adam loves his bed so much. He spends most of his time here.'

Sonya asked tentatively, 'You know why we have come?'

'Yes. And I know you. You are Doctor Simon's lady. You came to our church on Easter Day two years ago. And you are Maria Kabari. Your husband is the kind policeman. We have no mother. She died when we were born. Our father, Joseph, went away to Kisumu. We think he is dead now. Anna looked after us. She was a poor lady. We did not go to the school. Every day she read from the Bible to us. She is dead, too, this four years.'

'Do you know how old you are?'

'We think it is seventeen years. We are strong boys, but no one will give us work. We were sitting on the side of the road outside the Shell station on Moi Avenue. Patrick Uchome …'

'Patrick Uchome? How did you know this man?'

'The old lady who cared for us lived close by his family's plantation.'

Brother Adam startled Sonya and Maria for the second time. While his brother had been talking, Adam had lain with his back resting against the wall, dozing and seemingly uninterested. Suddenly he took up the story, speaking lucidly and with a good deal of passion.

'Uchome is a very bad man. He tricked us. He say, "Hey, Karume boys, get over here and pretty damn quick!" There were three of them in that big car coming out the Shell place. Smart fellahs, city folks. "How you like to earn five hundred shillings? Bet you never had so much money in your pocket".'

When Adam hesitated, Andrew took up the story.

'And what we got to do for this money? "Easy things. Take you no time. If you do good job, we give you five hundred each. Get in!" Tell you the truth, Memsahib, we were too scared not to get in.'

Adam gently touched his brother's arm. He was ready to continue.

'That car moved pretty damn fast, but we did not go far. It was coming to evening time. We went into a plantation. The workers were gone home. We stopped outside a hut just like this one. Uchome had a key. We all went inside. "Sit down on the boxes in the corner." The three of them were talking very quiet. We didn't want to hear their words. When darkness came he told us to get outside and tell him if we saw anyone getting near.'

There was a sudden silence. Both brothers seemed unable to continue. They looked out into the sunshine to avoid meeting the eyes of Sonya and Maria.

'I remember Anna, the old lady who looked after you. She was a good lady. You said that she read the Bible to you …'

'Until she learned us to read, Memsahib Maria, and then …'

'You read to her. Hosea and me read the book every night together.'

'Someone stole ours.'

'You shall have mine. It is in the car.' Maria paused and reached out to take the brothers' hands. She began again. There was a kindly wistfulness in her penetrating eyes. 'Have you noticed how every time God asks one of his prophets and even Jesus himself to do some hard thing, He is somewhere close by, ready to help them? It was hard for Memsahib Sonya to come here today. And now you have a hard thing. If we close our eyes we will understand that He is here, as usual.'

'There are terrible things.'

'I know, Adam, and I am ready.'

Adam and Andrew were far from ready to begin the difficult part of their story. They shifted along the bed until their bodies touched. They looked down at the paved floor, at each other and out into the sunshine. The effort showed in brief grunts of pain as if their lips, closed tight, were fighting to keep back the flow of words.

Sonya and Maria held hands and stared blankly at the whitewashed wall beyond the brothers' bed, waiting patiently, trying to shut down their active, vivid imaginations. When the words came, they gushed out in a pained duet as if they were actors checking their lines in a speed recitation of perfectly remembered lines.

'Memsahib, the big man opened the back of that car. I screamed.'

'We both screamed. The naked man was lying very still.'

'But he was not dead. His arms and legs were tied and they rolled him roughly and we saw his face.'

They broke off, this time in an effort to hold back tears.

'Mama Sonya, it was Doctor Simon. They took the cloth from his mouth and cut the ropes.'

'They pushed him into the room, kicked him. He made no noise. They screamed bad words into his face.'

'Then they argued. Uchome was angry with the other men. "You were paid to finish the job."'

'"Uchome, we have done our part. We are going back to Nairobi now and we are taking the car. And if you are wise, you will say nothing to Rubai!"'

'That was the name. Paul said that this was the name we must remember when the time comes. Rubai.'

Maria wanted to be sure she had understood.

'So the men went away in the car and left you with the doctor and Uchome who is a fat man?'

'Yes.'

'And you did not try …'

'Mama Maria, Uchome had a gun. He shouted at us.

"Damn you! Down on your knees in that corner. And damn you, Rubai!" He was very scared.'

'He kicked the doctor in the back. I still remember the noise as he hit the ground.'

'It was very quick. Uchome stabbed the doctor in the back two, three times.'

'Uchome screamed like a frightened child.'

'It was finished.'

'Uchome breathed heavy. Then he was calm. He said: "Now we wait. Then you will earn your money."'

'Much time passed. "You have one more job." Please, Mama, it was … the hands. We cannot speak this thing!'

'I know. I know. Sonya, darling, shall we leave these boys in peace?'

'Maria, a strange thing has been going on. You would understand it better than me. All the time we have been in this room listening, I have heard another voice.'

'Simon.'

'A whisper in harmony with the boys. I heard the voice but no words that I could catch with my mind. Maria, I feel so sorry for these boys. When this is all finished we will help them.'

Adam, calm again, had heard Sonya's words to Maria.

'Memsahib Maria, perhaps you will believe us. Uchome told us that we must hurt the doctor's hands.'

'We told him that he could shoot us, but we would not do this thing. He shouted and put the gun to our heads. We did not do it.'

'"Then you must carry this lump of meat and dump him where I tell you. Pick it up. Now!"'

Adam checked with his brother before he spoke again. Andrew nodded.

'By the light of the two candles burning on the floor, we saw the blood on the doctor's back, dried hard now. Andrew's words gave me courage. "We can do honour to this good man. We will carry him gently. Adam ..."'

'I said: We will tell ourselves that we are carrying Jesus himself, from the cross to the tomb.'

'There was no heaviness in this man. He was a handful of grass in our arms.'

'We moved quickly. Uchome followed with his gun in his hand.'

'We came to the place, near the gate of a big plantation. "Throw him down." We put him down gently.'

'"You like him so much, you can join him. The cops will find you all in one place. I like it. Neat!"'

'Andrew threw a handful of earth and stones into the fat man's face and we ran into the plantation and hid in the tea bushes. In the morning the early workers found us. They saw the blood on our hands ...'

# Chapter Thirty

'Obi, can you see the boys in the car behind?'

'They've caught up now, Boss.'

'And you do know where this place is?'

'My sister lives in the army camp. Married to an officer. She says to park by the police station. This … hospital is next door. She says the army boys call it "the loony bin".'

'The local MP, the man we have come to meet, would not approve. But Simon Nyache has a tender heart.'

'No, Papa, he is just getting soft in his old age. Why does he make such a fuss about this place?'

'Ask him yourself, Reuben. I think he wants to show us around. "Sorry, Mister Rubai. I cannot come to the city. It's my day for visiting my boys." My boys! Maybe you have a point, Reuben.'

'Nakuru South can certainly do with some young blood.'

'The McCall kid is about your age.'

'So you think he could win.'

Abel was amused by his son's demonstration of childish annoyance.

'Son, when you are in the public eye, you need to develop a tough skin. Tenderness is a fine thing in a parent but not in a leader. Lies, rumours, you learn to live with them. You have to know your people. Take this Simon. Is he a solid citizen or a traitor to the cause, to his people here in Nakuru South?'

* * *

'Simon, you look surprised. Something tells me that you didn't expect me to turn up today. Well, here we are, ready for the grand tour of Gilgil and district. And we would like to meet some of your people. Simon, do you realise that in the last ten years, you have submitted twenty requests for grants "to improve the lives of hundreds of forgotten citizens."'

'Abel, is there also a record of how much money was given to help the helpless?'

Simon had been talking with the duty sergeant in his office when the Rubai party entered the police station. He was surprised but not intimidated by the mass arrival. He put on a convincing show of affability.

'Abel, Reuben, surprised, not at all, but I was beginning to get anxious that there might have been an accident.'

'No accident, but we are a little behind schedule. But I am looking forward to meeting some of your friends. Perhaps we could start at once.'

'Homer, in here. Look after the place while I help to escort our distinguished guests around next door.

'I must explain, Abel, Reuben, that we have the sergeant with us as a precaution. Some of our boys can become agitated when they see a group of strange men on their … territory. Women never seem to trouble them. I can't explain that one, I'm afraid.'

The tour was brief. The party proceeded slowly into the large field where most of the patients congregated after breakfast. Most of them were preoccupied with what was happening in their own internal worlds. Some waved a friendly greeting. One or two tried to initiate a conversation but were ignored.

'Papa, why do you think they are all wearing these absurd little green tunics?'

Simon interrupted with an answer.

'They like them. They are easy to put on and it gives them a sense of unity.'

Abel was shocked by the sight of so many odd-looking characters gathered in one place.

'This is disgusting. What good does it do to lump together so many misfits. Give money to a place like this? I'd close it down and send them back to their families where they could receive some proper care. This is not the African way!'

'But, Abel, most of them have no families. That's why they are here in the first place.'

'I won't accept that European talk, the rubbish you can expect to hear from those ... idealists, to use a kind word, who have joined up with irritating groups like Serena.'

Abel fixed Simon with a challenging glare. 'Simon, where do you stand on this? Have you crossed over?'

'Become a traitor!'

'Reuben, shut up!'

'You don't trust me? I've given forty years loyal service to this party. I was working for KANU before you were born. I'm shocked, insulted.'

'Papa, I don't want a turncoat like this taking me around this town.'

Simon was playing a dangerous game and Abel had deep suspicions. While he admired Simon's bold defiance, it was not an attitude he could tolerate. Small infections could fester and spread quickly. But with the sergeant, an unknown quantity, present, he might have to cut his losses to prevent himself losing face. Simon had shown his hand by not denying a connection with Serena. Simon Nyache had sealed his fate. Abel could tolerate a brief delay. Yes, that was the way it would be. He announced a change of plan.

'So we will put off the tour. I have other business in the

district. Thank you, Simon, for your help. I now have a clearer perspective on one or two important issues. We will talk soon, Nairobi next time. Just let me know when you're in town next. Thank you, too, Sergeant. You seem to run a good station. Well done! If you will excuse me, I must speak to my boys in the second car.'

Abel was away less than five minutes. On his return, Simon Nyache was nowhere to be seen. The old fellow had outwitted him again.

'Sergeant, which way did he go?'

'He usually takes the back road which brings him straight out on the A104.'

'Have you got any cars out there that could pick him up?'

'Why would I want to pick him up?'

'Fool, I want him picked up!'

'Oh yes?' The tall, burly policeman sneered before striding away back to his office.

When he spoke to his boys a second time, Abel barked his instructions quickly and in a businesslike way.

'Get him! When you join the main road, there's a coach stop. Ask which way the red car went. Make sure you get this right. Nakuru, probably …'

Abel had guessed wrong, but the driver of the Mercedes was soon on the right track in pursuit of the terrified old man who was driving too fast and was praying aloud that he would reach his safe haven in Londiani along these rough back roads. 'Stop looking in the mirror, you old fool. Hit one big stone and you're finished!'

Meanwhile Abel was enjoying the ride along a familiar road. His mood was mellow. Those three boys were among his best and they would not fail him. He expected that he would soon be listening to a short item of news on KBS: 'We regret to announce the death of the popular and long-serving MP for Nakuru South. It seems that he was on his way to Naivasha when his car struck a tree. It is thought that no other vehicle was involved.'

And the old exhilaration was back. He presumed that hunters out on safari had something of the same thrill when they were on the trail of a dangerous animal. All the better that he never got his hands dirty. He considered that his kill was more practical, the elimination of an enemy who displeased him, rather than the execution of an innocent, often beautiful, creature.

'Papa, this isn't the quickest way home.'

'I thought you would like to look around part of your territory. What do you think, boy?'

'It's messy. The buildings are a shambles, but, okay, it's Kenya.'

'When your mother and I first came up this way, Gilgil was a lot smaller.'

'Why are we going back to Pembroke?'

'Got it at last.'

'Papa, why do you enjoy making out I'm a fool. I hate it when you call me "boy"!'

'You know, I never should have sent Julius to this place. I hope the headmaster will be around. Got some business to finish.'

* * *

'It's like this, Mister Foster. Those brass plaques on the wall in the chapel.'

'Memorials to boys who died before their time. Almost all violent deaths.'

'Got a hardworking girl to look after them? Shines the ass off the metal. I want her to shine a plaque in memory of my boy, Julius. Murder counts as a violent death, I suppose?'

'We never include the cause of death. Too painful for relatives. Morbid, too.'

'I'll pay extra.'

'Mister Rubai!'

'Thought not. Squeamish Europeans. Don't like the blood and guts, but that's all right. I want whatever you'll allow. Looking for closure. My wife and I have a new Julius, just a few weeks old. Perhaps you think that's morbid as well. Death, never pleasant but sometimes necessary, don't you think? Forgive me. My mind is elsewhere. Time to go home.'

* * *

Simon was on the downward slope and travelling even faster. The strain of concentrating so long was giving him a headache. 'At least you've still got a head to have an ache. Thank the Lord for a few trees. Ten k to go and still no sign of them. What if they aren't there at all?'

He decided to cross a narrow verge onto the main road. There were less than five kilometres to the turn-off. He looked behind to see that the road was empty, was empty until in the distance that black shape appeared, coming up fast. Without even thinking, he pulled out behind a truck loaded with charcoal spluttering along towards Nairobi. Simon whooped with delight as he slipped by safely well out of the way of the coach approaching him speeding to its destination up-country. How would the speedy black boy deal with that?

When he glanced in his mirror next, the Mercedes was coming up on the inside of the charcoal truck. The turn-off was just ahead, but so was the line of traffic completing its descent of the Escarpment. Two matatus sped by. Was there a safe gap in front of the lumbering milk truck? Hardly bearing to keep his eyes open, Simon swung the wheel hard.

The squeal of his skid as the car glided sideways towards the verge of the local road impressed the crowd standing around the crossroads, but the explosive thud of metal smashing into metal two seconds later did not.

# Chapter Thirty-one

Bertie Briggs, with the MP for Nakuru South sitting dazed at his side, arrived at Londiani in the early afternoon. His Pajero had Simon Nyache's car in tow and he drove straight to a newly restored motor pool on the farm side. John Marang who had steered the car in had been waiting in line with Bertie to join the A104. They had witnessed the crazy turn of the old man. How had he missed the bulk of the speeding milk tanker? That image was wiped out by the shocking sight of the full-on collision that happened a moment later when a black Mercedes was flung into the air and landed on the opposite verge to Simon.

Bertie and John leapt down onto the road and ran to the car that had been tipped on its side with the engine still being revved furiously. John reached across through the open window and switched off. Half a dozen young men righted the car. Just months before, a few kilometres up the Escarpment, Bertie had witnessed a semitrailer sliding out of control into three loaded matatus with the resulting horrific deaths of thirty-seven men and women. Body parts were scattered everywhere. Here, the three passengers, unconscious and probably dead, had suffered no obvious injuries. The front door opened easily for John.

'Bwana, look at this car! Hardly damaged. These boys could be just sleeping.'

'Bloody amazing! They almost got away with it.'

'Hey! See the driver of the other car. I think I know that man. Bwana Nyache, he don't look too good, bending over his car like that.'

'Go and check, John. Be there in a second. You chaps, help me get these three boys out. I know a bit of first aid. Perhaps we can do something to help. Then I'll phone the police.'

The last of the three smartly dressed young men was being laid out in the shade of a tree. 'Any of them still alive?'

'We don't know, Bwana. They are warm but …'

'Let me take a look.'

Bertie tried to find a pulse, then bent over to look for a heartbeat. He could detect nothing.

'Anyone recognise them, any of them?'

'Nairobi men working for some big boss down there.'

Bertie sat on the grass and dialled a number on his phone.

'Naivasha police station … There's been a bad accident on the edge of town … Any chance of an ambulance, just in case … okay. You'll be twenty minutes? Listen, Sergeant. I can't stay. Simon Nyache is across the road. I'm sure he was involved in the smash … Just shaken this time, I think. I know how careful you are about fingerprints, but I can't leave possible evidence lying around, can I? Okay, I'll do that and see you at the station later. I think we can't do anything to help.'

John was back and smiling. 'He's fine. He asked me to check if he was still alive. And he saw you had the four-wheel drive. He wants a tow.'

'John, get me a bag from the back of the vehicle. Make that two. Oh, John boy, what we do we do here?'

Bertie made one more stop before driving home. He bought a couple of cans of oil at the Shell station and dialled another number.

'Caroline? Bertie Briggs here. There's been a shocker of an accident on the road, just opposite Delamere's. You're at Londiani? No, it's all right. Your people are on to it. I've got something to show you. Afraid I've bent the law a bit. Anyway, see you in a minute.'

Simon had got used to being alive again, but his legs were unsteady when he slid down onto the concrete apron where Bertie had parked. He was breathing hard but happy.

'Look at these hands. I don't think they'll stop trembling for hours. God knows what my heart is doing.' He leaned against Bertie's car. 'I'm too old for these tricks. Look, I need some air. Can we walk over to the house?'

'If you feel up to it.'

At times it was more a stagger than a walk. Simon held tight onto Bertie's arm, moving slowly and thanking out loud a long list of beings, human and otherwise, for saving him, 'delivering me from evil!'

As they rounded the corner from the laundry garden to the front of the house, there was a surprise waiting. Bertie recognised the Welshmens' car. They had been due to set off for Gilgil a few minutes behind him. No doubt they had turned back when they saw that the road ahead was blocked at the crossroads. It was not the sight of the car that was the surprise but its additional two passengers. Two heavily-built young men were being carried up the veranda steps and laid out on two trestle tables.

'Almost Doctor' Iolo was in charge. He was shouting orders and constantly moving from one table to the other.

'Why can't you find a decent hospital when you need one? It's a miracle that these two are still breathing, Come on, Iolo boy! Just give it your best shot. Two volunteer nurses, please! Angela and Lydia, come around here! Thank God they were wearing their belts.'

Darkness was falling before the stories of the day's events were pieced together into a coherent whole. Inspector Caroline had been shuttling between Big House, her station, the accident scene and Naivasha Hospital.

'One sad piece of news. The other young man in the Mercedes is in the hospital morgue. The driver of the milk tanker has a few bruises and a sprained wrist. A big thank you to Iolo. You can drop the "almost" from now on! And to Angelo Conti, for coming down.'

'Lucky I was still on the Escarpment when I got the call. Another awful mess on our roads. That young man saved two lives with his very last action on this earth. Those other two? They'll live if we can get them to a decent operating theatre soon. David Daniels is willing to take them. I think we'll have risk travelling in the dark. But I understand that this is no straightforward story.'

An exhausted Simon Nyache lay back in an armchair with his head in his hands.

'My fault. One dead for sure and these two ... Doctor, I hope you are right.'

'Nonsense, Simon. Those three characters weren't after you to invite you out for a drink. Speaking for myself, I'm damn glad that you're here and not lying out on some hillside, another name ticked off on Rubai's hit list.'

'But surely there was some other way.'

'Yeah, right! Stop this madman dead in his tracks.'

'Alex is right, Simon. And the stuff we found on them could do just that. Paul has been on the phone. He and Daniel are on their way. Simon, check me on the story. We need to get it right for our lawyers. They think it could be our big breakthrough.'

* * *

'Unbelievable, Caroline. Simon, one thing still puzzles me. Why did you arrange to meet Rubai when you knew he was after you?'

'Paul, I am a stupid old man. I did not believe that he would turn up at the hospital. Incidentally, he hated the place. Said it should be shut down. But, Maria, you understand these things. Tell me who it was driving that car of mine?'

'Well, the first thought that comes into my mind is that it was Simon Nyache. There are witnesses. But witnesses rarely notice the higher self when He is at work. Of course, I would not advise you get ideas about entering the Safari Rally!'

'And where's your wife?'

'Safe with her sister in Nairobi, thanks to our good friend, the *Eldoret Express*.'

'Good. Rubai will know something has gone wrong. He probably passed the accident on his way home. I understand that there are some bits of interesting information. Could be very useful. I can give you some news. The "trial" is just weeks away.'

'Where is it going to be?'

'A bit complicated. Of course, we have to make sure that Rubai has no idea what's going on. Thanks to some quick thinking this afternoon, our case is stronger than ever. Tom, it could be in Nairobi, but we think it doesn't have to be in the normal court.'

Daniel took over.

'We've got Barnie on the job. He's checking on that. He says that Rubai's house could be an option. Wouldn't that be great? Bertie, great stuff! Thank John when you see him.

'Paul and I haven't met you boys from the "Land of Song". It's all right. I'm no brainbox, just a big fan of your Bryn

Terfyl! I know one of you is a doctor. But why didn't you take them to the hospital?'

'We did!' Ivor was still in shock about how they were received there. 'They took the corpse, no trouble, but they wanted fifty thousand up front, each, mind before they would take the other two! Rebecca, your hospital can't come quick enough!'

A thoughtful Rafaella aired her growing sense of confidence.

'Don't you feel that things are beginning to fall into place? Maria, is this what you have been trying to tell us all along?'

'The light on the path is becoming stronger. We are the sharp blade of a long spear. You are right, Rafaella. Hosea and I talked last night about how everything that has happened in these last weeks is part of an invisible driving force.'

'Maria, I'd like to plunge that spear straight into the heart of a certain person. Thank God he didn't get you, Simon, but those three young men ...'

'They had a choice, Bertie.'

'Yes, Tom, but poor boys ...'

Caroline returned to the room with Hosea, each of them carrying thick sheaves of paper.

'We've got copies of everything. We can take these two down to David now. Hosea is going to take my Volvo, again! Maria?'

'I've pressed his uniform.'

'And I'll follow, just in case.'

'Thanks, Angelo. Daniel and I will stay so that the rest of us can examine these papers together. One more thing. We need a volunteer to take this wallet back to the hospital. Sooner or later Rubai is going to catch up with that body.'

# Chapter Thirty-two

The Rubai machine had been in overdrive for several hours. Around the table in his conference room in the Pink Palace had gathered six security men and the chief of police for a night of hard work.

'Gentlemen, I propose we begin at the scene of the accident and move on from there.'

Abel, as usual, was selective in the information he passed on to supposedly trusted men who were trying to solve what was, essentially, his own personal problem. So there was no mention of failed phone calls to his men out on the road, nor a whisper of what they were doing out there.

Chief Shadrack Karui made his contribution.

'A report from Inspector Caroline Miggot of Nakuru Division: "An anonymous report from a member of the public alerted us to the news of the accident. Within minutes …"'

'How many minutes?'

'That is not stated here, sir. "Unfortunately there was no ambulance available to bring any dead and injured to the hospital. However, when our sergeant and constable arrived on the scene, there was no sign of any of the, we believe, three passengers who had been travelling in the Mercedes that we discovered, on inquiry, was owned by Mister Abel Rubai of Karen."'

'Blah, blah, blah. The next thing you are going to say is that inquiries are continuing and in about three weeks … Listen, we know that my three boys were lying on the side of the road. There were witnesses. Next minute, there is just one. Two disappear. How? Where? No witnesses. Did those two get up and walk away?'

'Sir, everyone who saw the crash said that the turn in front of the truck was suicidal.'

'Karui, are you telling me that fifty, a hundred Kenyans walked away from the free show of a terrible car crash? Unbelievable!'

Abel, intense with anger, glared at each of the security men in turn.

'The best in the business!'

The nominal leader of the security men, Colin Sitawi, had had enough. They had been called in to deal with a problem that, at this stage, was purely a police matter. They were being made to look like a bunch of incompetent fools.

'With respect, this problem is not in our line of business. We could …'

'Not? So what do we pay you people to do?'

Sitawi closed his lips tight and stared down at the empty first page of his notebook. His pose was self-assured.

Abel would not admit it, but he saw that he had been too hasty in calling the meeting. When the six men had been dismissed and had left the house, he sat quietly stroking his chin. That the meeting had been a failure was down to him. He had his ideas on what could have happened. In some ways the McCall family could have been involved. He shook his head. Paranoia, surely. He could chance his arm and order Karui to send a squad of his toughest cops down there. He shook his head again. It was far too big a risk. The scenario was easy to imagine. Karui's men arrive, rough up a few locals and find nothing. But Karui was no fool. He just might see some connections. Why was the Big Man linking the McCalls with these missing men? And why had Rubai been down at Naivasha on the night that the farmhouse had blown up? Two o'clock in the morning and he just happened to be down there with a top class rifle in his hands? But Karui would not dare to share any suspicions that had dropped into his mind.

Abel saw that, for the moment at least, he was on his own. He could not share his problem. He would have to put everything else on hold and work on this single dangerous mess. Two of his men were out there, dead or alive. Worse still, Nyache was probably hidden away in some godforsaken hole in the bush. The old man was on the loose and out of his control. This was new territory for him.

But there was a consolation. He picked up a couple of cold beers from the fridge and shut himself up in his most private room. He switched on a bank of screens, not to work on the money markets but simply for company. And so the wrestling match began. He turned his thoughts loose and let them fight it out, with the single stipulation that at the end of the struggle he would have a solution that would be workable and offer him the chance to regain control.

Just before ten pm an exhilarated Abel entered the western sitting room. He was delighted to find Sally and Reuben together.

'Abel, I wasn't sure that you were still at home. You have so many meetings these days.'

'Wait until we move into State House. The first lady will be a very busy woman with lots of meetings of your own.'

She frowned at the prospect but was more concerned with an immediate problem.

'Reuben and I have been talking about the accident today. He is upset, but you tell your father, Reuben.'

'Those three, they were my age. They were full of fun. We were joking just before they set off for home. It's weird. One hour later and they were all dead.'

'Only one for sure, son. There's mystery about the others. I still have hopes. But I don't have any hopes for that silly old man, Nyache. I think a lot of this is down to him. If he had kept his promise to show you around to the people up there, which was the plan ... But I've got an idea. I am also very hungry. Do you think it's too late for some supper, Sally? We could talk about it then.'

* * *

'Well, what do you think? We'll make our own tour of the region, all of us. You know how the little ones are always asking me to buy one of those stretch limos. And it would be Julius's first time out of Karen.'

'No tricks about buying flower farms, Abel!'

'A fun day out, David's preferred way of life.'

'But when?'

'What about tomorrow, Reuben? You're the key man here. I'm going to be busy later in the week. And, Sally, you could make a quick call on Maura McCall. Show off Julius and your war wound.'

'War wound? Oh, yes. Hey, Abel, you are in a good mood tonight!'

'Well, it's a long time since we all went out as a family.'

'As long as we don't have to visit that loony bin again!'

As the Rubai family was enjoying a congenial supper and making plans for the next day, less than half a mile away an old Volvo Estate, with Hosea Kabari at the wheel, was passing through the gates of Cartref. Stretched out on blankets in the back were two young men.

# Chapter Thirty-three

'But what else could I say, Alex?'

'Maura, Sally and the kids are fine and you women will be drooling over the baby, but I don't fancy another meeting with that shameless thug and his demented son. Perhaps they're coming to ask for forgiveness again!'

'Spare us! And what was it, two hours notice? And, naturally, he gets his wife to do the phoning.'

'We'll be all right, Tom. I'll be over the fields and you and Rebecca will be at the site. Debbie coming with you?'

'Yep. Two truckloads of materials are due at eleven. Jim Sawyer has taken all his boys over. They're pouring concrete. That's why Debbie left early.'

'Tom, I wonder what his real motive for coming is.'

'I think that's an easy one. He'll be sniffing around, looking for Simon.'

'And his two "missing" boys. Could be doing it in his trousers on that one. Have we got the old bugger on the run at last?'

'I doubt it. One slip up, one loose word on our side and the fox will be in with the chickens again.'

* * *

No sign of the father and his sons. Abel Rubai saw this as good news. They were keeping away from him. Probably had something to hide.

'Sally, Obi's taking me and Reuben over to the Shell garage. They've taken the damaged Mercedes there.'

The men were away for two hours. Abel was surprised with the state of the car. It was not a write-off.

'Tow it into the agent in Nairobi. Send the bill to my office, unless you want the cash now.'

Next stop was meant to be the site of the accident, but Obi pulled off onto the verge half a mile short of the junction.

'Boss, take a look to the right. A lot of folks over there are busy, busy, busy.'

'You two, stay inside.'

Abel stepped out and leaned his elbows on the car roof. He took in the activity with a narrowed gaze. The hard hats made it difficult to identify people moving in and out of the trucks and the machinery.

'Yeah, of course, the Florence Nightingale of Naivasha, but the other bitch, flashing the site plan around? Never seen her before. Old Sawyer. Mmn. I'll remember this Mister Building Man! And one, two, three white boys. Must be the illegals. I'm impressed. No idling there. Shame they'll soon be tearing it all up. Ah, well, can't say you weren't warned, you bunch of losers!'

At the turn-off there was plenty of evidence to show where the milk truck had hit his car less than twenty-four hours earlier – skid marks, bits of metal and plastic, the rearranged branches of a couple of trees. But he discovered nothing to help him with the mystery of the disappearance of his boys. In a lull in the traffic he clapped his hands and called out.

'Any of you people here yesterday when the accident

happened?! I'll pay for information! Come on! Come on! We're not the cops! Come on, you faceless country boys!' He waited, he glared, all in vain. 'Obi, get me out of this jinxed town.'

There was one more call to make before he returned to Londiani. He stormed up the steps of the town council offices and threw his weight around the central office.

'So sorry, sir, we are just office staff. We cannot ...'

'The name's Rubai, Abel Rubai.'

'We know, sir.'

'A very angry Abel Rubai. One of you write this down and pass it on to the first of your bosses who shows his face in this place: "Take a good look at what is going on in a field on the edge of your town here. This is an illegal build, as you should know. Let me know when the land has been restored to its proper state. That had better be sooner rather than later!"'

* * *

Sally saw that the children were unhappy to be going home early.

'But, Papa, we haven't been to the lake to see the hippos. Can we stay the night? We could camp out on that big field.'

'Hasn't Mama told you that the hippos come out of the water in the night? They sniff around all over the place. They would come and check out something new, like a tent they had never seen before.'

Sally was relieved. It was her first long outing since Julius had been born. She had been up early and the journey had been tiring. She made a mental note not to try another family outing until Julius was walking and talking.

Obi was a fine driver and gave them a smooth ride. The

children were more subdued than on the journey up and Sally was happy to come to the last crossroads before home. She glanced to her left.

'Abel, they say that the Daniels family have a beautiful garden and it is so close. Do you think they might invite us over? You know how Europeans love to have company when they, how do they say, "take tea".'

'Perhaps, but could we leave it for a time, until Julius is going to secondary school? I don't think I could find much to interest me in that place.'

# Chapter Thirty-four

Counting Sonya, there were five doctors in the Daniels family. All of them went out to meet the old Volvo Estate that arrived late into the evening of the day of the accident at the junction of the A104 and the lower turn-off into Naivaisha town. The two unconscious men were unloaded and transferred to the Daniels' private surgery. Work began at once. The large table that dominated that cool, airy room was wide enough to take two patients so that both men were stripped and examined simultaneously.

At Londiani Angelo Conti had been able to do no more than general first aid to prepare them for the potentially hazardous sixty-mile journey on less than perfect roads.

Sergeant Hosea had gone with Dorothy Daniels to the sitting room of Cartref, prepared for a long wait for news. Maria had gone in with a team of doctors. She had no formal medical qualifications, but all the trained and experienced people in that room welcomed her presence. They knew all about her healing gifts and her spiritual insight. If nothing else she would be a calming influence at a critical time.

It was soon agreed that one problem for both men was severe concussion. And David had a technical question for Maria.

'Do you know whether they were wearing their belts at the moment of impact?'

'Bertie, who was first on the scene, is definite on that. They were all strapped in.'

David was constantly on the move between patients. There was a great deal of very close observation and gentle manipulation of flesh and bone, particularly of the joints. Talk was in whispers and the preliminary work was painstakingly thorough. David, who was one of the best surgeons in Africa, with a reputation for very still hands and his unobtrusive work with the scalpel, was never eager to get to work with the knife.

'I've seen too many patients go down because the surgeon was too ready to get inside their patient to look around.'

But with those two strong young men everyone agreed that an entry must be made, and soon.

'There's blood sloshing around somewhere in this one. If we can't stop it soon, he'll be gone.'

Gareth was the Daniels who found it most difficult to preserve proper medical neutrality when treating patients. This usually meant that he was tender and sometimes passionate in the face of sickness and disease. But, on the other hand …

'Leave the bastard go. I wonder how many decent Kenyans he has knocked over for that boss of his.'

'Gareth, moral decisions aren't part of our job spec, thank God!'

'Sonya, these two hulks and their late, unlamented partner were minutes away from killing an old man struggling to do right in his last days. Sorry, Dad!'

'Come over here. I need your steady hand.'

Both wounded men survived the trauma of the next three hours. They would live. Everyone was pleased, even Gareth Daniels.

The men would wake up in a world alien to their way of

life. In two days they would begin to regain their strength. That would create a new situation. How to deal with it was now on everyone's agenda. There were several possibilities to consider, but it was too early to plan details.

A new day was not far off when the team joined Dot and Hosea in the sitting room for refreshment and relaxation. Maria did not stay long.

'Hosea, you are on duty tomorrow, so you will need to set off early.'

'And, don't tell me! You will not be travelling with me. What did I say, Dorothy?'

'If that is not a trouble to you, Dorothy.'

'We love having you here. But won't you stay in the house?'

'I will return later. Someone needs to be with those boys. Kwaheri for now.'

The lights had been left on low in the surgery and the naked bodies draped in white sheets up to the neck. Maria set up a chair on the platform surrounding the table, intending to watch and listen. Perhaps there would be some movement, perhaps some words would be spoken out of the deep subconscious. At each corner of table she lit a fat candle that she had made. As well as light, they gave off a faint perfume of orange blossom.

Maria had sat up with sick or wounded people many times. Her practice was to be busily proactive. Normally she began by focusing on the light of one of the candles to help her with a meditation. From there she moved on to a period of silent prayer, directed at each young man in turn.

Anyone standing outside would have been aware of her presence in the surgery only when she began to sing. Sonya had been sitting on the wooden bench set close to the door all the time that Maria had been inside. She had come to comfort herself with memories. Simon's body had passed its last night on earth in that place. Maria had convinced Sonya with her teaching that the essence of her husband, what others called the soul, was waiting to cross over. Then, as now, the evocation was at its strongest when the ancient words and the beautiful melody filled the air.

Sonya was not surprised when she heard her name called out.

'Sonya, please come inside. These boys need the help of your courage and strength.'

The two women embraced and sat side by side on the comfortable blue sofa, placed against the wall to the side of the table, raised enough for them to see across the bodies stretched out there. For a time there was no sound apart from the night breeze passing through the trees in the garden outside. At last Sonya whispered.

'Do you think that they could be aware of this … this power surrounding them here?'

'More than us. They don't have the obstruction of the conscious body to block their lines.'

The last time she had been in this room, Sonya had been looking down on the dead body of her husband, killed by Rubai men. In front of her now were two more of his people, alive because of the skill and care of her family.

'Maria, why can't I hate these men? They came close to killing Simon Nyache. Perhaps at other times …'

'Because you have travelled a long way down the road. When pastors pray for their flocks, why do they focus so much on sin and failure? This week their words ask for forgiveness and protection from the same sins as they spoke of last week, last year. Where is the progress? Is there anyone out there listening to these words? Or anyone listening when answers come?'

'So there is no point in praying?'

'You know better than that. The mystery is deep. Our task is to enter that mystery and wait. So many clever people see no road and think that when we pray we are simply deluding ourselves in some harmless way.'

'So why can I feel no hate?'

'Because you love them!'

During the long silence the followed, Sonya left her seat to walk around the platform surrounding the table. She peered down into each face in turn.

'Perhaps I am blind, but I see no murderers here. Their faces remind me of my three when they are in a peaceful sleep.'

'When deep pain comes, sometimes, if your mind is strong, it creates in your heart a wellspring of joy.'

'What will happen to these two when they return to themselves?'

'Paul has asked me to call him when I think the time comes. You know that he is a compassionate man, but he is also one who has a passion for justice. If you had seen poor Simon when Bertie brought him back to Londiani ...'

'But the law says that, for what they did, they could hang. Perhaps Gareth was right. We should have let them go when they were unconscious.'

'No, Sonya. We must hear them before they go to the court.'

'If Rubai knew that they were in the house next door!'

* * *

'My name is Elias and that is my brother Samuel. The other person with us was Saul, our youngest. Our mother was crazy for the Bible, like many poor women in this country. Tell me, where are my clothes, our suits? The boss had us measured for them specially.'

'Elias, your clothes are safe. You have had a serious operation. Loose clothing will be more comfortable.'

'Is this a hospital?'

'Almost.'

'And you are a doctor?'

'No. My name is Paul. I'm a friend of the family.'

'A family lives in a hospital? Is Samuel going to die?'

'Not at all. You know what sedated means?'

'Like when you are on something. My head is not staying in one place. Is Saul somewhere in this hospital?'

Paul hesitated briefly. 'No, Saul is dead. You remember the accident?'

'I thought so. It is my fault. He is not the best driver. Too wild. This thing will hurt our mother very much. He was her baby.'

'Elias, we must wait for your brother to wake up. We'll have a talk together.'

'So you are a cop? The boss has told us what to do if we ever get picked up by you people.'

'I am not a cop. And this lady is my sister, Maria. And standing by your brother, Sonya, one of the doctors who saved your life.'

Maria explained some practical details. 'Some comfortable chairs are being brought. And some food and drink.'

'You mean a Tusker?'

'Not quite yet. Your bodies are weak. This drink will have the vitamins you need.'

'So where is the catch, lady? Listen, my head feels like it's been hit by some big piece of wood, but the old brain is still working. I won't say nothing, drink nothing until my brother is here by my side.'

In the Pink Palace the next morning, the third email in

Abel's inbox at first startled him and then sent him into a rage. He was not used to having his commands dismissed lightly by petty bureaucrats. He had left a message for the Naivasha town council instructing them to get busy with the job of putting an end to the illegal attempt to put up a private hospital on the edge of town. The reply, in the name of the town's headman, was clear: 'We were so sorry to have missed you when you honoured us with a visit to our office recently. We noted your request, but we are sure you will understand that we intend to allow the building work to continue in accordance with a newly instituted local by-law that encourages sponsors to offer and support charitable causes that will benefit the local community. No doubt you will be pleased that the funds that our MP has requested from the government in Nairobi for the last twenty years will now be available for projects elsewhere.'

After a fifth reading of this graceless piece of impudence, Abel's rage was in the process of being transmuted into a decisive course of action. First he got his secretary to check that the message was genuine.

'Sir, it is from the council in Naivasha. I was told to inform you that the message itself was composed by a Mordecai Chambers, a writer/farmer who owns a block of land on the opposite side of town to the future hospital.'

Abel Rubai was not having a good week. There were no leads in the search for his two missing boys. And now some jumped-up local nobodies were spitting in his face by refusing point-blank to take his advice on a matter involving the law of the land. So they get some Jew boy who can string a few words together to do the dirty work, at some special price, of course.

*We never had trouble in that place until the singing whore came along. Now the fools have fallen for her. They can't see the Europeans pushing her on behind the scenes.* He slapped his hands together in triumph. *Got it!* It was so obvious. Why had he not worked it out before? They were pitching to win the election!

It was time to put an end to this nonsense, time to wrest back control. A plan was suggesting itself in the back of his mind. Give him an hour or two and he would have it worked out. Whatever it turned out to be he knew that he would have to hit hard and hit soon.

* * *

While he waited for a message from his sister to tell him that the second patient in the surgery was wholly back in the land of the living, Paul was talking with Daniel and his own brother, Barnaby, a successful lawyer from Boston.

'Daniel, do you still think it a good idea that just one of us confronts those two?'

'Paul, you are forgetting Maria is in there with you. She'll be better than any of us in getting them to cooperate. She's got the touch.'

'Oh, I haven't forgotten. What a sister, Barney! Yes, the gift, but I'm still not sure what it is. She loves people and … they understand that and warm to her. And she never gives up on anybody.'

Barnie pressed a large piece of paper flat onto the table. 'This is the list of headings of charges we have so far. If we get a fair shake in court, we'll nail him to the floor.'

'If they let us get him to a court, Barnie.'

'Right, Dan, our biggest problem by far. Marion says I'm worrying her with my worrying! I have these visions of a couple of brave policemen going up to him in the street: "Abel

Rubai, we are arresting you on the following charges …" Two fewer constables on the streets!'

'Sure, but if we get these two to sing, then they will be our most potent witnesses.'

'Assuming we can hide the pair of them until the trial.'

'And assuming his lawyers don't wipe them out in cross-examination.'

'And assuming that they'll even be willing to testify in the first place!'

* * *

'Paul, the boys want us to call them Eli and Sammy.'

'Good. More relaxed. Must say that you seem very relaxed, too, in those armchairs.'

'How much drugs did that doctor pump into us?'

'Maria, any idea? You were there all the time when David and the team were working.'

'Team?'

'Five altogether. A big accident needs a big team. All of them are from one family. One of them had her husband murdered just weeks ago. You must have heard about that.'

Sammy stirred from his torpor, leaning forward in his chair and pointing aggressively at Paul.

'Yeah, and Eli says that Saul is dead. Our brother was just a kid.'

Maria broke in with a raised voice and her eyes focusing her anger on each brother in turn.

'Listen a moment. Your brother and you two had a choice up to the last seconds when you collided with the truck. You were chasing an old man with orders from that person you call the boss. It is easy to guess what those orders were. Then your time of choice was over. You were close to being dead meat yourselves. Other people had a choice. You could say that they could have let you die, but they chose life for you, for you! Do you understand? In a few days you will be able to walk and go on your way.'

Like a fellow musician, Paul took up the theme from his sister and elaborated on it.

'Gentlemen, prepare yourselves to stand before a judge. As a lawyer I have to say that you must expect a verdict of guilty!'

'You don't scare us. We'll have protection. If we ever do get to that court, that judge, we know we will walk away.'

'Mmn, interesting that word protection! Let me give you more information. Sammy, when Eli asked me if this place was a hospital, I replied that it was "almost a hospital". The truth is that this is a special surgery, in a house where doctors live, doctors and the kindest people you could meet. They saved your lives. This house is in Karen. The Daniels family has a famous neighbour, a very rich man. He has very many men working for him. He likes them to wear smart, dark grey suits and to ride about in black Mercedes cars.' He paused for the information to sink in. 'This man is searching for two young men. They were in a car accident and they have disappeared. We think that he might be looking for them because he wants to give them … protection. You just used the same word.'

'Paul and I are sorry to have tired you with so much talk, but you have just had a life-changing experience. Do you know …'

'Yes, we know. We are not fools. And this mysterious man. Abel Rubai …'

'And, Eli, this is the boss you spoke of.'

'It is. You have said many things to us. We have a small

thing to tell you. Our parents live in Thika. They have a small farm there. They grow pineapples and vegetables. Ten years ago, when we lived in Kibera, our father gambled, with money he did not have. Some tough guys from Mombasa Road said they would kill him if he would not pay. Father had the green fingers and two days a week he worked in the garden of the Rubai family before they moved to Karen. He took us there to help sometimes.'

'Mama Sally liked Saul. He made her laugh with his stories. One day she did not laugh.'

'Sammy is right. He said to her: "Memsahib, men are coming to our house to kill Papa." When we got home Papa beat Saul with a big stick. We all cried, even Mama.'

'Next day a stranger came to tell us the money was paid.'

'Rubai?'

'Yes, madam. After that Papa did more work for the new boss, not often in the garden now. For five years all was well. One night Papa returned home drunk. Another man was in the house. There was a fight. Our Papa killed the other man with a panga and ran off. After two weeks, Papa returned and said we were moving to a farm in a new place. We brothers never went to school again. We were very happy. We were doing men's things. One year ago we learned to drive a vehicle.

'"Big strong men should always look smart!" The boss's son told us this, the one who was killed on the golf course. Obi, the main driver, took care of us and we were sometimes the backup men on big jobs.'

'This week, I forget how many days ago, we were at the police station in Gilgil …'

'And the boss told you that you must drive after the old man.'

'Who will tell our mother about Saul?'

Maria stood behind the brothers and pressed her hands into their shoulders. 'I will do it today. This will be the worst news she will ever have. I am a mother and I know this. Tell me where the farm is. I will tell her that you are safe and well.'

'We are going to give you a break from all this talk. You need a rest. When I was a boy, I fell from a tree and broke my leg.'

'And he slept for two days. I remember. I was his nurse.'

'You will leave us on our own? What if we just walk out?'

'Then you could go home and tell your mother about Saul yourselves!'

* * *

The only sound disturbing the peace of the surgery was the rasping snore of Sammy Akamba. Eli smiled and shook his head.

'Lucky again, Sammy. We've just lost our baby brother and we are too scared to go home and tell our mother. But you are lost in a dream. I wonder if it's a good-looking woman or a cold Tusker!'

Eli cleared his throat noisily and then clapped his hands without rousing his brother. A single sharp call of 'Sammy' close to his face did the trick.

When he was fully himself, Sammy rubbed his eyes and gave Eli a hurt look. 'Not nice! I think I was enjoying a happy dream and you drag me back to this hellhole!'

'That's the point, Sammy. Is this a hellhole or a safe hiding place?'

'What are you on about now?'

'Just that we are on our own now. Do we try to get out, or do we stay?'

'You decide. You're the brains. I don't care any more.'

'Okay. We have a choice. Rubai lives close by. He is looking for us. Perhaps we could manage to make it over there. Or we could phone for him to get us picked up. See, I still have my phone.'

Sammy pondered briefly. 'We don't feel too good now. He won't want us around. Mama will have three dead sons by nightfall, two of us out in some forest. What's the other choice?'

'Stay. These people want us alive. God knows why. Maybe they think we can help them to hurt Rubai in some way. Witnesses, I suppose.'

'No choice! I hope the food's good.'

* * *

'Paul, Mary phoned half an hour ago. I wanted us to talk before we replied. She will be in her office until six.'

'How did she sound, Daniel? If we've got the vibes wrong on this we'll be in very deep dudu.'

'You know Mary, Paul. The youngest high court judge in the country has got to watch her back. She was … pleasantly formal. "I understand you and Paul Miller are asking me for some legal advice. Strange question from the two best brains in our year in law school!"'

'Daniel, I say we take a walk around the garden for a few minutes, clear the tubes.'

'Mary, Paul Miller here … Yes, Daniel's listening in … Yes, a big problem. We want to know what someone on the bench would advise … No, it wouldn't work over the phone. Mary, perhaps it wouldn't be wise for you to be seen talking to us, not around Nairobi anyway. Okay, we won't move for the next half hour. Thank you, Mary.'

'You know, Paul, I have a sneaking feeling that she's still very much our Mary from the old days, always ready for some excitement.

'Excitement with a wig on!'

Twenty minutes later Paul and Daniel were checking out with each other the plan that Mary M'Tambo had given them.

'Let's get this clear. It's Mary's daughter's birthday this coming Thursday. The girl's husband is driving the three of them out to lunch.'

'You know that place, Daniel, Elementeita Lodge?'

'Didn't we have lunch there one time? Perfect place, well off the road, not too many visitors.'

'And a taxi driver she can trust. I had visions of us disguising ourselves and taking a matatu. Stop laughing. We couldn't take our cars, now could we?'

'Sure, but you as a bent old man with grey hair and a walking stick.'

'And you, a woman of the night. You always said you had nice legs.'

'Yeah, for a soccer player!'

* * *

'Daniel, Paul, my daughter Elizabeth and her husband, Jonathan. Paul and Daniel, the smartest students in our time at law school. How was the ride?'

'Marvellous! Emmanuel, best driver I've ever ridden with.'

'And Paul and I are often up this way. We are on the road too much, but with the election coming up …'

Jonathan, tall and skinny like a middle distance runner but with the heavy spectacles more typical of a successful manager of the Westlands branch of Barclays, was eager to make a point.

'It may sound a bit childish, but you two are my nomination for top men in the country. You are truly heroes.'

Paul and Daniel swapped amused grins.

'Paul, shall we ask him to put that in writing?'

'Sure. We could put it on our posters. Not everyone sees us like that.'

'Elizabeth and I are both members.'

As Jonathan spoke, Paul was watching Mary closely for any hint of a reaction. The eyes were impassive. He was encouraged that there was no sign of disapproval.

Lunch was taken on the veranda on an end table.

'The English, or was it Irish, lord chose the best spot on his estate to build his farmhouse, as usual.'

'Mama, imagine waking up to this view every morning. Pity Papa couldn't come today.'

'I wouldn't complain too much. Don't forget he's taking us out to dinner tonight because he wanted to play some important golf match this morning. The way he talks about them, they all seem important to me. Anyway, he's seen this view several times. He and Lord Delamere's Nose are on nodding acquaintance.

Though the restaurant and hotel were hidden behind rising ground, travellers moving up and down the A104 could see the soda lake and brilliant white shoreline with the extra treat that day of the ring of flamingos feeding around the margin.

As the young couple made their way down the grassy slope towards the monument and the lake itself, the three lawyers watched in a silence broken eventually by Mary.

'So, you two, what is the advice you want from me that you

cannot mention over the phone? More intriguing, why can we not speak about it in the normal, everyday manner?'

'Mary, it's a delicate matter.'

'I can see that, Daniel, but if you were pleading in front in a courtroom, I would be urging you to get on with the business, more expeditiously!'

'Yes, your worship! There is a case we want to bring to court involving, shall we say, a big man in this country. We know that there will be massive opposition.'

'Paul, the name!'

'Rubai!'

'Thank God! At last someone who is ready to rid our country of this scourge.'

She moved to grasp their hands and responded to their smiles though a lens of tears.

'No need to ask if the case is watertight, but you know that there is much danger here, too. Our strategy must be irresistible. But what a lovely place for us to begin our adventure. I've been hoping for a long time and many others as well. When I received your call …'

'Mary, our big problem will be getting him in front of a judge.'

'True, Daniel. But I know several judges who will be ready to take this on.'

'And thousands of supporters for the Big Man, ready to block us. Good logistics will be almost as important as good evidence.'

Mary shuddered as she punched her fist into her palm. 'We are going to win. I can feel it.'

'You sound as confident as my sister, Maria!'

'And, weeks ago now, Joshua Gombo said to contact him if we needed help.'

'He'd give Rubai a fair trial. Great choice.'

* * *

'Did you really go to Thika? Just three hours all that way?'

'I had a lift from Doctor Sonya. Your mother already knew about Saul. I don't have to tell you who told her?'

'Did he go himself?'

Maria's reply came in the arching of her eyebrows and a dismissive gesture with the palms of her hands.

'But she knows you are safe. That news brought out the smiles and the tears. She hates Abel Rubai, but you know that already. She's a lovely lady. I wanted to stay and talk, but she hurried me off, to check that her boys were all right.'

'Who are you anyway?'

'My name is Maria Kabari and my husband is a sergeant … in the Kenya police.'

'Ah, so you are keeping watch until he comes to arrest us!'

'I am also a healer. No one is coming to arrest you, but I want you to tell me about yourselves.'

'We already have told you about the past. The future, easy. Right, Sammy?'

'Yes. We walk across the road and report to the boss. He gets one of his boys to put one between our eyes. Most people think we are dead already.'

'Your mother knows better.'

'So says the healer woman, whatever that is. She and her friends want us to tell stories about the boss, probably to some old judge. That way we get to live a bit longer.'

'Right, Eli. That way we have company when we go down. Ever see a lion and his mate chasing after a wart-hog? Ever see the wart-hog win, even get away?'

'The boss knows all the moves, has all the top people, hit men, lawyers, you name it. Most of all he has the cash.'

'I agree. Everything you say is right. We want to get him, but we can't. His ship has all the big guns!'

'Memsahib, you are one very weird woman, but you're good-looking …'

'And you make us laugh.'

'Do you boys ever watch the television?'

'Course we do! Every day when we're not on a job. We love action movies, plenty of bang-bang and blood.'

'Ever seen real life stories? Say, someone climbing Everest or going to the moon? Or ever heard the story of Goliath and David?'

'Is that the same one as David and Goliath?'

'Sammy, you are such a idiot sometimes!'

'No, Eli. Sammy's right to check. The point is most of us would say: "Leave me out of that stuff. It is exciting but too dangerous. I can't do it!" But what if you could have people to try these things with you? We know the risks, but we feel something in the corner of our brains telling us that we can win.'

'So?'

'So your mother just lost her boy, Saul, because he took a risk for a bad thing. Would she want you to go over to the Rubai place and say: "Okay, Boss, we hear you been looking for us. Here we are"?'

The glum but thoughtful expressions encouraged Maria.

'But what would Mama Akamba think if she knew you were taking a risk for a good thing, with lots of people with you, all in it together? And you people just felt in the corner of your brains that you had a chance, that the big ugly, nasty bear could be put in a cage and your new friends might be able to send you back home to her?'

'I was right. You are weird!'

'Yes, Eli, weird, and stupid. You said that you are not stupid. Now that you know our plan, what's to stop you going across the road and giving the boss the good news?'

After a very long pause when the brothers exchanged glances several times and took time to look into the beautiful, compassionate eyes of this strange woman, at last Eli was ready to reply.

'Yes, we could go across the road and give him this news. Maybe he would offer us that Tusker, but, before morning, in the corner of our brains you were talking of there would still be a hole where the bullet passed through.'

Maria smiled. 'I have kept you from your rest. Tomorrow you will be stronger and the next day better yet. Perhaps you might want to sing one of my songs. But, if you do decide to cross the road, no one will get in your way.'

'I wish Mama was with us, Eli!'

'And poor Saul.'

'We've fucked up, haven't we?'

# Chapter Thirty-five

It would not be a long job, but it would give everyone in the town who saw it a boost. There would be a new hospital. There was the big slab of concrete laid out on the old field and now the sign to show what it was for. While Tom drove the heavy support posts deep into the ground, Rebecca buffed up the sign itself, a substitute for the original stored in a shed in Londiani. She rubbed the polished oak vigorously, concentrating on the gold lettering: THIS IS OUR HOSPITAL.

As Tom was tightening the last of the bolts, vehicles pulled up onto the verge to check out the words written on the shiny new piece of wood near the entrance to the old pasture land. One curious onlooker came from the direction of the large shed where building materials were being stockpiled. The tall, swarthy man held his hand out in greeting.

'Rebecca, Tom, forgive the informality, but I feel I know you so well.'

Tom was unsure only briefly.

'Mister Courtney, you know my, our, grandmother well.'

'It's Mordecai and yes, Rafaella is an old friend. We often swap books. She gave me Italian lessons when I was pretentiously keen to read Signor Dante in the original. And, please, forgive me for trespassing. I did tell old Jim Sawyer that I was on the site. I do have a good reason as well.'

'Mordecai, you are welcome, anytime. The more people interested in our work here the better.'

'Rebecca, it's an honour to meet you. Believe it or not, I saw one of your New York concerts. Breathtaking stuff! Toni Wajiru is a friend, too. This hospital is the best thing that has happened to this town in a hundred years. Seriously. You take a walk around the place, but I'm sure you do. Tom, you could win the seat here. The people are bubbling.'

'Ah, and you must know that KANU have Abel Rubai's son running.'

'Old misery guts, the father not the son! I suppose you heard that he ordered, ordered mind, the council to knock it all down.'

'No, we didn't know, but we are not surprised, Tom, are we?'

'Look at this. Copy of the email I sent in reply, at the request of the council, of course!'

They read together with mounting amusement.

'And what was his reply?'

'Nothing, so far! Do you have a few minutes? I know Abel Nathaniel Rubai, probably better than anyone in the country. Listen. Twenty-six years ago when he and Sally came down from the hills to work for Neisland, Kapper and Reed in Nairobi, I was on the staff. But, in those days, I was Mordecai Cohen. Complicated story, no crookery involved. I don't suppose he'd remember me. On second thoughts!'

'But you say you know him really well?'

'Yes, I know him. I'm writing his biography. True, true. It will sell a lot of copies when it comes out. It would sell millions if it came out tomorrow. But I'd be dead by the next morning!'

'That Rubai we both recognise.'

'Yes, you in the Kakamega Hills, Tom. Both of you with the unwholesome Julius.

Yes, AN Rubai is a first-class bastard, but he wasn't always like that. He is very bright and, in terms of finance, as honest a man as you could ever meet. He could have made a very good president. He had the strength to see off the many crooks with which this country, in common with most others, is liberally blest. Instead he became the number one crook himself.'

'But how do we get rid of a man like that? Look around you. He wants to stop all this work.'

'How do you get rid of him, Rebecca? There are two choices: a bullet between the eyes, or your way.'

'Our way?'

'But getting him in front of a judge will be a tough job!'

'How did you know ...?'

'About the court case? Complicated story, a bit like name changing from Cohen to Courtney. But if you need any help, I'm your man. I have a stack of useful stuff.'

'My grandma ...'

'Thomas, don't!'

'Sorry, 'becca! She knows that Rafaella hates that word. But ... my father's mother has talked about you. I thought you lived overseas.'

'Right, New York, where I saw that concert, but mostly in Nairobi. But I've decided to build my resting place on land I've owned for years, on the other side of the lake. I was asking Jim if he could fit me in to build it. Perhaps I'm hoping to be able to finish my book over there. Rebecca, you asked about getting rid of him. Tell you the truth, I think he'll bring himself down, sooner rather than later.'

'Can't be soon enough for us!'

'He's really lost it the last year or so. Rebecca, you've been a very big problem for him.'

'Me? But how?'

'I'm a student of the history of Rome, particularly the emperors. They couldn't stand it when they saw someone stronger than themselves come along. Rubai's just like that. He's no fool and he recognises that you are a stronger force than he is.'

'But this is plain crazy.'

'You are the most popular person in the country. You are beautiful. He still blames you and Tom for the death of his beloved spoilt son. He is mad with hate. It's an obsession.

'"Leave the country".' Ever had that advice given to you? Please, Jacob and Joseph, don't think of it! Now this place. My email didn't help. We could do with King Solomon to pass on some advice!'

'Think of it, Rebecca, we only came over this morning to put up our little sign!'

* * *

The sudden death of Julius had hit Abel Rubai hard, and more deeply than he realised. In quiet moments, he lamented to himself a loss of confidence. His favourite cliché that difficulties were opportunities in disguise had lost its lustre. He was besieged by two major concerns. Every effort to find the missing Akamba brothers had failed. He was beginning to feel tempted to believe the advice of his chief lieutenants that the boys were dead.

'Show me the bodies and then I will believe you.'

And the defiant reply to his instruction to the Naivasha Council to destroy the beginnings of the new hospital in the town was an even bigger blow. Many people in his camp knew the contents of the letter and were watching him closely. They had never seen him tested like this before. The inhabitants of the scruffy little town needed a thumping to bring them back in line. No doubt the boss had a plan of action, but they were anxious to see evidence of it.

Sally, too, had noticed signs of nervousness in her husband.

'Abel, perhaps we should call in the doctor. You are off your food and you are not sleeping properly.'

'Sally, there is no problem, just a dilemma, a win-win situation. I want to make sure it is a big win. That is all there is to it.'

To solve the Naivasha problem, he decided to take a chance on someone outside the circle of Nairobi hard men. His chiefs had been keeping an eye on a twenty-six year old man who had spent most of his life in the northern borderland. Nimosi Murroni was a young Turkana warrior with an addiction to very violent solutions to problems. His family were cattle herders and had suffered badly in defending their animals against marauding war parties from across the border with Ethiopia. As a fourteen year old he had lost an eye in one of these raids, but he had fought on and helped to drive the raiders back, and become a local hero. Over the years more and more of his family were wiped out in these same wars. At last he had reluctantly given in to pleas from his grandmother, his last surviving relative, to move south.

'Mama, I will take you to a safe place, but when you have passed on, I will return and fight again. But I will have money then and the pigs from the north will pay in blood for what they have done to us.'

They moved first to Marsabit, then to Isiolo and finally, drawn by the hope of making quick money, to Nairobi. When the offer came of a one night job with a big payout, he seized the chance.

'Look, Murroni, you got sixteen, eighteen boys ready to take with you? See, some people up north of here think they can mess about with a really important person who is rich enough to pay many thousands of shillings, American dollars if you like.'

'Yeah, sixteen, all Turkana. They don't like this city life. They don't like city people.'

'Great! The boss will like that. So you won't mind if there's a little blood about the place? The more blood, the bigger the payout. You fail, no money. The boss wants results. Understand?'

'No worries, man. Tell him to be down to the bank early.'

Two privately hired matatus pulled out of the ABC Centre on the edge of the inner city when Murroni decided that the night traffic on the road north out of Nairobi was light enough to allow them easy passage to the end of the dual carriage and down the winding hill to the valley of the Great Rift. Most of the passengers were younger than their leader and had followed him south from the homeland. They, too, shared his dream to return home one day and, as they saw it, to set their people free. Murroni had no trouble persuading them. For the first time since they had left the north, they would be working together and picking up wild amounts of money for one easy job.

'We are Turkana and we fight like the warriors we were and will be again.'

They were psyched up for a battle. With them were four southerners who knew the way to the place and would have their own jobs to do when they got there.

'Okay. You take care of the buildings and we will take care of the warriors.'

'Murroni, with any luck there be few warriors, just watchmen who will scatter to the hills as soon as they see us coming. You will never earn easier money than you will tonight.'

'My boys want there to be many warriors. They need the practice. See how excited they are! But this Boss, we can trust him to pay?'

'Always. He is excited, too. He heard that you are a bit crazy. His heart is in it. You boys will be able to buy yourselves beer for the next two years.'

'We will not waste the money. We have important work with our people.'

'Suit yourselves, brother!'

'And, Bwana, we are not crazy! Every one of these boys is special.'

There was no sleeping or nodding off on that journey. The young Turkana men had done small jobs in the city – hold-ups, burglaries, kidnappings – but they were convinced that in this country place they would have the chance to be real warriors again.

On the last bend down the Escarpment, the excitement mounted. No one had told them about the big lake in the valley. The large flat plate of water gleamed under a full moon, just like their lake at home.

The vans sped along the empty straight on the valley floor. At the first sighting of the lights of Naivasha, they began their final preparations, making sure that their weapons were to hand. As they passed over the level crossing, Murroni gave his boys an order.

'Bend low. As we go through this town, no one must see you. We must not spoil our little surprise. Izzy, flash your torch to the vehicle behind. They must hide, also. And be ready. The time is very near now. When we stop, do not move until I tell you.'

* * *

There was plenty of life in the centre of town. The large trucks on their way north from the coast, carrying goods to Uganda and the Sudan, were parked on the wide dusty verges. The bars were open and doing a good trade. Music blared as it did into the early hours seven nights a week at this popular staging post.

A few minutes later, with everyone upright again on their seats, they pulled up in front of a pair of metal gates secured by a chain and padlock. One of the city boys made quick work of getting through this barrier with his heavy-duty bolt cutters. The vans moved inside and parked under a tree away from the large, flat slab of concrete. The passengers waited inside on the lookout for the smallest signs of life in the shadows around them.

There was life, but the two askaris on duty had fled to shelter as soon as they spotted the white vans pulling up in front of the gates. Following instructions, they dialled the number of the police station. From there calls radiated to other parts of the town. The askari's mobile was kept open just in case there would be more news to pass on.

The vans emptied quickly and four Turkana stood guard while equipment was unloaded. Still there was no sign of anyone to give them a fight. Murroni sensed disappointment.

'First job is to dig holes under the concrete for the dynamite. That will wake them up around here. We'll leave the fire till later. Keep you weapons close to you. They could be all watching and waiting. And keep the noise down!'

In strategic positions around the block the energised warriors dug ferociously.

'Hey! Hey! That's plenty big enough. Now go and find some rock to hide behind, a hole, anything, that shed, but not too close! Try that old wall close to the fence.'

The charges were set and the deep silence of the night was broken by the distant sound of vehicles moving towards them from the town. There was a mixed reaction from the raiders. The city men older and more experienced calculated that they could finish the job and have an even chance of getting out of the compound and making the two hundred metres to the A104 without being discovered.

'Change of plan. Get back to the vans. Tell drivers to start up. We could be in luck here. We are ready to blow.'

Murroni's men despised this cowardice.

'No! We stand and fight.'

'Crazy savages! The job is done. Pick up your money and go home. Have a real war up there. Dead men do not collect their wages!'

'Go, but leave one vehicle for real men! We are not afraid of blood!'

'Nor us, as long as it belongs to somebody else! Right! Here comes the big bang!'

Six explosions were simultaneous and the shattered pieces of concrete flew high and the dust and earth flew higher. A final blast caused the store shed to collapse and burst into flames. Behind a single stone built wall, the remnant of a farmhouse built by a failed English farmer eighty years before, they were protected for the few vital seconds against the lethal blast and the chunks of concrete tumbling back to earth.

Car headlights were cutting through the darkness much closer now as the two white matatus skidded to their right as they left the compound in a panic.

The confused shouts and screams of the Naivasha men in the convoy of cars racing out of town signalled their fury and frustration that they had failed to protect their new dream project. They had been too casual, too lazy and let their children and women down.

'Henry, we saw those matatus pass us.'

'I swear there was nobody inside. I was watching carefully. Damn the beer!'

'Yeah, damn the beer. That's our problem. Blame somebody, something else.'

'Mother of God, look at that! I pity the one who will have to tell the Kamau girl.'

'McCall! Anyway I bet she's guessed. Everybody in town heard that noise.'

The dozen cars and pick-ups pulled up on the verge outside the compound. The disconsolate men stepped out and moved to the chicken-wire fence. With their fingers grasping the fence, they stared, incredulous, through the smoke and dust.

'Oh, no, I forgot! My uncle and cousin were supposed to be on duty in there tonight.'

'Someone was in there. That's where the police got the message from.'

'I'm going in.'

'We're with you. The cowards have run off by now. See, no matatus.'

In the restored silence of the night, names were shouted in a tangle of a dozen voices. When no reply came, the men scattered in different directions to search. But it was a search that was short-lived.

The wild screams coming at them out of the darkness to their left shocked them into silence and for a few seconds drained the energy out of their legs. The crazed pack fell on them, jabbing with the sharp points of their spears or swinging the broad, shiny blades of their pangas. The sudden frenzy of violence terrified them into running for their lives.

When the cries of pain of companions began, their own anger erupted into fierce retaliation. They hurled jagged pieces of concrete, picked up pieces of planking and rushed forward, ignoring the hurt of their wounds. Toe to toe, hand to hand, the savagery of the battle rose in a crescendo of fury of strained limbs and outbursts of obscenity and the agonised pleas for mercy from those fell under the weight of blows from a superior enemy.

The crack of pistol shots fired somewhere outside the tight ring of noise, dust and bloodshed brought a lull which grew into a prolonged cooling of the urge to fight on. Led by Inspector Caroline Miggot and Sergeant Hosea Kabari, still holding his pistol above his head, a crowd moved forward warily.

They laid the dead and the badly injured in separate lines on the dusty mix of grass and gravel away from the broken heart of the ruin of the hospital. Nobody had escaped unwounded. Those well enough to walk were herded into a group and forced to sit down in a circle, watched over by newly arrived Naivasha men. Other local men had been asked by the inspector to guard the closed gates to make sure that none of the hundreds gathered outside could get in. Tom and Rebecca McCall were led through. Rebecca was beyond tears as they moved forward trying to take the full impact of the horrors around them.

'Caroline, this is a place of healing and peace. Why ...' She heard cries of men in pain coming from close by. 'People have been hurt here?' Her eyes were staring in disbelief. She quickened her step and put her hands to her mouth when she saw the line of men stretched out on the ground lit up by the flames of the fire burning more quietly now.

'How many have died?'

'Many. We think twenty-five at least. Fifteen are from the town. The rumours are that the others are tribesmen. But, please, Rebecca, come away.'

'No. I must look at everyone here.'

She began her slow passage, stopping by each body and whispering what Tom and Caroline took to be a prayer. But her words were an apology, heart-wrenching grief for the men and for herself.

Tears filled Caroline's eyes. She knew that a deeper pain was about to strike her friend and that she could not warn her nor protect her from its impact.

'Oh, no! Please God, no!'

She fell to her knees and grasped the ankles of Iolo Jones, the 'almost doctor' from Wales. The tears streamed until the pain of cramp seized the muscles of her stomach. When Tom managed to lift her to her feet, she insisted on continuing her walk along the line, supported on her husband's arm. Her words were no longer spoken in a whisper.

'Please, forgive me. I have been so foolish, so arrogant. If only I could start again!'

Tom held back from saying a single word to her. He knew she would be unjust to herself and he was reconciled that he would not be able to follow her down to the lowest depths of her grief.

Caroline, on the busiest, most stressful night of her time in the police, moved to the group of men suffering minor wounds. She was shocked when a hand grasped her arm tight and pulled her 'round. Nimosi Murroni, his face disfigured by an empty eye socket, his clothes filthy with dust mingled with dried blood, looked her in the face and pointed towards Rebecca.

'Who is that person? I think I know her.'

Caroline pulled herself free and stared at her assailant. She replied coldly.

'Rebecca …'

'Kamau, the singer. Yes, of course. Why is she here?'

'Someone has just destroyed her dream. Perhaps the someone is you!'

'Her dream?'

'The hospital she wanted to build for her people here.'

'Hospital? Then they lied to us.'

The single startled eye would have unnervered someone less strong than the experienced police inspector.

'I must speak to her. Now!'

Caroline was spared the dilemma of making a decision. Tom and Rebecca were moving towards her. Murroni took his chance.

'Rebecca Kamau, my life has ended here tonight. My body is standing and you see my lips moving, but inside I am dead.'

Rebecca took Tom's hand and looked at the stranger, alert and composed.

'So you are telling me that this is your work. I think you have done all your speaking. I pity you'

'And I, too, can still feel pity in amongst the sea of shame. So many good men taken. Someone lied to me, but my lie is greater. Since I was a child I have known violence, the taking of lives. When my family was taken, I thought I knew how to honour their memory. My dream was revenge.'

'On innocent men like these, your people and ours?'

'If he came to me at this very moment, death would be a friend. In truth, there are no words.'

'No words.'

Rebecca turned aside and bowed her head. Tom, at a complete loss, looked to Caroline for guidance.

'Caroline, you have far more work than I can imagine.'

'Ambulances and doctors are on their way. Many policemen from the district. There will be no peace here for many days, perhaps never. But, take her home, Thomas. And, please, two small favours. Phone Paul and then Maria. There will be a tomorrow and we must try to prepare. But for tonight, let her emotions flow. Thank God for the warmth of family and friends.'

# Chapter Thirty-six

The media fest began early and spread far. *The Nation*, *The Standard* and local reporters from international outlets were in Naivasha before dawn. Television channels were allowed into the compound for half hour stints and low flying helicopters bearing news company logos confirmed to the people of the town that their suffering was a centre of attention for the second time within weeks.

The stories were graphic and, by and large, accurate. The photographs were suitably gruesome and persuaded editors to put them on front pages. Two east coast dailies in the United States managed to add personal touches. 'Rebecca Kamau, as she was then, will be remembered as the singing sensation at concerts at the Flamingo earlier this year,' said *The New York Times*.'

'Kenya born Debbie Miller, a graduate of MIT, designed the new hospital and is currently in Naivasha, supervising the early stages of the build,' reported *The Boston Globe*.

*The Daily Nation* of Nairobi probed deepest in an effort to find causes. 'One person stands out as the major link between three violent attacks this year: Rebecca Kamau. Julius Rubai, her fiancé, was gunned down on the night of their engagement party at Muthaiga Club last May. She and her family had close links with the McCall family of Londiani whose flower farm and house were blown up just weeks ago, with a horrific loss of life. And now this, the destruction of the hospital she planned and sponsored. To us at *The Nation*, this common thread in the attacks seems to provide a rich vein of clues to help uncover the culprits. When we inquired on progress to police headquarters in the city, we were given the old chestnut comments of "No comment" and "We are following several lines of inquiry". Hakuna matata, the boys in blue are hot on the trail.'

At the Rubai house, there was a strong sense of deja-vu. Sally had scoured the newspapers and followed this up with hours of Bible reading and prayers for the lost souls. She mused on the fate of Sodom and Gomorrah, for a few hours had no thoughts of new baby Julius and wondered if she might do some good by visiting her almost daughter-in-law and trying to offer comfort.

All these were solitary activities. Family discussion on the subject only took place in the evenings, just as they had done the last time disaster struck Naivasha and, that time, Londiani in particular. Sally, Abel and Reuben sat around the plasma. Sally, with her regular bouts of weeping and outbursts about the unfairness of life, soon began to bore her husband and son. Reuben stayed out of a sense of duty and made hardly any comment on the vivid scenes unfolding in front of them.

Abel was his usual two-faced self. His expression was solemn, but his words were few. Underneath the neutral exterior his mind was in overdrive. He had known about the destruction from a phone call from his regular boys on their way back to Nairobi. He had soon rationalised the possible problem for him with the crazy Turkana. There was nothing to link them with him and, as a bonus, he had saved a few shillings. The ten dead would not be asking for their pay and the other five were safe in a Nairobi lockup and likely to meet up with their brothers in the not too distant future.

As for the fifteen locals killed in what must have been quite a fight, he had no sympathy. If they had kept their noses out of his business, they could all be sitting that evening watching the television and seeing the fireworks display just down the road. And there was yet a bonus for him here, too. The smart-arsed songstress would be sitting in a corner somewhere, sobbing her heart out with shame and guilt, blaming herself for the death and destruction of the night. But now there would be no more sentimental drivel about putting up a hospital for the poor, unfortunate people of her beloved mess of her hometown. It was 'A win-win situation,' as he had predicted to Sally. He was as indestructible as ever, back in full control.

* * *

It had been a grim night at Naivasha. Home Grown, the nearest flower farm to the hospital site, had sent in two lines of mobile floodlights. At once the relief workers could move around more confidently, less fearful about where they planted their feet. The line of dead was watched over by priests and nuns who murmured their prayers and hymns over each corpse in turn. One by one the Naivasha dead were taken home by their families, still in a state of shock and unable to grasp the numbing reality of their own changed lives.

Ivor, Dai and Tom held their vigil over Iolo. They took turns to hold him in their arms. The spontaneous prayers in Welsh were the passionate outpourings of men hanging on in a whirlwind that had suddenly blasted into their quiet lives. Over and over there were pictures of home in their minds.

They visualised the moment when Iolo's family would hear the news. If they were thinking that bringing that news would be their awful duty, they were wrong. Sonya Mboya who knew members of their church in Llanelli had already passed on the news to the almost doctor's family. At that moment on a rainy night far to the north-west, their home chapel was filled with a congregation that was stunned and helpless. They prayed, sang hymns and waited. It was a small relief to them to be told that Iolo would be back in Wales by the middle of the next day. The KLM jet carrying the nightly cargo of flowers and vegetables to the Amsterdam market would divert briefly to Cardiff to drop off the four friends. Eddie and Rollo would travel with them.

* * *

'Thomas, I must go back. I should have stayed to help. At least then I should have been actually doing something instead of…'

'Rebecca, I'm ready to go now. But by coming home you helped. There were, are, so many practical things to see to over there.'

'So I would be no use for these practical things?'

'Better than anybody. You would have worked till you dropped. But I think that having you there right in the middle of a shattered dream would have broken a few hearts. I went back an hour ago to check.'

'And you didn't take me! Thomas, how could you?'

'There are big crowds all 'round the compound, making that low murmuring noise, that cry of deep grief. It is such a beautiful sound and I always cry when I hear it. Inside things are calmer. There are doctors and sisters from Kijabe, Nakuru, even Nairobi. I've never seen so many policemen in one place. Sweetheart, they are just like you. They are desperate to help in any way they can. And, they are angry!'

'I am not angry, Thomas. You know that.'

'I know it. That's because you haven't got an angry bone in you body, just like your father and mother.'

'Should I go, then, Thomas?'

'Get your clothes on.'

Dawn was close when they arrived at the gate. There was a pink glow on the rim of the Aberdares. But it was the after smell of burning that caught at her throat as it drifted through the car's open window and brought her close to vomiting.

Tom eased his way towards the locked gate. The sergeant on duty flashed his torch to check on the passengers. He turned sharply away and shouted, 'Open up! It's her!'

In moments they were standing in the compound again. Rebecca stood rigid and looked around. The news of her return spread quickly through the crowds on the fence. And there was a reaction. A heavily pregnant young woman began the wailing cry of grief.

'Rebecca, our special girl, do not forget your dream!'

Others took up the call with their own expression of sorrow. The confusion of sounds melted into a single outpouring, three words repeated over and over in an unhurried rhythm, the simple expression of ancient passion.

'Uhuru----Sasa-----Rebecca!'

Over and over in unison, the first two words heavy and emphatic and the last breathed out on a whisper. The repetition became hypnotic and softened the sharp edges of pain.

Against this soothing background, Rebecca moved first to the place where she had found Iolo. An American doctor and two sisters from Kijabe Hospital were preparing his body to be taken by ambulance to their mortuary. The doctor shook his head sadly.

'We must keep him cold. The hospital here can't take him. Their people have been marvellous. Strange isn't it? Someone told me that this bomb site was the beginnings of a brand new place for the town.'

A red-eyed Ivor Jones looked up from his kneeling position at his friend's side and motioned towards Rebecca.

'Sir, this is the lady …'

The doctor swivelled 'round to face Rebecca.

'I'm so sorry. Rebecca Kamau …'

'McCall. This is my husband, Thomas. No need for any sorry. We are so grateful that you are here to help our dear friends.'

'I have only seen photos of you on my discs of your music. I'm returning home next week. You'll always be the voice of Africa to me.'

'Thank you. Please, Thomas needs to talk to you. Important things about our Iolo.'

While Tom led the doctor to the empty space behind the open door of the ambulance, Rebecca grasped the hands of the other friends. By now the Home Grown lights had been switched off and in the glimmering of the new dawn, she pulled them into a tight circle. 'Why did he come?'

A weary shake of the head from the three of them. They had been over this ground so many times, since they found Iolo unconscious and cut up in amongst the jagged slabs of broken concrete.

'Bled to death.' David had an ironic smile on his lips as he spoke. 'Funny thing, he was the only person around who could have saved him. That make sense, Ivor?'

'Nothing makes sense! We should have been on our way

back to Gilgil. We were having a great time talking to a couple of truck drivers from the coast. Great blokes. Muslim boys.'

'Iolo got up on his feet. We thought he was going to make a speech. "Got to take a leak or we'll have to stop the car on the way home." We never saw him again. Alive I mean.' More tears slid from Ivor's reddened eyes.

'What's going to happen? Do you know anything, Rebecca? If we were home …'

'But you are home.'

'Before all this, Iolo was talking to the drivers about going back to med school. "One more year. The hospital will be open by then. I'm coming back to help a few Naivasha babies into the world." Gospel truth!'

'How did you four people come into our lives? Why does it have to be like this? Tom is talking to the doctor. His father has a plan. You know that a plane goes out to Europe every night, with a cargo from the farms?'

'You mean we could be on one?'

'Tonight, Iolo as well. I hope you don't hate our country.'

'Rebecca, we're not going. The four of us have been talking about it, the four of us!'

'I don't understand. Not the four of you talking, but … why stay?'

'There's a hospital to be built.'

Tom and the doctor had rejoined them and had heard David's last words. Rebecca turned to her husband in mild panic.

'Thomas, please explain. Friends, look around you. Destruction, death. What kind of a hospital can grow out of such soil? We have enemies. You know that. Thomas …?'

'I was in year three, I think. We had a teacher from South Africa. One of the boys said that when he grew up, he was going to be an astronaut or something. Miss Strauss allowed the jeering to continue for a few moments. Then she said, "Children, never trample on someone else's dreams. They are the most precious possession they have." This hospital …'

'No, Thomas, you are my most precious possession. Remember those days when I was the laundry girl at Londiani. It was easy then. When you have no money, you have more peace.'

'Rebecca, your father is the wisest man I know. Open your heart to him.'

'So my husband is unwilling …'

'Your husband loves you so much that he wants what you want and only that!'

'David, Phillip, Ivor, so sorry. I do not want to put you off …'

'Marriage? No chance!'

'Rebecca, you smiled!'

'Thomas, you are …'

'No I am not. I love to see you smile. And so do those ladies by the police car. They want to speak to you. I'll stay here. Sam's got more work to do. Perhaps I can help.'

'They are women from our church.'

* * *

'Rebecca, when are we going to start building the new hospital?'

She struggled to find a reply to a question that had startled her. She had expected the women to be angry with her. They sensed a reason for her hesitation. Their spokeswoman, Doris, well-known around the town for her work with the poor and the destitute, moved closer so that she could make strong eye contact.

'Girl, there is going to be a new hospital?'

Doris narrowed her eyes and challenged her young friend with her steely expression. She did not wait for a reply before continuing.

'Child, you know that this town loves you and rejoices to see that you have been blessed in your life in so many ways. The children, the women and the men I see every day do not have such blessings. Hope, that is a gift from the Lord and He has asked you to be His agent of hope here. So, we ask again. When are we going to start to build the new hospital?'

An already distressed Rebecca was now struggling not to break down in front of these women who had been part of her life since her earliest days.

'But there has been so much innocent blood shed here tonight.'

'You are not the cause of this. Wicked forces are always at work to destroy the good. The daughter of Stephen Kamau knows this. And shouldn't we honour the lives lost here tonight? Not to begin again will bring shame on all of us.'

'Perhaps I am not strong enough. Perhaps God has chosen the wrong person.'

'God does not make such mistakes. But I think you are right to say that you are not strong enough – yet!'

'So?'

'Yet, Rebecca, yet! Even at this moment God is making you stronger. Things that hurt us can teach us, if we allow it to happen. You have shown love. You have brought hope. Now, you must show faith. You are not alone.'

Felicity, Doris's twin sister, saw what was needed to ease the tension of the moment. As she threw her arms into the air and let her whole body sway slowly, she called out the command.

'Ladies, time to make a prayer circle around our beloved sister here!'

For a few moments everyone close by stopped what they were doing to watch ten respectable women from the town gather close around their younger sister. No words were said at first, but the constant rhythmic movement began at once. There was hand clapping, simple stepping from foot to foot and sinuous swaying from the hips. At last came the words.

Soon all activity around the whole site stopped except in those places where the wounded and the dead were being cared for. Those who were regular in their churchgoing and their prayers were first to move in close. They wanted to be a part of this huge change of mood that had descended on that place. Felicity, with her eyes closed and her face glowing in the early morning sunlight began.

'Holy Spirit, we know that you are with us in this place of pain. Be in our mouths as we pray, be in our hearts as we look for our words. Bring your tongues of fire to purify every word that proceeds from these mouths.'

Lips were unsealed and emotions began to build, but there was no wildness. Impromptu prayers, long and short, sang out effortlessly. Inside the circle Rebecca removed the scarf from her head and shook her long hair free. Matching the movement of her sisters, with eyes closed, she turned and lifted her head to face the sun. She was aware of the words but her consciousness was elsewhere. A comfortable lethargy enveloped her and images began to appear in front of her. They stayed only long enough for her to recognise them before each melted away, giving place to the next picture. She was being led through her own life story. The little girl who played on the lakeside became at last the woman who stood on the steps of the veranda of Londiani.

Suddenly the girl had tied a thick rope around the neck of a huge animal and was trying to draw it along the bank of a wide river. However hard she pulled, the creature refused to move. Again and again she tugged until she thought her whole body would burn up with the effort. When she became angry, the creature gave out a deep mocking peal of laughter. Another figure appeared, coming towards her slowly from the other side of the creature and not seen by it. Her father, in his working clothes, smiled and pulled a sharp knife from his belt. With one sweep of his arm he slashed at the rope and set the creature free.

New energy coursed through her body and she was wholly with the women of the church once more. Florence Ndoti who had been supporting Rebecca's limp body while her companions prayed, felt the strength return to the younger woman and stood back. As the women each embraced Rebecca in a warm hug, the crowd outside the circle clapped their hands wildly and punched the air. Above the noise, the penetrating voice of Florence Muthei rang out.

'God has been with us tonight! He will wipe away all tears and there shall be no more death!'

With her arms grasping as many women as she could reach, Rebecca began to sing, fixing her eyes on Thomas and the young Welshman who were now standing in front of her. They, too, were holding each other tight.

'Home to the Hills' had been composed by Toni Wajiru on a plane that was taking him, Mary and the band away from Kenya and on their way to try their luck in the United States. In the silence, Rebecca's voice could be heard clearly inside and outside the compound and far beyond on the cool of the morning.

When the last of the music died away, there was no applause.

The rawness of so many broken hearts was transmuted into the tenderness of genuine sadness. An overwhelming sense of compassion hung in the air like a perfume. A little bit of growing was going on in that unlikely place.

'Rebecca, when do we start to build our hospital here?' Doris's face was lit up with eager anticipation.

'We have already started.'

For her husband and his three friends she was able to share her new truth.

'It's all over. This hospital is not just the dream of Rebecca McCall. It never was and I understand that now. I have escaped from the foolishness that tells us that we can be in control.'

Tom embraced Rebecca and then pulled in the boys.

'The cameras are here, Rebecca. Look. Ten or more, I reckon, and blocking the gate. Don't worry. We'll wait for the ambulance taking Iolo and follow it out. We're going up to Kijabe with him.'

The argument going on at the gate had nothing to do with the media scrum trying to get a good angle on Rebecca. They were calling out, asking her to come over to them. Tom was surprised when the policemen on guard unlocked the gate briefly to let one through. The lucky man was a writer but a local one and no longer a reporter. A distressed Mordecai Courtney was hurrying to inspect the damage and calling out to no one in particular: 'I swear to God that this is the last time …'

'Tom, Rebecca, I didn't notice. Look, I can't find the words. I was spending the night in the Rift Valley Club. I've never driven from Nakuru so fast. Thank God it's early.'

Tom interrupted. 'Mordecai, I think you've met our friends from Wales.'

'Saw you working with Jim Sawyer on the site of … Just a minute, where's the doctor boy? We had a great chat about Methodists and those forbidding Welsh chapels …'

He broke off abruptly and smacked his head hard with his hands. 'No! Not possible, surely!'

He punched the air with his fists and screamed into the sky. 'Is there anybody up there?'

His white-hot anger cooled in an instant. He grasped Tom's arm and looked across at Rebecca.

'We know who's behind this. This is no act of God. I haven't helped with my smart email telling him to keep himself out of Naivasha's business. I never dreamed … Boys, I'm so sorry.'

The three young Welshmen looked down at the ground and shook their heads in tearful bewilderment. There was a bar of fire where their thinking mechanisms normally operated. The pictures that filled their memories were leaping from past to present uncontrollably. A Welsh chapel, full out to the doors and beyond, and an uninhibited outpouring of 'O, every hour I need thee!' became happy African laughter as strong young men hammered at the beams in the roof of the new Londiani.

A resolute Inspector Caroline, striding towards the main gate to check out security, drew up sharply when she saw the group of her friends. While colleagues from Nairobi sifted through the tangled mess for information and clues, she had set herself the task of looking after the human mess. She moved between the prisoners, the wounded and the dead, struggling to keep her emotions in some kind of order. When she came upon the body of Iolo, she hurried to the fence, let the tears run free and vomited.

Now she moved straight to his friends and grasped them

tight and pressed her wet cheeks to the faces of each of them in turn.

'Forgive me and forgive poor Africa. It is not meant to be like this. Some people are not happy unless they are spitting into the face of God himself!'

Tom saw that there was a danger of emotional floodgates being reopened. He forced himself to speak abruptly.

'We must bear this. Walls have come down here tonight, human walls. We all know that broken hearts can bring us to a place where we feel little more than anger, resentment, blame. But, but, at this moment when our hearts ache, in our time of failure, we can … (he was close to his own breaking point) we can find … healing … renewal. Rebecca, I wish your father were here now. I'm no good at this!'

Mordecai hugged Tom and spoke through his agonised smile.

'Great words for a gentile! Thomas, you're my man. I need this renewal. And our country needs renewal. But, sometimes, always, we have to flush a poison out of our system first.'

Caroline was able to offer Mordecai hope. 'It's the only thing that's keeping me going. I don't know how you hang poison, but we are going to manage it somehow. Fine talk from a policewoman.'

# Chapter Thirty-seven

The ambulance carrying Iolo and three of the dead Turkana boys eased its way through the crowds at the gate, followed dangerously and closely by Tom and his four passengers. He was wearing a white coat and Rebecca was hidden low down in the well of the passenger seat. On the back seat three mzungos sat, staring straight ahead. When they did not turn left towards town and the lakeside farms most of the onlookers were fooled, briefly. Moments later as the truth dawned that their big prize was getting away, the reporters and their assistants were back on the trail. They had barely got into top gear when the chase came to an abrupt halt, when they were waved down by the police patrol preventing unauthorised vehicles from joining the A104.

The five weary passengers had little to say on their journey up the Escarpment. The ambulance had long passed out of sight. Tom was driving well below his normal speed on the newly surfaced road. In his rear-view mirror he was glad to see that the three Welshmen were sleeping. If his own and Rebecca's thoughts had been presented in musical terms, they would have expressed variations on a common theme. The surge of passion sparked by the first shock of the news had eased back.

For Tom the recurring image was of Abel Rubai. In each memory, the large man was wearing an expensive suit and perspiring, and never without the confident smile, one of his main weapons of intimidation.

Rebecca was suffering another attack of guilt. Less than a year before if she had acted differently, been less selfish, so many deaths could have been avoided. If she had been more cooperative when Julius was pursuing her, the dream of a hospital for her people at home would have been much closer to reality. Poor Tom, poor Rebecca. The story of Romeo and his Juliet, an enjoyable, romantic read at school had become a bolt of truth. She looked across at her husband. Romeo and Juliet with a huge difference. She could smile, be happy. The guilt was ephemeral and already melting.

Tom checked his mirror. His back seat passengers were in a deep sleep. Their open mouths, their heads lolling backwards were proof. He whispered, 'Rebecca, I don't understand why we are doing this, coming up to Kijabe. We won't be able to see Iolo and if we could then … it's plain morbid. They should be away from all this. It sounds hard, but they need to try to separate themselves from what has happened tonight. We could take the boat and do some fishing out on the lake.'

'But, Thomas, they must have their time to grieve. Sitting out in the sun at Kijabe, it might help. Iolo would be close by.'

Someone was stirring from sleep.

'We're over halfway to Kijabe. Did the kip help, Dai?'

'Tom, could we pull over for a minute?'

'Feeling sick? We're about nine thousand feet up here.'

'No, no. I could do with some water though.'

'Just a tick. Safer 'round that bend. I'll cross over. You can look back on the lake.'

The strong chill breeze surprised the Welshmen.

'Wow! Goose pimples! I never expected to shiver in Kenya.'

'That's because you got used to being on the coast, Ivor. Turkish bath weather. Ready to get back in?'

'In a minute. Tom, would it upset things if we didn't go on to the hospital?'

'You want to go back to Londani?'

'No. Gilgil, the club, if you can spare the time.'

'Our favourite place, next to Londiani. The school, I mean.'

'We want to check Iolo's stuff. The family know, you said.'

'They do. It's four in the morning in England.'

'And Wales! You don't mind us staying on? We want to help with the rebuild.'

'Mind, Dai? Do we mind? That's settled, then.'

'There's something else. We want Iolo to stay with us. He prayed every night about the hospital and you, Rebecca. It bothered him that he was useless as a builder. He was excited about working in the hospital. That's why he went over there ... In a way he gave his life for it.'

'Let's get back in the car. ET's got some phoning to do.'

* * *

Tom had loved his Sundays in Pembroke. He laboured and played hard for six days and on the seventh day he rested. If anyone asked him why, his reply was always the same.

'Check it out with Mister Moses. I'm only obeying orders.'

While they had their home at the club, Iolo and the boys had been regulars at the club lunch on Sunday, the social highlight of the week with the community. They had never eaten so well, so much, and at a rock-bottom cost.

As they drove in through the top gate of the school, the first bell for lunch was ringing. In the staff room the duty master invited them to join the children for lunch supervising at a table.

'If you can stand the noise!'

'Funny thing, I ate thousands of meals in that place and never thought it was noisy.'

Sitting out on the veranda with a coffee after lunch, while children were at rest in their dormitories, Tom made a suggestion.

'Ready to do your checking at the club? We'll come if you want us to.'

Dai answered for the three of them. 'Can we leave it for a while? I tell you, I'm dreading it.'

Ivor added, 'That time with the kids. Tom you must have loved it here!'

'When I left and went to Oundle, I cried for days. Homesick for Pembroke not Londiani! Tell you what, let's stay for chapel. A couple more phone calls home and we can be kids again for a whole afternoon.'

The unexpected therapy continued until they drove back out onto the Nyharuru Road. The evening skies were made darker than usual by the heavy storm clouds blowing in from the north-west.

'Do you think we can race them home, Thomas?'

'Could do. On the other hand the rain might hit us before we reach Gilgil. The canvas cover won't do much to protect your bags on the roof.'

'Tom, don't rush for our sakes. We've had a fantastic time. If you had told me twelve hours ago that this was possible …'

'I know it will all hit us again soon, but for a few hours I felt … just normal. Yet there wasn't a single minute when I didn't remember Iolo.'

'Especially in the chapel. Remember those two services he did? I've never heard kids laughing so much. One of the older girls asked me where he was. That was the one who said a prayer for us.'

'That cracked me up for sure. If you hadn't sung straight after, Rebecca, we … Wow, did you see that lightning?'

And after the lightning, the barrels rolling across the sky. And after the thunder, the teeming rain and finally the cool stillness and the return of the millions of stars hanging low in the African sky.

'I hope you can get some sleep tonight. Mum's organised everything. I know that it's not safe to make predictions, but tomorrow, we have some visitors. Rebecca, Maria's returning from Cartref. Paul and Daniel are coming.'

'Is it beginning, Thomas?'

'It is. Earlier than planned, but, after last night we can't give him the time to do more damage.'

'And we can win?'

Tom smiled and looked up at the stars.

'The answer is up there!'

# Chapter Thirty-eight

Iolo was not flown out on the KLM flower plane that Sunday night. Calls had passed between Londiani and Llanelli since late morning and the final arrangement was that a group of Iolo's family and friends would get themselves to Amsterdam and travel back to Kenya on the empty return flight.

On Monday the flow of telephone calls and emails increased to a flood. The many that offered sympathy to Rebecca each included offers of support as well as cheques for thousands of shillings. Eddie and Rollo volunteered to be temporary hospital accountants. Jim Sawyer arrived early with a complete set of plans.

'I always keep duplicates at home just in case. On the way here, I stopped with a few of my boys. The two policemen on the gate let us in to have a look around. The young lads were in tears straight away. They were back in the truck in five minutes. I didn't last much longer, but I saw enough to tell me that, if we do go on, we'll have to start from scratch.'

'Jim, no ifs!'

'Great, Alex. If you don't mind, the boys and I will go back to the site. Yes, I know, but when they find out that we're on the move, they'll be ready for anything. I just hope we don't find anything … difficult. On the way here, they told me they were willing to work for nothing. That was a first for me!'

The rebuilding of Londiani was almost complete. Maura

and Rafaella had asked that the dining room and the kitchen should be the first places to be made ready for normal living. So it was in the dining room, with a whiff of fresh paint still in the air that thirteen friends sat around the oval oak table, ready for the most important meeting of their lives.

At one end sat Paul Miller, flanked on one side by his sister, Maria, and on the other by his brother, Barnaby. Directly opposite were Daniel Komar, Rebecca and Tom. Across the middle, Stephen faced Rafaella, Hosea looked over to Caroline and Maura had a direct view of Alex and his best friend, Bertie. Paul spoke first.

'We could be here for some time, so before we get down to business, does anyone have something relevant that we have not heard?'

Maria was first up.

'As you know, I have spent the last few days in Cartref with the Akamba boys, Eli and Sammy. Physically they have recovered well after the car crash on the A104. We talked a lot about the death of younger brother, Saul, the driver of the car. I made two visits to Thika to see their mother. She's a wonderful woman, grateful to us for managing to save two of her boys. She's on our side. She blames Rubai for ruining the lives of the family. When I left them they were on a tour of the garden with Dorothy, learning about flowers and shrubs and how to look after them.'

Bertie was anxious. 'But, Maria, what's to stop them just walking through the gates to join their old boss across the road?'

'Nothing! And that is one reason why they won't go. They are free and have the chance of staying free. It may sound naïve, but I believe these two kids are discovering that life can be different for them.'

'Bloody hell! But, Paul, I thought these two could be our strongest witnesses.'

'Right, Bertie, but if we want things to change here, we can't use the old ways and lock these kids up until we need them and when they've done their bit, throw them out on the streets.'

'Bit risky, isn't it?'

'Right again, but what isn't risky about what we are trying to do?'

'Sorry, Paul. Letting the side down and all that.'

'No, Bertie, you're not letting anyone down. Daniel, Barnie and I have been working on this plan day and night. Perhaps it's getting through to me more than I realised.'

Daniel continued to build the picture of what they were letting themselves in for.

'Barnie put it well. "We are trying to get water to run uphill." Impossible.'

'Thank you, gentlemen. That's very encouraging.'

'Worst case, Maura. We have to think about that.'

'Ladies and gentlemen, five of us here are law people. I'm just a farm boy, not very clever, but there are thirteen of us around this table. For me that's a good sign. Best case. There were thirteen around that table a long time ago. They turned the world upside down. We only have one foolish man to teach a lesson to.'

'On the nail, Stephen. Just thirteen here, but I thank God for the thousands who are not here who will make sure that Abel Rubai discovers that he is not top of the class in Kenya. We are taking our country back. So, bwana of bwanas, boss of bosses, your time has passed. Barnie, you start.'

'Thank you, brother. Once we get our friend in front of a judge in a courtroom, we have a great bunch of evidence to hit him with. Eight big bombs, at least. But how do we get him there? Do we drive up to his front door at his mansion in Karen and say, "Abel Nathaniel Rubai, this is a warrant for your arrest. Will you please accompany me ... etcetera"?'

It may surprise you, but that is exactly how we plan to make our first move, but a little more subtly and at a time that we chose. Caroline will explain.'

'We make our first move next Sunday, very early. Three cars will draw up at the front door of the Rubai home. The charges will be read out to the defendant in front of a magistrate and we shall read him his rights. Paul will be our lawyer and we will have his lawyer there. Three weeks later, there is a court booked in Nairobi. We have been advised from high up that this is the minimum notice we can give.'

'Caroline, in three weeks, in three hours more like, his people will be all over us.'

'Correct, Tom, if we were trying to hold him in his Karen home. But within an hour of his arrest he will be on his way to one of six locations we have prepared for His Majesty.'

'Is that legal?'

Caroline smiled. 'Probably not, Alex, but we've got good reasons.'

Bertie offered a quick solution.

'We could say he made a dash for the door and we had to shoot the bastard. Sorry, Raf. Slipped out and all that!'

Tom was highly amused. 'Then we'd have riots on the streets and we'd be making a run for it.'

'That's why there will be late editions of *The Nation* and *The Standard* plus special early morning television and radio programs, all carrying news of the arrest and a full list of charges. That will hold off the riots for a while. And in the three weeks we will drip out little bits of news, "from our special correspondent", telling the world how the brave Abel is standing up to his captors and looking forward to his day in court.'

'And back here in Londiani?'

'Life will move on at its usual leisurely pace, except that you, Bertie, with Ewan and Lydia could be on a short break for a couple of days, just as a precaution.'

'Njoro, Kisumu, Nanyuki, so many people want to help, even though they have no notion of what's really happening.'

'No, no, Paul. Not a good idea. Naivasha is the safest place in the country for us right now.'

'Fine, fine. This town will be off his radar. He thinks he has won again. In five days he will learn a new truth.'

* * *

'In case someone is not sure, the people from Wales arrive tomorrow, with Iolo's funeral on Wednesday. There will be twelve altogether. I'm dreading it in one way, but they are in for the best up-country welcome we can give them. Iolo has given us so much, too much.'

'Memsahib, Angela and I would like to be here.'

'Stephen, no more memsahib. We are all family now. You must be here. The Welsh are good singers … I tell you something. I'm ready to go. No more fear. But Alex is giving me lessons on how to shoot straight. Sorry, Stephen, Caroline, but if anyone does stray down this way and starts threatening …'

Barnie took advantage of the emotional lull to add another piece of news.

'Perhaps some of you don't know it, but the story of the attack has gone all 'round the world. Debbie has received dozens of emails. Rebecca, you're a good part of the reason for this. Two weeks ago, *The Globe* in Boston ran a story about you, the famous singer – yes, their words, not mine – and 'This is our hospital'. It's not important just now, but the dollars are flowing into the trust fund Debbie and some friends set up when she was working on the plans for the hospital.'

Paul added, 'And next Sunday morning after we've presented Rubai with our list of charges, that list is going global, too.'

* * *

'Maura, Iolo loved this country, the people. He told us that he was coming back when he qualified. The funny thing is that, as soon as we heard the news, Albie and I were sure that he should rest out here. Now that we've seen how beautiful it is here … I'm sorry.'

'We'll look after him. Remember, Londiani is your home, too, now. We'll take you into the town. When they find out who you are, you'll see how much everyone loved him.'

But first came the funeral. The young Reverend Billy Rees was the only one of the Welsh party who saw the grave before the burial. Tom explained about the garden.

'It was planted just a few weeks ago. We lost the old one when the house burned down. You'll see the difference when the rains come.'

'Breathtaking!'

'He'll be on the edge. He'll have a Welsh oak for shade and a view of the lake.'

It was no surprise to see so many mourners gathered on the grassy plain studded with flat-topped acacia. The handsome waterbuck looked up from their grazing before deciding to move closer to the lake to finish their lunch. The crowds sat on the ground to wait. The collective whisper of their voices created a buzz. The silence was instant when the procession appeared from around the corner of the new house. Even from the last rows the view was clear. In front their own Stephen Kamau towered over the pale mzungo pastor at his side. Iolo's three friends and the McCall boys shouldered the dark coffin.

The sight of Iolo's family triggered the tears and the sobbing, but there were none of the uninhibited individual calls of pain usually heard at country funerals. When the coffin was laid on a wooden stand close to the grave, the mzungos, men and women, gathered around and sang a song in a strange language. By the third verse, many in the crowd, now standing, swayed slowly and hummed the haunting melody.

When everyone sat down again, the young pastor placed one hand on the coffin, bowed his head and cried out in a voice that surprised them with its power, incomprehensible words but with unmistakable longing and passion.

The tears of the mourners began again, pierced this time with the shouts of anguish and sometimes anger, even cries for revenge.

The small platform set up by the coffin had last been used at the wedding of Rebecca and Tom. This time three men spoke the last words over the dead 'almost' doctor. The first was Paul Miller.

'Brothers and sisters, I will not keep you long. Londiani is one of the most lovely places in our part of Great Rift Valley, but we all know that it has been the scene of much tragedy in recent months. And now you good people of Naivasha have more suffering to bear. Still fresh in my memory is a funeral that took place in the township of Kibera not very long ago. Some words I spoke there come back to me now. I say that we should not be in this place today. Back then we were crying for the loss of Doctor Simon Mboya, a great friend to the poor people of this country. Today we honour the memory of 'almost Doctor' Iolo Jones. No need for the word 'almost' to your friends here. But we will not seek revenge. "Vengeance is mine, saith the Lord", Jeremiah tells us. But we demand justice. And I pledge to you people who have come to us from a faraway country that Iolo Owain Jones will not be forgotten by the people of Kenya in its struggle for peace and harmony.'

The Reverend Billy Rees was in front of them again. This time the power of his voice was muted. 'Ivor Jones, David Davies, Philip Jones and Iolo Jones made us very proud on the day they announced that were coming to this country in the Lord's service. We listened to the reports they sent back to us with great interest and usually with amusement. Four days ago a report came to us in the middle of the night that shocked us deeply. Iolo had been taken from us and from you. Words cannot help too much at a time like this and I cannot see the Lord's hand in this. But Iolo came to this beautiful country to offer his talent and his warm heart. In the end, he was willing to offer his life. And, Rebecca, our whole church blesses you for your wonderful dream and for letting our young men share it with you.'

Stephen put both his hands on the coffin.

'Let us bow our heads and listen. The Spirit blows where the Spirit chooses. Today, perhaps he will choose you.'

For the youngest, the silence was long and puzzling. They half understood what was going on but were disappointed that Bwana Kamau was not telling them one of his stories that always made them laugh and usually taught them something, even when they did not realise it. Most of the older ones maintained the silence with a special effort and certainly did not expect anyone up there to choose them to speak to. A few who heard nothing more than their own breath rising and falling felt the touch of calm that they had not brought with them to Londiani.

# Chapter Thirty-nine

At three-thirty am, three cars met at a crossroads in Karen. They had travelled by separate routes from the city to avoid any possibility of creating suspicion. From where they had parked on a wide verge, they took a right turn. Headlights were switched off for the last few hundred metres to their destination, the large pink house clearly visible under its bright security lights.

The advance party had done their job well. The gatehouse was not manned and there was no sign of any guards in the parkland surrounding the house. They parked on the lawn far back from the main door and the twelve occupants of the cars, not all of them there willingly, hurried on using the thick grass to muffle their steps.

Within five minutes of entering, the intruders had calmed the shocked household and persuaded Abel Nathaniel Rubai to leave his bedroom to join his unwelcome visitors downstairs in his conference room. Paul Miller explained their presence to their furious host.

'No one will be hurt and no damage will be done …'

'Miller, get your thugs out my house this minute and maybe, just maybe I will be willing to forget this outrage. Is that you, Alfred? Don't tell me that you are …'

'Mister Koyane is here as your advocate to see that everything is done according to the demands of the law.'

'Get out of my house! Now!' Rubai screamed. The sound of a child crying in the distance drove him close to apoplexy. 'Get out! Get out! When my men get here, they will shoot you down like the wild animals you are!'

With no sign of emotion, Miller continued.

'This is Mister Collins Roberts, a magistrate whose area of responsibility includes the township of Kibera. Normally business of this nature would not be held in a defendant's house, but for the sake of public order.'

Rubai's manner turned instantly, but his roar of laughter had a hollow ring to it.

'You are trying to arrest me?'

'And Inspector Caroline Miggot will read you your rights and then the list of charges. Your lawyer will have a copy of these, of course.'

'Haven't I seen you before? At least you've given me one good-looking out of three. Just as well for you, sister. When you are dismissed, probably by this evening, you will find it easy to get customers downtown.'

'Mr Rubai, I must caution you …'

'Yeah, blah, blah, blah. And don't forget you are not allowed to have more than two shits a day except on Sunday, etcetera. Naivasha, yeah, that's where I saw you. A Rift Valley stitch-up …'

Alfred Koyane broke in.

'I've had a scan of this list of charges. Murder, murder, attempted murder … Are you being serious?'

'I tell you that your client will have his chance to refute these charges in court …'

'Miller, stop talking like a constipated arsehole and get real. Suppose I behave like a good little boy and allow myself to be taken to some lockup in the city. Once news gets out, you idiots won't make it as far as the Ngong Road. You've ruined a Sunday morning for me and my family. I'm about to ruin the rest of your lives. I'm going upstairs. I need to check on my wife and kids.'

Miller blocked his path. 'We have no beef with any of them. We've got good people up there looking after them. So, I'm sorry ...'

'Out of my fucking way ...'

'Put the cuffs on him!'

Two lanky but strong policemen used the impetus of Rubai's charge to spin him 'round. One pulled Rubai's hands behind his back and the other closed the manacles on his wrists. Neither of the sergeants was wearing a uniform. Of the five police personnel in the room, only Inspector Caroline could be recognised as such.

'Reasonable force, Mr Koyane?'

'Mr Miller, do you know who you are dealing with here?'

For the first time, Paul Miller dropped the bland, formal manner.

'We certainly do. This is no game. This is an honest attempt by the people of this country to put this murdering scourge where he belongs!'

Rubai detected a tremble in the venom of Miller's anger. He replied calmly in a tone of sneering contempt.

'Go ahead, you fool! In a month's time, you and your puny comrades will be history. Treason is still a capital offence in this country.'

'Treason! You megalomaniac! Who do you think you are? You have never been elected to any office of state. You have gathered around you a bunch of cronies who are shit-scared of you but hang around for the crumbs you throw down for them!'

The theatrical silence that followed was disturbed by the

sound of a powerful engine approaching the house. Paul smiled and pointed his right index finger towards the ceiling. 'The way out!'

The scowl on the face of Abel Nathaniel Rubai revealed that a new truth was dawning in his mind.

'Who gave permission for that vehicle to fly so close to this house?'

'The same person that ordered this puny group of citizens to pay you a visit to let you know that you are about to become part of the history of the dark side of this wonderful country.'

'You intend to kidnap me?'

'Mr Rubai, ten out of ten for quick thinking! You will have to forgive us that you will not be able to enjoy what I have been told is a marvellous view of the city and the country from your seat in the aircraft that I hear has landed on your back lawn. We have the blindfold ready.'

As soon as the hum of the engine and the whirr of the rotor blades had died away, Paul Miller led everyone from the sitting room to the back lawn. After Abel Rubai was safely on board, helped up by two policemen, Paul said his goodbyes to Alfred Koyane and Collins Roberts who left at once to join the cars waiting at the front of the house to take them home. Before Caroline was driven back to Naivasha in the third car, she and Paul had a brief exchange.

'Too late to change our minds now, Paul.'

'It's really do or die for us. A first in my life. I had expected to feel some strong emotion when we came face to face with him, exhilaration or, maybe, apprehension. Nothing, a dull day at the office, except that once or twice I felt close to bursting out laughing.'

'And I kept on seeing pictures of the headlines in the papers tomorrow. A bit crazy?'

'Couldn't tell you. This is another first for ... all of us. But I'm rock solid ready to go. Glad the waiting is over.'

'Well, a big kwaheri to all of you. I'll report back to Daniel and we'll all keep in touch. You're off to the hills and I'm returning to the world.'

The air force pilot flew some aimless miles before homing in on his destination, a landing circle in an open space in the forest high in the Aberdare National Park. Abel Rubai had been a silent passenger the whole time they had been in the air

Two cars were waiting as arranged. The pilot kept his blades moving while the transfer was made and the party of seven joined their drivers to set off along a trail that brought them to the Wanderia Gate and the road to Nanyuki. Abel spoke his first words in two hours.

'Forest trail, then a good road. Too cold for Tsavo or the Shimba Hills. Kagamega, I don't think so. I go for somewhere in the Aberdares, as traitors like you call them, but Nyandarua to true Kenyans. You know there's no point in keeping me in the dark. I will outwit you every day of the week.'

The prisoner was relaxed and confident. His silence on the journey had not been wasted time. In his mind he had gone over the events of the hour between the brutal entry of these clowns into his home to the moments when he had been dragged along the soft turf of his lawn and then manhandled up into that smelly, uncomfortable metal box with wings. From tiny fragments of conversation he guessed that there were seven or eight on board. His key realisation was that they would not harm him in any way for the three weeks leading up to his planned appearance in court. He was safe, whatever threats they mouthed against him. The hunt for him would be on already. The searches would be extensive and the questioning relentless. His own boys knew how to threaten effectively. Oh, yes, he would be a free man again within days, if not hours.

Before they reached Nanyuki town, the cars turned off onto a dirt track and started climbing steeply. The large, low farmhouse, set in the trees, would have been out of sight to other dwellings, had there been any. It was an ideal spot for a quiet retreat from the world, where these holidaymakers would be able to take care of their blind brother and complete a few canvases for their imminent Nairobi exhibition.

When the news came out of the disappearance of Mister Big, it caused a huge sensation in Kenya and further afield. There were rumours by the hundred to keep the media and the wananchi excited and even a limited version of the true story took a long time to come out. There were interviews, mostly with nobodies but a few with somebodies. Abel would have been annoyed and upset to learn how many of the wananchi expressed satisfaction that the country's kingpin had been removed from the scene. Once it was known that he had been flown off from his Karen home, one rumour spread quickly that he had he had been pushed out into a part of the Mara River that was infested with crocodiles.

Next morning there was a collective sobering of national opinion when *The Standard* and *The Nation* published identical versions of the charges laid against the richest man in the country. Most readers were stunned and incredulous, but a sizeable number nodded quietly and hoped that this single event might mark a new beginning of a new era for the people of the country which had once prided itself in the title of 'The jewel of Africa.'

On the Tuesday after the disappearance, TV networks in Kenya and neighbouring countries drew a huge audience for an exclusive live interview.

In the same sitting room of the Karen house where Abel had been introduced to his kidnappers, the camera was focused on the surprisingly composed remaining members of his family. Reuben sat next to his mother on a large settee. Sally, heavily made up, was holding baby Julius in a white lace shawl. The children in between smiled shyly when they knew they were in shot and at that moment as popular as film stars or famous sporting idols.

The single lady interviewer was well-known to the Rubai family and was chosen for her sensitive manner and her way of putting at ease the shyest and most reluctant of those who sat opposite her in front of the cameras. After almost three days with no news of her husband Sally was ready to open her heart in the hope that it might help to bring her beloved Abel back home.

'I cannot understand who would do such a thing to a man who loved his country and wanted to serve her.'

'So what message would you like to send to those people who took him away from you all?'

'Please, bring him back or, at least, let us know that he is well and in good spirits. There are so many stories of good men snatched away from their homes ...'

Sally could not contemplate the ultimate horror. The interviewer turned to Reuben to confront him, reluctantly, with the most difficult question she had on her prepared list.

'Reuben, we have seen in the papers the list of charges being made against your father. Do you have any comment on these?'

Without hesitation Reuben, looking straight into the camera, dismissed the accusations.

'Garbage! My father has many enemies out there, envious people who are ready to make up a string of lies to bring him down. And I would add that it is quite disgraceful that these rags are willing to give space to this stuff just to sell a few more copies.'

'So what about the trial to be ...'

'Madam, there will be no trial, unless it is of these cowardly thugs who saw fit to invade the home of an innocent man for whatever corrupt motives they have. I am working to bring my father back to where he belongs.'

Many of the millions watching the interview were so won over by the actual presentation of the family that they did not need to hear any opposing point of view. Abel Rubai was being foully treated, but the authorities would soon put this situation right. At that moment many of the viewers would have been happy to have raised these people who bore their suffering with such dignity to the level of royalty.

Viewers gathered in front of their set in Londiani were impressed with the program. They were aware, too, that this shameless makeover would make their task that much more difficult. Next morning at breakfast Tom expressed his fear.

'Say we manage to hang onto him for the next nineteen days. How will we get him to court with the local rent-a-mob in action?'

Daniel reminded him.

'Tom, we always knew that this was not going to be easy. We will not be given the chance to reply to that sentimental hogwash.'

Maria was able to bring good news.

'Hosea has heard from Inspector George Simpson up at Nanyuki. Caroline reached the farmhouse safely last night.'

'Thank God!'

'Yes, Maura, that's one worry less. When I tried to tell her that it would be dangerous for her to read out the charges to

Rubai, she reminded me that someone from the police had to do it. "Daniel, I am not willing to hide away. That way Rubai will survive again."'

'Right now we stick to our jobs down here. There is much to do. Debbie and Rebecca are over at the site. And think of all those people of the town helping with the work. Every piece of the old site is gone. Jim Sawyer has got the concreters sending their stuff in by the truckload. And, listen to this. No charge for material, time and transport. I wish we could let Paul and the others know about that.'

'Maria's right, Tom. Things to be done. It's over to the fields for us. Stephen is going to be late this morning. He's down at Iolo's grave helping the masons to finish the work. There'll be no spelling mistakes on the headstone when he's around. It should be all done by the time of the sunset farewell.'

For most of the day, Abel Rubai remained in his cosy room up at the farmhouse high above Nanyuki. No one made any effort to coax him out. When he did appear, he was either complaining or boasting.

'Why do you have to keep those hideous black curtains on the windows? And I see that there are steel shutters outside. Are you growing mushrooms in there?'

'Why don't you check that out? Give you something to do. But sir does not seem to be in the best of spirits today. By the way, could you stop the shouting and screaming? Nobody around for miles.'

'Miller, I'm going to make sure I'm in the front row when they string you up!'

'For trying to save the country from a psychopath like you?'

'For treason and kidnapping!'

'Don't be tedious. We've been over that one already. Hey, perhaps you do need some air. I hope you breathe through your nostrils. The gag will be tight and we'll have to have someone guide you on a rope. That blindfold is made of special material.'

Rubai picked up a china ornament from the table, hurled it into the fireplace and stalked back to his room. 'You uncivilised bastards!'

'And that ornament was expensive. It will go down on your bill. You can pay before or after the trial. And we do take American Express!'

'Shut the fuck up!'

The bellow was muffled by the thickness of the heavy door.

* * *

There were more tears at the farewell service than at the funeral. Fifty people at most were gathered around the white marble grave. The gold letters on the headstone dazzled, as they were caught by the last rays of the setting sun.

Ivor sang a Welsh song much loved by Iolo, a lament for the lover's beloved Myfanwy and Rebecca responded with the 'Ave, Maria' that she had first heard on her first morning in Santa Maria College. At that moment, in that place with a pink and mauve afterglow filling the western sky, Myrtle would have been happy to join her son on his journey into eternity.

'Nos da, Cariad!'

* * *

It was fortunate that the visitors from Wales flew back home later that night. Early next morning, at around four am, a party of policemen burst noisily onto the gravel driveway at Londiani. They had made one other stop in Naivasha and now they were fully prepared for the task of the day.

Hosea Kabari was thrown out onto the ground from one of the vehicles, in his night clothes and barefooted. The loud bass voice of a constable called out towards the upstairs windows. 'You inside, get down here at once! We need information!'

Lights went on upstairs, but there was no sign of movement inside. The inspector in charge of the twelve man group, angry that obedience to his command had not been instant, called out himself. 'Do not try to skulk away like the cowards you are! We have a traitor here. All come now, or he will suffer.'

Rollo and Eddie were the first to appear on the veranda. Rebecca and Tom followed. The veranda lights were switched on only when Maura and Alex came in.'

'And the old witch? We know she is here.'

A silent and tense two minutes passed before Rafaella, in full make-up and dressed immaculately, made her entrance. Her ladyship peered distastefully into the darkness and called to her son in a loud stage whisper.

'Alex, who are these boorish people who don't know that it is bad form to make a call at this unearthly hour?'

Eddie and Rollo could not resist a smile that they tried to hide from their visitors by lowering their heads. The inspector was furious and attempted to win back the high ground by grabbing Hosea by the neck and throwing him forward onto the veranda steps. If he felt any pain, Hosea did not show it. He knelt silently, aware that he would be the whipping boy these invaders would use to have their way.

Self-control was becoming an issue for the number one cop in the Central Nairobi District. He had expected instant submission, not the casual defiance that was raising the levels of his anger.

'You Europeans are not in charge now ...'

'We are not Europeans. We are Kenyans, just like you!'

'McCall Junior, if I am not mistaken. I've been warned about you. These three officers with the guns know how to shoot straight! Be very careful!'

Before Tom could reply with a sarcastic jab, there was a disturbance from the direction of South Lake Road. In seconds, a breathless woman appeared in the circle of light. A dishevelled Maria ran to the steps and cradled her husband's head in her arms.

'Darling, I am so sorry to be late. If I had only taken time to learn to ride the bicycle of yours properly. Your head is bleeding! I'm taking you home at once. Alex, can you help us?'

'Maria, I'll do it. I don't care for this company.'

'Rafaella ...'

'Mokubu, fire one at the steps!'

The whirr of the bullet and the ping of the ricochet had the desired effect for the increasingly angry inspector. At last he had the serious attention of this arrogant bunch.

'Joseph, grab the mad woman and throw her up the steps to be with the other animals in this zoo.'

The inspector removed his hat and replaced it after giving his head a nervous shake. 'To business! We want information. The traitor here, this disgrace to the police force, has been involved in a very serious crime against the state. You all have. We know this and you know it. Where is Mister Abel Rubai, our next president, being held? Answer at once!'

Nothing.

'Joseph, the little finger on his right hand!'

The inspector was unmoved by the gasps and screams of pain as a heavy boot stamped down on Hosea's hand.

'Now then!'

No words.

'Little finger, left hand.'

The screams were louder and Hosea collapsed. Rollo sprinted forward and managed to get a kick into the face of the snarling Joseph. Two swinging punches and he lay unconscious on the gravel.

'Bastards, are you going to kill all of us? We don't know what you are talking about!'

'Totally predictable response from Thomas McCall. But perhaps you, Mrs Kabari, are beginning to understand. How much do you value this man's life?'

Maria took several deep breaths and stepped forward. The unflinching glare did not move from the eyes of the inspector's face. One step down, two and her head was level with the inspector's. She knelt and touched her unmoving husband. Standing again she looked along the line of the whole group in front of her. 'God, forgive these men for their foolish ignorance.'

She turned and was immediately grasped by the arms of Rafaella. Tom and Rebecca helped Maura to lift Rollo and carry him to the sofa against the wall of the veranda.

The inspector, more disturbed than he showed, chuckled nervously. 'Hey, boys, we have found us a nest of Christians. But, just because you people are soft in the head is not going to help you.'

Alex, speaking quietly and with nervous passion, spat out his words.

'You mean you are going on with this … this unspeakable crime?'

'Sir, you have fine words, but your brain must be blocked in some serious way. I will spell it out for the last time. Tell us where Rubai is or, yes, this Kabari will receive summary justice for his treason, bone by bone. Notice, no numbers on our shoulders and the names you have heard are false. When we are finished with him, he will go for a sail on your lake and provide breakfast for the little fishes. Do you understand?'

'Perfectly!'

The reply did not come from anyone on the veranda. Before anyone could turn, the voice continued.

'There are four of us. We know which three of you have the guns and we can see you clearly, Mister Big Mouth. Our guns are pointing straight at you. I must warn you that our weapons were made by the finest gunsmith in London. They were used in the old days for bringing down bigger boys than you. Understand? Buffalo, elephant, dead with a single shot. Very messy. Big holes in those fat bodies of yours.'

The inspector turned and made a nervous attempt to call a bluff. From the circle of light he peered into the early morning darkness. He saw four shadowy outlines and the glint of four well-oiled barrels. What he could not realise was that three of the four gunmen had very little idea about discharging shells, let alone pointing their heavy weapons confidently at even the largest targets.

'Now, look here. You are …'

Bertie fired at the veranda wall and gouged out a big chunk of plaster and stone.

'Sorry about that, Alex. I'll get it fixed later. Get your guns out, please. Then we can take out eight at a time. Big Mouth's mine! Now, gentlemen, if you three sharpshooters would just step out towards us and place your guns on the ground quietly. Then return to your colleagues and lie on the ground stomachs down.'

'You will hang for this!'

'Of course we will!'

Alex, Tom and Eddie, all good shots, moved to the top of

the steps carrying their own guns. Alex raised the butt of his rifle to his shoulder and pointed it at the inspector. By now Bertie and his Welsh companions had moved to the veranda. On his way around the line of prone bodies, Bertie took out a moment to inspect the damage in the veranda wall. By now the women were focused on helping their wounded patients.

Alex lowered his gun and grasped his old friend's arm tightly. His stomach was still churning and his heart racing as his terror began to subside. He stood in awe at Bertie's casual confidence. Bertie himself sat on the top step, cleared his throat and began.

'My friends, we have a dilemma here. What can we do with you … policemen? Whatever. But you cannot invade innocent people's homes at dead of night.'

'You taught us these bad ways when you or your friends took off our boss. You have him hidden here? Or have you killed him?'

'You mean bone by bone? Not so. Not guilty. But whoever managed to prise him away, well, he has our blessing. Anyway.'

'We are twelve. We have two police vehicles. Too hard to hide.'

'Not so either. Here's the choice for us. We each put a single bullet up the spout. Eight down. Then reload for the remaining four gentlemen! Yes, we are well prepared. We shoot you in the head, strip you, drive you 'round to the far side of the lake. We know just the place where there are many hungry little fishes. We burn your cars and drop them into the lake and disturb a few hippos. All finished before dawn!'

One or two of the younger prisoners began to shudder and to sob. Bertie consoled them.

'But we are not barbarians. We will not harm a hair on your heads. I have a friend. He lives close by. Until a few years ago, before the flowers came to the lake, he owned a vineyard here. Made good wine. To keep it cool and safe he got his men to dig out cellars out of the rocks. Six in all. I inspected them just last week. I won't tell you why. Heavy doors and the lights are still working. Lo and behold, the keys.'

He stood up. His tone changed dramatically. He was firm and threatening.

'One at a time you will stand up and take off your clothes. Keep your underwear, boots and socks. We presume you all carry that policeman's best friend, a strong pair of handcuffs. You may keep those, too, carried on your very own wrists. Then we will escort you to your accommodation. Yes, it is cold, but not as cold as the waters of the lake.'

The reaction of the prisoners on the walk across the fields varied. Four tramped in silence. Boss man ranted and raved, spat and cursed. The others, the youngest and the oldest, walked submissively, seeking assurances that that they would be unharmed and freed soon.

Bertie promised nothing.

'Just remember that if something should happen to us, then there will be nobody to check on you, and, more important for you, to make sure you eat. You can shout as much as you like. No one will hear you.' He added with an angry warning. 'And, do not forget that you are getting a much better deal than you deserve, you bunch of savages.'

At breakfast around the large oak table in Londiani, the atmosphere was one of relief, not of triumph. Maria had been home to fetch her ointments and her powders. The damage to Hosea's fingers was less than she had feared. The large sofa on the veranda was the hospital bed and soon she was singing her ancient melodies in the Aramaic language that soothed the minds of the two patients, but of everyone who heard them. Bertie was assuring them all about the security of the cells.

'If you three had gone back to Gilgil last night, that bit of cheek would not have worked.'

Maria's voice called out from the next room.

'Synchronicity, Bertie! It never stops! That's why we are going to win out!'

'By the way, where's Tom?'

Alex smiled. 'Bertie, did you notice that the cars have gone? Tom and Stephen are over the yard, doing a little paint job. Plenty of room over there to hide them in a corner, in case they send another lot of snoopers.'

Alex hesitated and took a wry sidelong look at his schoolboy friend before continuing.

'Bertie, how long have we known each other?'

'Ah? Forever, thank the Lord!'

'It's just that I've never seen you like that before – smooth, calm, like a Naivasha version of James Bond.'

'Put it like this. You remember that new bottle of Famous Grouse on my sideboard?'

'The one we were keeping till the trial?'

'Well it's half empty now! Two long pulls and I was ready to take a few scalps. The lads were fantastic. Glad they didn't have to fire at anything. Thought you were going to ask me about the cellars in Johnny de Souza's old vineyard, me checking them over and all that. Tell you the truth, I was thinking of us hiding in them, if the balloon went up.'

For the next two weeks, life in Naivasha slid back into a kind of normality. The dead were given the funerals of heroes. Some of the bereaved families reluctantly moved away further north.

The newly planted garden in Londiani looked healthy and

happy and sprigs of bright colours were beginning to peep out of the rich soil of the farm.

Over at the hospital site progress was fast. Jim had had to turn away skilled volunteers for fear of having too many people working at one time who would most likely begin to get in each other's way.

One mystery was that, as far as they could judge, no one turned up at the farm to ask about the disappearance of the platoon of the boys in blue. Their uniforms had been laundered and the contents of the pockets locked away. Perhaps undercover agents had been sent to find where the missing men were. Perhaps they had not been proper policemen at all. Perhaps an entry had been made in the personnel rosters, saying something like 'lost in action'.

With each day that passed on the way to the fateful Monday, the tension became more taut. Paradoxically, as the days were counted down, there was also a growing sense of relief that the moment of make or break was closer.

On the first Saturday of their imprisonment, two policemen sharing a cell received a visitor. Inspector Victor and Constable Joseph were surprised to hear a key turn in the lock of their door and shocked when they recognised standing in front of them the wife of the sergeant whom they had been brutalising. She was coming to take her revenge.

They scrambled to the far corner. Maria smiled at their predictable reaction. For the first time and in poor light they noticed what a beautiful woman she was. Her slim figure was emphasised by the tight-fitting black polo shirt and trousers. But, like many before them, their main attention was caught and riveted by the power of her eyes. As she flicked a glance from one to the other, they became conscious all in a second of their mystery, their humour, and, most important in their circumstances, their compassion. They carried no threat except to their own deeply felt anger and aggression.

'Do you find it cold down here?'

They replied by looking down and shuffling their feet.

'I have to say that you look quite ridiculous in those outfits. And it is a pity that you do not seem to be too fond of exercise.'

Joseph, still finding it hard to believe that no harm was about to come to him, blurted out a garbled sentence or two that sounded vaguely like a request for forgiveness.

'Madam, I was foolish. I ask myself … Please, pick up a stone and strike me on the head. I want to be hurt, to be punished. The inspector and I have been talking here …'

The inspector narrowed his gaze and reminded Maria of a remark she had made on the steps of that farmhouse.

'Why did you say those words? You forgave us. We came to hurt you, to kill you and you look after us. Joseph and I ask each other many questions. What are we doing in this place? So many other puzzlements.'

Maria cut in.

'Do you know that there is a hospital being built in Naivasha?'

'Nothing about a hospital.'

'And a young person from this town is paying for it? Have you ever heard of this person called Rebecca Kamau?'

'Everyone knows her. I have heard her sing. I was on duty at a concert at the Bomas.'

'It is her money. She is over there at this very minute. There was a fire. Many men died. Your boss man, Rubai, was the person who wanted this fire.'

'There were pictures on the television. Yes, I remember this thing now. But, Madam, I must tell you something, too. The top cops in HQ tell us to do this thing or that thing. If we won't follow instructions, next day we are looking for a job on the big estate on Mombasa Road.'

Joseph sat on a fragile chair that creaked under his bulk. He looked at his boss, then at Maria and finally at the open door.

'How many guards you have with you out there?'

'Nobody, out there.'

'So, Victor and I could hurt you and escape?'

'Yes.'

'Do you think they would let me work on that hospital? I am very strong.'

'I will ask.'

'Will you come again? Perhaps it is not so bad to sit down here in our underwear. I think that I could learn things.'

* * *

Many visitors came to Londiani in those last days before the trial. Families came to put flowers on the mzungo boy's grave. Every evening just after five, three men on bicycles turned off South Lake Road. Two men from the rondavel village were escorting a man they only knew as Joseph back from a day's work at the hospital site. They handed him over to Stephen Kamau who rode with him across the fields to the site of the old vineyard and locked him in for the night.

'Bwana Kamau, do you think that your daughter will allow more of the boys to work on the site with me?'

'You must ask her yourself.'

'But she is such a famous lady and I am ashamed.'

Stephen smiled at the thought of having a 'famous lady' for a daughter.

'Do what I do. Think of her as the most special wash girl in the whole of Kenya!'

Stephen and his companion were still visible when the last visitor for the day parked his familiar red car on the gravel close to the bottom step of the veranda. It was several minutes before the driver was ready to get out.

Rebecca and Tom were enjoying their coffee together while sharing the events of their day, she at the hospital and he on the farm. They had not noticed the small car parked nearby and were surprised to see Simon Nyache suddenly materialising on the top step of the veranda. He seemed reluctant to move towards them and Rebecca hurried to him when she saw that he was in some distress.

'What has happened, Simon? Please, come, sit down and tell us. You have just missed my father, but he and the others will be here soon.'

He accepted a coffee but only toyed with the queen cake that Rebecca set before him. He admitted that he was deeply unhappy but firmly refused to give any reason until more of the family arrived.

'I do not wish to be rude to you people who have always been so kind to me, but I do not believe I have it in me to tell you, to explain my grief more than once.'

'Try that cake. Rebecca is using me as a guinea pig, trying new recipes out on me every day. But perhaps you would prefer to hear how the new building is going.'

'The new building?'

Simon was trying to steady himself in his moments of distress.

'Oh, yes. I heard about the fire and the deaths. You are building again? I hadn't heard.'

Rebecca raised the old man's spirits a little with her account of the new things happening on the other side of town. She was happy to cut herself off when the Londiani family gathering was complete. Making an effort to stay composed, he began.

'You see a man who is full of shame. When I was a young man, the idea of me reaching the ancient age of eighty seemed impossible. But the mzees I saw around the village in those days all seemed to be content with themselves and their lives. But then I don't suppose that any one of those ever came close to betraying their kindest friends. I see that I am puzzling you. Rubai took my wife and my two granddaughters.'

'The bastard! Is there any single foul, disgraceful thing in this world that he wouldn't stoop to?'

'Thomas, it happened two days before he himself was taken from his own people. God bless them for having real guts. Rubai told me to give him a list of the members of Serena. Now Rubai is gone, one of his … thugs wants me to tell him where his boss is being hidden. If I want to see my …'

Rafaella sat next to him and placed a glass of brown liquid in front of him.

'Warm brandy and a big spoonful of honey. Don's favourite.'

'This morning I went to tell them. They had given me an address on Moi Avenue. I was going crazy with worry. Olivia, our youngest, has the asthma and needs dawa. I was so scared it took me four hours to drive from Nakuru.'

'But, Simon, do you know where Rubai is?'

'No, Tom, I do not. I did not know who took him. There have been rumours.'

'But when you named some place.'

'Yes, they would check and find out I was lying. So they add another one to their list of dead men. But perhaps, they would let my girls go. I would have been happy to go to give them a chance.'

'But you are here now. Did they believe you?'

'I parked my car at the Norfolk and walked to the address. I thought the fresh air would clear my brain. On my way it came to me. They believe it was …'

Maria finished his sentence.

'Yes, it was us. We have him hidden. Five days to the trial. Our hopes are rising.'

'I was shocked. I went through the nearest door. It was a bank. I sat down with my face towards the wall. One of the tellers came over to me with a glass of water. And now I am here.'

Maura knelt in front of Simon. 'So you have not betrayed anyone.'

'I was ready to …'

'To save your family. Who could blame you?'

'Maura, there has been enough death in this town. I am supposed to be the protector of these people. Listen to me. On my way here I had an idea. You tell me where he is. Can I drive there? Alex?'

'Yes, but it's a long way.'

'It will be dark soon and the roads will be clear. I have a gun. What people are there?'

'You know some of them.'

'Good! So they will let me in.'

'Perhaps but …'

'I can be a good talker. All those years in parliament. In ten minutes, he will be dead.'

'Simon, you must stop this.'

Simon was being carried away on a wave of excitement. 'And the best part is that I would strap him into the front seat of my car, drive him down to Nairobi and wait outside that address in Moi Avenue. You see, no need for the risk of a trial!'

Maria and Rebecca sat up with the tired old man until after midnight. Maria began one of her ancient songs. Rebecca was soon able to pick up the melody and soon the sweetness of their harmony had Simon dozing into a deep sleep. Holding hands, they sang on, soothing away their own anxieties, wondering what the next few days would have in store for everyone in that house and in every other part of their beloved country.

# Chapter Forty

Everyone involved in the dangerous attempt to bring a rich and powerful man who expected soon to be the next president to trial in a Nairobi court had agreed that, from Thursday on, they would be willing to use the up-country radio system to keep in contact. From its crude beginnings during the days of the Mau Mau troubles, it had developed into a more sophisticated means of keeping tabs on even the remotest settlements in the Rift Valley and the Highlands.

Daniel's first contact from the radio in Bertie's guesthouse was with High Court Judge, Mary M'tambo. She had important pieces of news, but she needed to know about Rubai.

'He is still with our people? Good. We have three possible courts on standby for Monday. We'll choose one on the morning we start. I've had dozens of meetings in the last fourteen days, most of them in secret. Daniel, you will appreciate that a trial like this is unprecedented. That is why the city is jammed with reporters from all over the world. A big plus is that Koyane, Rubai's man, has agreed to the starting day, mainly because he thinks that it will be impossible to get him to court. There will be five judges and no jury. There's no need to ask if you and Paul have your case ready. There is a huge risk for you, of course.'

'Mary, this is our chance. Serena would have taken years to work itself into this position. And, at bottom we owe it all to a beautiful twenty-something. I call her the Kenyan Joan of Arc, only to myself, of course. She would never see it that way. Everybody loves her, except a certain Mister Big who will soon be losing that title.'

'God willing! Right, we will organise the Nairobi side. You get him down here. Could we speak again on Sunday morning on this wavelength?'

'Sure. We will be moving out from here in the afternoon.'

'I've never seen the city so excited and tense at the same time. Much worse than Saba Saba Day.'

* * *

Daniel and Paul kept their first conversation for almost three weeks very brief.

'Paul, what time do you plan to arrive?'

'Two am. We have two helicopters. One will start from here. The other will be a decoy, setting off from Kijabe and flying low. We might fool someone!'

'We plan to leave Naivasha near sundown. You won't believe this, but we are going down to the Daniels' house in two police cars and dressed in police uniforms, even the ladies. It's true! Shall we say that we are borrowing them for the day! Tell you the whole story when this is all over.'

'Maria is still confident?'

'She talks as though she has a special line to someone in authority!'

'That's my sister.'

'Paul, between you and me, I find it hard to believe that all of us will come out of this. But the adrenalin is pumping and there's been a lot of praying. Ivor has contacted his chapel people in Wales. Apparently, they've spread the word and there are hundreds behind us. Those three have been great. They have regular quiet times around Iolo. Sometimes they are out there for hours. I'll stop now, just in case, by some fluke, someone will pick up this wavelength.'

'See you soon, Dan. We all make a great team, don't you think?'

'That's for sure. And the best is yet to be.'

'Mister R Browning?'

'Who else?'

They set off at intervals of fifteen minutes. When they reached South Lake Road, Hosea turned right towards Longonot and Daniel left towards the town. There was not a white face to be seen in either car. Young Ewan had cackled with amusement as Maria had smeared his face with dark chocolate, happy that all the big people were joining in the game.

Daniel drove fast up the Escarpment. Rafaella looked down towards the lake far below on her right. The water was dark under lowering, dark clouds that matched her mood when she considered that this might be her last sight of the stretch of water that had played such a large part in her life. They avoided the dual carriageway which would have brought them into the city centre and took the back road that led down to Dagoretti Corner and on from there to Karen.

The wooden gates at Cartref were open and the night askari waved them through with a smile. Ewan had fun dog-licking the chocolate from the faces of Eddie and Rollo. Bertie looked on with mixed feelings. He loved watching his son enjoying himself, but being in the Daniels' large sitting room always brought back to him the saddest night of his life. In that place he held the newly born in his arms. His Anna was gone and her beautiful body was alone in some cold, dark place.

The grief would never leave him, but he was able to join in the hilarity at the buffet supper laid on by the Daniels family. The room was crowded and, to start with, the conversation was loud and frantic, the constant rush of noise often heard in playgrounds when children have been set free for a break between lessons.

Midnight passed and gradually the mood began to change. Though it was far too early, ears began to tune themselves in for the sound of a helicopter descending and landing. Conversation mellowed and thoughts became more private and meditative. Time for action was near.

Eli and Sammy Akamba made a brief appearance. The Naivasha contingent saw for themselves the changes in the two young men that Maria had described. They had last seen them in Londiani when they were suffering from the trauma of their horrific car accident. Their eyes lit up when they caught sight of the woman who had turned their lives around. Maria had introduced them to the joys and responsibilities of true freedom. More than that she had brought hope into the life of their mother and restored trust between her and her two surviving sons. When the trial began they were ready to be key witnesses for the prosecution. For now they were happy to help out by patrolling the garden and to report to those inside as soon as they heard the first sounds of the approaching helicopter.

Not long after they left, those who were going to be inside the grounds of the Pink Palace got themselves into their black sweatsuits and balaclavas. Watches and torches were checked. Then all the men and Maria, Maura and Rebecca sat around and waited for the return of Daniel and Tom. These two had been in the Rubai grounds checking that everything was as ready as it could be.

The house itself was empty. Sally had taken family and staff up to one of the farms in the north-west. She had never been separated from Abel for so long. She spent much of her day with her Bible, remembering Paul's advice to his followers in Philippi that they should pray without ceasing. She was confident that her innocent husband would soon return to put an end to the turmoil and discomfort of the previous three weeks.

The guards in the area of the landing triangle had been briefed yet again. There was little more that could be done except to wait and keep a tight hold on the nerves.

Up in the farmhouse near Nanyuki, everyone was glad that the three weeks of inaction were coming to an end. Abel had not found it difficult to work out that he would soon be on the move again, probably back to Nairobi and his home in Karen. His ordeal was almost over. He had given up warning the desperate fools holding him captive that they had made a terrible blunder in trying to get him to court. The mass of the wananchi would never let that happen. It was time to be patient and let events unfold. Simple logic pointed clearly to a win for himself in every way. In the election in four weeks there would be a landslide victory for KANU and Rubai.

His captors were concentrated on the immediate business of making a safe getaway, hopeful rather than fully confident that they would bring their plan to a successful conclusion. There were many imponderables, and unforeseen problems would test them to, and perhaps beyond, their limits. In those three weeks of isolation, there had been time enough to contemplate that there would be deaths on their side. They could expect no mercy from the other side.

It was time to set off. The helicopter had been silently waiting to be in the air and flying south-east to its home base.

Paul drew comfort and confidence from the young people around him. They were excited, light-hearted by the thought of the adventure that lay ahead. It was a privilege to have a chance of being part of a big day in the history of Kenya. Win or lose, it was a bigger day for them than for him.

After a brief call to those waiting in the Daniels' home, they lifted off.

'Mister Rubai, notice that we are not using a blindfold for the return journey.'

'I will return the favour when I see you lined up on the scaffold in the near future.'

'We thought we'd do the decent thing and let you look down on the country as we pass over. You will be able to create some memories for you to recall in those long years behind bars. Sorry it will be pitch-dark all the way.'

* * *

The dark clouds that Rafaella had seen hanging over the lake as they left Naivasha had followed them and worked themselves into a storm. Thunder crackled and rain poured. David Daniels saw gloomy faces all around his sitting room and made a confident prediction.

'We often get these little bursts of weather around this time of year. The gardener loves them, brief but heavy. He won't have to water for a week. Trust me.'

Half an hour later he led his guests out into the garden and lifted his hand skywards.

'Have you ever seen the stars looking brighter? Dad told us as kids that God had been rinsing the dust away from the sky.'

Dorothy Daniels saw that the Akamba boys were dripping wet and sent them inside to change their clothes. They emerged dry and warm, but within minutes they were calling in through the front door.

'Memsahib, come quickly! There is a noise in the sky. And little lights are dropping towards us.'

Ten frantic minutes later and a large group had gathered on the back lawn of the Rubai house, lit up to guide the pilot down to a perfect landing. The army major in charge of the reception group held his arm up to let the pilot know that he wanted time to make sure that everyone was in position. He did not see the old man outside the circle of light hurrying towards the helicopter. He was breathing hard from the effort of moving faster than he had done for thirty years.

Simon Nyache had spent the previous two days at the house of his sister-in-law in the city. He had travelled there straight after leaving Londiani in a state of mind that made him a bigger menace on the road than usual. He had willed himself to believe that, when he arrived, he would find Margaret and the girls waiting for him and asking to go home. He had found Velma alone in the house, afraid to come to the door until he convinced her that he was not another potential kidnapper. Even then the two old people spent long hours trying to convince themselves that the Rubai men would be knocking at the door at any moment.

'The boss says he's got no more use for these three. He made a big mistake. Have them back! They have been driving us crazy with their screaming and shouting.'

*Huh!* The 'boss' was in no position to give orders, wherever he was. Wherever he was? But there was a trial on Monday. Simon had an idea. If he could confront Rubai face to face….

He waited outside the circle until he saw his opportunity. He kept a close watch on the officer giving out the orders. At last, the major waved to the pilot and pointed his thumb towards the ground. The door opened and the passengers stepped down.

'Abel Rubai!'

The disembodied voice moved quickly into the bright light of the circle, repeating his call as he went.

'Abel Rubai, over here!'

Taken by surprise, the escort guiding their prisoner to the back door of his own house paused and allowed him to turn to face the unshaven man in the torn dusty suit.

'Come closer! Let me see you!'

Returned to his home and power base, Abel was his old disdainful self. Recognising a former colleague, he snorted dismissively.

'Witness for the prosecution, I see!'

'Sir, I beg you to tell me where they are!'

'You pathetic excuse for a man, now do you understand what it means to betray your party and your leader? As for the rest of you, I can see that you are beginning to feel the heat for your embarrassing stupidity. Don't worry. You will be dealt with justly.'

'Mister Rubai, please step inside so that we can go through procedures with you.'

'All very polite now, Mister Komar, Mister Miller. Procedures! What a joke you are! I have been very patient with you ignoramuses. I'll tell you about procedures. The people decide procedures. Perhaps they will gather around this house tonight. Perhaps they will wait until morning. But again I tell you. There will be no trial tomorrow or any other day. I am tired. I am going to bed right now.'

'As you wish. When you wake, there will be one or two surprises waiting for you.'

In half an hour the house was quiet and in darkness, except

for the conference room. Natural adrenalin and many cups of coffee were helping to keep energy levels high in the dozen people gathered around the polished oak table. Maria was in good spirits.

'These police uniforms and the cars are a gift from heaven. Synchronicity again! Paul, I only wish I could come with you but …'

'Synchronicity, yes, but are you sure that you didn't plan it like this? I really believe that we are going to win out here.'

'No planning, just waiting, Tom. Strange how you have to wait for the last minute for the mist to clear.'

'Two cars, four policemen. Sorry, Caroline. Four police personnel will get through to the courtroom more easily than six tanks. Does Judge Mary know about this?'

'Tom, it's her idea! She'll have friendly officers waiting at the door.'

Something that those in that room did not know was that Reuben Rubai was in the house and had been for three days. He had found it easy to evade the patrol sent to check that the Pink Palace was empty.

* * *

The hunched figure of a forlorn Simon Nyache was halfway down the driveway when Rebecca caught up with him.

'Ah, Rebecca, thank goodness! I thought it was one of his thugs coming to finish me off!'

'But, Simon, he is locked away for the night. Have you forgotten about the trial?'

'Dear Rebecca, I have not forgotten. I hope that you can pin the snake down. It has come too late for me. Three weeks since my girls were taken. Do you think it is possible that they are still alive? No, that is not a fair question. All I know is that my life is over.'

'Simon, I truly believe that they are hidden away somewhere. You are on edge. We all are. But where were you going? Come back to the house with me. Or stay with the boys down in the gatehouse. But do not go out on the road. There are leopards about.'

'Perhaps you are right. Let's just stop for a moment. Look up there. When we were younger, Margaret and I spent many hours watching the stars without saying a word to each other. She knew the names of the constellations. She thought of them as people. She was sure that they must be displeased with us for spoiling our world.'

'Thomas and I can see Old Longonot from a little hill behind Londiani. We think that the mountains and stars are our guardian angels watching over us.'

'My granddaughters love your songs. They love you. "I wish I was beautiful like Rebecca Kamau. If I could sing like her, I would be happy."'

'When we were young, my friends and I wanted to be like film stars.'

'Rebecca, thank you.'

'For what?'

'Tom is a lucky man. So many people say it, that just being near you makes them feel better.'

'Simon, remember I am just a wash girl.'

'But it is true. Look at an old monkey like me! Show me a tree I can climb and I'll prove it.'

Simon closed his eyes and sighed deeply before continuing.

'Please, do not be angry with me. That man who is in this place somewhere, he is so full of hate. Margaret says it is envy and fear. All those things, they are the same. He blames you for the death of that rogue of a son. I was at the engagement party at Muthaiga. Remember I am your MP! The bitterness drove him crazy. Yes, crazy. Think of the deaths on the farm. And now more deaths at the hospital. Any person, any thing that you love, he feels he must destroy it.'

'Simon, can a man have so much hate in him?'

'I think it. And when such a man has wealth and power, he loses control. Megalomaniac. That is a word my Margaret taught me. She was a clever lady.'

'Is, Simon!'

'If you say so.'

The spark that had briefly lit up Simon's whole being had vanished like the brightness of a falling star.

'Simon, look, a bench. Let's sit. It will be easier for us to watch the stars.'

He bent his knees wearily, placed himself on the edge of the bench and stared into the distance.

'I want to give you some news. Thomas and I are expecting a child. It will be many months before this happens. Already I feel different. Do not laugh, but when we are alone, I sing to her, or him, of course.'

Simon became more animated. 'That's a lucky child. I think that hearing such a voice will be a great gift.'

'Every time I sing the same song. It is one of Toni's songs that has no words, 'Lullaby of peace.'

'I have heard it. The girls play it often for their grandmother. As I said, a lucky child.'

She took Simon's hand and began. It was based on a melody that Toni had heard down at the coast, in Lamu, a mingling of African and Arab cadences. She began softly, enjoying again the rise and fall of the music. Gradually, the presence of the stars, the shadowy outline of the trees around them and even of Simon himself slipped from her consciousness. She heard her voice becoming stronger and floating away on the still night air.

Tom was the first one in the conference room to pick up the familiar sound as it came to him through an open window. He smiled and turned to his companions.

'I'm for some night air. I think I'll just take a stroll around the garden. I'm ready for whatever … you all know the rest.'

He and Rebecca persuaded Simon that he must spend what was left of the night inside the house. They left him at the table where Sally Rubai kept her Bible. A lamp was on and he pulled the large book towards him and opened a page at random.

Long before sunrise, there was a lot of quiet movement downstairs. Paul met the CNN camera crew, the only one invited to film inside the grounds of the Pink Palace. He explained the plan for the departure of Abel Rubai.

'You must realise that our friend is a very unpredictable man, so be prepared. He's still upstairs. We were surprised to discover his son, Reuben, with him. We didn't ask how he got in.'

'Mister Miller, there's a big bunch of people just outside the gate, reporters mostly. And the crowds were gathering in the city as we left. Are you taking him down by chopper?'

Paul replied with raised eyebrows and a cagey smile.

'That's one of our options.'

Earlier, in the conference room, it had been decided that strategy must be flexible and that their plan would work best if they could keep everyone outside the group wondering what would happen next. Paul added, 'You can take it that he will be stepping out at seven.'

The early sun cast the shadow of the house across the

dew-soaked lawns at the front. Most of those gathering outside the main entrance were security men with their weapons loaded. They were nervous, still fearful of a surprise attack of some kind. The Daniels stood to one side and close to the front door.

The entrance of Abel, with Reuben close behind, was impressive. Both men wore identical, expensive, dark suits. The father's tie was in the Kenya national colours and his black shoes had been buffed up until they gleamed. The two men stood on the top step of five cut from black granite and looked around imperiously. When he became aware of the television camera, Abel smiled and waved with that air of confidence he would show on his first appearance after being elected president.

During the short pause while Mister R played up to the camera, a small, unshaven old man appeared on the bottom step. Abel groaned with impatience, but the little man was determined to have his moment.

'Abel Rubai, we spoke last night about my wife and grandchildren ...'

'Will someone take this old fool back to his cage?'

Abel was ignored and Simon Nyache continued.

'I know you have a busy day ahead, but last night I wrote ...' Simon slipped his hand into his pocket.

'Papa, this is a trick! There is a gun!'

Abel's face contorted into a grimace of panic. He pulled out the same pistol he had held in his hand on the golf course, preparing to shoot Stephen Kamau and Tom McCall. This time there was no Sally to stay his finger. Two bullets entered Simon's frail body and he crumpled to the ground. The dramatic silence was broken by a scream from Reuben.

'You all witnessed it! That maniac was about to kill my father! Papa, you were right to defend yourself!'

The stunned witnesses watched Tom McCall hurry towards Simon. He sat on the bottom step and lifted him against his body. In a few seconds he looked up at Paul and shook his head grimly. Simon's hand was still in his pocket. Tom eased it out gently. He searched the pocket and took out a letter.

'It is addressed to Abel Rubai.'

From his sitting position he handed the letter to his father. Alex stepped up and handed it over. 'I believe this is meant for you.'

The CNN camera had Abel and Reuben in close focus. Paul Miller and Inspector Caroline moved into camera range. Paul stood in front of Rubai.

'You're a bigger fool than I thought. Cold-blooded murder in front of millions of witnesses.'

'You all saw him put his hand into his pocket. It was obvious what was going to happen.'

'He was going to shoot you with a letter!'

'Paul, do I charge him now, or wait until we get to court? This is new territory for me.'

'Book him, Caroline! We'll sort out the protocols later.'

The murmuring began. Arms were thrown out, pointing angrily towards the Rubais. Abel, knowing that he had no friends in the crowd, tried to turn to get back into the relative safety of his house but was held firmly by two Nairobi policemen in plain clothes.

'Let me go, you oafs! Come on! Come on! I can make you rich!'

As he stared around wild-eyed, looking for help, or at least some sympathy, he caught sight of Rebecca McCall kneeling over the body of Simon Nyache and looking straight up at him. In a single moment he recognised a truth that sent a shock of pain through his whole body. In the purity of the compassion revealed in that beautiful face, he was overwhelmed by a sense of his own selfish, filthy arrogance.

Distracted as he was, he did not notice two young men hurrying out of that part of the crowd where the Daniels family was standing.

Eli and Sammy Akamba threw themselves down onto the steps right in front of him, determined not to be moved. He vaguely recognised them. Eli reminded him.

'Bwana, do you not know us? We are two brothers.'

The bitterness in Sammy's tone was sharper.

'We had a younger brother. He was the wild one. Remember that day at the loony hospital in Gilgil? The three of us were wearing clothes that you had bought for us.'

'The old man down there. You told us to take your car and follow him. Bwana, you did not like to soil your hands.'

'Bwana, we failed and broke our mother's heart.'

'See those people over there? We know them. They are healers. They brought our broken bodies back to life. To life, Bwana, to life! They paid attention to us and tried to bring peace to our minds.'

'And we came so close, so close. But the wildness was too deep.'

'Sammy, Eli, I remember you so well. I saw to everything after Saul was taken. Ask your mother. I owed you money. I still owe you money! I can give it to you now, if these gorillas let me have five minutes. Where have you been? I've looked everywhere for you.'

'Bwana, it is good that you are ready to pay your debts.

Next time you want to find us, you must look in that place they call hell!'

It was over quickly. Abel was still in the grasp of the policemen when one knife ripped across his throat and the other plunged into his heart.

# Epilogue

So the battle was over. The shock of the swift, brutal dispatch stunned everyone who was close enough to see the gush of life-blood as Abel tumbled down the steps of his own home, dragging his guards with him. The head of the falling corpse struck the bottom step, inches from where Rebecca McCall held the body of Simon Nyache in her arms. The sound of the cracking skull sent an electric shock of horror through the length of her body. She feared for the life of her child. She drew the lifeless body of Simon tight to her as though it had the power to protect her against the sight of that leer of terror frozen on the dead face of the man who, in life, had tested the goodness of her heart to its limit.

The single cry of 'Thomas!' cut the morning air like the scream of a lion on the point of death, but it was Maria Kabari who was first to her side. She released her grasp on Simon Nyache, lifted her and passed her into the arms of her husband. As he turned to take her away, back to Londiani if that had been possible, he found himself looking into the warm, comforting eyes of Dorothy Daniels.

'Tom, my car is close by. We'll take her over to Cartref. There is going to be a lot of noise and activity here soon.'

Messy. Physically, mentally, spiritually messy.

The dark red blood from Abel Rubai's body was spattered down every step with splashes and spots on Simon Nyache.

The blood of the old man made no more than a stain on the coat of his dark suit. Even in that moment of deep crisis, Rebecca was concerned that the blood be cleaned away quickly before liquid congealed into a permanent mark in the surface of the granite. She was led off before she could think of some way to do the job herself.

The doctors who were already gathered around were concerned only with making a last check that the men were dead before having them carried inside and laid head to head under sheets on the large table in the conference room.

The numbing confusion generated by the shock of the two deaths affected everyone close to the entrance, even the CNN crew who had experience of death and destruction in war zones in Asia and Africa. But for those whose minds and bodies had been concentrated in making sure that their defendant be presented on time in front of a judge in a Nairobi court, there was no luxury of taking in events slowly and musing on them in some philosophical, leisurely way.

In particular, Paul Miller and Daniel Komar were landed with a crisis of their own that might prove more dangerous to them than getting a living Abel Rubai down to the city. A whole new series of events lay in wait for them. New thinking and planning were needed and their instincts and anticipation must be accurate if they were to be able to present the truth to the people.

Convincing the legions of Rubai supporters presented a massive, if not impossible, problem. First there had been the kidnapping and now the ritual execution of their beloved leader. Vengeance would be the top item on their agenda. Blood must have blood, if possible in a public way.

Up there in the relative safety of Karen, issues were being dealt with competently. The Daniels family knew how to deal with everything associated with the dead men. Two policemen were guarding Reuben Rubai in a small room at the back of the house where he could carry on screaming out his grief and his curses and not be heard in the front of the house.

Maria Kabari sat alone with the Akamba brothers. She felt no danger from the two powerful young men, although she had just watched them make a savage attack on a defenceless man. Yes, there was a kind of madness in them, but she was confident that the heat of their passion would cool and they would return to themselves and perhaps be ready to unburden themselves to her.

Outside, quick decisions were being made.

Daniel asked the CNN producer to stop transmitting pictures but to use her experience and judgement about continuing to film.

Paul's first call was to Mary Mtambo.

'Have you seen the television pictures on CNN?'

'No. They are not going to be shown inside Kenya until this evening.'

'Mary, listen to this ...'

Half an hour later a newscast went out that the trial of Abel Rubai would not be going ahead that day. The speaker of the parliament had been asked to call a meeting of the house for noon with as many members present as possible. He was given only a partial reason for the request.

Daniel had a sister living close to the Rubai farm in the north.

'Susan, ask the reverend to make a casual call on Sally Rubai and her family. Ask him to take his wife. Give me his mobile number. We will phone when we know more.'

* * *

Hosea, with Caroline at his side, drove one of the borrowed police cars into the city. The other passengers were Paul Miller and Daniel Komar. They were surprised and delighted that their journey was totally without incident, an easier drive than on a normal weekday morning.

By noon more than a hundred and fifty members had gathered in the house. The excited hubbub in the chamber was not calmed when the speaker announced that members would be addressed by the leaders of the Serena Party. He silenced the shouts of protest and outrage with a threat to call off the meeting. Paul began.

'Honourable members, my name is Paul Miller and this is my colleague, Daniel Komar. We know that you are not happy about our presence in this chamber today. We have some important news, but we will be brief in relating it. Daniel will explain.'

'You will probably know that the proposed trial of Abel Rubai will not be taking place today. Paul has something to read to you.'

'I have here a letter written last night by a member of this chamber, Simon Nyache, the representative for Nakuru South. It is addressed to Mister Abel Rubai, whom I note is not a member of this parliament.

'Dear Abel, we have known each other for many years now, most of that time as good friends. You are a man of intelligence and energy. When you became financial adviser to our late president, I considered that this country was fortunate. You guided our country through many difficult times. You grew more powerful and, in time, in my humble opinion, too powerful. I fear that you became more and more estranged from the interests of our country to the point where you, with your small army of paid men, have seen it as satisfactory to run Kenya as your personal fiefdom. Rubai's interests took priority over the interests of the state.

'That is why you are facing trial tomorrow. For the sake of our people, I hope you will be found guilty. Abel, you have misused your gifts. What a great leader you could have been!

'On a personal level, I know that I have displeased you and you have seen fit to punish me by taking from me my beloved wife, Margaret, and my granddaughters. Please, God, they are still alive! So, in hope I beg of you, once more, to restore them to the family. I solemnly offer my own life in their place. Take this worthless thing from me in any way you choose. Take it now!'

There was a pause. When Daniel judged the moment to be right he looked 'round the chamber very slowly and went on.

'This evening, make sure that you are near a television set that shows CNN news. Let me explain. Four hours ago, Simon Nyache stood in front of Abel Rubai. He reached into his pocket to take this letter out. As you will see, before he could do so, Abel Rubai, in front of millions of witnesses, drew a gun and fired two bullets into the old man's frail body.'

The chamber erupted. The shouts of anger and outrage drowned each other into a chaotic roar of noise. All over the chamber fights broke out between doubters and believers. Order was only restored by unusual but effective action by the speaker. He fired one shot into the floor and another into the ceiling. While the members took refuge behind their desks, Paul moved forward with his arms outstretched in a gesture of supplication.

'My fellow Kenyans, I have one more piece of news, one more important thing to say. Abel Rubai will not face a court today, nor on any other day. He, too, is dead. Abel Rubai is dead.'

A moment of silence and a collective gasp of shock were followed by a wide range of personally instinctive reactions. Most KANU members were on their feet hollering, jumping up and down and waving their arms about. Others sat quietly grieving, but Daniel and Paul were taken aback that not one member was pressing them to explain how the great man had died and by whose hand. Perhaps they were preoccupied with working on how the cataclysmic event would affect their own lives. They seemed to have lost interest in the messenger. Paul turned to Daniel and shrugged.

'Why were we so worried? The king is dead. Long live self-interest!'

In the confusion, Paul and Daniel slipped out by a back door and were hurried away from the city centre by Hosea Kabari.

Next morning there were thousands of wananchi on the streets, but what took place out there could not be described as riots set off by the death of a beloved leader. Long rows of young men and women stomped down Uhuru Highway and into Kenyatta Avenue, smiling and chanting rhythmic war cries. But there was no fire, no passion. No cars were turned over, no shops looted. Most of the marchers had watched the evening broadcast on CNN news. As they sat in front of their screens, any anger they felt had been directed at Rubai. In the morning, when they had read the list of charges against him as republished in *The Nation*, there was a ring of truth about them that they had not acknowledged when they had read them before.

Three short weeks later and the country had settled into a kind of peace. The people of Naivasha had returned to work, many of them on the lakeside flower farms. It had become a custom for families to take evening strolls to the edge of town to check on the progress in the build of their new hospital.

Sally Rubai had taken her family back to their home in Karen. She grieved at the loss of Abel. Every day, visitors came to offer their sympathy, many of them giving well-intentioned advice on how she might cope with the shock of her loss. Most were surprised with the new widow's composure which they saw as some kind of reward for her life of prayer.

Sally herself hardly dared to admit to herself that with Abel's passing, some tensions in her life were lifted. She no longer had to pretend about certain aspects of her married life. Abel's secretiveness, particularly in the last year, had troubled her. She had been afraid to bring her suspicions out into the open. It was becoming more difficult to play the role of the innocent, trusting wife. She looked forward with a kind of hope, surprised that she felt no guilty feelings about this readiness to let herself be changed. She thought many times about her up-country friends. Perhaps one day she might be able to visit Londiani. She sent a very large cheque to her much loved Rebecca for her new hospital.

The hospital fund administered by Barney Miller was drawing money from all over the world. His daughter, Debbie, took a year off from her studies in Boston to supervise the build of her design. On a short visit home she had taken Lydia Smith and helped her with the formalities of beginning her nursing training in the hospital on the university campus. Jim Sawyer had helped his three Welsh friends to build a chapel next to the new hospital, Capel Dewi Sant.

The first baby born in the new maternity wing was later baptised Stephen Alexander McCall.

# Best-selling titles by Kerry B. Collison

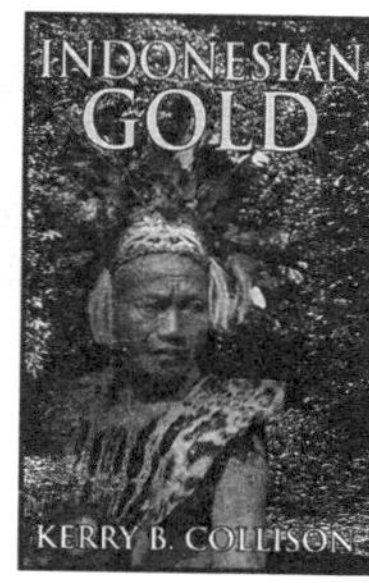


SID HARTA
PUBLISHERS

Readers are invited to visit our publishing websites at:
http://sidharta.com.au
http://publisher-guidelines.com/

Kerry B. Collison's home pages:
http://www.authorsden.com/visit/author.asp?AuthorID=2239
http://www.expat.or.id/sponsors/collison.html
email: author@sidharta.com.au

Purchase Sid Harta titles online at:
http://sidharta.com.au